# Lives of Magic

✦ SEVEN WANDERERS TRILOGY ✦

# LUCY LEIDERMAN

# Lives of Magic

**DUNDURN**
TORONTO

Editor: Allister Thompson
Design: Courtney Horner
Printer: Webcom

Leiderman, Lucy, author
    Lives of magic / by Lucy Leiderman.

(Seven wanderers trilogy)
Issued also in electronic formats.
ISBN 978-1-4597-0846-4

    I. Title.

PS8623.I37L59 2014        jC813'.6        C2013-902951-6
                                          C2013-902952-4

1   2   3   4   5       17   16   15   14   13

    Conseil des Arts   Canada Council          Canadä          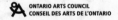   ONTARIO ARTS COUNCIL
                        du Canada          for the Arts                                   CONSEIL DES ARTS DE L'ONTARIO

We acknowledge the support of the **Canada Council for the Arts** and the **Ontario Arts Council** for our publishing program. We also acknowledge the financial support of the **Government of Canada** through the **Canada Book Fund** and **Livres Canada Books**, and the **Government of Ontario** through the **Ontario Book Publishing Tax Credit** and the **Ontario Media Development Corporation**.

Care has been taken to trace the ownership of copyright material used in this book. The author and the publisher welcome any information enabling them to rectify any references or credits in subsequent editions.

*J. Kirk Howard, President*

The publisher is not responsible for websites or their content unless they are owned by the publisher.

Printed and bound in Canada.

VISIT US AT
Dundurn.com | @dundurnpress
Facebook.com/dundurnpress | Pinterest.com/dundurnpress

| Dundurn | Gazelle Book Services Limited | Dundurn |
|---|---|---|
| 3 Church Street, Suite 500 | White Cross Mills | 2250 Military Road |
| Toronto, Ontario, Canada | High Town, Lancaster, England | Tonawanda, NY |
| M5E 1M2 | LA1 4XS | U.S.A. 14150 |

*To all the giants whose shoulders I stand on.*

# Chapter One

I wasn't always doing exercises in the rain, jumping around with my feet submerged in mud. The water dripped into my shoes a long time ago, and when I'm finally allowed to come in, I know I'm going to smell like damp earth for the next week or so.

I was just like any other teen. I had a family, I went to school, and I used to go out. Then my family moved to this little town and I met Kian on my first day of my senior year.

I'm telling this story all wrong. I should probably start from the beginning. My name is Gwen Carlisle, and I'm still a little mad about never getting to high school.

Last summer was rough. Global warming was going full speed, and every other week someone was predicting the end of the world. Washington State was hit by a giant tsunami. Then some houses in Florida were carried away by hurricanes. Small towns were levelled in moments. Honestly, I didn't know where half of these places were before they were destroyed.

We lived in San Francisco, right near the water. Mom and Dad had CNN on in the kitchen all the time. Tornadoes popped up everywhere from Arkansas to Vermont, and the California coast was hit by an earthquake practically every week. Finally, my parents had had enough. They decided to uproot and work from home amidst what they liked to call nature.

They were both veterinarians and hated the commute to their downtown clinic. They wanted to get away from the shakes of San Fran, and I guess we were pretty lucky we could. Tons of people were stuck in the rubble, and though people still lived their lives from day to day, the sound of sirens was getting a little too familiar.

At first I couldn't imagine leaving the city. I loved my hometown of San Francisco: the nightlife, the sights ... okay, so I was only seventeen and didn't get out much, but I liked looking at that stuff from my window. We had a little house with a great view, and I still miss the city very much. Now that I look back on all the things I've seen since then, it's strange thinking I never wanted to leave. But it was home.

My parents decided to make a new home a few hundred miles up the coast, in a little town in Oregon called Astoria. The trees grow tall and untouched there, balanced precariously on the precipice of North America and the Pacific Ocean. Wood-chip trails lead to wooden homes, and the town's skyline is kept low on purpose, all the better to admire the grey ocean. It's also known for being the setting of movies about a whale.

Most houses in Astoria are built along the ocean. Ours was no exception, and my parents were extremely proud of their successful relocation. My room was on the third level of a little old house, and my former view of the bay was replaced by trees, the ocean, and the formidable garage.

With such a tumultuous summer, I wasn't angry with my parents for moving me out to the middle of nowhere. In fact, for the first few days, I liked the quiet. But after a few weeks, I realized we weren't leaving — so I tried to make the best of it.

This fall was supposed to be different. I was prepared for a new high school, new friends, and a new life. I was going to make an effort to be more sociable and connect with my classmates. Join groups and toss Frisbees during break. Needless to say, I had never in my life done any of this and had no real desire to. I was once locked in the library, and had my mom not given every administrator she could find a thorough tongue-lashing, I daresay no one would have been the wiser when I walked out of there the next morning. But like I said, this year was going to be different.

My last high school hadn't been receptive to my hobby of archery, the one thing I could do well. It wasn't as high-profile as cheerleading, and was even lower on the social ladder than field hockey. I had been resentful in San Francisco, but my era of high school was running out. This year, I vowed to stop being so invisible.

The night before the first day of school, I arranged all my pens and pencils and sorted my notebooks by subject into my backpack. I made a lunch and put it in the fridge, and laid out my clothes for the morning. I was excited, what can I say? I even dragged a brush through my sandy hair, effectively ending up with a lion's mane.

My parents were large people. Larger than life in personality and bigger than most in size. They held the attention of anyone around them, and when they weren't on the latest fad diet, they were always in good humour. And even in my teenage years, I still liked my mom and dad pretty darn much. However, I was a little different. A head shorter and a fourth the width of either of them, I held no attention at all.

I surveyed with distaste the clothes in my closet — I hadn't gotten anything new in ages. That's what happens when you're the same size for years on end ... still waiting for that growth spurt. I was a little too skinny, and a little too short. My reflection in the window was a ghostly kind of pale in the moonlight. The San Francisco sun was fading off of my skin, and my grey eyes looked dusty out of my newly pale face. After a short bit of excitement and thinking I wouldn't be able to sleep, I was passed out by ten thirty.

✦

It was raining when morning came, of course. My parents had already started setting up shop in another area of the house, so I got my umbrella and trudged the two blocks over to where the school bus would pick me up. The wind was stronger here because we were right on the coast, and it made it rain from all angles.

Disgruntled and dishevelled, I made my way down the driveway and onto the road. There were no sidewalks in these parts.

My rain boots were covered in mud within seconds, and my coat was doing nothing to keep the rain out. After a few steps away from the house, my hair was already dripping and any make-up I had bothered with was gone.

Only yards from the house, I was already considering the opportunity to reinvent myself gone. I hadn't ever bothered to make friends at my last school. If I showed up looking like a wet cat at this new one, I didn't really see a bright light at the end of my dark social life tunnel.

*Slosh. Slosh. Slosh.*

I trudged on, convincing myself I was better off continuing as the recluse I was by nature. A few more yards and I was in a deep funk. I had never turned any heads. I mournfully noted that I didn't even have any brothers or sisters I could rely on to marry and have children, so that I could come to their dinners and be that crazy spinster aunt. I could chat about the cats I would inevitably own, and give them socks for Christmas.

When my thoughts had turned as dreary as the day, it happened. It was like a twitch in my chest, a shaking in my eyes, and goose bumps all at once. I had never felt anything like it before, and it made me stop dead in my tracks. I thought I was having a heart attack and clutched at my chest through my soaking wet jacket.

Something was off. Something somewhere was strange, and today was going to be different. I felt it in my bones, even with all that rain. It was like the rain fell on my face from one direction, but the wind blew from another. My senses were buzzing. After a few seconds of standing still, internally examining what the hell was wrong with me, I decided I wasn't getting any dryer in this weather.

I had to think about moving. A strange feeling washed over me, like an emotion that makes you want to know all of the world's secrets at once. I felt like my brain was trying to jump out of my head, and my heart out of my chest. I tried a foot forward, then another, and then I was walking. Happy with my success, I realized I was going crazy.

Walking while under this spell, for lack of a better word, felt like an accomplishment. I was uncoordinated, tripping, and it began to feel like when I had two glasses of wine at my uncle's second wedding. I didn't handle it well then, and I probably wouldn't handle it well now.

A prickling on the back of my neck made me turn around, and of course I lost my umbrella immediately to the wind. It flew away in a turned-out mess, like the antithesis to Mary Poppins, leaving me in the rain and mysteriously incapacitated.

When I turned at first there were only leaves all around, swaying with the awful weather. And that's when I saw him. The moment that would change my life forever.

I had to stare at the trees like I would at one of those abstract images, where if you cross your eyes and squint, you see a unicorn. But there he was. Standing a little into the trees was a man I had never seen before. He was older than me, but his face was so clear I could see every feature, even with the wind and rain.

I felt off balance, my eyes becoming like a telescope and zeroing in on his features while seeing my surroundings, all at once. His eyes shone out at me as he stared in my direction. His dark hair dripped with rain, and he wore a stern expression that forced his eyebrows to link together in a frown just over his nose, which was just slightly too long. His brown eyes stared me down even over the yards that separated us. With my new vision, I could see every raindrop as it fell from his eyelashes onto his cheek.

In the cold weather, he wore a jacket and jeans. Plain. But something about him was very different. I watched him for only a few seconds, because that's how long it took me to realize he had followed me ever since home. I just knew it.

Panicked, still wobbly, I decided to keep walking as if unsuspecting. My heart racing, I stupidly turned down a bunch of random streets and away from the main road to make sure he was indeed following me.

When I turned back and saw he was nearer than before, I couldn't help it. Even in my inexplicable state, I started to run down the lane, tripping and teetering every few feet. I had no idea where I was. I could hear the ocean on my right, and steep mountainside climbed up the left. All I could focus on was moving my feet forward, which resulted in staring stupidly down as I tried to run.

My instincts were going crazy. I could have sworn that in those moments, I could feel his running footsteps echo in the asphalt behind me as he closed in on his prey — me.

I was soaked and the rain pricked my face as I moved down the leafy road. Continuing my total stupidity of that morning, I decided to turn around to see if the stranger was still there. To my absolute horror — my heart was beating nearly out of my chest by now — he was only a few yards behind me.

I panicked and turned too quickly. The edge of the cliff edge must have been closer than I thought, and I tripped over my own feet into the ravine below. The last thing I saw clearly was him coming closer, reaching out to stop me toppling, head over feet, down a cliff. But topple I did.

Oddly, as I fell and fell and fell, I could only think about that look on his face. He didn't look much older than me, but his face seemed *ancient*, like some kind of Roman statue. When he reached out to stop my fall, it was the first time his eyebrows had un-knit, and a genuine look of worry came over that strange face. It seemed ridiculous that I had been frightened of him.

Falling hurt a lot, and some injuries I can still see and feel today. As I was going downhill at top speed, I didn't see much but the sleeves of my red coat flopping around like a rag doll. It was the kind of pain where all you can do is wait it out. The branches cracked near my ears as I rolled, and the leaves were a pleasant respite from sharp rocks that stuck out of the hillside at painful angles.

I only vaguely remembered that the ocean lay at the bottom. The rocky, deep, dangerous ocean. I shielded my face with my arms, tried not to land on my neck, and rolled until all of a sudden I was airborne. There was a bit of a drop, and then a crash.

I was on my hands and knees, eyes shut tight and already holding my breath, waiting for the cold to come and sweep me away. But nothing happened.

Slowly, I opened one eye at a time. To my extreme surprise, I was on the water. That's right, *on top* of it. I had stopped my fall with my hands and knees and now crouched on top of the Pacific Ocean. My hands were just in the water, and I could see a trickle of blood dripping down my arm — the sleeve had torn — and landing in the water between my fingers. I knelt there, gasping, for longer than I care to remember.

My hands and legs were freezing. They were submerged in the water, and waves much smaller than the ones that were hitting the bluffs broke against my legs. But I could only stare, afraid to move.

My first thought, naturally, was to wonder if I had died and become a ghost. But my heart was pounding and I was way too cold for that. I couldn't feel any of my injuries just then. I think I had too much on my mind.

I crouched there, on top of the water, afraid to move a muscle. My hands, knees, and feet were numb by the time I looked up. I heard my named being called.

"Gwen!"

While his voice reverberated even among the bluffs and waves, he was not yelling. The one who had been following me, who had driven me down the hill and into the water, was standing at the edge of the cliff. He was cut up on his arms a bit but otherwise seemed to have come down the ravine unhurt, probably following in my path of destruction.

I was still too afraid to move. My teeth chattered. I didn't answer.

"Gwen Carlisle," he called, "you can stand!"

I did not trust him and was too scared anyway. So I just knelt there some more. He waited patiently for a few minutes. My eyes were set straight ahead at my hands on the water, somehow kneeling on it as if it was hardwood flooring. Cold and wet hardwood flooring.

Suddenly, I heard a little splash, and two shoes came into my vision, standing in front of me, walking on the water. I dared to move slightly and tilted my head upwards to look at him, and he was staring at me, stern but concerned.

"Gwen Carlisle, I am called Kian," he told me in a voice as cool as ice. "You need to come with me."

# Chapter Two

I don't remember any more than that. My body gave in to pain and exhaustion and I promptly passed out. I couldn't make sense of what was happening, or what Kian had said. He picked me up off of the ocean and swung me over his shoulder like a child.

I opened my eyes briefly to see his feet gingerly walking on top of the water, every now and then getting a splash from the waves. I was wet and freezing. His body only warmed me slightly. I didn't realize I was being kidnapped. I hung there lazily, drifting in and out of consciousness. Way to go, Gwen.

✦

My mind came back to me slowly. As soon as I began to feel my body again, I felt restrained, tied up, and tried to sit up in a fit. I couldn't remember exactly what had happened, only that it had been something very stressful.

I gasped as soon as I tried to move. I hadn't been tied up, it was just that everything hurt, especially all the parts in my torso that had to move in order to go from sitting to standing. The pain was too much and I lay back down. I felt trapped in my clothes, which had dried hard and stiff from the sea salt.

"Hello!" Kian exclaimed happily.

We were in a tiny little shed, which was more of a hovel than anything. The wood on the walls was peeling, and even as I stared directly up at the ceiling, trying to keep the tears from my eyes, I saw a dozen little bugs crawling in and out of the low roof.

The walls were bare and thin but looked to have whole ecosystems going on inside them. Other than that, the only furniture in the place was a little fire pot and three chairs that I lay across. Definitely a shed. .

And then, to my surprise, there was a sleek little suitcase in the corner and Kian coming towards me. He was wearing a plain white t-shirt and was carrying a mortar and pestle. He was too tall for the little shack; his head brushed up against the ceiling and sent a few spiders cascading over his forehead. He didn't even flinch.

Forgetting earlier events, in that moment, I was sure a serial killer had abducted me. You don't know panic until you wake up in a shack with a serial killer. I was in too much pain to move and had been brought to some hovel in the woods. My heart beat so hard against my ribs that even that was painful. I grimaced in a most unattractive way.

"Don't move," he told me. It was a suggestion, not an order. "I am Kian," he added when I stared at him in confusion. He pointed to himself to make it clear. "Remember?"

His voice was deep and I liked it, despite myself. I slid my eyes over to what he was doing. Holding a big bowl in one hand, he was mashing something that smelled earthy. He scooped up what he had made and started towards me. My eyes must have widened, because he stopped.

"This is salve for your wounds. You have a lot."

I eyed his bright green concoction for a moment then nodded, resigning myself. I was in too much pain to run away anyway. His presence calmed me a little bit. At least I wasn't alone, but the mystery of the entire situation did more to unnerve me. Kian spoke soothingly, almost pityingly, and I was sure it had something to do with how I looked after taking that fall.

When I remembered falling down the mountain, I recalled bits and snippets of other things — wetness, falling through the air, landing in the water. It had hurt. My knees and wrists felt as if I may as well have landed on concrete. But I landed on the water. I couldn't make sense of it so I pushed the thought to the back of my mind.

Less than three feet away, the same person who had terrified me this morning was busy creating a green paste. My stomach did somersaults. As soon as I realized I had no idea how long I had been unconscious, my panic doubled. The shack had no windows, only a little mosquito lantern and the small flame in the fire pot. No rain crashed down on the roof. Enough time had passed for the storm to subside.

Kian came towards me with that green stuff in his palm, but first put another hand just underneath my throat. Before I could ask, a soothing feeling swept over me and I relaxed. His touch convinced me everything was okay. The situation didn't seem so bad anymore. My mind, frenzied, had to surrender to the calm that came over my body. I was totally conflicted.

He smiled, more to himself than to me, satisfied with his work, and gently picked up my arm. As I looked down, I realized it was the last bit of me that wasn't covered with the stuff. Kian's goo was being absorbed by my body through my clothes. He hadn't undressed me, though at that moment my salty, damp jeans were getting increasingly uncomfortable.

It was awkward, lying there, helpless, with a strange guy covering me in some kind of earthy-smelling goop. While I could only stare, I took in his face again.

The face I had seen following me through the rain had been a slightly distorted version of the man who stood in front of me now. He looked much younger, and though his nose was still a little too long for his slim face, his expression was pleasant and friendly.

I looked up at his brown eyes. His eyelashes were exceptionally long and swept up towards dark brows, which were knitted together in concentration. His pale face brought out full lips, and my eyes were embarrassingly on those when I realized he was speaking to me.

"Sorry?" I asked hoarsely.

"I asked how you are feeling," Kian said.

His face was stony — not mean but impossible to read. But I could have sworn there was some laughter going on under all his layers of tranquillity. He was being so calm it was frustrating.

Cautious, still under suspicion that he could be some kind of cannibal serial killer lurking in the Oregon woods, I did the only thing I could think of: comply.

I wiggled my fingers and toes and realized nothing was broken. I might even be able to make a run for it. I smiled in relief, again despite myself, and he took that for an answer.

"You should lie still for another little while," he told me, getting up off the floor and gently releasing my arm. It was covered in a fresh layer of green goo. He stood up and had to duck between the low rafters as he threw the leftovers into the fire pot. The smell filled the small room.

"Perhaps it is better that way, however," he said as he cleaned the little area. "You may want to be lying down."

"What?" I asked immediately. My voice was flat and nervous.

Kian came over to me again and sat cross-legged on the floor. His face was level with mine and he looked at me so seriously I was sure he was about to tell me someone died. It's the kind of face that makes you instantly nervous and upset, and definitely makes you want to ask more questions instead of listen patiently.

My suspicions about him forced me to back up as much as I could into the row of chairs I was lying on, as he sat in front of me inches from my face. He eyed me again with a patient, stern look and I calmed down some more, wary that I was falling into his plot.

Kian shook his head, and grasping the chair legs pulled all three chairs closer to him. I immediately realized he was strong, and my chances of bolting diminished greatly.

"Don't be afraid of me," he told me, almost pleadingly.

His face was so close to mine that I held my breath. I wanted to believe him. The urgency in his voice and his honest face made it hard to imagine him being a serial killer. But I had watched too many crime shows to let down my guard. I continued to stare at him silently, my mind in total conflict.

"I'm here to rescue you," Kian said finally.

A thousand sarcastic replies flew to my lips but I swallowed them down. "From what?"

"Three magicians." He raised three fingers to illustrate the point. "They are trying to conquer this world. But they need more power."

I continued to stare blankly, so he went on.

"Magic is rare today. Only you and a few others have it." Kian looked up at the ceiling, searching for words. "The magicians want to capture you and steal your magic."

*That's not so bad*, my thoughts tried to reassure myself.

"Your magic is attached to your soul. If they succeed in stealing your magic, your soul will be enslaved forever."

Very little of this made sense to me, and I opened my mouth to tell him so. I didn't like words like steal, soul, and enslave in the same sentence. I thought of a few classic arguments to make, such as *you've got the wrong girl* or *you must be confusing me with someone else.* Magicians and past lives weren't something I dealt with.

Kian must have seen my protest forming so he rushed to reassure me.

"It may not be easy to hear, but we're running out of time. Your consciousness mixed at our proximity. I saw it. Your power will not stop developing. I am here to help you."

His gaze fell back to me, and I nodded stupidly. He was urgent, as if this news was the most important thing in the world. His hushed tone drew me into him.

"You are very special, Gwen Carlisle," he said. "Many things you believe are truths are not. But you need to run or risk being captured, though I had hoped you would have more time to grow."

A silence stretched between us, and finally, I could only manage another weak, "What?"

He cocked his head to the side, the universal symbol of someone trying to be understanding and sensitive. I felt like he was trying to examine me, figure out how to approach whatever it was that he wanted to reveal. My nervousness grew by the second.

"What if I told you that you are not actually who you think you are?"

Again, I opened my mouth to interject but he kept going.

"What if I told you that with my help, you can unlock memories and capabilities inside of you that could save your life and possibly countless others?"

Kian was staring at me like the cue had happened for me having a revelation. On my part, I was only getting fed up and nervous. This sounded like a speech he had rehearsed.

"I don't follow," I told him flatly.

"Gwen ..." Kian leaned in and looked into my eyes. I could feel his breath on my face. "I can only show you."

Before I could flinch, he placed his hands on my ears, as if trying to keep me from hearing. But after an instant had passed, I felt a searing pain in my head. I winced and tried to squirm out of his grasp, but he was too strong.

Even prone to migraines, I had never felt anything like this before. As if my brain had exploded and taken my eyes and ears with it, I thought I would pass out from the pain ... again. I don't know if I cried out. But as soon as it had started, it was over. I gasped in relief and like with migraine, felt a giant weight being lifted. Dragging in breath, I saw what was in front of me.

While Kian still held my head and I lay on his chairs, covered in goo, it was as if a projector was playing a movie directly in front of my eyes. But the movie made no sense. It was emanating from me. The images had no sounds, and they moved too quickly to decipher them. I stared, barely blinking, straight ahead and up.

Glimpses played in front of me of someone who looked familiar, even like me, but different. Different in the way that Kian was different, like some kind of statue or Renaissance painting. It was the depiction of a person whose age is unknowable and face unreadable: an obscure person.

In my confusion the image made me sad, though I couldn't understand why. I stared, mouth hanging open, at what I saw. What I somehow knew had come out of my own mind.

The movie was on fast forward. Too fast, and I couldn't make out a single thing being played in front of me. The images moved quickly, and I saw people. Places. I *saw* emotions. Loyalty, love, family. I saw an entire life, as if through some kind of new generation of role-playing game. I realized, shocked, that the world was spinning around me, moving quickly, but in this movie, I was always at the centre of it.

I imagined this must be like having your life flash before your eyes, seeing nothing and everything at once. But this was not my life. I had led a quiet existence in Northern California, a place where most people lead quiet existences.

Slowly, the images faded off the screen of silver light, and then it was gone, leaving only the dust around the ceiling slightly illuminated.

I choked. My mouth had been open for way too long. I didn't know how long the images had played out, but I noticed my limbs and torso feeling a little better. Was Kian's goo working? It must have been several minutes at least.

He let go of my head and sat back, looking at me expectantly and rubbing his hands together like they were cold.

"What was that?" I whispered.

My breath billowed out in wisps of steam as I spoke. My voice was feeling stronger, but it felt like a quiet occasion. I couldn't explain what had just happened.

By this point, I had written off Kian as some kind of lonely Oregon wanderer, and my walk across the ocean as inexplicable reef activity. But this was something else. I couldn't explain this at all.

It was the question he had been waiting for.

"That was your past, Gwen," he said, "And unfortunately, your future."

# Chapter Three

"Y ou're wrong," I told him immediately, but Kian
only sighed.

"It is no coincidence that magic is dead in this
world and yet you have it deep inside of you," he told
me. "You were once a great magician. A warrior in
our tribe. That soul resides in you. You have heard of
ancient lands and people?" he asked. "Your history?"

I nodded, lying, and wondering what he was driving at. I never paid attention in history class.

"You have probably not heard *this*." Kian sat back
and crossed his legs in front of him. He continued
looking at me in an eerily imploring way, and I had no
choice but to listen to his story some more.

"In my land," Kian began, "we lived in a place
where the roots of time were deep beneath our feet.
We walked the same soil as our ancestors, and their
ancestors, and their gods. We were so intertwined
with our past that some of our tribe still retained the
magical strengths of their forebears."

Okay, not so bad.

"We had a good king, and he had noble warriors," Kian went on. "They were gifted and formed a group of men and women who had powers greater than any man could hope for. Some people said they were descended from the gods and had inherited their unique traits."

Kian smiled to himself as if recalling a happier time, perhaps when he wasn't keeping a teenager hostage in a shack in the woods. When he looked up he seemed to remember I was watching him.

"They could do incredible things," he explained as if trying to convince me. "In that time, magicians were known to exist. They were not common, but they were certainly real."

It was getting weirder than I had anticipated. The tale of why I needed rescuing was very detailed for a crazy man. But I was determined to listen to his story. If I could find holes in his logic, maybe he would let me go. And I wanted to find out what that movie thing was that seemed to have come out of my own eyes. As if reading my thoughts, Kian explained.

"What you just saw was a glimpse of that life," he said. "I have very limited magic, and I can only unlock some of the reflections of memories you already have inside of you, but that was your past."

He sighed and scuffed his foot on the ground, as if telling the story pained him. I almost felt bad for him, and then I remembered I was being held captive, and his story was sounding crazy.

*Stockholm syndrome*, I chastised myself.

"Our tribe, however, was besieged. This was two thousand years ago," he said.

*Red flag*, my mind warned. *He's definitely crazy.*

His tone implied talking about two thousand years ago was as normal as talking about the neighbourhood dog.

"We were fighting a neighbouring kingdom that had three very powerful magicians," Kian continued. "They were using the earth against us. They had enough power between them to roll the hills beneath our feet and dry the earth for our harvest. They washed the salt water of the sea over our people and many were lost. Our own gifted warriors were fighting them, but then another problem arose."

Kian looked to see if I was following then went on. "At our borders, another type of beast was trying to break in. The Romans had come and had waged a war against our people, in a land where they had no business. We had very little gold or silver, no roads — none of the things they admired. But we had a love for our way of life and that was why we fought them. While the Roman machine was nearly at our doorstep, the magicians in the north were growing stronger. They shook the earth and brought ice and snow crashing over entire villages, and there were not enough children of the gods to stop them."

A vivid picture had manifested itself in my mind. A snowy landscape, narrow mountain passes, shaking earth, terrified people. The sound of marching Romans echoed in my ears, and a panic I had never known until that day filled my heart. A thought seeped in slowly —

I had never even watched the History Channel.

"Against all odds, our warriors braved the spells cast by the magicians and captured their tribe," Kian said. "But they were too late. The magicians had sensed a losing war and had done what no man had dared before."

His tone had gone hushed and the gravity of the situation pressed on me like a weight on my chest.

"What happened?" I asked.

"They cast a spell on their own souls," Kian whispered. "The three magicians were found dead. But a strong magic had stolen their souls and sent them forward in time to where they could be reborn to try their plot again."

"What?"

I should have guessed that when Kian had first mentioned anything to do with magic, anything else was possible in his story. He must have been expecting my bafflement, since he seemed to have an answer ready.

"There is a magic," he explained, "that can capture your soul and keep it intact into your next life. Your memories, and more importantly your magic, are all locked away under the surface. It is called metempsychosis in this century, but for us it is an ancient ritual. In myths, the gods used it to live forever."

He paused to make sure the information had sunk in.

My clothes were now nearly dry thanks to the warm fire, and the pain of my ravine wounds was coming back at full strength. Lying on the chairs was beginning to be very uncomfortable, but Kian's presence and story enveloped me like a blanket.

I lay listening, his words filling my head with images I had never seen before. My logical mind told me to run. A strange rebelliousness I was not accustomed to wanted me to stay. It wanted to see that life again, and to feel magic.

"The three magicians had cast a spell to send themselves forward in time, where they would attempt to take over our lands once more." Kian's smile had turned into a wince. "We were naïve," he said bitterly, "thinking they had skipped a few years into time and would attempt to claim our small kingdom. We could never have known how large the world would become.

"Our good king was torn by the decision he had to make. The Roman power was at our door, and his warriors could now gather strength to defeat them. But if the warriors risked themselves in the war against the Romans, then there was no protection for the tribe in the future when the magicians would return in their next lives."

"What did he do?" I asked. It seemed like a lose-lose situation.

"The king was selfless and decided that surrendering to the Romans might be better than being defenceless against the magicians when they returned to their full power in the future. He asked his most prized warriors to complete their duty by performing the ultimate sacrifice."

"What?"

"Dying."

I gasped despite myself. Small strings of comprehension were making connections in my mind. The noise of thoughts resulting from Kian's story was so loud that I fought to think clearly.

"They were sacrificed in a ritual. It was a terrible solution," Kian continued. "But their souls were cast in magic and sent forward. Nothing but faith promised that they would land in the same time as the wicked magicians, but our warriors were servants of our king, and they did as he asked."

I inhaled deeply, trying to settle my nerves. It was calming, but the smell of the green goo filled my nostrils and I could not avoid facing my situation. Then I realized I was getting a bad case of the crazies if I believed Kian's story. Why was he telling me this?

"The magicians have arrived in this time," Kian told me, the stern look settling over his face once more. "Though ahead of you. And they seek power." He spat the words. "They are the one final challenge for our king's warriors."

I nodded. Okay. Fair enough.

"The Romans invaded, taking everything," Kian said, "and destroying the magicians now will be the only way to make the king's sacrifice worthwhile."

He scuffed his foot again.

"So ..." I tried to make sense of his ramblings. "You think I'm an ancient warrior..." The word felt foreign in my mouth. "... that can fight some ... evil ... magicians?" It sounded ridiculous. How could he not think it sounded ridiculous?

"No," Kian answered, and I exhaled in relief, thinking he was going to say something saner. "I need you to run away with me so that I can keep them from gaining the power they need."

So much for that theory.

"They *can* destroy this world in the effort to capture it." Kian reached over and gripped my hands while he said this. It was like he was pleading with me, but I had no idea how to help him. "If they get your magic before you are strong enough to defend yourself against them, then all is lost."

The panic rose again in my chest and into my throat. Fear washed over me and I thought I would vomit. I couldn't help but feel like his emotions were bleeding into me through his hands, and I wanted nothing more than to retreat.

"What does this have to do with me?" I asked, trying to be calm. I was clamping my jaw shut, afraid of being sick. My main thought was to get out of this cabin and leave Kian behind with his supernatural problems.

"There's no reason to keep me here," I told him, trying my luck.

Kian slumped down again. The emotions that played out on his porcelain face were at the same time varying and muted. I tried desperately to read him, but it was impossible. The statuesque face was solid and set.

"The king was a great man, Gwen," Kian told me, trying to persuade me, as if I had disagreed with him. "He risked everything to save a future he knew nothing of."

When I clearly wasn't getting his point, a look of sadness floated across his face. He obviously had thought he was making some progress with me. His forehead crumpled up into a frown and his voice took on a new sense of urgency. I couldn't help but feel like

I had disappointed him — even in my situation, lying in some shed in the middle of the forest, covered in goo and probably broken in several places.

Kian could tell I was getting distracted. "You *are* one of those warriors, Gwen. We had no way of knowing how far into the future you would be carried, but the magicians are here. And you need to run. Recover your memories and gain your strength before they destroy you."

Now the air definitely did stop dead in my throat and I stared blankly at him. I could not believe I was hearing this correctly. The threads of understanding in my mind tied themselves into a neat bow as Kian's story and my involvement were made official.

"You have all been scattered. Born into new places and homes some seventeen years ago," Kian explained. "You began new lives, but it is my responsibility to remind you of who you are, and why you were sent here. You have been reminded, your memories have become unleashed, and you have no choice now."

The stubborn set to his jaw told me he wouldn't back down. My logical mind took over and I slowly started to understand. Kian, mysterious, handsome, and absolutely crazy, thought he was on a mission to collect magical warriors from the past who were sent ahead in time so that magicians would not take over the Earth. He was so convinced of this that he had managed to get me to listen to all of this without trying to escape once. He was good. But like I mentioned, I had seen too many crime shows.

Things were getting too delusional for me. I sat up slowly, in case he tried to stop me.

"No," I said sternly. "Not me. You've got the wrong girl. Sorry."

"I knew you wouldn't believe me," he said, sounding truly disappointed.

I felt an undeserved guilt and willed it away. My strength seemed to be coming back to me exponentially, and now that I was sitting, I was panicking. Was this what an adrenaline rush felt like? I assumed being able to sit up was equal to being able to run, and I eyed the door as my temper rose. I had probably missed the first day of school by now.

A feeling that I can only describe as an itch settled over me — I had to leave. Now.

"You thought I wouldn't believe you when you told me that I'm some kind of magical warrior sent forward in time to stop world-destroying magicians?" I said, perhaps more snippily than required. If Kian noticed the sarcasm, he didn't comment on it. I tried to grip the chairs to steady myself but couldn't because my hands were covered in that green goo.

"And what is this?" I asked. I was getting frantic and fed up with the entire situation. The stuff was all over me. Kian did not seem dangerous, at least not now, and I was getting braver.

"Avocado," Kian answered simply, "and some other ingredients." He hadn't moved, even with all my fidgeting.

"You made me into a human chip dip?"

Now that I look back on it, it was probably not the time to be focussed on this. I had just been told that everything in my life was leading up to this moment and that I was in danger. But I was covered in avocado.

Kian's calm demeanour was making me seem like the crazy one, trying to wipe as much of the guacamole off of me as possible.

"Avocado is a miracle vegetable. I was only able to discover it recently, but since then have found its potential in healing remarkable," he said plainly, seeming unconcerned that I was trying to leave.

"I —" I stammered, unable to reply.

He was calm and still and it drove me crazy. I just wanted to go home, and the urge to do so swept over me like an uncontrollable craze. I was tired, hungry, and sore. All I wanted was a shower and my own bed. For the moment, I forcefully pushed all thoughts of magicians, world destruction, and magical powers to the back of my mind.

Eventually, I was able to wobble onto my feet and slip into my boots, which were waiting by the door. I expected Kian to try to stop me, but he sat and watched my struggle to move after the long fall down the hill.

"You have been reminded, Gwen," Kian said, still cross-legged on the floor. He was covered in bits of avocado pulp from when I tried to clean the goo off myself. "The process has begun. Restoration of your memories and powers will not stop."

I was already outside the shack, but I turned around one last time. "Avocado is a fruit!" I yelled and slammed the door.

# Chapter Four

I stumbled through the forest for only a few feet, blinking in the late afternoon light. Late afternoon! I still couldn't believe my luck at being able to get away, and the fact that Kian had let me go made me all the more paranoid. Was he after me? The thought kept my feet moving and my heart pounding.

I imagined my parents had already put out a missing person's report on me. I didn't want to think about explaining my appearance and blowing off school on the first day. But as I stumbled a little further, dark thoughts sinking my already sunk mood, I suddenly realized where I was.

Just through the trees in front of me was a little house with an add-on in the back. VETERINARIAN, it said.

"Ha!" I barked one small bit of laughter and the noise scared some birds out of the trees. The shack I was held prisoner in had been in my own backyard.

I suddenly stopped and swallowed hard. Kian was still hiding there. My mind raced. *Call the police.*

*Run. Get out of here.*

*No,* a voice said in my head. I was shocked to hear it was my own. I supposed he hadn't done anything wrong. In fact, he had saved me from drowning and didn't keep me against my will. A blanket of comfort wrapped itself around my mind, easing my worries, and I forgot about asking for help. In fact, I forgot all about Kian being so close.

The hoarse noise that had escaped my throat had gotten some attention inside the house. A window opened from the vet clinic and my mom popped her head out. I had never been so happy to see that round, curly-haired woman in my life.

"Gwen?" she called, squinting in the fading light. Her eyes widened when she finally saw me. "Good heavens! What *happened* to you?"

She grimaced when she saw that I was covered in green slime. My clothes hid most of my injuries.

I didn't have the energy to respond. Instead I trotted to the house, the several yards between the shack and my new home making all the difference in the world. My clothes caught on leaves and my wet-and-dried rain boots were leaving blisters on my feet, but I didn't care. I ran through the short bit of woods and right into the house.

My mom was already at the door when I ran up. Luckily for me, most of my appearance was hidden in the dusk of the evening.

"How was school? Goodness, did you run into something?" she asked me. I tried to slink around her in the darkness to avoid more questions. No one had called from the school. I had been lucky.

"School was ... good," I improvised. "I fell in the mud, Mom. No worries."

I was almost at the stairs.

"You sound absolutely beat," my mother called. "Where were you?" I rolled my eyes while taking the stairs in twos. If she only knew....

"Tired. Going to bed," I called back, wincing at the small amount of information I was actually giving. As I turned into the hall I set our burglar alarm. My mother raised her eyebrows at me and I shrugged, trying to get away as fast as possible.

I remembered Kian's neat little suitcase, all shiny and new. He did not have the appearance of one who lives in the forest. I briefly tried to convince myself that he had in fact left my yard. After all, there was no reason for him to stay.

At the top of the stairs, I waited to see if there were any more questions from my mother. Breathing heavily, more due to stress than to stairs, I listened for any restless-mother signs. Luckily, a cat in the vet clinic began to howl and my mom rushed off, muttering something about teenagers.

Now I felt absolutely awful. I hadn't gone to school and made friends. Instead, I had been chased down by Kian, a lunatic I was drawn to empathize with. I had lied to and avoided my mom, and I was pretty sure I had just tracked avocado all up the stairs and against the walls too.

I sighed so heavily that I thought my chest was going to collapse into itself.

My parents were battling with the angry cat downstairs. Their voices came muffled through the old floorboards of the house. Somehow I felt safer, and as I walked towards the shower I began to peel off my clothes.

Wincing and in pain, I eventually managed and climbed in. Naturally, the water ran green within seconds. I stood for ages, thinking about my day and at the same time pushing everything Kian had told me out of my mind.

I couldn't explain how I had done what I did. I met the Pacific and I sat on top of it. I had seen images play in front of my eyes. I shook my head with the wonder of it all. But out of all things, I was most confused about Kian.

He was eerily handsome and calm. I remembered how he had carried me off the water, walking on top like it was ice. Slinging me over his shoulder as if I weighed nothing. He radiated warmth, but his face was cool, unreadable. He had told me I was special.

I opened my eyes in shock as I realized that I wanted to believe him. I pressed my palms against the shower walls to steady myself. He must have drugged me. His story was so unbelievable and fantastic. I watched the water drip off of my eyelashes as I stood there, thinking about the possibility of being extraordinary.

Suddenly my ears popped like water had flooded them. The sensation was painful and I covered them with my hands on reflex. But then my eyes started to smart and I squinted until spots appeared in my vision. Confused, vulnerable, and being pelted by the suddenly freezing water, I started to shake. Reaching for the temperature knob, I groped at something that felt like rock. My ears were now thundering and I chanced opening my eyes.

I was standing under a torrent of water, but I was no longer in my shower. To my surprise, and extreme fear, the water pouring over my head was icy cold and heavy, as if it fell from a great height. It made my breath catch in my throat. I swallowed some water in shock — it was cool and fresh, unlike anything I had tasted before.

My feet ached and I realized I was standing on stones, round ones that shifted every so often with the weight of the water. The thundering in my ears had been these waterfalls.

There was no doubt about it. I was not in my house anymore, not safe in my shower. I noticed I still lacked any clothing at all, and suddenly felt that much more exposed. Goosebumps covered my arms as I raised them to my eyes, trying to clear my vision and see my surroundings for the first time.

Unexpectedly, the first thing I saw through the water was another person. Blurry, but definitely there, someone was approaching me. I gasped and choked on a lungful of water. Collapsing, struggling for air, I grabbed a hold of my shower curtain and pulled it down with me.

After another coughing fit, I stood up at home again, in my own shower, clutching at my torn shower curtain. The water was spilling out onto the floor where my avocado-stained clothes still lay.

I sat for a minute, doing nothing, thinking nothing. I could only stare, gasping a little bit. My heart was pounding wildly, and despite myself, the only mystery I could think of was who that shadow had been coming towards me. I had not felt afraid … I couldn't put a name on how I felt, standing in the freezing water. It was as if I rode in someone else's body.

I remembered Kian's words. He told me that whatever memories I had would not stop. I briefly considered believing his story but decided against it. If such a thing existed in the world, there was no way I could be a part of it.

I climbed out of the shower and threw my clothes in after me. Some items were torn beyond repair, but I thought I'd rinse out as much avocado as possible to avoid more questions.

Surveying myself in the mirror as the steam filled up the bathroom, I knew whatever vision I had just had was due to a possible concussion. I was obviously confused and disoriented. My body was like a bad tie-dye: all yellows and reds that would soon turn into blues and purples. I washed the blood off the bigger scrapes on my arms and legs, but my torso was still covered in bruises. The pain was such a constant throb that I could not tell where it was coming from.

As I lay in bed that night, I couldn't keep my mind off what I had seen. My body was in agony, to such an extent that I had debated asking my mother to buy a few avocados when a handful of Tylenols hadn't helped. I was sure some ribs were fractured if not broken, since lying on my back and breathing at the same time was excruciating. But distractions from the pain floated around my mind.

A waterfall ... it was so real! I could feel the uneven rocks underneath my feet, the strain on my neck as the water poured down on top of my head, the cold rush through my body and into my bones! There had been someone else there....

I had spent a large part of the evening thinking about what I had felt as I saw that figure. It was the strangest feeling. I was terrified, panicked ... but that seemed like only one mind. It was the mind that was attached to everything around me in Oregon: my room, my parents, and my ordinary surroundings. But in that moment I had felt a second mind, one that was calm, confident, and absolutely overjoyed at seeing that figure through the haze of water. Was that love?

For an embarrassingly long time, I lay in bed, closing and opening my eyes. I was hoping to reignite whatever had made me see that other place. I wanted to go back, explore. The need to see that place again and experience those feelings grew in my chest and ate away at me. Scared, I noted that something inside me had awakened — something wild and uncontrollable that longed to get control.

✦

*I was wading through a creek. The cold water went up to my waist and I wearily scanned the riverbanks on either side of me. I towed a small, round, floating thing behind me. It was only big enough for one and looked as if it was a giant shield turned on its front. I knew someone would track me sooner or later, but I wanted some time before getting discovered.*

*I picked my way carefully along the rocks in the river and avoided the middle due to the strong current. I was worried about being seen. Frightened of the consequences. Very aware of the fact that I was unarmed, I tried to make as little noise as possible.*

*Suddenly, in the distance, the bushes on my right rattled slightly. I hugged the riverbank and tried to tuck myself into its side, hiding. A hand reached out for me from the bushes. I gasped but my panic turned to exhilaration in a heartbeat. I knew that hand. I loved that hand. Overjoyed, I grabbed it and was pulled onto dry land.*

✦

I awoke expecting to be somewhere else but was still in my dark room. Tossing and turning, I eventually fell back to sleep.

Surprisingly, I felt rested in the morning. The sun was beating against my eyelids as soon as I woke up, and I knew it was late in the morning. Suddenly, a shadow blocked out the sun and I threw my eyes open.

"Ah!"

I screamed and jumped back, kicking at my bed sheets. It hurt. Kian was sitting on the end of my bed, looking perfectly at ease. The previous day's events, the pain in my body, and my memories of those visions came back like a torrent. Whatever magic he had used to make me forget his presence evaporated in an instant.

I heard my mother call from somewhere in the house.

"Is everything okay?" she asked. Then, "Why aren't you at school?"

I was breathing hard, torn between curiosity and not wanting to believe any of it. But he looked so trustworthy.

I'm not going to lie. I debated telling her to call the police. Screaming help, fire, etc. But he was looking at me so imploringly, and my chest started fluttering with memories of what I'd seen yesterday — the other place. I had no idea why I wanted to go back there so badly, but I did, even if it meant trusting Kian. I mentally kicked myself.

"Gwen?" My mother was still waiting for an answer. I realized time had passed while I thought through my next course of action.

"Everything's fine!" I yelled back. "I saw a spider. And I have first period off."

"Geez — sounded like you saw a ghost or something," she called.

I rolled my eyes and listened for more, but that was it. My lie seemed to satisfy her, and I was left to stare at Kian, thankful I had remembered to put on pyjamas the night before.

"Okay," I told him. All my doubts and misgivings were pulsing in my throat and I swallowed them down, leaving room for the uncontrollable urge to see that other place again. My next words came from that overwhelming desire.

"Tell me. Everything, this time," I said, and couldn't believe myself as I said it.

## Chapter Five

Kian looked just slightly surprised as his eyebrows lifted, but he regained his normal cool composure. He was wearing the same denim jeans with the white t-shirt as the previous day.

My mother's assumption had not been far off. He seemed like a ghost, pale and immune to all the elements around him. It was like time didn't matter for him. I felt certain that his pitch-black hair would never go grey, and his porcelain skin would never wrinkle. The thought scared me, but he seemed helpless at the moment.

He scooted a little closer to my end of the bed and looked at me with such earnestness that I thought I would melt.

"Everything I told you was true, Gwen. You are the first I'm collecting. You must help me find the others like you. The magicians are here and they need your power. Your soul. If they get it, you will not only be enslaved but they will have what they need to continue destroying the world. Millions of lives depend on you."

I stared. My mind was buzzing and I knew I had to get some answers before I could sort things out. It was too early.

"The magicians," Kian went on, "are trying to do the same as they did in their previous lives. They will destroy the world to own it. They will cow the Earth into submission. They have already begun."

"But ... but ... global warming...." was all I could say.

Kian shook his head. "There is something happening to the Earth, and it is unnatural. But they will crumble away the pieces until there is so little left that they can grab hold. In the process, millions could die."

"When did these ... magicians ... or whatever ... get here?" I asked, still feeling foolish. A part of me expected a camera crew to jump out and tell me I was in some MTV show.

"They were born approximately half a century ago. They have prominent positions in this country," Kian answered obediently. "They have recovered their memories, and hence their powers, decades ago. I'm afraid you have a lot of catching up to do."

*Okay*, I thought, *I have no idea what that means. Next.*

"Why are you here then?"

To my surprise Kian actually seemed at a loss at what to say and bowed back a little bit. I instantly felt sorry for my question; he looked so hurt by it. I was debating whether to take it back when he looked at me with a set chin and sorrowful eyes.

"I am here to collect you all. I am the perfect collector," he said, but it was not a boast. "I knew you all in your previous lives. You have retained some of your appearances, but you will be drawn to your own kind."

"Are you my own kind?" I asked, feeling like an alien.

Kian shook his head. "Only you have had previous lives. I am here through other magic, and only to do this."

There it was again. Those words set me on edge.

"Previous lives?" It came out it a whisper. I cleared my throat.

Kian sighed. I knew what he was going to say. I dreaded hearing the words. "You are not your body," he said sternly. "To send you forward in time is to send your soul."

*Relax*, I told myself. *It's a past life — of course it means I died.* Still, being told of your death was never pleasant. Figures. Last year I told my parents I was an atheist. My mom had asked me if I still wanted Christmas presents. So much for all of that.

Kian's cold demeanour had been falling apart since yesterday. He lit up with a crooked smile when I nodded. It felt like the right thing to do. I suddenly became very aware he was sitting in my bed.

His story was insane, but it explained so much. I had walked on water! (One half of my mind said) I had never fit in at home. But, on the other hand (the other half reminded me), I didn't know if I felt this way because I was a warrior on a mission travelling through time, or because I was a teenager.

My previous day was coming back to me in waves. I remembered the terrifying and paralyzing sensation of losing control, the pain of falling down the hillside and hitting the water. The images Kian had shown me playing from my eyes now seemed familiar, like memories. Like when you can't remember if you've dreamed something or if it happened to you.

I looked Kian straight in the face and said, "Okay. I'll do it."

In that moment, I was sure. I was sure the visions wouldn't stop, and I was sure that whatever I had felt in that vision — or whatever it was — were the strongest and most real feelings I had ever felt in my life. I had to see where this would lead.

Kian was overjoyed. He looked like a little kid at Christmas. He jumped up and grabbed me out of my bed, spinning me around. I was reminded of how strong he was and how my short-shorts pyjamas weren't really appropriate for this kind of thing. It was odd being held fast to his chest.

*Gwen Carlisle*, I said to myself, *your quiet days are over. And stop thinking about how nice and strong he is.*

After some negotiating and wiggling, I got him to put me down.

"What do I need to do?" I asked, smiling despite myself. It was a journey of self-discovery, and I was determined to find out who the stranger in the water was. Kian's awed and ecstatic look made this feel like a joyous occasion, and not my agreeing to run away with a stranger.

"Pack your things," he told me. "The others are in this country. We will need to find them."

I obediently began dragging an old green suitcase out of my closet when I suddenly realized something.

"How did you find me?" I asked. "How are you going to find anybody?"

While I struggled to get the tattered green suitcase out from underneath some shoeboxes, Kian dug around in his pocket.

"The world is big. But I have this machine."

I turned around to look and immediately sighed.

"That's a cell phone.".

He nodded. "I receive messages written in text with the location of the next one to be found. Like I said, you were scattered."

"So how did you find me?" I asked again.

"The location was given to me as this town," Kian answered simply, "and you were the only new young person here. I followed you, and here we are. You all performed the ritual at the same time. You are all the same age. Probably born on the same day."

I nodded. It seemed so obvious when he said it like that.

"How old are you?" I asked.

"Older than you," he replied, smiling like it was a joke.

I gave up and began throwing things into my suitcase, keeping my panic down by pretending I was just going on a family vacation. It was the new rebellious side of my personality that had agreed to this.

I packed everything from boots to sandals, dresses and pants, jackets and sunhats. Twenty minutes later I was almost done and marvelled at how quickly I had packed up my whole life.

"Wait," I said, climbing on top of the dingy thing so that I could close it. "Who sends you the text messages?"

Kian came over to help me struggle with the zipper. Together, we managed to close it and it sat on my floor, more like a sphere than a rectangle.

"I don't know," he answered, shrugging. "Magicians exist today, though they hide. Our cause has supporters. They finance our journey and provide me with locations."

"Doesn't that seem odd to you?" I asked him. "Are these other magicians the ones who brought you here?" When he only smiled, I shrugged and relented.

"You're right. That's the least odd part about this. So who told you it was your job to find all of us? How did you get here?"

I circled my room a few more times like a hawk, looking for necessities I had forgotten, but found I had none. After a few moments, I noticed Kian hadn't said anything.

"Well?" I asked, turning to look at him.

He was sitting on the edge of my bed, an awkward sight. I could only imagine what my parents would say if they saw him just sitting there as I rushed around in front of him in my little pyjamas. My eyes drifted to my closed bedroom door and I realized how suspicious my parents would be if they knew he was here at all.

"Hmm?" asked Kian.

I somehow doubted that he hadn't heard, but repeated myself nonetheless.

"I said how did you get here? What's your story?"

"It is what I need to do," he answered simply, looking out the window at the sun. "It has been, I think, seven years since I came here."

His voice had changed somewhat — he sounded bored when he answered me, like he wanted to change the subject.

"Okay...." I replied, patting down my suitcase. "I guess I have less here than I thought. Turn around."

Kian obediently turned while I got dressed. When I announced I was finished, he got up, and taking the suitcase in one hand as if it weighed nothing, crossed my room before I could realize what he was doing. Soon, he had opened the door and was about to go downstairs.

"Hey!"

I chased after him, my heart jumping up into my throat. I didn't know how I was going to tell my parents that I was leaving for a while, all because some magicians might want to steal my magical powers.

"What are you doing?" I whispered fiercely.

"We have a flight that leaves this afternoon," he answered, calm as calm could be. He started descending the stairs, having to manoeuvre my oversized suitcase carefully since he and it did not fit onto the narrow stairway together.

"Hey!"

I immediately followed. Even in my panic, I marvelled at how his different moods washed over me like waves. I could feel sympathy for him one moment and be furious the next.

"You knew I would come around?" I half-yelled. The house felt too small to full-on yell.

When I caught up to him on the stairs, his mouth was set and his dark eyes feigned innocence. Struggling with my suitcase made him look a little more human —

especially when he missed a step and nearly crashed on top of the green thing that held my belongings.

"I had an inclination that you would not deny your true self," Kian replied calmly, but I could see frustration play across his face as he reached the first landing of the stairs and had one more to go. I nearly growled at him.

"That was a little presumptuous, don't you think?" I was still chasing him down the stairs at about zero miles per hour. "To think I would just jump on a plane and leave the country? This is a lot to take in, you know!"

"But your memories are convincing, are they not?" he asked. By the way he looked at me, I wondered how much he knew.

"Besides," Kian added, pretending I wasn't shouting in his ear, "we are going to New York City, not leaving the country."

"New York?" I cried.

My resolve weakening, I had to remind myself of the waterfalls. The hand on the riverbank. My selfish — and foolish — reason for following Kian into the unknown.

He finally reached the last few steps and shoved the big suitcase unceremoniously down into the kitchen. He followed it down then picked it up and headed for the back door. I was on his heels.

"Listen, I don't even know if I have a passport…." I lied, knowing I had packed it in my backpack. It was all just going too fast.

"Gwen," Kian finally turned at the back door to face me full-on, "what happened to your sense of adventure and wonder? And, moreover, what happened to your willingness to come with me?"

I didn't know if he was talking about me in a past life or in the present. I bit my lip. All I wanted was to learn about the visions — the other place — and maybe see it again. I had naïvely assumed that Kian and his search would stay rooted in Oregon.

"Well?" Kian asked.

"I just didn't think of leaving and going ... far," I replied.

"You will get used to it," he told me. "Think of how I felt when I first learned of all the new lands and how you could travel across them!"

I sighed again. He was trying to make me feel better, but we could not relate to each other. I looked back at him but noticed his eyes focused on something over my shoulder. Kian pursed his lips, and if he were anyone else, I was sure he would be blushing. I knew what it was before I even turned around.

"Hi, Mom, Dad." I nodded to my parents, trying in vain to place myself in front of my suitcase. The thing was twice my size.

At the small kitchen table, my parents sat with toast on their plates. They had gone on a diet the week before. My dad still held a knife in mid-air, the low-fat, no-sugar jam having already fallen to the table. No one had come in — they'd been there the whole time. Their mouths hung open.

# Chapter Six

"Who's your friend, Gwen?" my mother asked politely. "And what was he doing upstairs this morning?"

"This is Ted," I improvised, "from school."

My mother raised an eyebrow. "You're in high school?" she asked Kian skeptically.

"No," he answered.

I choked.

"And where are you and Ted heading with your suitcase?" my father asked, standing up.

*Oh, no.*

I could see the questions play across their faces. Slowly, my mother put down her fork and wiped her mouth with a napkin. Kian looked as if he was being cornered by wolves. His eyes darted, looking for an escape route, and fell on some horseback riding trophies on a mantle in the living room. I hadn't ridden in years, but back when I was eight, I was tough to beat. They were sandwiched between some pictures of me in my ballerina outfit from childhood and my archery trophies.

"Gwen has been selected to attend a school for the arts — a very prestigious one," Kian told my parents. "But unfortunately, the deadline to apply was in July, and Gwen filled out her application in August, so the school's acceptance is rather short notice. I am a ... representative ... of that school. I booked her a flight for today, but unfortunately couldn't reach you."

In unison, my parents turned to me. I was surprised at his improvisation skills but felt my mind go horribly blank.

"Surprise...." I said weakly. It was all I could manage.

"Gwen ..." my mother began, "what's going on?"

I couldn't think of anything the way a rebel brain does on a vital exam question. I stalled the inevitable.

"Like he said, Mom, I applied to this school and now I've been accepted, but the semester started today and I really shouldn't miss more than one day...." It was such a weak lie.

"And where is this school?" asked Dad.

"New York," I answered immediately.

"And what is it called?" he asked.

I looked to Kian for inspiration.

"The ... Academy for Gifted Young People?" It came out as a question.

In my mind, I was kicking myself furiously, holding my breath as I waited for my parents to realize I had stolen the name from *X-Men*.

"That sounds familiar," my mother said, putting a finger to her chin, contemplatively trying to remember where she had heard the name before.

The *X-Men* DVD on the TV cabinet burned in my vision. I wished it out of existence, but it did not budge. I looked at Kian, desperate. He took a deep breath.

"You will not worry about Gwen," he told my parents. "Nor will you check the school, or speak about it to others. You will know she is away and will expect her letters. But Gwen *is* away."

I held my breath — I had no idea what he was doing, what he was trying to pull. There was a long pause while my parents seemed frozen in time, then my mother broke into a loud sob and grabbed me in her arms.

"I'm going to miss you!" she exclaimed. I would have gasped had I not been crushed in her large arms.

"You take good care of her, Ted," my dad said to Kian then shook his hand. Kian smiled in return. Dad gave me a hug, for which Mom had to move out of the way, and then tried to include her in what he called our family bear hugs.

After even more hugs and promises to write, Kian and I stepped out of the house. We did not speak as we walked down the driveway, and he put my suitcase in the trunk of a rental car that I was not surprised to see parked on the road.

It was a heavy moment for me. I had just lied to my parents and left home with a stranger. My rebellious mind pictured the *America's Most Wanted* episode which would feature my photo next to Kian's.

I got into the passenger seat of the Ford Focus and leaned my head against the headrest. A big part of me wanted to run back into the house, screaming that

I had been abducted by a lunatic. But another part was curious, and for the first time in my life, really courageous. I blamed it on an adrenaline rush and low blood sugar. I hadn't eaten anything in a long time.

Kian got in next to me and slowly, with my heart aching, we began to pull away from the house.

"So are you a Jedi or something?" I finally asked. I could tell he had been respecting the gravity of the situation for me, not pressing me to talk.

"A who?" he asked.

I rolled my eyes in the morning sunlight. I sat hugging my knapsack, looking at the sky above. "What did you do to my parents?"

"Magic," he answered simply. "Though I am not like you. I can do simple things like play on the power of conviction and belief. I do not like to do it," he added when I turned around to look at him. "I do not like to take advantage of the human mind, or its weaknesses. But it was necessary."

"You did that to me yesterday, didn't you? To keep me from calling the cops or something?"

"It was necessary," Kian repeated.

"Yeah," was all I could say in response. Then, "So I can do more than that?"

"Yeah," Kian said, smiling and emulating my tone.

"You know, you're really annoying," I retorted, looking away. I saw him shrug in the window's reflection.

"Yes, I was told that a long time ago."

He seemed happy enough and I turned on the radio, scanning the channels until I was able to find something that wasn't talk radio or country music. It was surprisingly difficult. And there we sat for upwards of an hour — an apparent magician from two thousand years ago and a seventeen-year-old descendant of his gods, who was, in all respectable terms, plain as cheddar cheese.

When we finally pulled up to the rental car garage at the airport, my heart lurched a little. I was inundated with anxiety about (of all things) missing school. How much was I going to miss? Would they call home? What would my parents say? Would I have to stay back a year? My resolve was weakening.

I opened my mouth to ask this last ridiculous question, but Kian turned at that moment to deal with the garage attendant. I scuffed the ground with my foot, dejected. When he came back he frowned at my expression.

"Don't worry," he said, leading me into the airport. "You are brave for trusting your true self above all others. You will be fine."

"Where are you getting this?"

"My father," Kian replied, finally getting a printout from his jeans pocket. He also produced a passport. "He was a wise man, and I remember his words, even now."

I felt unfit to comment, so I just stood, stupidly staring at the escalators and desks with airline logos as far as the eye could see. Kian went to an electronic board with desk numbers then walked until he found the desk he was looking for. I followed all the while, feeling like a lost child.

"Delta," Kian read aloud, "New York."

He smiled at me with an accomplished look. I couldn't tell if I was getting used to the statuesque eeriness of him or if he was letting down his guard. His mind-bending magic kept me nervous — I wasn't sure if my emotions were my own. I kept second-guessing my decision to go with him and run away from the apparent threat of some magicians. Had it really been my choice? Yes. I wanted to see that place again. To feel like I had under the waterfalls.

"Hello." Kian had walked up to the attendant at the desk and passed her the printed paper.

She was a young woman, at least ten years older than me, and she smiled at him coyly and made small talk for nearly five minutes, even though there were people queuing behind us. I was getting annoyed.

"What's the matter?" Kian asked me when she had finally turned back to her computer to do her job.

"Nothing," I replied automatically. He frowned at me.

"Your jaw is set," he said.

I made a point of turning away from him. All I could hear was the little computer tap-tapping of the flirty attendant at the Delta desk.

"And will your ... little sister be travelling with you?" the woman asked.

Before Kian could open his mouth, I had slammed my passport down on the desk. Neither of us said a word. The flirty woman tapped in my information, and the machine spat out two boarding passes.

My head was throbbing and my injuries were causing my entire body to ache and tense. The combination made me irate.

"Here you go." She gave the passes to Kian.

We walked away towards the gate we needed.

"What's the matter?" he asked again.

I did not underestimate his naïveté, so I was about to tell him when I turned and saw a wide smile on his face.

"Oh, you're such a jerk!" I rushed forward, pulling his dainty suitcase behind me. Unfortunately, there was no getting rid of him.

While we sat in the uncomfortable airport chairs, he badgered me.

"Why did you not like the desk woman?" he asked, smiling in a way that made me want to punch him.

"Her smile," I finally answered.

"What about her smile?"

"I don't know," I answered honestly. "It had too much *eye*."

Kian frowned, genuine confusion playing on his face. "Gwen," he answered, quite seriously, "she had two eyes."

"Oh, forget it!"

## Chapter Seven

Waiting for a flight isn't like usual waiting. You're excited, nervous, and every once in a while, you entertain thoughts of a fiery death in a plummet to earth from thousands of feet above. Your activity is limited. You can only watch little children get on their parents' nerves, or elderly people sit reading a book or businessmen tapping away on their laptops. Sustenance is limited to greasy fast food. Your smell is restricted to the cinnamon bun place down the hall mixing with the toilet at the other end of the hall. The five senses are crippled.

I was bored — going through security had been less than fun. Getting a pat-down from a retiree while Kian just smiled his way through was all the more annoying. I had been excited to have time to think about my vision, but my head was aching and I was grouchy.

Too many questions about my practical future — school, my parents, etc. — were plaguing me.

And while Kian sat and texted with the mysterious all-knowing someone, looking like some historical character given a twenty-first century gadget, I groped at my forehead and squinted at the brightly lit ceiling.

"Where are you going?" Kian asked when I stood. He was back to hostage-taker mode in a second, but then remembered I had agreed to come willingly and relented. I felt bad for being a grouch.

"Restroom," I replied. With my head pulsing, it was the most I could manage.

I walked into the even more brightly lit restroom, where only one stall was occupied. Grasping the sink to steady myself, I washed my face with cold water. But when I looked up, to my panic, I could not see anything but vague shapes and lights. I was gone in the mirror — then the mirror and the bathroom were gone too.

I felt blinded and started panicking. Now that I think about it, it probably lasted all of five seconds, but it felt like an eternity. Then, just as my sight was leaving me, my sense of hearing kicked in full force, but only in one ear.

Laughter. A man's laughter sounded in my ear as if he stood behind me. My heart exploded all at once with the same excitement and love that I had felt in my previous vision and dream. The truest of true feelings.

"You know —" the voice began, but I was slipping, falling. I tried to grab at it, but I was too far away. My hearing and sight impaired, I was losing balance, and soon I hit the cold ceramic floor.

"Gwen!"

This voice was real now, concrete, and in both my ears. My sight was still blurred, but I felt around with a hand and grasped Kian's hair.

"Is she okay?" a woman's voice asked, and somewhere far away, a toilet flushed. For a moment, I thought how dirty I must look, lying on a bathroom floor in an airport. Classy.

"She's okay," Kian replied. "Just hasn't eaten today. A little faint, is all."

I heard the woman tsk.

"Young girls and eating disorders today," she said disapprovingly. "I blame the media." And with that she was gone. Had I not been incapacitated, I would have rolled my eyes.

Kian dragged me up and we hobbled over to the cinnamon bun place. He force-fed me a sticky roll as my vision came back in increments.

"You haven't eaten," he scolded. I shrugged. As much as I hated to admit it, the food was making me stronger. And he was being quite sweet, hovering over me like a mother hen.

"I heard a voice," I told him when I had regained some strength. The flirty desk woman from before was calling rows to board. I was surprised when he said nothing. I looked up at him, suddenly suspicious. "Can you laugh?" I asked.

"Why?"

"Please, I just want to know you can laugh," I said, giving the worst argument of my life.

Kian chuckled a little dutifully. Not even close. The

voice I had heard was completely different. I sighed as Kian dragged me up.

My heart skipped a beat when he wrapped an arm around my shoulders. My body must have stiffened because he looked at me to explain.

"It will look strange if I have to carry you onto the airplane," he said. I nodded, but the walk onto the plane still had my heart beating a little faster than normal, and I had the embarrassing feeling that Kian knew it.

✦

My first flight in many years went by with little excitement. My head was still pounding and after Kian practically pushed me into my first class seat, he promptly fell asleep and I began buzzing the attendants for some Aspirin. My body felt like a punching bag. It was like all I had done after seeing Kian for the first time was fall down.

It surprised me a little that Kian slept, or ate for that matter. He had eaten a cinnamon bun and was now snoozing with his mouth slightly open. Fast asleep, leaning his head against the window, he looked more statuesque than ever, but more human as well. It was a strange juxtaposition.

We were airborne by the time a young flight attendant came around, asking what I needed. She eyed Kian, smiling, and came back with my Aspirin in less than a minute. I cradled my head and envisioned the Aspirin dissolving, its magic bringing me back to life a little. Annoyingly, the flight attendant came back.

She dawdled in front of our row for a moment before finally leaning over to me.

"Hey," she whispered, as if we were long-time confidantes, her bright blue eyes shining. "Between you and me, that guy is really, *really* cute."

Pause.

She looked from me to Kian, and then leaned over to me again. "Is that your brother?"

I raised my eyebrows at her and looked as stern as I could. "Between you and me," I said flatly, "no."

She smiled again, politely, and walked away. However, not before looking me up and down again, most definitely wondering what I had that others didn't. My sandy hair and plain, dusty eyes; I didn't look all too spectacular.

"*You* be a descendant of the gods," I muttered smugly into my airline pillow, and promptly fell asleep too.

✦

I awoke on my side, my head in Kian's lap. Realizing where I was made heat flood into my face, and by the time I sat up, I was blushing insanely. The sun was rapidly setting and the people around us were putting on their shoes and hiding their books and laptops. I noticed Kian had put a blanket over me and felt a fresh pulse of heat in my face.

"Please put your seatbelt on, miss," the flight attendant from before said to me. Her eyes drifted over Kian then settled onto the aisle. I was trying to hide my face from him.

"Gwen, would you like to look outside?" he asked.

I did. I pretended to be searching for my seatbelt while I pressed my cold hands to my face, trying to get the red out. Mustering my best neutral expression, I looked out the window onto New York City.

My eyes widened with all there was to take in: the brilliant lights shimmered like a galaxy, while tall buildings rose like giants from the landscape. Darkness had fallen while we flew and the night made the Hudson River glisten, an enormous snake slithering through the city. It all shone like a jewel against the dark of the Atlantic Ocean. I could think of no other word for what I was seeing than a miracle. A conclave of happenstance and opportunity had created this mammoth, living city. And I was about to set foot in it.

Giddily, I noticed my headache had gone and I was actually very excited to be in New York. I had always dreamed of coming here. My thoughts of leaving home, school, and running away with Kian dissolved as I looked out the tiny window.

Kian touched my arm and I was brought back to the present.

"Have you been here before?" he asked.

"No. Have you?"

He shook his head.

Even with the visions, this stranger, and magicians threatening my life, I took a chance.

"Let's go do tourist things tomorrow," I said.

The words came from the part of me that wished to stall the inevitable. No magic for now, and no danger — just New York. Maybe I was so adept at normalcy that I was trying to restore some even in my ridiculous escape with Kian.

He raised a perfectly black eyebrow at me but had no chance to respond as the plane began to descend and the noise of the wheels coming out from under the cabin scared us both into gripping the seat dividers. I looked over at Kian trying to mask his fright — his demeanour was falling apart. It was nice seeing his human side.

✦

Leaving JFK airport was an adventure in itself. We picked up our baggage and Kian once again stuck his little suitcase into my hand and picked up my giant green one. We walked through the glassy airport looking for a way out, until finally stumbling upon a taxi service.

"Manhattan," Kian said to the driver, "8th and West 42nd — Hilton Hotel."

I sat nervously in the back seat, a little portion of my mind still going crazy at my actions. It was like the old Gwen was trapped in the mind of this new Gwen. The old Gwen was screaming and stomping and wanted to go home to somewhere sane, and the new Gwen wanted to see where this adventure would lead. She was dangerous. I frowned disapprovingly at my reflection in the window. The new Gwen wanted to see if Kian would touch her arm again.

By the time we arrived at the hotel, it was past eleven at night. The time difference quickly caught up to me and I found myself exhausted. The cab driver silently unloaded our bags, but I didn't even notice. I wanted sleep. The giddiness had seeped out of me as I sat in the car, and now a proper rest was in order.

As I got out of the taxi, I was reminded of the pain I was in. I hadn't noticed it while sitting in the plane, but as I stood, everything hurt. I could hear my elbow crack and my knee snap in ways they never had before. Kian paid and led the way into the expansive lobby of the Hilton.

I missed the name he gave at the desk, and I didn't even notice the shiny credit card he fished out. I was standing off to the side, dreaming about a pillow and a bath to soak aching bones and muscles. In my mind, the old Gwen was beginning to sound like a senior citizen. Not paying attention, I also missed that Kian had only gotten one room.

We travelled quietly in the elevator, the bright lights beginning to sting at my eyes again as the headache returned. I felt like one big mess of pain. I followed Kian to a door then stopped.

"You only got the one room?" I asked, the force having left my voice. My stomach did somersaults.

"Just to make sure I don't lose you," Kian said, smiling reassuringly. His crooked smile again reminded me of the demeanour he had shed in the past day. Even with the smile, his words unnerved me. What did he think could happen to me?

Before I could ask, he opened the door to reveal two double beds and other components of a standard hotel room. I was relieved to see the double beds, and all questions were forgotten as I fished my pyjamas out of the tattered green suitcase, changed in the bathroom, and climbed into bed. I had reserved some thinking time to ponder my day and figure out what was happening inside my mind, but as soon as my head touched the pillow, I fell asleep.

✦

*I was standing on a clifftop, overlooking a dark and angry sea. Waves were hitting the shore unnaturally, as if no longer an effect of the tide and wind, but rather a deep rage that was threatening to break onto the land. Every wave that smashed against the rocks far below was like a hammer to my chest. The wind rose around me, and soon I was struggling for breath as it blew past my face so quickly I could not catch time to inhale.*

*Terrified, gasping, I still looked over the edge onto the jagged rocks beneath. I did not want to see them — did not want to increase my fear, but could not turn away. The wind picked up and blew even harder against my skin, whipping my thin dress against my legs and back. My hair stung at my face and eyes. Any moment now, I would be carried away.*

*As if on cue, the wind reached out to me with solid hands, and I could feel the tendrils of air pinch and prod into my sides. I gasped as the human pain of my aching and abused body protested against the assault. I could not fight it — the power was too strong. Panicking, I realized I was failing. I was not strong enough to stand against this, and I would be destroyed. My heart tried to pound against my ribcage, but a tendril of wind had wrapped itself so tightly around my torso that it could not. I felt like my heart would burst as I was lifted off my feet and carried into the air above the deadly bluffs below. I hung, suspended and in pain.*

*Then, I felt the stirring inside me like electricity in my bones. My magic would fight this unnatural storm. My power was the power of the storm. I would survive.*

*A voice was calling my name. He fought with me. The sound of him brought me back to my senses and I searched inside me for the spark of magic. It flooded me like a fire, and the heat spread to the cold wind. Slowly, the tempest began to die down.*

## Chapter Eight

T he dream released me like a switch being turned off. My eyes opened to the darkness of the hotel room, and I sucked in the air I had been deprived of in the dream. There was still a weight on top of me, making my sore muscles ache and my bones groan with the force holding me down.

I fought on instinct, kicking and managing little screams between my gasps for air. It was probably a few seconds, but felt like hours, when I realized I was on my back on the floor, and the weight on top of me was Kian. He was saying something — something that I hadn't been able to hear because the rush of wind and the pounding of waves had remained in my ears long after the dream had gone.

"Gwen! Come back!" he was saying. "Come back!"

His voice was low and forceful. For the first time since we'd met, I was truly frightened of him. The growl in his tone suggested a character I had not yet seen.

I calmed down enough to stop struggling, though my heart still pounded and I was still short of breath. This was more to do with his weight on top of me.

In the darkness, Kian's eyes found mine and softened with recognition.

"Gwen?" he asked softly.

I nodded.

"What happened?" I asked, my voice hoarse. I could remember the sensation of the wind suffocating me, drying my throat.

Instead of answering, Kian climbed off me. Before I could reach out for his hand, he scooped me up and placed me back on my bed. It was soaked with sweat and the sheets had been torn off. The same kind of headache I'd experienced in the airport was setting in. He didn't have to tell me.

"Memories?" I said. It was more like a moan. I had accepted my fate. Somewhat. Why was I still being bombarded?

I placed both arms over my face and sighed with the relief the pressure brought.

"You didn't want to leave me alone because you knew this would happen." I couldn't decide if I wanted to say it as a comment or as an accusation.

I managed to sit up, swaying slightly, on the edge of the bed.

Kian did not look much better than I felt. His appearance made me wonder how difficult it had been to restrain me. His t-shirt-and-shorts ensemble matched mine, but sweat dripped from his dark hair and he gasped slightly. His eyes shone, but his mouth was set in a grim line. I remembered that he had chased me, carried my suitcase, and performed magic without ever breaking a sweat. My own apparent strength scared me.

As I set down my hands to steady myself, I felt crumbs beneath my fingers. The substance was flaky and white. Wearily, I looked up towards the ceiling where it seemed like something had clawed and beaten at the hotel plaster. In turn, I saw my hands and fore-arms were covered in the stuff.

"Was I …"

He nodded, looking exhausted. Before I could ask anything else, there was a hard knock on the door. Putting on his best stoic look, Kian went to answer it while I sat, dumbfounded.

He opened the door to two security guards in the hall, both huge, both looking very stern. The wedge of light from the hallway made me cringe as a new wave of pain brushed across my eyes like a curtain. I could barely see their serious faces, but their tones made up for it.

"Sir," one security guard said gruffly, "we had a report of a disturbance in this room."

"What kind of disturbance?" asked Kian. His voice held worry, and I couldn't decide if it was fake for the security guards or real for me.

There was silence from the door, as the security guards looked him up and down. I could imagine their appraisal of him — doesn't look dangerous, doesn't look crazy. But you never know.

Finally, one of them spoke. "One of your neigh-bours said they heard screaming, sir. Is there anyone else in the room?"

Just then an unwelcome flashlight shone into my face, and I found myself stumbling into a complimentary bathrobe and coming to the door.

"Ma'am." They both gave one curt nod. My head still pounded so I squinted into the hall, doing my best to look tired and not pained.

"I'm sorry," I said, blurting out the first thing that came to mind. I just wanted them to go away. "We'll try to keep it down."

Shutting the door on their suspicious faces, I slunk back into the room. My stomach had been against getting up so quickly. I could hear Kian saying something behind me, but I rushed into the bathroom and was sick all over the sparkling hotel toilet.

I hated throwing up. My knees and hands shook and it felt like ages before I was done emptying the contents of my stomach, which hadn't been a lot since we had again neglected food. When I was done, I leaned back only to find a weight against my back. Kian had been holding my hair.

He helped me wash my face then scooped me back into bed for the second time that night. I lay there, listening as he moved around the room, cleaning up whatever I.had destroyed or moved while in my dream state. Finally he sat down next to me.

"Sleep will help you. You should not have gotten up. My small bit of magic is still enough to work persuasion," he said.

"Hm," was all I managed in reply. He sighed.

"Your past life was…" he paused, searching for words, "more than on this human level. Your memories will be strong, intense. And they will interfere with the power you have."

"How … stop?" I mumbled.

Kian shook his head. "If they stop, you die. There are bad people coming to get you. You need to be strong enough to defend yourself. As bad as this feels, having it taken from you is worse."

I lay prone, listening without the capability to consider his words. Storing the information away in a part of my mind, to be dealt with later, I listened as Kian explained how I had flown from my bed and began to convulse as my dreaming state flowed over into the real world. He told me how he had to drag me from the air and pin me down — wake me up so that I would not hurt myself.

"You are somewhat different," Kian said, changing the topic. His voice was tired, but there was a hint of strong emotion behind it. Was he upset? "You speak with humour in this life, and you smile faster." Then, after another pause, "Gwen?"

I lay with my eyes closed. He thought I was asleep. I did not reply, wondering what he would say.

"In the days before the Romans came," Kian began, "you had become more mysterious. I always wished to ask you about it, but never did. And then it was too late." He paused. "Maybe if you remember, you will tell me."

He sighed then and leaned in closer. I didn't know why I held my breath, but I did, and in the darkness, Kian placed a single kiss on my forehead. He moved into his own bed, and soon I was fast asleep, the pain in my head having blissfully dissipated.

✦

"You're different," I told Kian over our complimentary continental breakfast.

Around us, businessmen, families, and wealthy looking housewives conversed over their buffet meals. I was absolutely delighted the pain in my head was gone and revelled in the noise of the room.

Kian looked better as well. He wore a collared white shirt and black pants, giving him the look of some banker who has run out on his day job. He had smoothed down his hair, and his features were becoming more human to me. When he looked up at me over his bowl of cereal, his lips were pursed.

"You've been different since we left," I repeated after not getting a reaction. He put down his spoon and shrugged. I was about to press further when he sighed and leaned in close.

"You are changing me," he said. His voice was a mixture of revelation and resignation. I must have looked confused, because he went on. "Being with you feels … human again. I am becoming what I once was. It was different when I was on my own. I forgot what it was like to be with people."

"Oh," I said stupidly. I didn't know if it was a compliment. The conversation over breakfast had just turned heavy.

"You said you were here for seven years. What were you doing before you found me?" I asked.

"Waiting," he said.

Before I had time to think about it, he got up and

cleared his dishes. We were out of the hotel and into the bright morning sunlit streets of Manhattan within minutes. Even in September, the weather was particularly hot. I was already warm. My heart skipped a beat when I realized it was a weekday, and I was missing yet more classes.

To hide all of the bruises, cuts, and bumps sustained over the past few days, I had worn a long-sleeved flowing shirt and tights. Just enough to cover all of my injuries, but I was already baking on the sidewalk. It didn't help my summer wear that many of the fresh bruises on my arms and legs were in the shape of handprints from Kian's attempts to get me off our hotel room ceiling.

I sighed and was about to complain when I realized his wear wasn't meant for summer either.

We had decided that to find someone on an island of over eight million people, we would need to cover as much ground as possible. My suggestion to split up was instantly rebuffed as Kian reminded me he did not want to leave me alone. And, after last night, I had been hoping he would say that and not leave me to fend for myself.

Convincing myself it was for the good of our mission, I talked him into taking me to the Statue of Liberty. Every time I remembered what I was doing, panic would flare in my chest and my heart would race.

My reckless, irresponsible behaviour over the past few days was still foreign to me. The part of me that kept being inexplicably magical, no matter how much it harmed me, was tempting me. Kian's warm looks and attention didn't help to deter me from following him either. I realized I hadn't even thought about the loom-ing threat Kian had said awaited me. I knew nothing of magicians and needed to stay focused on the moment.

Last night had been jarring and painful. If having my magic stolen by any of the ancient magicians was worse than that, I wanted to avoid it happening to me or anyone else like me. Kian insisted we keep an eye out for anyone my age. I wondered how soon he would realize that we needed a new plan.

The pain of the night before had made me remem-ber how real my situation was. If I didn't survive the memories, I wanted to see the Statue of Liberty before I died. That was my logic. So, a short and sweaty cab ride later, we were waiting in line for a boat that would circle the Statue of Liberty and then return to shore, as the statue itself was closed to visitors.

I had bought an ice cream to pass my time in line, while Kian text messaged on his little phone again. Finally, I had had enough.

"I don't believe you don't know who's on the other end," I said sternly, while a chubby six-year-old pushed past me to join his parents in line. All around us, people chatted and looked annoyed at standing out in the heat.

"Why not?" Kian asked, putting away his phone.

"You're not curious to know whose orders you're following or why?" I lowered my voice, realizing tour-ists surrounded us. "You've never seen or spoken to any of the magicians you said are on our side?"

He looked out onto the ocean for a long while before speaking. "Facing this direction," Kian said, "I could almost imagine seeing home." He sounded so wistful it nearly broke my heart. He turned around to face me, his back to the sea.

"I came here by a magic that has kept my body and soul intact, and I have been given a magic and strength that is not mine. My responsibility is to collect those that can challenge the magicians. I told you that."

The statement sounded well-rehearsed, like he had assured himself of this many times. When I was about to open my mouth, pointing out I had still not gotten any answers, he continued.

"So I know why I am doing what I do, and I know why I am going to the places I go," Kian said. "No magic goes unnoticed. That's how the others, stronger magicians than I, know of you. I don't have that strength. I could not help you without them. So I do not ask any more." He smiled, but when I clearly didn't understand, he went on.

"At home, I had no magic. Anything I have is to do this one task. Your life, Gwen, uses your magic. The person you are, how you live and feel, all of those things use your magic whether you notice it or not. And powerful magicians can locate this magic in the world. The existence of our power is rare enough that when it is used, magicians feel it and where it comes from."

"And then you go and track the person down," I supplied. Kian nodded. "But ..." I stammered. *I'd been using magic my entire life?* "I'm so boring!"

"Perhaps you wanted to be," Kian suggested. I opened my mouth to argue, but then a thought struck me. It was the old Gwen, still sitting in my mind, fighting and kicking for things to go back to normal. Grudgingly, I had to admit that Kian was right. It was old Gwen's nature. I did just want to be left alone.

"Four months ago," Kian said. His words brought me back to the present, waiting in a hot line to sit on a hot boat.

"What?"

"Four months ago, there was an earthquake in San Francisco after the magicians had disturbed the earth with their magic. The houses around yours crumbled. You watched from the window and willed it to stop."

I remembered that day. I had been so scared, home on the weekend while Mom and Dad were at their clinic downtown. Everything shook while I watched TV, and the plasma crashed down onto the living room floor. I had run to the window to see the entire bay not shaking, but rolling. And then the houses to the left were collapsing into their foundations. My heart had pounded, I had held my breath, and the rolling had stopped. We were safe, and I had never thought anything more of it than luck or coincidence.

"But I ..." I began.

"You have a natural magic, which makes it pure and strong. You did will it to end."

"That's when you were sent to find me?" I asked. Kian nodded again.

We shuffled forward as we had been doing for the last hour. We reached a portion of the line where we were near to the front, underneath a canopy and in front of some TVs playing various news channels. Apparently, meteorologists were warning of an extremely brutal winter for the Northeast. But I would be home by then. A thought struck me.

"Kian!" How could I not think to ask? "How many are there? How many people are you going to find?" My actual burning question was how long I would be away from home.

He shrugged dismissively. "I don't know," he said quietly.

"What do you mean you don't know? I thought you knew all of us." I was annoyed, hot, and probably sunburnt. When I turned and saw his face, however, I understood. Kian turned back towards the television screens.

*He doesn't know how many he'll find because he doesn't know how many are left.*

I pondered all of the events that could have befallen me had I never met Kian. What if these memories came back, and I didn't know what to do? What if he hadn't been there last night to drag me down by the ankle? What if I was just overrun by magic and collapsed under its weight? What if something else had happened to my human self? Has this happened to any of us?

I checked myself after the word "us." No turning back now.

"BREAKING NEWS." The television screens behind us flashed red. The muttering died down and people turned to the screens to watch and listen. I could hear a few parents shushing their children.

The noise of the crowd was still too loud to hear the announcer, but the closed captioning on each screen was flashing wildly. Suddenly, each of the dozen screens began showing an image of the Atlantic Ocean, with a red target sign over top.

"What …?" I began, but my question was cut off as the pier beneath us lurched and I toppled to the side. Kian caught my arm in a painful grip, but others weren't as fortunate. Frantic screams erupted as people fell into the water, which was swaying in uneasy and violent waves.

"There's been an earthquake somewhere offshore," Kian said through gritted teeth. I instinctively looked up towards the screens for the news anchors confirming this, but everything had short-circuited.

The pier jolted and I lost my footing again. This time, for a terrifying few seconds, the pier groaned and shook as the water was sucked out from underneath it and into the ocean. We were faced with a giant wave forming offshore. More screams cut through the air. The wave broke but its tide still hit the pier and raised it. Through my panic, I saw more people tumble into the swelling ocean. The only thing keeping me away from the water was Kian's death grip on my arm. He was hanging on to the railing of the pier with his other hand.

We rose with the water until the pier stood nearly vertical. The only thing louder than the roar of the sea was the grating of metal and wood as aged infrastructure gave out. And when I thought we were about to flip, the wave was gone and the pier crashed down.

Water engulfed us and I inhaled it in terror. The feeling of the pier slamming into the ocean was akin to when I had fallen into the Pacific only a few days ago. The ache reverberated off my heels, up my spine, through my neck, and into my head. I was disoriented and half drowned when Kian dragged me up.

"Run!" he shouted over the noise. I tried to scramble away, but my gaze kept turning back to the sea. People were in the water. Some struggled, some did not. I stared hard at the dangerous dark surface, expecting the magicians to emerge from within it.

"Gwen!" Kian was still yelling at me. "*Run!*"

I finally gathered the strength to run towards the end of the boardwalk and land, but not before I saw the Statue of Liberty violently rocking and shaking with the ocean's surges.

# Chapter Nine

The slippery and uneven wood did not make running easy, especially since I was still sore and aching. I eventually had to stop. My breath was becoming ragged, and my chest seized as the blood pumped through to my head, each heartbeat like a hammer blow.

I pulled Kian to a stop and realized we had been holding hands as we ran from the ocean's fury. He let go and knelt in front of me, looking worried, while I doubled over and heaved. Something unfamiliar tugged at my chest. It threatened to overthrow me, but I couldn't figure out what it was.

When I regained some energy and air, I straightened. We stood on a street that must have held lots of banks and offices, since the people who flooded the streets and crowded the windows were all dressed in smart black suits. Everyone eyed the sea nervously and spoke amongst themselves. I was at a total loss. So much for seeing the city.

Kian seized my arm again, his favourite spot where he liked to hold me as he saved my life, and I winced as the bruises deepened.

"Let's go," he said grimly.

A cold wind had swept over me, and I was suddenly glad to be wearing the long sleeves as I shivered like a wet cat. When the smell of salt touched my nostrils, it was sickening. I should not smell salt. Not here, not among the concrete and hot-dog vendors and cars. The magicians, if they were doing this, for the first time since I had allowed myself to believe, seemed wholly real.

Dripping with sweat, we eventually made it back to the hotel. I didn't know how Kian remembered the way, but my side ached and the heat and dirt of the city pricked at my skin. He seemed unfazed. The streets we had passed were loaded with people gawking and whispering in the direction of the pier. We stopped outside the big doors of the hotel, where life seemed to be business as usual.

Kian gave me a look I hadn't seen before. Was it meant to be reassuring? He took my hand and led me inside.

The screens in the lobby were all playing the same footage of the horror we had come from. Underneath the images of a rolling pier, a headline read, "Fifty-four dead in latest natural disaster to hit east coast."

Kian was saying something. When I didn't answer, he said, "Gwen?"

"Hm?"

I was embarrassed to be caught with my gaze lingering on our intertwined fingers. He ignored the red that quickly spread over my cheeks and led the way to the elevators. Luckily, our horrid appearance didn't attract any attention as each face was turned either to a TV screen or a window.

I was refusing to look outside. I felt exposed and unsafe, as if the sea was about to surge and swallow Manhattan. The force had seemed so huge. The power to control that would have to be enormous. How did I ever stand a chance?

"What was that?" I asked in the elevator. My voice shook.

"In ancient times, people believed they were a product of the earth," Kian said, pressing the button for our floor. "So to control the people, one must control the earth. That is what *they* did to our home, and now they are doing it to this land. They think if they cause enough confusion and fear, they will have enough power to take control."

"How?"

Kian gave me a look that made it clear I did not want to know, but I would not back down.

"They campaign on fear. They believe to lead this country is the most powerful position in the world, and they want it."

"Oh."

The answer seemed obvious but I was still shocked an ancient magician would want to be president. To destroy the country seemed extreme.

"That's why they need me," I said. It was a statement. My power to control the earth meant political power to the magicians.

"Yes."

Once in our room, I bolted for the shower. I could nearly feel the day's events clinging to my skin like the heat and dirt. My cheeks and nose were sunburnt. I climbed into the shower and stood under the cold water.

My body and mind felt disconnected but not in the magical past-life kind of way. A thought slowly emerged: I was in shock. Stoically, with precision, I examined my emotions to determine if I was actually in a state of shock.

The headlines repeated in my mind. *Fifty-four dead.* The ache in my chest began anew, and I realized what the mysterious feeling tugging at me had been. All my energy left me and I sat in the shower, hugging my knees to my chest. Guilt.

It washed over me like the water from the showerhead. It was heavier, though, and caused me to struggle for air while tears rolled down my face. The barriers of protections that the shock had created were crumbling around me as the gravity of the situation wore in.

*If I am all-powerful, why didn't I do something?* I scolded myself. Then another thought interrupted. *If that was an indication of the magicians' power, how am I ever going to survive?*

Fear mingled with my remorse about being so helpless and running away. I sat in the shower and sobbed, unaware of the time.

*There's nothing you could have done. You're not trained, you're alone.* The logical portion of my mind spoke to me, but it was too quiet to quell the onslaught of revelations. It was the first time I had approached my supposed enemy — and I had run away, terrified.

*The first time was the earthquake near your home, and you stopped that with your magic,* the logical half said. Again, I chose to ignore it.

The cold water kept striking my skin, but I could no longer feel it. Steam started to rise in the bathroom. I felt hot. My natural instincts kicked in and the terror was replaced by fury. Fury at the magicians for ruining lives, fury at my inability to help, fury for my situation. I told myself this was different than self-pity.

Suddenly, I was too hot. I reached out to turn off the hot water completely, but the knob sizzled when I touched it. Carefully, I stood. As I touched the shower curtain to pull it aside, it ignited in my hand. In an instant, I was boxed into the ceramic tile by a wall of fire.

A scream tore from my lips before I could think. The bathroom door banged open and Kian darted for the showerhead, pushing the fire aside with towels and spraying the flaming curtain. It was over as soon as it had begun.

We were left in a room filled with thick grey smoke, both gagging and coughing on it. Amazingly, though not reassuringly, the fire alarm in the hotel room hadn't even gone off.

That's when I realized I was completely exposed. Kian noticed at the same time and quickly turned away. For an instant, I even thought I saw some red creeping up his neck and into his ears. He turned towards the door and held out a hand to me. I took it, frowning, and practically skipped into the room to dive under the sheets.

"You keep doing that, you're going to let the magic consume you unless you are more careful!"

It was the first annoyance I'd seen from him. He sounded angry in the way your parents get angry. Concerned.

"You need to learn to control yourself. Aren't you frightened?" he asked.

My sob-fest in the shower was still fresh on my mind. I wanted to stall talking about it, afraid I would break out in tears again.

"Okay." I stared at him defiantly. "I'm terrified. I have no idea what's happening to me. If it's not crippling visions, then I'm catching on fire or something...." I waved my arm around the room while speaking and found the scratched ceiling. I sighed. My hands still held the cuts from last night's expedition up the hotel room wall. "And," I continued, "you can't teach me."

"But I can help you," Kian said. "Powers like yours went elsewhere in the family." He smiled at me in the same crooked way I saw earlier, though I didn't get his joke. "Besides," he added, "you are not going to escape the magicians or even survive your memories if you let your emotions set you on fire."

His features implied he was joking, but a hard lump suddenly appeared in my throat. He was right. I didn't stand a chance.

✦

Later that evening, when I had dressed, eaten, and calmed somewhat, we watched the news until the day's events began to be a monotone. When night was beginning to set in, my heartbeat quickened. Tonight I would try Kian's method. As the darkness swept over the city, Kian closed the curtains and turned towards me, looking determined.

"Your magic is natural," he told me. "You have never had to struggle for it, steal it, or lie for it. It is your birthright. As far as I know, your powers lie within your soul. They are yours to command. No magicians' rules. No laws. The only thing I can tell you is that if you try to expend too much, or if you don't consider your human body, your magic can kill you."

Great.

"Once," Kian continued, "you and a handful of others were strong enough to defeat the magicians, even as the Romans were calling your attention away — you were stretched too thin. You were fighting two wars. You controlled your power, and only you can rediscover how. I had hoped that your memories would unlock your abilities, but I suppose you must unlock your memories first."

I opened my mouth to protest. Each so-called memory that had returned to me featured a man I did not know, overwhelming and confusing feelings, and more often than not, pain. And what about my dream from the night before? What was that?

Kian saw I was lost in thought and cut in. "You must find a way to initiate your memories and find your power. Perhaps if you can control them, they won't cause you such pain."

I thought over his words as I chewed my bottom lip. I had changed in the past few days — had it only been few days? Before then, I had experienced nothing. Now I felt like I had experienced everything. Kian, sitting on his bed a mere two feet away from me, had changed too. He was still handsome, still eerie and magical, but he was more human now. Did he just appear that way to me? Had he shown me his human side?

I kicked myself when I realized my thoughts were lingering on Kian rather than how to unlock my memories.

"My father used to tell me," Kian said, one eye on the television, "that if you think long enough about any problem, the answer will come to you."

I sighed. "So your wise suggestion is to ... think?"

Kian nodded. "That, or be torn apart by your own soul."

✦

One week after arriving in New York, I was starting to long for home. Kian and I explored the city by day, and during the evening I lay prone, trying to regain some memories of my past life. I missed my parents and being constantly surrounded by animals.

After the incident at the pier, I was amazed at how life went on as usual. The president declared a state of emergency due to flooding in New York and a few other states, and a week of mourning for all the people who died when the sea surged. There had been an earthquake off the coast, just like the news said. No one mentioned any magicians trying to destroy the world.

"They are using the earth, just like last time," Kian had said, pounding a fist into his other hand. I watched him pace our small room. "They are setting the pieces into motion, but it's impossible to know how much time we have."

So I had some time to learn, at least. I was getting fed up with my efforts. Lying on my back in the hotel room, I tried to blanket my mind in the knowledge that my soul held a strong power, and that another life was residing inside me.

Sometimes I succeeded in transporting my consciousness to the place where I could see through the eyes of my previous self. The visions were blurry, and the world spun. I threw up over the side of the bed on one occasion. Still, Kian assured me we were making progress.

Other times, I fell asleep. Kian would prod me awake with his foot if I began to snore. For someone who was bent on collecting every one of my kind to save the world and ourselves, he seemed very content staying with me in the hotel room. He even began to ignore his phone when his mysterious magician contacts would begin to call.

I had tried to look inside myself like I had done in my dream and find the power there, but more often than not, all I saw when I closed my eyes was grey. Boredom seized my mind and I found myself dreading the evenings when Kian forced me to try to find my memories. To my frustration, he would not let me give up. He read magazines and books quietly while I lay. I found my mind drifting to him when I would run out of things to think about. I always pushed him to the back of my mind. I realized it was because I didn't want to hope. Hope for what, I didn't know. But my thoughts would linger on when he took my hand.

On our eighth evening in New York, I closed my eyes. I figured on the occasions I had worked magic, I was scared. But what did it feel like?

I tried to bring myself back to the events when I knew I had used my magic: the earthquake in San Francisco, the fall in Oregon, in the shower. Each time I had been under emotional duress, pulled beyond my limit. I put myself in all of those terrifying scenarios again. *What did I do? How did I do it?*

Minutes passed before the silence in the room weighed on my mind.

"Can you turn on a radio or something?" I asked Kian. He fiddled with the radio near the television until rock music played clearly. He raised an eyebrow at me.

"Too quiet," I said.

"Must be horrible to concentrate with," he muttered, but I chose to ignore him. He turned the volume up, sprawled back out on his bed and resumed reading his book, a historical account of World War I.

I closed my eyes again and focused. Soon the music was seeping into my mind, driving me crazy, yet I could not get up to turn it off. I realized I was driving it into my thoughts — it was a welcome distraction from what I was doing. The noise forced its way in like it was trying to corral whatever was hiding to come out. Thinking about the music and my magic at the same time was stirring something in my heart.

A new song came on. A piano played a few bars of a frantic intro before the other instruments joined in. I focused on that, but the power in me kept building. Stunned, I realized being distracted helped.

My magic was locked off to me if I searched for it. As is the way of the universe, I found it right when I stopped looking.

By the time the song moved into the chorus, my chest was seizing. It became hard to breathe. I fought the urge to cough and sputter. I knew where my magic was now. I could feel it buzzing in my blood, my muscles, and my bones. It was like a spark that ignited throughout my body. I developed a new perspective that allowed me to see it and separate it from my human self.

I took myself back to the time Kian had chased me. I had pushed the ocean away from me when I fell, creating ice. When the earthquake struck near my home, I had shoved its power away, at least subconsciously. Now, I experimented.

I mentally pushed and squeezed at the magic, moulding it, forming it to my body. The concentration of it in my chest would kill me, I was sure. I could feel sweat running down my face, but I continued. Eyes tightly closed, I mentally eased the magic into me. Soon I wore what felt like a suit of magic. It pulsed in an unfamiliar way, out of sync with my heart.

Slowly, I opened my eyes. Kian was still on his bed, but he eyed me curiously. Stunned, I saw night had fallen. I sat up. My magic suit vibrated.

"What …" Kian began.

I tried to open my mouth to interrupt him, but my throat vibrated. My teeth chattered. It was all I could do to keep the magic with me.

"Gwen?" Kian asked.

I sat staring at him, wide-eyed. I was unable to speak for fear of letting go of the suit would either fade the magic or have it explode from my body. I held up one shaking finger, telling him to give me a minute.

I lay back down again and closed my eyes. This fragile state of mind would not do. Now I could see myself from the side. I could see the power that had taken me over.

*I controlled it once*, I said to myself, *I can do it again*.

The memory of the people on the pier came back to me. I had been helpless. I would not be again. Seeing myself from the side allowed me to imagine the magic like an aura, hanging around me, suffocating me. I began mentally kneading it back into my body. The resistance I found in my mind scared me.

Finally, I had pummelled it into the depths of my soul, where it belonged. Before opening my eyes again, I searched around for any hints that memories had been unlocked.

*Nothing yet*, I sighed to myself. Then I sat up.

Kian still watched me. His book was put away. The radio played more rock music. Gripping the edge of my bed, I stood. I extended my arms out towards the window and pushed at the magic again, this time through my fingertips. As if on cue, the window curtains blew open to reveal the rising sun as if a gust of wind had disturbed them. It was dawn.

"Wow," I breathed.

## Chapter Ten

"**S**o you just stopped thinking about it?" Kian asked me skeptically.

I nodded.

We were walking through Central Park on a sunny afternoon, days after my experimenting with fitting into magic. Belief had finally started to seep into me, and I felt like the very knowledge of who I had been (whoever that was) was giving me strength.

After sleeping off my initial fatigue, I had been trying new things every chance I got. The buzzing in my bones hadn't stopped — it was there every time I looked for it, like an electrical current. I got used to it eventually.

Kian tested me, but moving objects was not a skill I possessed. Any time I tried to do something it was as if a small wind hit my target object and disappeared. It seemed a stereotype of possessing magic that I had to make rocks fly around. Kian assured me there was more to it, and I would find out with more memories.

Regardless of my weak magic, I felt empowered for the first time in my life. I felt strong. And despite myself, I revelled in Kian's approval. Though I did not always pass his tests — he began warning me after he threw a lamp and nearly hit my head — I was adjusting to the life of a magician. The security guards at the hotel, who knew us by name at this point, were called again every so often, but only eyed the wreckage suspiciously and left.

I was only disappointed that I could not increase my memories faster. Since fitting into the magic, I had bits and snippets of the past thrown at me. It was either pieced together or too abstract. A tiny mud house. Fog. Green everywhere. A grey sky. Always, a grey sky would loom above me.

I had two coherent visions. In one, I was riding a horse. The world was quiet. The sound of hooves and the smell of horse filled my senses. In the other, I was cold, wet, and annoyed. I waded through an extremely cold stream with people all around me, leading horses and holding weapons above our heads.

Both memories felt lonely to me. The emotions were simple, nothing stood out. I longed for another memory of *him*.

"Your powers obviously lie in the physical world," Kian told me, eating one of the three hotdogs he had bought from a vendor. "Which makes sense, since your magic is of a past world. The old will have control over the new. Such is the way of the world."

I didn't get it, but sometimes I just let him talk to hear his voice.

"And yours?" I asked him.

He hadn't used any magic, as far as I could tell, since we arrived in New York.

"Not natural," he said simply. "I wasn't born with any."

He looked to see if I was following, and saw that I was not.

"Magic is simply manipulation," he explained. "You were given the gift of manipulating your surroundings, and you never sought magic outside of your own talents, so that is all you know. Others," I could have sworn I saw him shudder, "want to grow their magic, exploit it. Use it. They learn and perfect ways of moving beyond the realm of their natural abilities, becoming ..."

"A magician?" I asked.

"A monster," Kian answered. "Magic is addictive just like any other strength that feeds the body and the mind. It is hard to have enough."

I didn't probe his comments and instead focused on the day.

It had been a few weeks since I was supposed to go to school. Around me, teenagers who had just gotten out of classes wandered home in large gangs, usually smoking and cursing. It seemed so counter-intuitive to the positive hum of the park.

We walked back to the hotel, each lost in our own thoughts. We were almost back to the hotel when I stopped on the pavement.

"What is it?" Kian asked.

I could feel the subway train rumbling below my feet. A small fear at the back of mind thought of the surging sea or the rolling bay in San Francisco. The underground thunder rumbled through my shoes and into my spine. What if the magicians tore through the earth with a power much greater than this train? All I had been doing was moving pebbles with small pulses of magic.

My thoughts shifted to escaping the magicians. At this point they were just black blobs in my mind, like abstract images — I had no idea what to actually expect. The vibrations of the train matched the buzzing of my magic until they became one.

Suddenly, my stomach dropped and I gasped and grabbed for Kian. I was submerged to my thighs in concrete, as solid as it had ever been. Below, I could feel my legs encased in concrete and my feet dangling painfully over the subway tunnel.

Kian's eyes were so wide that it would have been comical were I not so panicked. He grabbed my arms and tried to shield me from the public, luckily sparse at this time of day. Everyone was either hurrying with heads low or walking determinedly.

It was something I had remarked on earlier about this city: people feared to look at each other or to notice each other. Well, it worked out for me since this was a hell of a situation to talk myself out of.

"What did you do?" Kian whispered at me frantically.

Hanging there hurt. My thighs were pinched and Kian's tugging at my arms and torso didn't help.

"I don't know!" I had tried to whisper but my voice came out high and shrill. "I was just thinking about the train."

Kian reached down and hugged me around the torso, then pulled hard. My body, aching after everything I had put it through in the last weeks, protested. His dark hair was in my face.

"Kian, that's not going to work!" I nearly shrieked at him.

The light turned green nearby, a crowd of people who had been waiting at a stoplight were about to cross our path at any moment. He leaned down again to me.

"You use your magic by pushing, right?" he asked.

I nodded. I hated myself for the tears welling up in my eyes, and his panic wasn't helping.

"Well," Kian's bright eyes were on the group coming towards us, "*push!*"

I forced my magic into the ground around me and popped up like a fish out of water. Kian caught me and we fell, landing sprawled on the ground. He put a hand to his head, wincing, but smiled at the stares we received from passersby.

✦

When I got up to turn off the light in our hotel room that night, Kian motioned for me to use my magic instead. I sat reluctantly back down on the bed. After all, what if I fell right through?

"Don't lose faith in yourself," Kian said, reading or guessing my thoughts. "Today was an accident. You need to hug your power close to yourself, and not let anything else intrude. If your magic becomes connected to something else, then you're giving it away, aren't you?"

So many things I didn't know — and didn't really understand. Kian spoke about the supernatural as if it was all clear as day. This was normal to him. Not to me.

Focussing on the light switch, I imagined my fingers over the knob and pushed down. To my surprise, the lights went out. Smiling, I lay down.

✦

*I was in the darkness. Moonlight beat down on me like a ray of fire, urging me on. In this light, I was ashen. My long, pale hair floated near my face as I ran. I could feel the dirt and sweat on my skin. A power beat at my back — keep running, keep running. It was as if a hand pressed against my back and pushed me forwards. But I wasn't being chased. I was chasing. I was the hunter, and I sought the only thing in the world that could satiate my yearning.*

*The anxiety in my chest built even as my air became strained. I was running too fast — but nervousness filled me. I was late for something. I was going to be late. I ran through the forest until I lost track of time. How was I still running? Magic. Hours passed.*

*I felt the hum of magic in my feet, moving me forward. Could it make me faster? I ran as if with a strong current. I felt like the wind. I could feel every twig and stone that I stepped on — every branch that I leapt across. I could not remember feeling my body so vividly in my human life.*

*Finally, after what seemed like an eternity, I came to a clearing in the woods. No one. I searched with my eyes, knowing I was the only one there. My magic had already searched for life, and found none but the animals in the trees and the bushes.*

*My heart dropped into my feet and a steady ache replaced my shortness of breath. It grew and grew until I thought I was going to cry out. It hurt. Disappointment, sadness, and worry washed over me. I sank to my knees in the tall grass.*

No, *my mind cried out in a voice I did not recognize,* no no no no no.

*My hands gripped stalks and I looked down at my short nails as they tore through the earth and dug up the grass, tearing it away. Fury. A large ring with what looked like a sapphire glinted on my hand. Suddenly, I could not bear to look at it. I tore it off and threw it into the darkness of the surrounding woods.*

No, *my mental voice said,* not yet.

*Weary, I got up and walked through the clearing, my feet feeling like lead. The moonlight was my only guide as I began roaming the forest. Searching for him. I loved him and wanted him more than life. I would wander here for eternity if it meant I would find him. A distant voice told me he was gone, that he had done something ... something horrible ... and would not be coming back again. But I refused to accept it. I wandered until the night grew too dark, sobs threatening to break through my throat, tears spilling out.*

*The moonlight faded.*

✦

I opened my eyes to darkness but was still in my dream state. I felt more alive than I ever had, yet my mind was far away, still thinking and reacting like my other self — my dream self, my past self. I felt my human body as vividly as I had my dream body.

I had torn the sheets off my bed and was sweat soaked. Again. My mind raced with thoughts that weren't mine, though the mesh of people and places just turned into one humming sound that I chose to ignore. I gasped for air, but a longing crushed my lungs. In the darkness, someone leaned over me. I could not hear what he said. I felt a weight on the corner of my bed and knew he was near. The longing was threatening to flatten me into the mattress. Decimate me.

I reached out blindly and touched his arm with my fingertips. A chill ran through me as I felt skin.

WHAT ARE YOU DOING? STOP! A part of my mind screamed at me. That was the old Gwen from Oregon, kicking me from the passenger seat in my head.

*It's him! It must really be him!* another part yelled back.

I was at war with myself, and my body was not paying a bit of attention to my rational mind.

Running my hands up the arms, I hugged the shape and pulled it down towards me. The broad shoulders stiffened and resisted, but only for a moment. The weight of another person came down on me, yet the pressure on my chest lessened. The longing was gone and replaced by the person in my arms.

I felt breath on my face. An instant later, wet lips touched mine. I could only issue a tiny gasp as he kissed me, hesitantly at first, and then with a greater urgency. His touch was warm and exhilarating. All reason was gone. I squirmed underneath him and shaped my body to his, clinging to him as if for dear life.

Fully understanding that I had better judgement than this did not stop me. My other self had been quiet for some time, curious, but I could not resist. He soothed my soul with his kisses. Our breaths became ragged. For the first time in a very long time, I felt truly happy, even in my precarious situation. I ran my hands through his hair and down his neck. And stopped.

My other self was back in a heartbeat. A memory. An instinct told me to feel his neck again. Annoyed at being distracted during such a wonderful moment, I ran my hand once more over the smooth skin under his chin. All at once my mind erupted with memories and the other self, the person I had been in the dream, unleashed the full force of her emotions on me.

*"No!"*

A scream escaped my lips before I could control myself. I pushed and kicked at the person on top of me, the person whose love I had wanted so dearly only a few moments before.

## Chapter Eleven

Kian flipped on the light and the room was flooded with brightness. We both winced as our eyes adjusted to the light. He stood looking confused and, for the first time, scared. He stared at me wide-eyed, his cheeks flushed, panting slightly. I realized the mistake my other self had made and what I had done.

"Oh my god."

I buried my face in my hands, too embarrassed to be seen. "Oh no, no, no."

As I was starting to return to my regular state of mind, I could feel my suit of magic again. I resisted the temptation to sink myself into the floor for fear of what would actually happen to my body. Instead, I could only be mortified.

I heard Kian sit down in his own bed. I owed him an explanation, but I couldn't bring myself to look at him. I was willing to bet that I had never been so embarrassed in any of my lives.

Finally, when his breathing slowed, he spoke.

"What happened, Gwen?" He said my name with so much care that it made more blood rush to my face and pulse in my cheeks.

I debated what to tell him of my dreams and memories, of what my past self had been thinking. What *I* had been thinking. Deciding that I couldn't be any more embarrassed, I vied for the truth.

"In my dream ... I think it was a memory ... I was searching for a man, in a forest."

Even after deciding on the truth, I just couldn't bring myself to divulge my feelings for this man to Kian. Not now.

"I couldn't find him, and I began to panic," I said. "When I woke up, I was still half in the dream. When I saw someone near me, my mind returned to the memory-dream, and I thought ..." I didn't know what to say. What *did* I think? "I thought you were the person I had been searching for," I finished.

Kian looked thoughtful. Was he disappointed or relieved? I couldn't tell. Before I could move, he came and sat next to me on my bed. My heart skipped a beat and then raced. Carefully, slowly, he reached out and placed some wayward hair behind my ear.

"You must be careful with your dreams and memories. You were thrashing around in bed. I thought you would try to float away again," he said quietly.

When he spoke in near whispers, his words embraced me like his kisses had. I pushed the thought to the back of my mind.

"You must also remember," Kian added, "that this life is yours to lead. You are one soul, spread over two lives. You must remember, always, where you come from. I know it's difficult, but you need to remember your other life, and then let it go. Don't lose the person you've become. With two lives, who is to say which is more important?"

*The louder one*, I answered in my mind immediately. The girl who had screamed and pushed Kian away had not been me. It had been an echo of a former me, who longed for someone else. Did I long for him?

When Kian stood and turned off the light, returning to his own bed, I could not decide if it was to my relief or regret.

As I lay fidgeting, the bed felt lonely. I scolded myself for even thinking such a thing, but the longing in my heart came back. I touched my lips, thinking about the night's events.

*I am so stupid*, I thought, exasperated. With very confusing thoughts, and the partial knowledge that Kian was still awake, I eventually dozed off.

✦

The morning was awkward, and we ate at the breakfast buffet in silence. Kian made himself look busy by playing with his phone, staring at it intently. I tried to focus on other things than last night. Every time I did, I felt a deep blush creeping up my neck and into my face. I still had the intense desire to sink into the floor, but had to stop myself from this train of thought for fear that I actually might.

Suddenly, Kian's phone rang. His eyes widened and he looked at me in surprise. He quickly left the table and flipped open the phone. He wasn't speaking, just listening. I sighed and shoved a piece of cantaloupe into my mouth.

Yeah, I could move things around with my mind and I could feel magic now. But I had seen people on the Discovery Channel claim to do the same thing. At the time I thought they were lying, but now I wasn't so sure. After running away with Kian and ditching everything I had known for the journey, I had attained the level of expertise of a late-night novelty show host. Perfect.

Kian came back to the table looking thoughtful and worried. Only the person on the other end of his phone made him look like that.

"What's up?" I asked, glad for the excuse to talk like nothing had happened.

Kian frowned some more into his plate. "He says we are taking too long," he said finally.

"Well," I replied, "your magician friend is more than welcome to come to New York City and find one unknown person in less than two weeks."

"The senator is very busy," Kian told me with a knowing look.

"What?"

"One of the magicians from our time is influential here," Kian explained.

"Yes, you said that," I replied. "And when were you going to tell me that I've probably seen him on television?"

"When the time was right."

I stared at him, torn between asking more questions and storming off. I needed to know anything useful.

"Gwen," he said, "now that you have your magic, at least in a small way, you can understand that other people with magic may be hiding in plain sight as well. You must also be wary of everyone. Remember that."

"Great. How does a magician from the ancient world get to be a senator?" A part of me was dying to ask which one.

"I told you, they have lived and remembered and accumulated power," Kian answered. "Just like you are trying to do."

I noticed his eyes straying to the ceiling. He was holding something back. I was shocked to realize I knew him so well after a few weeks, and mulled over if it was worth prying what he knew from him, one question after the other. Then decided I probably didn't want to know.

"Kian, are you telling me," I leaned in to whisper, "that there are magicians in the government keeping other magicians a secret?"

"Of course," he replied simply. "We play with politics to keep people from finding out the truth. Now you're like the rest of our people here. You're hiding and you can't let anyone know the truth."

I felt like I had been tricked into something without realizing it. I didn't like what I was hearing so I did the only thing I had become accustomed to over the past weeks. It was easy. I just did as Kian told me. I finished a small strawberry, got up, and picked up my bag.

"Where are you going?" Kian asked.

"I don't know," I said. "But apparently we're taking too long, so let's go find me a magical friend. I don't want to be fighting anyone alone."

A look of guilt flitted across his face.

*Good*, I thought.

In hindsight, I think the magic made me feel powerful and cocky. At first I congratulated myself on my newfound self-confidence, but every so often I would stop and wonder if this was me or *her*.

Kian was annoyed all day. Everything about New York City seemed to bother him. We found ourselves spending the afternoon at the park again. Kian's bad mood did not interfere with his logic, which was that this was where to find a lot of people. I told him we should ride the train, but he hated the subways and said they felt like a dungeon. I wondered how many dungeons he had seen.

He barely talked to me and I was fine with that, since I was still trying to erase last night from my memory. We were walking out to 5th Avenue when Kian gave me a sidelong glance.

"What?"

"You look hot," he said. I stopped and stared for only a moment, before he added, "You're sweating very much. Are you alright?"

Something inside me deflated when he added the last bit to his sentence, but I felt fine and told him so. Apart from being horribly self-conscious of looking gross, nothing felt strange.

It was still warm for the beginning of October, but not overly so. We were at the gates to the park when Kian put his hand to my forehead.

"You're burning —"

I didn't hear the rest because all sound was

drowned out. My legs crumpled beneath me and my vision blurred as I felt Kian grab my waist to keep my head from slamming against the asphalt.

It was like the feeling of falling you sometimes get right before falling asleep. Then you wake up. But I couldn't wake up. A part of me was terrified, while the other part was running.

*Always with the running*, modern-day Gwen thought. All I knew about my past life was that I had done a lot of running. At least I could control the panic of slipping into a memory now, because I knew that it would end. Eventually.

The emotions and sensations of the memory slowly washed over me, but when they did, they had me completely.

✦

*I could smell the damp earth and trees around me. I could feel every footstep against the uneven earth beneath my feet. My hands were cut and I swatted at the flora in my path. I only cared about one thing. I was looking for him again.*

*I searched in my mind for a picture of him. Who am I looking for? But I couldn't control the memory. My former self wasn't thinking. I just knew I had to get somewhere before something terrible happened. Feelings that I had never felt so strongly were thrust onto me like a suit of armour. I could not escape from guilt, sadness, and an overwhelming sense of regret. The regret burned like a fire in my soul and my torn hands stung as I pushed more leaves and branches out of my way.*

*I was already mourning in my mind. The sobs escaped from my chest like gasps as I ran, and tears flew back into my hair. I was mourning him, and I was mourning me. I knew that we were both as good as dead.*

✦

I snapped out of it like coming out from a bad dream. Before I even knew where or who I was, I was on my feet, groping for any constant. I found Kian's shirt and grabbed it in my fists, burying my head in his chest and sobbing. The feelings were slow to melt away, just like a headache. I knew it must look strange to passersby, but I didn't care. Let them think he had just broken up with me.

Finally, when I had gotten myself under control, I asked how long I'd been out.

"A few seconds," Kian answered confusedly. "What did you see?"

*A few seconds! That felt like hours!*

My throat was hoarse and I felt like I would breathe smoke if I exhaled with enough force. I didn't know what to tell him, and I didn't want to talk about it for fear that the feelings would come back.

"Same," I answered. "Running, forest ..."

This time, though, Kian pressed for more. "Why were you running?" he asked.

I shrugged. "It doesn't make sense," I answered. It didn't. "I felt like I was late for something, and something bad was going to happen because of it. But ... I just felt doomed. Like the world was over."

"How did you feel about that?"

I straightened up and released his ruined shirt. Where my nails had dug into the cotton, there were singe marks and his skin was red underneath. I'd burned him and he hadn't even said anything. I wiped wet smears off my face with the back of my hand.

"What do you mean?"

"Well, how did you feel about the world being over?"

He fixed me with the look that could make me tell him my deepest secrets. I realized he already knew pretty much all of my secrets, but I still didn't know what he was driving at. Around us, cars and pedestrians sped by, oblivious.

I frowned. "I felt pretty awful about it," I answered. "How do you think I'd feel?"

Thankfully, he let the subject drop. I was getting annoyed and my head was starting to throb yet again. I felt like my brain was literally trying to split into two.

Kian ran a hand through his dark hair then poked a finger through the singed holes in his shirt. "Well, you appear to have a gift for fire, which is always useful," he said, frowning. "It's also something new."

✦

After having a nap, I felt like myself again. Or whoever I was these days. Kian was starting to drive me insane with his nervous pacing and I even began to feel guilty for not really trying to find the next one of my kind. I realized I had enjoyed the time getting to know Kian and gaining my magic. The task of finding a nondescript teenager in New York City seemed immense. I didn't know where to start.

"Let's go out," I told him.

It was more of a statement than a suggestion.

"Walk?" he asked.

"No, *out* out."

He stared at me.

"It's Friday," I told him.

He continued staring. "You mean to one of those dark places where people meet?"

What he was describing sounded a lot more ominous than the restaurant I had been thinking of, but my nap had given me a lot of energy so I went with his train of thought.

"Sure. A club." I waited a bit, and then added, "Besides, we might find who we're looking for there."

Guilt flared and I hoped Kian didn't know enough about clubs to realize you probably wouldn't find a teenager in one.

To my immense surprise, he agreed. Excited, I ran to get some make-up on. The desire to be in a crowded room with loud noise, dim lights and uncomfortable shoes had never taken over me like this before. But I had never had Kian before. The prospect of going out on my own was unappealing. A small part of my mind complained that I was being selfish, but I pushed past it.

I wanted to go out and act like a grown-up. I reminded myself that I had basically been cooped up in a hotel room with Kian for nearly three weeks. So this was what cabin fever felt like.

I found the one dress I had taken and smoothed it out with my hands. It was simple and black and I had bought it for a veterinarian dinner my parents were honoured at the previous year.

The low neckline of the dress, ending at a V just at the limit of appropriateness, was still too low for me. I had to remind myself not to tug on the dress as I applied my make-up and started trying to arrange my hair on top of my head. It was never a skill of mine.

Kian came into the bathroom dressed in a nice shirt and pants that I didn't know he had. I was beginning to wonder about the magical properties of his little suit-case. He was dressed completely in black, and it made his eyes shine. He frowned at the blush I was using, and then shrugged, accepting it.

"No one used to wear black," he said, commenting on my dress and his own clothes. "The colour was considered only for mourning."

"Now it is considered for *slimming*," I told him.

## Chapter Twelve

It felt a little surreal to be preparing for a night out with Kian. We stood side by side, looking at our reflections in the mirror for just a moment before he moved behind me and began to take out the bobby pins I had stuck randomly into my hair. It all seemed arbitrary to me, and I guessed that I looked ridiculous.

Kian laid the small metal pins onto the counter and began braiding my hair intricately from the top of my head. His fingers felt nice in my hair, and I leaned back into his hands before I caught myself and gave myself a nice mental scolding. When he was done, my hair was interwoven in a pattern I could not follow and pinned to the back. Its pale sandy colour made me look sophisticated, for once.

"How did you do that?" I asked. I hadn't thought braiding was one of his talents.

Kian shrugged, smiling.

*Hm,* I thought, *what else don't I know?*

We went out and got hot dogs, yet again, then

spent the evening walking around until it was time to choose a club.

"You know, no one knows for sure what's in those," I told him as he downed his third hot dog. I had been a human pocket for him, carrying his drink and napkins.

"I've probably eaten worse," he said absentmindedly.

Loud music, flashing lights, and fancy cars that seemed to go around in an endless loop brought us to the nightclub area of Manhattan.

We found one that was just the right mix of intimidating and exclusive and got into line behind a velvet rope. Everyone around me looked considerably older. As we approached the security guard, I was feeling more nervous.

"Uh, Kian?" I tried to whisper. We were surrounded by people.

"Yes?"

"I may need you to work some magic on the guards."

He looked at me suspiciously. "Why?"

"Well …" *Am I wringing my hands?* I'd never done anything like this before. "They may not think I am old enough to come in."

I knew he had realized that I was taking advantage of him, but I only had a second to feel guilty because we were at the front of the line and my heart leapt up into my chest. He sighed and rolled his eyes.

The balding man at the door was about a foot and a half taller than me, and twice the width of Kian. I imagined him holding me in a headlock while waiting for the police to arrive because I was underage. I gave him my driver's license and Kian gave him a passport.

I waited in silence for the worst. But he looked us over and gave us back our IDs.

With my heart hammering in my chest, we moved into the club, where red velvet curtains surrounded pedestals on which scantily clad men and women were dancing much closer than would be allowed at my old high school.

I felt the red flush into my cheeks before I trained my eyes to avoid the pedestals. On a stage in the centre, surrounded by people sitting on bongos, a fire breather inhaled and swallowed flaming swords.

"I'm going to look around," Kian said, leaning in so that I could hear him. His breath smelled sweet, and again I had to give myself the mental scolding. "Maybe we can find *another* here. The magician said you'd be drawn to be nearer to him or her."

I watched him walk away, feeling slightly guilty. I had hardly been drawn to this place and was already regretting coming. Even with my new abilities making me cocky, I knew I didn't belong here. But Kian still had not put two and two together. Teens wouldn't hang out here. No one my age was in the vicinity.

I made my way to the bar, partly because I did not know how to dance and also because I was wearing heels and my feet were already killing me. I had brought the only nice pair of shoes I owned and now I remembered why I had never worn them. I sat staring at the bartenders moving quickly behind the bar, and the thousand or so bottles they had to choose from.

A few minutes passed as I watched the fire breather. A bartender came over to me with a pink drink in a small glass.

"Sorry, I didn't order this," I yelled at him over the noise. *I'm also underage,* a voice yelled in my mind. The music was like a steady beat in my chest. It was monotonous and I couldn't tell when it rose and fell. How did people dance to this stuff?

"It's from him," he called back to me and pointed to a man sitting four people away.

I stammered and had the drink shoved into my hand before the bartender sped away. The man who was now eyeing me with a faint smile was blond, with a square jaw and almond-shaped eyes. His best features were that he had no noticeable features. I could see how he would be found attractive, but to me he was bland. He was also at least ten years older than me. I smiled politely, not knowing the etiquette on such things, and accepted the drink.

It tasted sweet and I stupidly assumed they hadn't put any alcohol in it. My only previous drinking experience was at the aforementioned uncle's wedding. Soon, Blond Man had come over, sat next to me, and ordered me a second drink.

It turned out his name was Neil and he was a photographer. The more drinks he got me, the more I became interested in lenses and light and angles. I let him talk my ear off about cameras — he even had a fancy one with him — while I enjoyed the warmth in my stomach and the buzzing in my ears. The alcohol went a surprisingly long way towards shutting out the horrible music, which I could feel beating through my seat and the floor. Time passed by as if I floated on a river.

I think on drink number five or six, a hand snatched the pink glass away before I could have any. Testosterone exploded in an instant and my blond friend, Neil, was out of his stool, puffing himself up like a peacock.

"Hey man, what's your problem?"

I didn't have to guess who was behind me. We had spent so much time together that I could feel him like a temperature change.

Kian ignored Neil and rounded on me. "How many of these have you had?" he asked me angrily.

"You know this guy?" Neil asked at the same time.

In my state, the two questions were too much to handle. I wobbled up from my stool and looked at both of them. They were quite opposite to each other, but both stared at me waiting for their answer.

"Neil," it took extra thought to form words, "thank you for the drinks. Your camera is lovely." I emphasized my point with a nod. "Kian, just enjoy yourself for once!" I waved my arms at the club around us and smacked a girl in the head by accident. "Sorry!"

She glared at me but didn't think I was worth the trouble. I was okay with that.

My first idea was to join the pedestal dancers, but on second thought I realized there were not enough pink drinks in the world to make me do that. Instead, my eyes fell on the sticks of the fire breather, who was taking a break on the side of his stage.

I made my way over there with surprising speed and got to his sticks before he could protest. I also managed to beat Kian, who was on my heels. I climbed onto the stage, knowing that Kian wouldn't follow me.

He had shown me over the past weeks that he did not like attention, and now I used that against him. A small bit of guilt sprang up again, but I quenched it down with drunkenness.

"Gwen, what are you doing?" he yelled.

"Don't worry! I'm having fun!" I yelled back. "Like you should be. Tomorrow we could be ensnarled!"

"Enslaved," he yelled.

"Whatever."

The sticks felt sticky in my hands and were wrapped in some kind of black cloth. I unwrapped it until I could hold just the metal. It still felt hot in my hands from the earlier show.

The fire breather finally noticed.

"Hey!" he yelled, setting down his beer and climbing up to the stage.

He saw Kian yelling at me too and told him, "Don't worry, the lighters and fluid have been put away. They're harmless. But your girl is going to burn herself holding the steel like that!"

Kian did not seem reassured.

I pleaded with him. "Please can I try them?"

Somewhere off to the corner of my vision a flash went off. Neil had his camera out. The fire breather noticed and acquiesced.

"Fine, but I'm not lighting them, so don't even ask," he said to me.

It didn't matter. I didn't know if it was the alcohol or the magic flowing in my veins but it pulsed and wanted out. I felt the energy flow through my hands and into the metal sticks, and suddenly they were aflame.

The fire breather cursed in ways I won't repeat and jumped off the stage in shock.

"Drop them!" he was yelling. "Drop them!"

Neither the sticks nor the fire were hot to the touch. I enjoyed trying to flip them around like I had seen him do. The whole club just fell away and I was alone with my fire. This thing that had nearly consumed me on several occasions was now manageable.

I felt proud of myself, and it burned the alcohol out of my system. My head was clear and I loved every moment of it. Kian had talked about having magical talent. I knew this was mine.

"Gwen, watch out!" Kian's voice brought me back to the present. I dropped the sticks and jumped back just in time to avoid being sprayed with smelly white foam from a fire extinguisher. Two security guards stood over the smoking fire sticks, not looking pleased at all. Behind them, the fire breather groped comically at his short hair, yelling.

I quickly scrambled off the stage and Kian and I were shown the door. We were asked not to return in the near future. I protested when a large security guard gripped my arm and handed me my shoes, which I didn't remember abandoning before climbing onto the stage.

Outside, I shied away from Kian's inevitable fury. We were on a mission, and I had been an idiot. We walked for a while in silence before I realized I was starving. It was nearly three in the morning.

"Are you mad at me?" I asked sheepishly.

"No," Kian answered, but it was an angry no.

"Yes you are."

He stopped me in the middle of the street and put his hands on my shoulders. "You're young, and I can't be angry with you for idiotic decisions. You are allowed to make mistakes and have fun. The least I can do, after taking your youth away from you with this journey, is to allow you that."

I frowned at him. "Wow," I said, "that was incredibly reasonable."

"Yes. Well, in the future I'm going to have to forcibly drag you out of any establishment where you're accepting drinks from a stranger. He could have been dangerous! He was a complete stranger *feeding* you a *mysterious* substance. It could have been poison! Not to mention that you legally cannot drink alcohol in this country! Which you failed to mention, by the way. It was also stupid to show your magic in front of all those people. I just hope they'll think it was some fire-related accident!"

*So much for reasonable*, I thought.

I knew he had a point. But so did I. He had taken away any chance I had at a last bid for teenage freedom and stupidity. I was only trying to claim a little back.

At three in the morning in New York City, there was a surprising amount of restaurants open. I was insanely hungry. I had given up on my shoes and carried them in my hand while I walked barefoot on the sidewalk, which Kian kept reminding me was a terrible idea.

It's strange how in a city, with a light every few feet, it's possible to forget that the sun has set. We wandered around because I kept changing my mind about what I wanted to eat. Suddenly I stopped dead in my tracks.

*You're crazy.*

The words rang clear as day in my ears. It was a young, male voice. And I knew him.

*No way! You don't know what you're talking about!* another male voice argued.

I stood stock-still, afraid the voices would come tumbling out of my head if I moved too quickly.

*The X-Men are mutants, they can take any shape they and they can be anything because they're mutated. That's the whole point.*

*Yeah, but newer issues depict them as some kind of novelty hybrids, apart from the initial main characters who could actually have talents that can be considered evolution!*

*It's a mutation!*

*But it's supposed to be evolution, too. Having fairy wings because they're cute isn't a mutation. Evolution says we'll get stronger and adapt to our surroundings. How do dragonfly wings make you stronger? If I touch them, the oil from my fingers will make them too heavy to fly with!*

*That only applies to actual dragonflies!*

*No difference!*

# Chapter Thirteen

"Gwen?" Kian's voice interrupted the argument.

I had been listening intently and only then realized that Kian had walked on ahead without me. He came back looking puzzled.

"I think I'm hearing people talking," I said.

What would have sounded insane to anyone else made Kian's eyes light up with excitement.

"We might be near someone!" he said. If he were anyone else he would have been jumping up and down. "Which way?"

Trying to drown out the argument, which still went on even though I had lost track, I followed the voices like a hound on the trail of a fox. Several times I made us turn around and go back, and we ran into two dead ends.

About twenty minutes later, I knew I had found the place. Nearly running, I felt my body being pulled to an all-night coffee house. Like a puppet on a string, I felt dragged along, certain that I no longer controlled my feet. I hadn't believed Kian when he told me I'd just know, but I did. This was it. The next one of my kind was in here.

My bare feet made no noise on the pavement as I ran across the road and skipped to avoid stepping on painful pebbles. I felt like a fish on a hook. The voices had shushed in my mind but had been replaced by a pulsing need to reach whoever had been speaking.

Before I even got to the door, my imagination caught hold of me. I thought of how good it would feel not to be the magically impotent one anymore. I couldn't wait to actually feel like I knew what I was doing, as it became someone else's turn to learn they were on their second life and had to escape power-hungry magicians.

We entered the coffee shop where about twenty young people were sitting in armchairs and at wooden tables. They were drinking coffees and either reading or chatting. A few faces were staring at computer screens. No one was arguing about anything. I looked around, but I couldn't guess whose voices I had heard.

*Am I in the wrong place? Am I too late?*

The shop was decorated to look like a wooden parlour room, and I felt the grain of the wood panelling on the walls with a finger as I walked around suspiciously, eyeing every customer. Kian was hot on my heels and I could practically feel him breathing down my neck. I finally snapped at him when he asked, "Is that him?" for the tenth time.

"Will you please just give me a moment?" I whispered furiously.

He shrugged and backed off, but only a little bit. He still followed me around. I wondered how long it would take before people would notice that we were circling like vultures. I would have given up and left but the dragging feeling on my insides, which was acting like a compass, would not subside.

I walked up to the cash register. "Can I get something with a lot of caffeine?" I asked the barista.

The buzz in my head was turning into a warm, fuzzy feeling. It was lulling me to sleep.

"Espresso?" the guy at the counter suggested with a smile.

My eyes widened as I recognized the voice. Kian saw my face and gawked at the teen too, who, now that I noticed, looked to be exactly my age.

We were, of course, not very subtle.

"What?" The teen stepped back, looking ready to run.

An all-night café in New York City must get its share of crazies, and I had just turned into one. When neither of us said anything, and the silence became awkward, I turned to Kian.

"*Well?*"

Just then the back room door opened and someone else came out. He wasn't dressed like an employee and carried a backpack. As I turned around, the world seemed to turn with me. Everything blurred except for him. In those few seconds, I couldn't even describe what he looked like. It was like I was seeing through all that, and into the past.

The world fell away as I saw into all the memories I had recovered. It left me dizzy on my feet. He was the missing piece. As if one eye had been hidden throughout any recollection I had had of my past life, I now saw him there — at every moment that was worth remembering.

We were older then. He was a man with a beard and eyes that held every shade of green and brown. I couldn't tear myself away from those eyes. His black hair made his face look all the more pale, and I was bombarded by the weight of the entire emotional spectrum crashing down on me. I remembered my dream. This was who I'd been running for.

Moments passed and I was shocked to realize that I still stood in the coffee shop. It seemed strange that the universe hadn't *actually* melted away as it had in my mind. My heart was pounding in my chest as the stranger walked over to me. He probably looked like an ordinary person to everyone else, but to me, he practically glowed.

As he set his backpack down, I noticed the same angular features, the same pale face, and a familiar mop of black hair above his face. I thought I was going to fall through the floor again when he smiled at me. It was a small, hesitant smile, but with the next step it grew to a big grin and the familiarity of it nearly killed me. Another step and he was within reach. I suddenly remembered my booziness and my make-up, which was most likely smeared, but it was a passing thought.

He was standing right in front of me. He paused for a just a second and then grabbed me in the tightest hug I've ever received in my life. It was like an elastic band had been wound around my heart, keeping me calm and contained for my entire life. It burst now as I was squished against his chest, where I could feel his heart beating as loudly as mine. He hugged me more completely than I could imagine and my face was buried in his sweater. I felt tears well up in my eyes and a huge sense of relief, though I didn't know why.

I don't know how long we stood there until he released me. I turned to find Kian and the other teenager absolutely wide-eyed.

"Gwen?" Kian said slowly. To my surprise, his low voice was nearly a growl. His body language suggested suspicion.

"My name is Seth," the stranger said. It didn't seem to fit quite right, but I couldn't think of any other name to call him.

"I'm Garrison," said the one behind the counter. "I think you're looking for us?"

I didn't understand. I stepped back, staring from one to the other.

"Both of you?" Kian asked.

Garrison nodded confidently, and a wide smile spread across his face. "We knew someone would eventually come looking. I guess you're the welcoming party," he said, rocking backwards and forwards on his heels.

I squinted at Garrison and tried to imagine him as he once would have been, without the apron or the cash register. There was something vaguely familiar about his curly brown hair and lanky stature, but I was trying and it could have been my imagination. He was tall and skinny, but his round face held friendly dimples.

Seth was another matter. I knew him and I felt that conviction in my bones. His dark hair and pale skin brought me back to a place of stormy skies and wind.

Kian turned to Seth and me. I felt glued to his side, like I couldn't be close enough to him. Moving an inch would be like losing him all over again.

*Get a hold of yourself,* I scolded.

"You know each other?" Kian asked skeptically.

We nodded. I noticed they were the same height when Seth left my side and moved towards him. Kian's wide eyes and behaviour suggested that he had had no idea what this reunion would entail. A flutter of panic brushed over me as I imagined him as clueless as me. Surely that wasn't possible.

"Who are you?" Seth asked him. "I don't know you."

I had been travelling with Kian long enough to know that the statement upset him. His shoulders drooped slightly. Something turned off in his eyes, and he was the stony-faced kidnapper I had first met in Oregon.

"I was sent here to collect you," Kian said in a monotone. "You need to tell me what you remember of your past. We can begin working to recover your full strength so that you may succeed in your mission. More importantly, the magicians from your past will try to steal your magic. They need your power, and you need to get stronger before that happens."

I was relieved but annoyed to see that neither Seth nor Garrison were the wide-eyed novices I'd hoped they'd be. They looked at each other warily, but with understanding.

"Can we outrun them?" Seth asked. My jaw dropped. He spoke like all of this was old news.

"Only for a while," Kian replied without emotion.

"No more waiting, right?" Garrison said to Seth, taking off his apron and motioning for a waitress nearby to take over.

"Where are you going?" she called, but we were already near the door.

"I quit," Garrison called back.

Great. Everyone was a professional except for me.

On the street, I put my shoes back on while Kian, Garrison, and Seth talked. I felt pretty useless when I realized how much they knew. While I had been terrified, the two new additions to our group were excited.

Garrison was loud and outspoken. He questioned Kian about every aspect of our past lives, including where we were from and what happened to us. I felt a bit better when I heard that neither of them fully remembered anything, just bits and pieces. They had led different lives but were able to put pieces together to form the story Kian had told me.

Seth listened more than spoke. I observed him and noticed Kian's eyes slide back and forth between him and I even as Garrison bombarded him with questions. I don't know how long we stood on the street, but when Kian had run out of ways to dodge Garrison's questions he announced that we should all meet in the morning. We agreed to a place, and I reluctantly left Garrison and Seth walking in the opposite direction.

The distance between this new stranger and me was like a cold gust of wind. As Kian practically dragged me back to the hotel by my elbow, I felt the brush of loneliness creeping up my side where I had stood next to him.

I vowed to think over everything that I'd felt that night. Kian's words about living my own life were prevalent in my mind. I didn't know this person, and he didn't know me. If I let my feelings for him control my life now, then where would it end? Would the past Gwen take over and forget myself as I had been my entire life? But those kinds of feelings had never happened to me before. How could I just throw them away? Seth was the reason I had come with Kian in the first place — he meant that much to me before I had ever even seen him.

*No*, I scolded myself, *I don't know him.*

This train of thought went around in my mind until it made me dizzy and I lay down in my dress. I placed my arms over my eyes to avoid the light while Kian moved around. The sun was rising, I hadn't slept, and I was emotionally drained. He finally shut off the light and I heard him lie down. I was worried about being able to sleep, but the alcohol was still in my body and caused a warm feeling in my stomach. Soon, I was asleep.

In the afternoon when we finally woke up, Kian was in another dark mood. I could sense it from the moment I got up. We got ready in silence and walked down to a small restaurant Garrison had picked the night before for lunch. It was strange meeting for food to discuss escaping magicians. But the only thing on my mind was how Kian was avoiding me.

He sped past busy streets, full of people either selling something or rushing somewhere. I had to struggle to keep up with him. When I nearly lost him, I jogged to catch up and stopped in front of him. He looked down at me as if surprised to see me there.

"Hey!" I called to him. "What's the matter with you?"

"Nothing," was the short answer.

I ran around him and stopped again. He turned to me with an annoyed frown.

"What happened between you and the one named Seth?" he asked. His hands on his hips could have been comical were I not irritated and out of breath. "Do *you* know *him?*"

Was this jealousy? Crazy, ancient jealousy? I decided that lying would get me into more trouble later.

"I do," I said meekly. I still didn't know what I had seen and hadn't had the time to properly think about it. "I remember him. It's like all of my memories are about him."

Kian's eyes narrowed further, making his nose look even longer. He was like a bird staring down the mouse he would have for dinner.

"What?" he asked quietly. The word came out like a whip and I instantly felt like I had done something wrong.

"What?" I retorted, defensive. "I'm just saying that ... the few memories I've had ... seem to revolve around him somehow. I just know it."

I would spare him the long-winded explanation of feeling it by the ache in my heart.

Kian walked past me in a huff.

We got to a small restaurant with aluminum tables and chairs arranged in a wide room. The metallic counter up front was busy with people ordering their meals. It took me only a second to locate Garrison and Seth sitting at a round table near the back.

I made my way over, feeling Kian's glum presence at my back. I still hadn't figured out what was wrong with him, but it would have to wait.

"Hello, fellow time travellers!"

I jumped and immediately turned around to see who had heard. No one paid attention. Garrison was smiling widely and waving to us enthusiastically. His tall, thin frame was eclipsed by a giant backpack. He looked like a twig supporting a cocoon. I realized that I liked his plain brown hair and honest face. If this was someone I knew in a past life, I could bet that we had been friends. Behind him, Seth was carrying a similar backpack and smiled, but hesitantly.

"What did you tell your parents?" I asked.

Kian and I took seats as Garrison flung an arm over Seth's shoulders.

"The truth. Magicians trying to steal my magic. Need to escape. Recover a past life, you know...." Garrison said as his eyes met mine. I hadn't understood the joke. Kian and I stared at him blankly.

"Tough crowd," he muttered, turning to Seth. "My talented friend helped convincing them that we were taking the last year of high school off to travel Europe. And that it's okay." He smiled wider. Seth shrugged.

"Oh come on," Garrison chided, "it's a gift and you knew you'd have to use it!" He turned to me and explained, "Seth can influence emotions and thoughts. He can also sense them and hunt them down!"

Seth only scowled.

"But he doesn't like to," Garrison added. I could understand how the argument I had heard last night would have come from them.

I tried to smile supportively but that was the last thing I had wanted to hear. I would rather think that Seth's ability was to turn into a pile of goo than to sense my feelings and thoughts.

A waitress came over to take our orders and I realized I hadn't even seen a menu, though I was starving. Kian and I ordered whatever the other two were having. Once he was sure that the woman was gone, Kian leaned in conspiratorially.

"How much do you remember?" he asked. "Really? Specifically."

Seth and Garrison looked at each other. It was nearly a full minute before either answered.

"Bits and pieces of a former life," Garrison replied. His smile had vanished and he looked troubled. "We figured it was somewhere in Western Europe. I remember ..." he ran a hand over his face, "just everyday things, I guess."

He was obviously holding something back, but Kian didn't press him; instead, he changed the question.

"But what do you remember of why you are here?"

"There was a war that was going to destroy everything?" Seth answered, but it sounded more like a question. He frowned at the table, recalling the memory. "Magicians."

"And Romans," Garrison added.

"And Romans," Seth said. "I have this nagging feeling like everything was over. We were all going to be destroyed. I've been dreaming about it for years. Just the most horrible feeling of everything being for nothing."

Silence stretched at our table as I remembered how I had felt in my dream when I was running. I knew that feeling well. I wanted to reach out and hold his hand but today the modern-day Gwen was in charge, and she wasn't that daring. Last night's outburst from past-life Gwen had shown me just how much I needed to always keep myself — or her — in check.

"There was something special about us. I guess it was the magic. But we still couldn't fight something like them and the Romans too. I've been dreaming about feeling like we lost," said Seth.

Garrison nodded.

"And I remember being with you, Gwen," Seth said.

# Chapter Fourteen

W hile my heart skipped a beat and I searched for something to say, opening and closing my mouth like a fish, Kian ignored him completely.

"How long have you known?" Kian asked Garrison, pointedly ending whatever conversation Seth's comment could have caused.

"A few years," answered Garrison, and it was Seth's turn to nod.

I didn't know if I felt jealous or lucky. Was it good that I didn't have to live through years of these memory attacks and magic without knowing what to do about it? Or was it bad that I could have been preparing myself for this moment, and didn't know?

Kian looked around to make sure no one was listening. "You did have magic, and you were special," he said. "And you couldn't win against the magicians. Mistakes were made. You were weakened from fighting the Romans. Now this world is in danger."

The gravity in his voice brought me back to the shack in the woods, lying in pain and looking into his eyes. Was that really less than a month ago?

I sat and listened patiently as Kian retold the whole story of our past. In a way, it was good to see Garrison and Seth nodding along. While my memories and abilities had convinced me I wasn't on some reality TV show, I felt validated that someone else was going through the same thing. It offered some credibility for my having run off chasing the memory of someone now sitting in front of me. Again, I longed to reach out and take hold of him.

*Control yourself,* my own stern voice warned in my head.

"You all have different talents," Kian was saying, "and the key to unlocking those talents is to regain the memories of your past lives and sync those lives with your own."

"And the phone?" I reminded him.

Seth and Garrison didn't have to pry every little piece of information from Kian's locked-down mind. I had already done all the work. He shot me an I-should-tape-your-mouth-shut look.

"Magicians help our cause," was all he said. "They brought me here to find you. They keep the magical plot a secret. They finance our efforts."

His face looked like he was sucking a lemon. Why was it so terrible to explain? I assumed Kian did not like being bossed around by whatever magicians were helping us.

"Why bother hiding it?" Garrison asked. "Can't anyone do anything about them? Surely going after a few magicians would be better than cleaning up all the mess they're making?"

Kian shook his head. "To destroy the magicians is difficult. They are influential in this world, and respected. It would also take all the strengths of this era and would mean the destruction of the world itself. Probably, nothing would be left."

It was grim, but we absorbed this new information while the grey clouds rolled in. News of the pier incident still played across some TV screens in the corner of the restaurant.

We ate our food, each lost in our own thoughts and occasionally stopping for Garrison to ask Kian more questions. Seth and I kept quiet, though I felt as if he stole glances at me over his omelette.

When the waitress came to collect our plates, Kian followed her to pay.

"Not very happy, is he?" Garrison asked, staring at his back. I only realized it was a question directed to me when I saw both of them staring.

"Oh...." I thought of what to say to avoid telling them he was in a bad mood. "He just takes a while to get used to new people," I replied. They both seemed happy with this, though I felt I had just made Kian, the two-thousand-year-old, sound like a cat.

We walked back to the hotel, where Kian had gotten a room for Seth and Garrison next door to ours. He didn't seem as paranoid about them either running away or going crazy with memories, but still wanted them nearby. They were taking leaving their lives very well. I guessed that's what happened when you had years to prepare yourself and a friend with whom to share your experience. A pang of jealousy reverberated in my chest.

I was worried Kian's foul mood would mean another walk in silence, but Garrison wouldn't let that happen. He spent the long walk telling us how he and Seth had met while on a school trip to a museum. They were from different schools but had recognized each other at once.

"Friends ever since," Garrison said.

Seth had little input in the story but now eyed the flags all around us as we walked by an office tower. They flew at half-mast after the incident at the pier.

"The tsunami the other day ..." he began, but Kian must have sensed his question.

"Yes," he said.

"Why don't we just fight them now?" Garrison asked. Even I knew the answer to that.

"You're not strong enough," Kian replied.

"But you know who they are," Garrison pressed.

Kian looked at him sidelong, not appearing very pleased. His face flickered between irritation and that sour lemon look he wore earlier.

"Yes," he said, and before Garrison could open his mouth, he added, "but I will not tell you."

Garrison relented and I could have sworn I saw a smile flit across Kian's face. He saw me looking and quickly replaced it with a frown.

We reached the hotel and Kian gave them the key to their room, pointing to the left of ours. I felt red flood my face as they noticed Kian and I shared one hotel room. If they thought anything about it, they didn't say anything.

Regardless of the sleep I had, I was exhausted. We had agreed to meet for dinner, but as soon as I lay down I couldn't move. A million and one questions floated across my mind about the new additions to our group. How much did they know? Did their memories shake them like mine? And how did I feel about Seth?

Kian settled onto his bed and kicked off his shoes. He was either very quickly absorbed in his book or pretended to be absorbed in it by the time I looked up. Though I had many questions, I felt like I needed to talk to Garrison and Seth in private. Kian might know more about my past life than I did, but I wanted to find out on my own terms.

"I think I'll go over there," I said, starting to get up. My body protested.

"Don't."

Kian's intervention was surprising. A small part of me was happy to lie back down, but the other part was riled at being bossed around.

"Why not?" I asked. I may have snapped a bit.

Kian must have realized I didn't appreciate his tone, so he put his book away and sat up. "Let them relax. You need to relax too."

He was easy to agree with when I was this tired.

"Fine," I said, making it sound angry on purpose. I lay back down and in an instant was lightly dozing. Knowing Kian was a few feet away, watching over me, made me feel eerily better.

*Stockholm syndrome,* I thought and smiled.

✦

A hard knock on the door startled me into a sitting position. I was up before I was fully awake. I saw quickly that evening had fallen and Kian had closed our curtains and turned on the light.

He walked past me to answer the door.

"Seriously," he said with a slight smile, "relax."

I tried to sit and soothe my pounding heart with calming thoughts. Garrison and Seth piled in, looking like I felt. There were bags under their eyes and they moved as if with heavy limbs.

While Kian held the door open, a procession of squawking girls dressed in little itty-bitty dresses filed past. They yelled and screamed and laughed all for no reason. One wore a tiara and held balloons that said "Birthday." They eyed Garrison, Seth, and Kian as they milled past, giggling and squawking some more. I remembered it was Saturday. I did not want to be on the street.

"Room service?" I suggested.

The other three nodded.

As Seth came to sit next to me, Kian plopped down on my bed, blocking his way. I frowned at him. He had only ever come close to this bed when he was saving me from one of my memories. The memory of the last time threatened to send a flush up to my cheeks, so I pushed it away.

Seth and Garrison sat on his bed, and within the hour we were eating burgers and French fries while watching a movie. It was a nice respite into the realm of normal, until the movie ended and Garrison turned to me.

"So Gwen," he said, "what can you do?"

I nearly choked on a fry. Sputtering, I sipped my soda, stalling. "What do you mean?" I asked finally.

"What are your abilities?" Garrison asked. When I still didn't reply, he continued. "For example, mine involves using my magic to move objects. That's pretty common, I guess, applying the energy like a force. Seth can affect people's moods, read them, and convince them."

Seth still scowled at this. I understood that he was not happy with his mental connection or powers of persuasion.

"She can alter matter," Kian said.

It startled me, and I turned to him, staring.

"Don't look at me like that," he scolded. "You are capable of it. You've seen some of what you can do. Sinking through the asphalt, creating fire ... Recover your past self and you all of your powers will be returned."

*What if I don't want those powers?* I thought rebelliously.

Kian had meant to be encouraging but I was beginning to frighten myself. If I had even a percentage of the power it took to cause a tsunami, then I thought it better to go without.

Eventually, Seth and Garrison left, and Kian reverted back to silence. I couldn't sleep when I was so annoyed, so as he took out his toothbrush I blocked his way to the bathroom. I placed my hands on either end of the doorway and did my best to stare him down. Kian's eyes flashed.

"What are you doing?" he asked. There was an undercurrent to his voice that almost sounded like panic.

"What's the matter with you?"

It felt good to confront him. A thrill shot down my spine, but it was followed by self-doubt. What if it was all in my head? Taking a steadying breath, I continued. "You've been quiet ever since we met them. Is there a reason you dislike Seth so much?"

I had hit a nerve. Kian's face fell and he stared at the floor intently.

"I don't dislike him," Kian said quietly. "It's just that ..."

"Just what?"

His eyes held electricity as he looked up at me. A vibration hummed between us like the air had been charged. Was this magic?

"I am just afraid to lose you." Kian opened his mouth to say something else and then reconsidered, closing it again. "Whatever you think you know about him, you're risking losing yourself in the process. Your life is split between the present and the past. Who is to say which is more important? Besides, you're different too," he accused.

My head spun with what he had just said. Lose me? I didn't know he had had me to begin with. The vibration pulsed between us and I had to ignore it to think clearly. When I looked up at Kian's face, I knew how I truly felt.

"You're not going to lose me," I said. "I'm still myself. Maybe you just need to remind me of it sometimes."

He smiled and my heart melted. I longed for him to take my hand again. Kiss me again. Hold me again. But instead he pushed me aside like one would a sibling.

"Good," he said, shutting the bathroom door.

✦

Our routine began. In the morning we would walk around New York City, and Seth and Garrison would show Kian and I the places they liked to go. They had given up on school and had to duck on several occasions when they were about to run into teachers or friends who thought they had flitted off to Europe. Kian's mood eventually improved.

Sometimes, he would have us use our magic when no one was around. He remained tight-lipped about the magicians, but I noticed he ignored his phone more often when it began to ring. He would occasionally answer it and run off to take the call in private, and those days his mood would be ruined for good.

We waited patiently for our next move, practising some simple magic and trying to piece our memories together. Seth and Garrison didn't have much to add. The main story, the reason for our existence, had been clear in their minds, but we didn't have time to get into much else. Kian would always think of another lesson to teach us or another errand we had to do.

Seth, Garrison, and I got to know each other, though Kian never left my side. I waited over a week to sneak a moment alone with Seth. Our initial meeting had been like an explosion that had died out quickly. Now, I wanted to know what the smoking embers held for us.

Garrison had convinced Kian to take him out to practice moving larger objects. Kian insisted Seth go with them, but when Seth said he was too tired, Kian didn't have a good reason not to leave him alone. Casting me a pleading look as he walked out the door, Kian left me alone in our hotel room.

I waited until I was sure they were gone then went to knock on their door. Seth answered, dressed in pyjama pants and a concert t-shirt. He looked surprised to see me there but smiled and invited me in.

"I thought Kian would have forbidden you from seeing me without his escort," he said, sitting down on his bed. I cringed.

"Is it that obvious?"

Seth nodded.

Suddenly, I was nervous and awkward. What was I here for? Corroboration of my memories to prove I wasn't crazy?

"I just wondered ..." I could already feel the blood rushing to my face, "how you know me ... and ..." *How do I put this without it making me want to hide my face in a pillow?* "If you have any memories of me that you ... didn't mention?"

Well, I couldn't get more embarrassed than I was. I was asking expressly about the second half of the waterfalls vision. Something I wasn't in a rush to tell Kian about.

Deciding there was nothing to lose, I faced him head on.

Seth smiled at my awkwardness and his hazel eyes glinted. He got up and went to his large backpack, which looked like a grenade had gone off inside of it. Clothing and shoes were scattered all over his corner of the hotel room. He began digging inside the bag.

"My memories of you are more emotional than anything," he told me, "and I'm still trying to sort that out."

I swallowed.

"Kian said we have to live our own lives. That it's important we don't forget who we are here," I blurted out.

"Yeah, well ..." Seth sat back on his heels and produced a worn leather book with pages sticking out of it at odd angles. "The problem is that sometimes that past life influences who we become, and what we do."

He moved over to sit next to me on the bed and opened his book.

"Garrison has known since he was small. Nine, I think. Me, I've been dreaming this for a few years now. So I did this to pass the time until you showed up."

My jaw dropped as he opened the sketchbook onto the first page, where a place I knew in my soul was depicted in pencil crayon. I quickly shut my mouth and focused my attention on staring.

A low wall of stone marked the entrance to a small settlement that looked no bigger than a farmer's field. Conical houses made of mud with straw roofs sat strewn about haphazardly. He flipped the page to a grey sky with a sun coming out from between the clouds and casting a direct glow onto a small inlet.

As he turned the pages, I felt like I was being absorbed into a world I had once known. We travelled together through fields, houses, and even along dirt roads.

Finally, Seth looked up at me with a question in his eyes.

Taking a deep breath, he flipped the page to a picture of me. This time, I full-on gasped as I was presented with an image of what I might look like in a decade. My hair was loose and I sat staring off into the distance in his portrait.

"Don't worry about what I remember," Seth told me as he flipped to more pictures of my past life. "This is how I see you. Now, and then."

✦

The next week passed similarly to the first. It was now well into the semester and I had pushed all worry about high school to the back of my mind. It was gone, like any chance of a fun senior year. What I got instead was daily marathon walks with Kian, Seth, and Garrison.

After we spoke in private, Seth became more open with me. Relief and disappointment battled inside me. I didn't know what I wanted, but Kian's suspicious glances in my direction and my past life's yearning for Seth made me very aware of how much I had to struggle just to stay true to myself.

On one of our walks, we ended up in a dark corner of Central Park at night. Kian had been driving me crazy by staring at his phone every few seconds and glancing around in paranoia. His magician hadn't called in a few days, and I was assuming he had heard of the park's reputation. Mainly the "don't go wandering into dark, deserted corners at night" part.

"We'll be fine," I told him, placing a hand on his arm.

He looked down in surprise. I felt slightly guilty for distancing myself from him since finding the others. His mood had helped to drive me away, but my feelings about Seth may have distracted me enough to annoy Kian further.

Kian relented and I held on to his arm as we paced the darkness. Sharing his warmth stilled the complaint on my lips. Garrison had wanted to explore his magic on larger objects, which meant rocks in the park. After an hour standing in the cold, I was shivering. There was no moon and the darkness enveloped the park.

Kian took Garrison aside. I could only make out their shapes in the distance as they rolled large rocks backward and forward. Garrison was pushing around some more of these rocks with his magic when Seth grabbed my arm. We had been watching from a distance.

"What is it?" I asked.

He sniffed at the air and then stood stock-still. Nervous, I dragged him over to the open area where the other two were.

"Something's wrong," I told Kian.

I pulled Seth behind me like a puppy. He was still staring off into the distance but his body had stiffened.

"He stopped," he said confusedly, and began looking around the darkness in vain.

"Who?" I began, but my next words were cut off by something whizzing past my head.

Kian grabbed me and pushed me down. I found my face in the wet grass. Only after I was already down did I realize the loud crack I heard was a gunshot.

## Chapter Fifteen

It's amazing how quickly your heart can begin to painfully hammer in your chest. I tried to look up to see Garrison and Seth, but Kian's hand was on the back of my head and pushed me back down.

As gunshots rang through the park, I fought Kian until he finally allowed me to sit up, all the while dragging me to a sitting position behind one of the rocks Garrison had been rolling.

"What's going on?" My voice was a frantic mix of whisper and shriek.

Kian didn't answer me. Instead he looked over my shoulder to where Garrison and Seth were crouched behind a tree. I could barely make out their shapes in the dark.

*Crack. Bang. Crack.*

The tree was chipping as bullets flew past. Whoever was after us knew where they were hiding. Worry washed over me, and I was seized with the desire to run and help them. That's when I noticed

Kian was at my side, an arm tightly wrapped around my waist.

"Let me go," I whispered.

"No," he said firmly. "They are taking care of it."

I argued that I couldn't see anything of the sort. As more and more bullets rang out, the medium-sized tree in front of them chipped further. Soon there would be nothing left to protect them.

"If they are magicians, why are they trying to shoot us?" I asked. I still couldn't pull my eyes away from the two figures hidden behind the tree.

Kian pointed to Seth.

For a moment, I panicked, thinking that he had been hit. He sat against the tree trunk, body limp. I gasped.

"He is trying to find our attacker," Kian whispered. "He is sensing him. Let him."

I gaped at Kian.

"This is another lesson?" I nearly cried out in disbelief. The look Kian gave me implied a deep concern, and I regretted my words.

"No," he growled through gritted teeth.

Despite my anxiety, I sat quietly, counting each bullet as it flew past the tree. The pressure in my chest was building, and soon I began to feel my magic buzzing through my fingers. I looked down to where my hands were firmly planted in the earth. I was clutching mounds of grass.

Every heartbeat pounded in my ears, and it grew until I knew what I was going to do. Kian's overprotectiveness could not stop me. In the distance, sirens rang out, coming our way. But it would be too late. Our attacker was determined.

Slowly, carefully, I let my magic seep from my mind into my eyes. My vision expanded to see the world anew and illuminated the night. I was able to focus in on Seth, who was still immobile, though I could see every bead of sweat that lined his forehead. He was struggling.

Garrison was huddled beside him, hands over his ears to drown out the loud bangs that would not cease. Then I turned my attention to the bullets which flew past, blowing small bits of tree away from my friends' defence.

I was like a hunter. I chased the shots upstream to get to their source. As I was still well aware of Kian's tight grip on my waist, I ran through the park in search of life in my mind. The birds had flown away due to the noise, and all the other animals were hiding in their boroughs. Then I felt the presence of magic.

It was not like mine. While I felt sparks and light, this was dense and dark, and even as I approached it I felt like I was nearing quicksand. It threatened to suck me in and capture me. The weapon had been superficial. The attacker wasn't here. This was a trap.

I felt a familiar flicker nearby and I knew that Seth and his magic were here somewhere. I sent my awareness into the surrounding area and found him struggling with the dark thing: the void in the night.

Panic interlaced with fear as the threat Kian had first told me became real. The magicians were here. My mental footing began to slip, and I found myself being sucked in. I panicked for an instant and then remembered Kian's hold on me. I used the sensation to anchor myself back to the physical world. In this mental place, he was my foundation in the real world.

I tried to reach out to Seth's energy somewhere nearby. He was being dragged in by the dark power. I was terrified, but Kian's grip sent calming energy through my physical body and into my awareness. My grasping for Seth became a tendril of energy that I saw floating into the darkness in front of me and grasping a small spark. Then, with all of my remaining strength, I pulled back like my life depended on it.

My ears popped and my lungs strained. It felt as if the world remained stationary and I was moving backwards. Like I was rising too fast from the depths of a dark sea. I was catapulted into my body with such force that it sent both Kian and I rolling backwards. When I finally found my face in the ground once more, I listened. No more shots.

Before I could decide if it was a good idea or not, I pushed myself up and ran to cover the space between Seth and me. He was still immobile, and Garrison sat next to him, shaking him and calling his name.

My knees buckled beneath me. Shocked, I realized how weak I was. The effort to use my magic in that capacity had sapped my strength completely. Kian ran up as I brought my ear to Seth's lips. They were slightly parted and my heart seized as I listened and waited. A shallow breath brushed against my ears, and I relaxed somewhat, knowing he was alive.

Then, I heard what I had been waiting for: inexplicably, I now knew the sound of his magic. The little spark that I had wrestled away from the dark thing sounded in my ears as if a bell was rung, and I knew he was intact.

I sat back on my heels and smiled. "He's going to be okay," I said as Seth started to choke and sputter.

Garrison tried clapping his back to help the coughing, regardless of my protests.

"It was a trap," Seth rasped as soon as he could talk. "Whoever it was, the magician, knew we would try to find him with magic. It was like a black hole. I couldn't get away."

Kian blanched while Garrison looked terrified.

"I was going to get sucked in if Gwen hadn't saved me," Seth said.

All eyes turned to me.

"How did you do that?" Kian asked me.

I looked away from him and searched the trees for an answer. I didn't know how to put it and didn't have the strength to speak more than I needed to.

"You kept me here," I told him. "You were ... uh ... holding me and stuff and I just had something to grab a hold of. Like a rope when I was being sucked into quicksand."

Seth nodded.

Recounting what happened was painful. The dismal feeling of the dark shape that had nearly consumed us stayed with me long after I felt I had escaped. Like a bad taste in my mouth, it persisted in my thoughts and feelings.

Kian and Garrison both looked confused and horrified as Seth and I described the thing. When we were done, I turned on Kian, even though my eyes were drifting shut.

"Why would they do that? Shoot at us?" I asked him. I knew he kept secrets, but I never thought they could be the kind that would put us in danger.

"I don't know," Kian said. "The noise and shots are to frighten you. Do you feel any different?"

"Exhausted," I said. "Why?" My suspicions were growing but I could draw no conclusions. When Kian shrugged, all I wanted to do was go back to the hotel.

"Are you saying the magicians know where we are?" Seth's voice was still weak.

Kian nodded. "Maybe."

"Then why don't they just grab us now and get it over with? They must have more power than that?" I asked. Shivering at the implication, I imagined being dragged into something like that and not being able to get out.

"They could," Kian replied, not making me feel better, "or they could wait until you are stronger so that you would give them more power. Don't forget that only you have access to your memories. You will be at your most powerful when you have recovered them."

The night pressed heavily on me like a dark blanket, stifling my emotions and impairing my breathing. I took little gasps and squinted in the moonlight to see my friends. Something didn't feel right.

"Then aren't we doing exactly what they want by trying to regain our memories?" I asked. It felt like a classic scenario of you're damned if you do, damned if you don't. A lose-lose situation.

"Your efforts may be the only thing keeping you alive," Kian said quietly. "If they thought your power was not on its way to improving, then you would be caught by now. They know where we are, but it's impossible to say where the attack came from, or how close they may be."

I felt like a lamb being fed and cared for just to be slaughtered. All we could hope for was a brief moment between getting magician-level power and being kidnapped. Then we could escape, ward off their attacks, and what? I had no idea what I would do then.

I thought of how the bullets were meant for our bodies and the black hole meant for our magic. Suddenly, I felt fragile. We were too exposed. Even if the magicians didn't succeed in destroying both, our bodies could not function without our magic and vice versa. I felt that to be true and it made me shudder visibly. Kian saw my face.

"You've put it together then," he said grimly. "Your magic is attached to your soul."

"What's going to happen?" I asked. Would I ever be able to sleep peacefully again?

Kian shrugged and stood, crouching low. Garrison followed him and they helped Seth stand. He was sweat-soaked and swayed on his feet. I crept behind them, staring into the shadows as if I could actually see anything that might be lurking there. My feet dragged.

"You have shown them your strength," Kian said as we walked and hobbled out of the park. His voice contained a mixture of pride and resignation. "They will not stop. You just have to keep beating them, until you are capable of ending them completely."

"But that black hole —" I began.

"Could have been a trap. The guns were a distraction. Probably an illusion."

In the dark, I huffed. "Probably?"

Kian didn't answer me.

We came onto the street where the streetlights felt like we had just broken into daylight from a dark abyss. I felt the park at my back, ominous and dangerous. I glanced at Garrison's watch. It was only one in the morning.

I was paranoid and couldn't stop swivelling my head uncontrollably as we walked back to the hotel, dishevelled and silent. My feet felt like they weighed a ton and I realized how much magic I had expended. I was exhausted.

At the hotel, Kian pushed a foul-smelling liquid into my hands. The cup steamed as it warmed my hands but turned my stomach. The avocado spread in Oregon had been the first of his medicinal creations. The teas were new.

Kian was under the impression that he could improvise remedies because he had once been able to, but he couldn't find the right ingredients here. So he threw together a bunch of herbs and whatever looked right to him at the moment and would make me drink the result. If Seth or Garrison saw him putting on the kettle in our hotel room, they would bolt. I didn't have that luxury.

I looked into the cup. It looked like he had tried to make a disgusting loose leaf tea and hadn't bothered with the tea bag. The water had barely changed colour.

"Drink it," he said. "It'll make you sleep better."

"Are you sure you got the right ingredients?" I asked, trying not to sound too skeptical.

Kian stopped brushing his teeth and looked at me for a moment, considering. "I had to think of a few substitutes, but it should have the same effect."

I sighed.

✦

The next few days passed by in a blur. The morning after we were attacked, the news began covering a story of a drought affecting half the country. Scientists were baffled and everyone was yelling that we had to stop global warming. I knew better.

We watched the coverage of dust storms that could have been an apocalypse descending on towns. Drinking water was spoiled and hundreds of thousands of farm animals died. Farms were abandoned. Politicians came out and began blaming each other.

I felt violated. Kian confirmed that whatever trap Seth and I had fallen for probably seeped some magic and gave the magicians strength for this latest disaster. I had to control my shuddering at the thought.

✦

Kian kicked a hockey bag towards me. It looked like it could contain a body.

Five days had passed since the attack. It had taken this long for Seth and I to get our energy back, and

Kian wasn't wasting any time. He had dragged us back to the park, despite our protests.

"They won't strike twice in the same place," Kian assured us. I thought he was taking the attack on our lives very well. Still, he showed up one morning with this giant hockey bag and dumped it in front of us.

"What is it?" I asked wearily.

He knelt down to open it, and before we could react, he began tossing various heavy objects at us.

"Hey!" Garrison protested as he skipped out of the way. He then bent down to pick up a metal sword. The sun glinted off of the blade like a strobe light. The weapon seemed out of sync with the crowded park.

My eyes widened as I noticed I was standing in the middle of swords, daggers, and other paraphernalia that made me believe my troubles with assassin magicians were nowhere near over.

"Seriously?" Seth asked, eyeing the weapons skeptically. "People are going to think we're role playing some video game."

Kian crossed his arms over his chest and said nothing.

Garrison had picked up the sword with both hands and held it up to the daylight. The thing was longer than his arm and nearly as broad. I noticed, thankfully, that the edges were dull. The thick metal hilt was worn from use.

"Where did you get these?" Garrison asked.

"Borrowed them," Kian replied obscurely.

I doubted that. They looked to be relics stolen from a museum. He had left us for hours the night before.

"Legally?" I asked. He raised an eyebrow and ignored my question.

Garrison tsked and shook his head, putting down the sword. His struggle implied it was heavy.

"This is literally like bringing a knife to a gun-fight," he told Kian. "Look at that tree!" He pointed to a maple that looked as if careless beavers had had their way with it. The bark near the bottom centre was gone and it curved into the middle, dangerously leaning to one side. It was the tree they hid behind days earlier.

"That could have been our heads!" Garrison exclaimed.

Kian placed the sword back into Garrison's hand. Then he fitted one into Seth's hand and my own. The steel felt cold against my skin and my arm and wrist began to ache within a minute.

"You won't win this war with weapons," Kian said. Garrison opened his mouth to protest but Kian silenced him with a hand. "You need your magic to get stronger, quickly. You've been found by the magicians, which limits your time to learn considerably."

"So what's with the Highlander sword?" Seth asked. He still looked tired and the bags under his eyes hadn't disappeared.

"You need to stay in shape," Kian said simply. "If only to run, but this is something you were once very familiar with." He looked each of us in turn.

"Swords?" Garrison cut in.

"War," Kian said. "Perhaps if you fall into similar rhythms, you will regain your memories faster." He seemed proud of himself for thinking of the exercise, and I couldn't bear to tell him that I felt nothing from this other than a cold heaviness.

Despite our lack of enthusiasm, he lined us up in a row and began to explain, pointing to various parts of the heavy swords.

"This is the blade." He ran his finger along the dull edge. "Where your knuckles face is called the true edge, and this will be your striking edge most of the time. The side of your thumb is your false edge. This bar is the cross-guard, which keeps blades from sliding down to your hands. Where you hold the sword is the grip, and that round thing at the bottom is called a pommel. You can hit people with it."

The rest of the afternoon followed in the same fashion, with Kian spouting information and us listening patiently. He showed us a few simple moves and made us practice until sweat ran down my forehead and into my eyes. They stung, and as I watched Kian shouting directions to Seth and Garrison while they sparred, I saw something come to life within him.

Our group had gathered a small audience that came and went throughout the day. The teenaged girls stayed longest, batting their eyes at Kian while he made us struggle under the weight of the swords. When I complained my arm hurt, he told me it was because I wasn't strong enough.

*No kidding,* I thought.

Another week passed. We ate like savage animals after having our lessons with Kian, where he drilled us endlessly and exhausted us to the bone. He kept us so busy that I did not have time to worry about anyone being after me. It was now mid-October, and I consoled myself that only one attempt on my life in a month and a half of travelling with Kian was a pretty good record.

Seth and Garrison had small glimpses of memories, but my mind remained blocked off. I blamed Kian's rigorous training schedule, but I also felt my own resistance. Since meeting Seth, I was afraid to let myself go. If I opened the floodgates, I was worried I could never close them again.

I was eating yet another hot dog in the evening with Seth and Garrison, contemplating time travel, when Kian came back. He had left to talk on his phone, which had been unusually quiet lately. I knew by the set of his jaw that he wasn't happy.

"We are leaving tonight," he said.

## Chapter Sixteen

Seth and Garrison looked at each other. Though they had abandoned their lives, I guessed that it was a small change since we'd stayed in the city they knew. Now, they were surprised to hear their lives would be changing so suddenly.

"Where are we going?" I asked, feeling like the travel veteran.

"I don't know yet," Kian said, "but there is going to be an unexpected hurricane hitting New York in the early morning. We need to leave before they know and start cancelling flights."

"Unexpected?" Seth raised an eyebrow.

"How do you know?" I asked.

Kian ignored both of us and started to walk away towards the hotel. Grudgingly, I followed him to our room. The evening was spent quietly, packing as I removed my belongings from the hotel wardrobe. We had been here for over a month now and it was beginning to feel like home. I had worried that coming with Kian would mean turning into a nomad, and was beginning to believe that that wouldn't be the case. My own dark thoughts made me grumpy.

The way Kian had neatly put all of his things away and fitted them all into his small suitcase annoyed me further.

"Why are you being so cryptic all of a sudden?" I snapped at him, knowing very well that cryptic could have been his middle name.

Kian zipped up his bag then tossed it near the door as if it weighed nothing. "You know what you need to know," he said.

I could have hit him.

Then, without warning, he spun and took both of my hands. His eyes met mine and my heart stopped in its tracks, all of my thoughts tumbling out of my head as if they weighed nothing.

"You need to be very careful," he said, his eyes imploring.

"Okay," I replied. It was a stupid reply but I felt like the moment had escalated to something serious between us, and I didn't know how to handle it.

"I'm serious, Gwen." Kian brought both my hands up and touched them gently with his lips. "You could be the strongest."

My eyes widened. What was happening?

When a knock sounded at the door and Garrison impatiently called out to us, Kian dropped my hands as if they had burned him. He got his bag and left the hotel room. I followed him again, still unsure of what had just happened. My hands tingled where he had held them.

When we got to the airport, the sky was turning a strange shade of dark as if someone had turned the dimmer switch down on the western hemisphere. The airport, made of glass and lit brightly, made it feel even more eerie. My eyelids began to droop. After a silent taxi ride, we stood in the international departures hall.

Kian was on edge. He kept checking his little cell phone and looking at the clock. My head felt like it was filled with cotton as the knowledge of a hurricane slowly crept up on me. The weather was giving me a headache and making me sway where I stood.

I turned and realized Kian was gone. I spotted him at a flight desk, paying for tickets. We stood in silence waiting for him, like children waiting for their mother, until he returned and handed out boarding passes to us all.

"I never gave you my passport," Seth said, frowning.

Kian smiled at him. "You are not the only one with a power for persuasion," he replied.

"Manchester?"

Seth was looking at his boarding pass. I realized I hadn't known where we were going either and looked down to find it was England.

"What's in Manchester, anyway?" Seth asked. "And when do we get to find out why we're travelling around? Are we looking for someone or is this visit about something else?"

"We should go somewhere," Kian said over Seth to drown him out.

In the airport, I doubted any one was listening anyway. But we obediently dropped the subject while our group made our way to the baggage drop-off, and

I was glad to get rid of my bursting green suitcase.

We filed quietly through security and bought snacks in the shop on the other side. Then Kian led us to the first class lounge, where we showed our boarding passes and walked through to an empty blue room full of empty blue booths.

Kian chose one near the window, where the sky could be clearly seen. It was looking more dangerous by the minute. I sat next to Kian while Garrison and Seth sat across from us. In hushed tones, we discussed finding more of our kind in order to be stronger and fight the magicians.

Time crawled as I kept my eyes on the clouds rolling in. It was nearly midnight when the sky was illuminated by orange as if lit with fiery electricity. I did not yearn to be up in those clouds.

"How did you know about the hurricane?" I asked Kian.

He pointed out the window. "That," he motioned to the orange clouds, "takes a great deal of magic. Magic they got from you." I shuddered. "All part of their plan. Soon, you'll be able to feel it before it acts. For now, you'll have to trust me." He smiled at me and it didn't seem like a crazy request. I had already clung to him for dear life on several occasions.

Time passed and my headache grew. After an orange juice and snapping at Kian for looking at his watch every three seconds — it was making me nervous — our flight was called for boarding. I was surprised to find that Seth was sitting next to me, with Kian and Garrison in the row in front of us.

The sky was nearly erupting with energy.

The flight attendants ran through the safety pro-cedures, checked our seatbelts, and asked everyone to keep their seat upright. The pilot introduced himself and told us that the flight would take six hours and forty minutes. Sitting next to Seth and looking out the window, my tiredness was abated for the moment.

He smiled at me reassuringly, and I saw that he was gripping the armrests of his seat.

"Fear of flying?" I asked.

"Not fear," he answered, "I just hate it."

I smiled, keeping to myself that the two were probably the same thing.

"Tell me something distracting," he said.

I thought for a while, but nothing came to mind. We were warriors from an ancient land who died to come to the future in order to, most likely, die again fighting some magicians who wanted to take over the world. In the end, I could only think about us and the connection we had felt weeks ago. It still seemed peculiar that it could flare to life and be extinguished just as suddenly.

"It was very nice to meet you," I said.

He smiled at me. "It was nice to meet you, too."

It was like an inside joke that had spanned two thousand years. I knew everything about him, but I just hadn't figured it out yet. And I knew he could say the same about me. I felt a comfort in that.

The plane, after driving around for a while, finally came to a standstill. The engines went full power and we started to speed down the runway. Seth's grip on the armrests made his knuckles white.

Hesitantly, I placed my head on his shoulder, though it bounced as the plane lifted off. He glanced down at me in surprise. I don't know why I did it. I felt sure that I could seep my calmness into him if I just touched him. He did relax slightly and leaned back into his seat. The incline of the plane pushed us back, and I relaxed into my place near his side. This felt natural. He was quite a bit taller and as I looked up at him I saw a mark like a scar under his chin.

Without thinking, I gently touched the mark with a finger. It was raised like a scar.

"What's that?" I asked.

"Birthmark," he replied through gritted teeth.

Suddenly, the small incline turned into a big one as the plane jerked nearly straight up. We were seated at the front and heard some cries from behind. What was most alarming to me was seeing the eyes of the flight attendants widen and their hands move to grasp their seatbelts. Seth winced. I leaned over to look out my window and my heart dropped to my feet.

We were flying through the hurricane. The black and orange clouds around us were shaking the plane and lightning was shooting through the clouds. The wings and engines shuddered with the pressure as we ascended too quickly. My ears roared and popped. The lights in the cabin dimmed and more people screamed. The metal of the airplane's body made a groaning sound as we moved higher and higher, never able to break free from the hurricane.

"Oh, no."

"What is it?" Seth asked. His head was pressed back into his seat, hands gripping the armrests and eyes closed.

"Uh ..." I didn't know how else to put it. My heart was speeding up too. At a loss, I punched the seat in front of me. Kian turned around.

"What?" he asked.

I motioned out of the window and widened my eyes at him meaningfully.

"We are flying through the hurricane. I was afraid we would be grounded, but at least we can get above it," he told me. Then cast an eye at Seth. "This is not dangerous," he told him in a flat voice. It was not reassuring.

"Sir, please sit down," a flight attendant called from a few rows ahead. She was still strapped in.

Kian did as he was told and I leaned forward to whisper between the seats.

"You scared?" I asked. I saw the side of his face turn towards me.

"I don't understand how we are up in the sky," Kian told me. "To me, this is already being logical. I don't see how a hurricane is more frightening."

I sat back, dejected. I could see Garrison rocking backwards and forwards in the seat in front of Seth.

"You okay?" I called.

"Fine!" came the reply. It was strained and hoarse.

In the next five minutes, it was all I could do to not join Seth in an absolute panic attack. In a way, I was glad that I was seeing a more human side of him than just the person I felt I knew from my dreams and memories. But whenever I would get on this train of thought, the plane would rock, drop or incline steeply and my chest would seize up in terror.

Finally, the plane seemed to level out and the lights came back on in the cabin. Seth tentatively opened one eye and then the other, releasing his grip on his seat. I found myself able to breathe again.

The sound system in the airplane beeped for attention.

"Well, folks," the pilot said through some static, "it's been a bumpy ride with a turn of unexpected bad weather, but we're past the worst of it now and will continue en route to Manchester. Enjoy your flight."

Some people around us clapped.

"Well, that was embarrassing," Seth said, sitting back. I smiled at him again.

The flight was uneventful because I passed out as soon as we had gotten over our escape from the hurricane. Emotionally drained, I slept for most of it and woke up when Garrison was tapping me on the forehead. I opened my eyes.

"What?"

He was leaning over the back of his seat and looking at Seth and me.

"We're talking about memories," Garrison said. "Wondering what snippets you've come across that perhaps are new."

I winced, not wanting to share anything I remembered. I had not fully explained my dreams and memories to the others. No one knew about my frantic running through the woods.

"I think I remember most," Garrison was saying.

When I looked at him questioningly, he continued.

"My name is Dylan. Really. But I think that Garrison used to be my old name. I introduce myself by it." He shrugged.

"Do you remember my name?" I asked suddenly. I hadn't known that I wanted to know.

Garrison shook his head. "No one else's, sorry."

Right then the seat belt sign came on and the pilot announced we would be landing shortly. I was glad. My back ached and the left side of my butt was completely asleep.

"Have you ever been here before?" I asked Seth. He shook his head.

"I've never travelled anywhere," he said. "Garrison's been around the world with his parents. They're very ..." he searched for the right word, "progressive. When he started calling himself Garrison, they went along with it. They barely needed any convincing at all."

Through the crack between our seats, I could see Kian was listening. He had put down his magazine and his head was turned in our direction.

"And your parents?" I asked.

"They are very protective. I hate it. But I hated having to put thoughts in their heads too." Seth looked ahead at the tray table. "It doesn't feel right. How did yours let you leave?"

I motioned my head in Kian's direction and lowered my voice so he wouldn't hear.

"He did the same thing to mine. Put thoughts into their heads or whatever. I guess it's better than them worrying. I know it's wrong, but it's for the best. They think I'm out at some private school or cruise high school or whatever. I don't even remember what I told them anymore. Something about *X-Men*."

Seth looked at me questioningly but didn't press. Instead, he also motioned his head towards Kian.

"How long exactly have you two been ... travelling together?" he asked. I didn't miss the hesitation.

"He found me in Oregon," I said quickly. "That's it. I came to New York to find you."

I remembered how the memory of some kind of ridiculous love and wonderful past life had made me set out on this adventure in the first place. I had been so naïve.

In a way, I felt like I had been lied to by my memories. Ever since that initial first glimpse into something wonderful, I'd been plagued with memories and feelings of endless running, despair, and helplessness. Not to mention that the initial memories nearly killed me.

"What do you remember about us?" asked Seth suddenly. "Exactly...."

There was a glint in his eye that I could fall in love with in a heartbeat.

*Snap out of it!* I chastised myself. I was very aware of Kian straining to listen, but Seth has lowered his voice.

"Not much," I answered. *Am I blushing?*

I had never told a more blatant lie in my life. Worst still, I knew he knew. I knew we both had felt it.

Seth raised an eyebrow at me. His hazel eyes stared me down, unconvinced. "Really?"

I felt the heat rise to my face like an unstoppable torrent of evident embarrassment. *You look like a freaking tomato.*

"I just need to … uh … sort it out," was my short answer. Thankfully, Seth let it go. He smiled knowingly and then began flipping through the safety pamphlet, something he had done about a dozen times already.

I couldn't figure him out. For all that I felt like I knew him down to every wrinkle, his character was a mystery.

The next hour or so passed mechanically. We landed, went through border control — where I explained at length that I was visiting family whose address or hometowns I couldn't remember — and got our bags. Waiting at the carousels for our luggage to arrive, all eyes were glued on the televisions.

New York had been hit by a horrible hurricane. Apparently it had gathered so quickly in the Atlantic that very few people had seen it coming. We knew better.

A lot of the city was flooded, included the memorials set up for victims of the recent tidal wave on the piers. The entire east coast was flooded, and the images of houses and cars being swept away were projected from a hundred different locations.

Kian had said the magicians dragged on the weather and threatened to pull the Earth apart with their powers. It was part of their plan to cause enough havoc to gain control. The images I now saw on the TV were horrible. In the last six hours, cities were nearly drowned and blown apart. I couldn't help but wonder if this was my fault. Had I given them the strength?

"They shook the mountains, and they crumbled," Kian said under his breath. His voice sent a shiver down my spine. He stood behind me and leaned in close. I felt the vibration again between us. "What were once great snowy peaks now remain as foothills. Many villages were buried and many people died, and the great king lived to regret his decision about casting all of his warriors into death and an uncertain future. But the greatest tragedy would be if all was for naught, and the magicians will inherit the Earth."

He looked around to see if Seth and Garrison were nearby, saw that they had gone to stand at the other end of the conveyor belt, and wrapped his arms around my waist in a quick hug. He rested a cheek on the top of my head, and while the gesture would have made me swoon, his words buried themselves deep into my skin. He held on to me as if he knew I would not be around much longer.

# Chapter Seventeen

"**L**et's go."

Kian dragged me away from the TVs and we all piled into a taxi van after handing our luggage to the driver.

The all-night flight had taken a toll on me. It was early morning in New York but already the afternoon in England. I was feeling exhaustion setting in, so I leaned my head against the window and got ready for a nap. It was only three o'clock in the afternoon but the sky was a sleepy kind of grey, and Seth and Garrison, who felt warm next to me, bunched me in. The motion of the car lulled me to sleep.

To my dismay, we stopped five minutes later. I opened my eyes to find an airport hotel.

"Really?" I asked sleepily.

Instead of answering, Kian paid and got out of the van, motioning for us to do the same. We waited, silent and exhausted, as he got us keys and we went upstairs. We had a large family suite in the airport hotel, which looked more like a spacious apartment. I tossed my stuff into a room I assumed would be mine and came out to the living room, where Kian was turning on the TV.

"Why are we here?" I asked sleepily.

The news coverage of the hurricane could be seen on every channel as he flipped from one station to another. The images were steadily getting worse and worse. I saw numbers on a scrolling marquee on the screen, but didn't want to think what they represented. Casualties? More deaths that could have been avoided if we could just get our act together faster?

Seth and Garrison came into the living room as well, settling down on the couch. It was two teenaged boys, a two-thousand-year-old grumpy man, and me. Great. An itching for action came over me.

"Let's go!" I was half shouting and half groaning. I had reached the level of exhaustion that makes you slightly crazy. "Things aren't getting any better!" I waved an arm at the TV. Seth and Garrison just looked from Kian to me, and back again. I was about to start yelling again when he finally lowered the remote control and turned.

"I don't know where to go yet," Kian said simply.

He sat in an armchair next to the couch. His stony demeanour was driving me insane. "The magician who has been in contact with me is silent today — he must be busy with this." He motioned to the screen.

"Well —" I was going to yell at him to think of something else, but he cut me off.

"Besides, you need to rest," he said.

"I'm fine!"

The three of them cast unconvinced glances in my direction.

"You look kind of pale," Seth said.

"And crazy-eyed," Garrison added.

I was getting too irritated. I went into my room and slammed the door, glancing at the mirror next to the bed. I was indeed pale, and my eyes were bloodshot and puffy from lack of sleep. This had to be one of the longest days of my life.

I climbed into the bed with my clothes on and promptly fell asleep.

✦

*The wind and branches whipped my face. I wasn't running anymore. I was riding. I looked down to find a brown horse with a pale yellow mane. The ground was blurring past me. It made my head spin so I looked ahead to where a man rode in front of me on a black horse.*

*Slowly, the trees cleared and I could see greenery up ahead. I rode through onto a hilltop. My heart skipped as the man ahead descended off of his horse, and I thought it might be Seth. The mind of my former self stayed stoic. I felt nothing. The contrast was jarring. Confused, I realized I was getting more of a presence in my memories. I could feel myself be myself. It was a small comfort as I sat, still a useless passenger in my own former body.*

*The man turned and it wasn't Seth. He was older and had thick brown hair that was windswept behind a widow's peak. His eyes were blue but there was something heavy about them. He was handsome enough, but I couldn't figure out who he was. My past life wasn't giving me any indication. He came closer and took my hand. I got off my own horse and followed him to the edge of the cliff. He spoke to me.*

*At first I felt myself staring blankly at the sounds coming out of his mouth. I certainly didn't understand this. Then, slowly, the meaning began to form in my mind.*

*"You have to understand why we do this," he said. "Everyone is beginning to see the war is lost."*

*"We still have time," I replied.*

*The man's eyes hardened. "You are my wife and you will do as I say," he said.*

*I pulled my hand from his grasp. "Do what you want, but my magic belongs to this people and I will not use it against them," I said. "Husband, you will offend the gods if you go ahead with this."*

*He stared at me then waved his arms at the land below the hill.*

*"Look at them!" he whispered fiercely. "The Romans have conquered the world and they do it with their gods. Ours are too weak! You are too weak!"*

*He pulled me close and held me even as I struggled.*

*"Do not be as blind as our foolish king. I do not want to see my family ruined. Sent away into slavery. I am doing this to save you."*

*He pulled me towards the edge and I saw the vast camp below. Canvas tents, dozens of horses, hundreds of men, wagons, and supplies. The fires that burned were cooking meat from our lands. They were using our water to drink, and our wood to build. Deep inside, the old me finally awoke and was furious. Something bubbled in my heart. The sight was shocking — there were so many of them. The familiar feeling of helplessness crept up on me.*

✦

"Gwen." A hand was shaking me awake. "Are you okay? What happened?"

"Nothing," I replied. "A dream, but I forgot it."

I opened my eyes. Seth and Garrison were standing over me, while Kian was at the door. I could see the flickering light of the TV from the living room.

"You were saying something totally incomprehensible," Seth told me. He looked concerned, and I still marvel at how our shared secret brought three complete strangers so close together.

"Yeah — I don't know, I was having a dream, but I don't remember," I said again.

I didn't know why I lied. Well, that is a lie. I lied because I couldn't keep things straight anymore. My grip on my past-life — let alone reality — was totally slipping.

I came out to the living room to watch some show about pawnshops. We watched TV and paced the room until night fell and eventually everyone went to bed. We had a few meals throughout the day, but I was too distracted to notice. I tried to fall asleep but the dream was playing over and over in my head.

*Married?* My thoughts were going around in circles. I thought I was supposed to be with Seth! *Okay, married ...* But was I a traitor? Was the man in my dream a traitor? I kept thinking about the Romans and how many there were. I knew, somehow, that our population was small. Their huge numbers could easily swallow us up. This was a truth I couldn't deny.

When the shadows cast by the ceiling fan began to take on shapes of their own and started to turn into menacing figures, I decided it was time to get up. Tip-toeing so as not to wake anyone, I crossed the hall to the bathroom and got into the shower.

The hot water felt relaxing after I had spent so long sitting in the plane and on the couch. I stood with my back to it, letting it pour over my head and trying to empty my mind of any thoughts at all. After a few minutes, the water became cold. I danced around to avoid it and turned the hot water tap completely up. Still nothing. The water was freezing now. I sighed and rolled my eyes. Even in a hotel, they run out of hot water.

I felt a gentle pull at my body and especially my eyes — a little like vertigo. I stumbled for only a second and then realized what was happening. I was falling into a memory, and I already knew which one.

✦

*I was back to the waterfall from my very first memory. I felt the rocks underneath my feet and the weight of the water as it fell onto the back of my neck. This time, I stepped out from underneath the water and saw that mysterious person. My eyes blurred and stung from the downpour, but in the haze of the summer day, I could clearly make out an older version of Seth coming towards me.*

*He was standing on the bank, beckoning to me. The difference was striking. The older Seth had a beard, he was more muscular, and there was something different about his walk. Confidence. His broad shoulders matched his height and I was drawn to him like a moth to a flame. The hunger I felt deep within my body scared me. Despite my feelings for the Seth I knew, I had never felt this.*

*I stepped towards him, unable to stop myself. My heart melted when I recognized the glint in his eyes, which, over two thousand years later, I would see in New York City. The modern me celebrated as I received confirmation that I had been right. I was supposed to be with Seth! What about the other man? What about my husband? I pushed those thoughts away when another interrupted my stream of thoughts. What about Kian?*

*The past me wasn't concerned. I made my way over to the bank. It took me a shockingly long time to realize he wasn't clothed. My inner self wanted to cover up and avert my eyes, but my past life just stood there. I felt the muscles in my face smiling at him. I loved him.*

*We were in a forest clearing and while I stood in the freezing water of what I saw to be a small waterfalls cascading over a larger hill, past-Seth stopped coming towards me and sat on the bank. He was still pronouncedly naked, and I saw my hand come up to motion him towards me.*

*He remained seated on the bank and smiled at me, laughing a little. I wondered if it was normal to just hang out naked in the ancient world. Clothes were probably much harder to come by.*

*Eventually, my past self got fed up and began wading through the shallow water towards him. I felt every rock as my feet found the safe places to step in the murky water. Some were slippery, some were sharp. A few times I grabbed some reeds to help me make my way to the bank and I felt them stinging my hands.*

*I was seated deep inside my past body, shocked at my own brazen daytime nudity and frolic in the water. I held my breath for what would happen next. My past life finally approached past-Seth and I saw the Roman uniform — just like the ones I'd seen in my previous dream — lying on the ground behind him.*

*Uh-oh.*

## Chapter Eighteen

"Gwen!"

I opened my eyes but couldn't see a thing. It took me a moment to realize I was back in my bathtub and someone was banging on the door — hard. Then I couldn't breathe. Choking and sputtering through the smoke I climbed out and ran to the door, tossing myself out of the bathroom. Oh, and I was naked, of course. All the nudity!

"Are you okay? What happened?" Garrison and Seth were holding their arms to their faces to prevent breathing in the smoke that had seeped into the suite from under the bathroom door. The fire alarms were going off and someone was knocking on the door.

"I'll go deal with that," said Garrison, avoiding looking at me.

"I'll come with you," Seth added.

My eyes were watering from the smoke and I was still finding it hard to breathe. Kian dragged me up by my arm and helped me to my room. I leaned on him and stumbled to my bed, climbing under the covers. It was still night outside.

"What happened?" he asked. He was confused and worried — I welcomed it. His human side drew me to him like a moth to a flame. He opened all the windows in the room and the sound of highway traffic seeped in. Somewhere nearby, an airplane took off.

"I had a memory again — not a dream this time," I replied. It hurt to speak. "What's all this smoke?"

Kian picked something white off my arm and showed it to me. "The bathtub was lined with something rubber. When you heated up or used your fire, it must have melted and began to burn."

I suddenly became very aware of random bits and pieces stuck to my arms, legs, and back. I squirmed in the bed until deciding to investigate further when I was alone in the room. I noticed Kian stayed by me, reluctant to leave. I could hear the other two explaining the smoke to a man at the door.

"Why am I having so many of these memories?" I asked him. *And what do they mean?* a voice yelled inside me. "I've had two in the past few hours. Why?"

I got one of his looks of worry and tenderness that made my heart flutter a bit. "We are coming closer to where everything first began."

I pieced it together. We hadn't just come to England to find another one like us. Kian was hoping that bringing us back to wherever our old home used to be would ignite some memories and abilities. I felt bad for yelling at him earlier — he had had a plan.

"But how do I stop them? How do I control them,

at least?" I realized I sounded desperate. I *was* desperate. It was not only embarrassing, seeing as how Seth and Garrison had not nearly burned down our hotel, but also exhausting and confusing.

Kian shrugged and looked truly remorseful. His eyes were downcast and his lips were pursed. "I'm sorry, but I cannot answer that. And you need to remember how to use your magic," he said.

That sounded strange. It was like he was implying he knew but could not tell me.

"But what about all of the other stuff?" I asked. His eyes widened and it dawned on me that he didn't know what I knew. It was the first secret I had kept from him.

"What other stuff?"

I needed to change the subject, not wanting to talk about anything I had dreamt or seen. "I don't feel like myself anymore," I told him sternly. "There are too many memories. Too many things are getting mixed up."

He opened his mouth to ask me more questions I probably didn't want to answer, but luckily Seth and Garrison came in.

"We convinced the hotel manager that the smoke is not coming from this room," Garrison announced, sitting on the corner of my bed. "Which is a lie, of course, because Gwen nearly roasted us."

He meant it kindly and Seth laughed at his joke. Even Kian smiled and I was very thankful that this was the company I kept, and that they had changed the subject.

❖

The next day was the first of November. I felt only slight anxiety this month about being absent from school. It felt silly, but I imagined all the classes that I wasn't taking and how my future was effectively postponed. If I had a future at all after this.

Kian rented a car in the morning and we piled in, with Seth and I in the back. No one had asked me what happened the night before but I felt the questions hanging in the air. We drove for about an hour until we reached a town called Chester.

The town was large and the overcast weather fit in perfectly with the stout brown buildings. I could only stare out of the window as we drove through many pedestrian-only streets, all of which looked posh. However, I could tell this town was old. The streets and shops looked like the twenty-first century had been smashed in with ancient times, as a medieval church stood next to a half-buried ancient coliseum and a very modern parking lot. The whole town had the look of an ancient fort revamped to serve the functions of a shopping mall.

Our car ride had been silent, and as we stepped out onto the street with our luggage, a feeling of restlessness buzzed inside me. I should have been exhausted after last night, but I felt like I could run a mile. I looked left and began to cross the street, but Kian grabbed my arm. A car zoomed by from the right.

"Oh yeah," I said.

My wrist tingled where he touched me. It warmed me and I scolded myself. I was supposed to be with Seth. Or the man who said he was my husband. Definitely not Kian. I had had no memories of Kian, even though he said he had known me. Another confusing twist to my story, which I pushed to the back of my mind. When I had time to think about it, I would examine my options. For now, I only smiled stupidly at him.

We got to our new hotel and were led up narrow flights of stairs to two rooms.

"Sorry, only two left," the woman explained. "It's usually quiet this time of year, but we've got a lot of shoppers down for the weekend."

She handed two keys with oversized key rings to Seth and Kian, and then looked at me with a raised eyebrow.

"If you let me know in which room you'll be, I can have someone bring up your luggage, dear."

I stared for an instant, not knowing what to say until Kian replied for me.

"She will be in my room. Thank you."

The woman smiled and left without further comment.

I didn't look at the other two as they shuffled off to their room next door. My cheeks were too pink. I didn't know why it should be different now than in New York, but the restlessness in my heart beat against my chest. I felt an excitement and I didn't know what for.

Kian unlocked the room and we went in. I gaped at the bed. The only bed in the room.

"I can sleep on the floor," he told me, then moved to look out the window.

The room was decorated like a bed and breakfast, with a floral pattern on the quilt and pastel ceramics on the dresser and night table. The ceiling was the same colour of wood as the floor and slated with the roof. Kian had to duck as he moved towards the window.

"It is amazing how things change over time," he commented absentmindedly. I smiled.

My feelings for Seth had cooled since meeting him, but the vision of the waterfalls showed me that my previous self had been deeply in love with him. In this life, Kian had got to me first.

*But how do I feel?*

I didn't know, but as I watched Kian duck and twist in order to see all the way out of the window, my heart warmed for him. For the first time in a while, I felt a clear distinction between my past life and this one.

"What?" Kian asked.

"Hm?"

"I can feel you staring a hole through my back, Gwen," he answered. "What is it?"

Embarrassed, I fought to find something to say that wasn't what I had actually been thinking about him.

"How close are we to our former selves?" I asked.

Kian's eyes narrowed and I wondered what he knew about my memories. "What do you mean?"

"You know … appearance … personalities …"

I figured if I was a traitor in my past life that frolicked in forests with men who weren't my husband, I couldn't have been a stellar person. Kian sat on the windowsill.

"Like I said." His hands were clasped. "I knew you, but you are considerably different in this life. How you feel, think, and live changes how you look. You're also much younger than I remember you …" he thought about it for a moment "… and changed. But you have retained the appearances of your former selves. You have been scattered into safe places where you can blend in and disappear until you are needed. You are close in every aspect to your past life, except ..." He walked over to me and touched a finger to my heart. I held my breath and looked up at him as he stood over me. He loomed like a cave enveloping me but I welcomed it. "Your character. Your soul is divided. But," he gave me a crooked smile that weakened my knees, "remember that you are not your past, and only you determine your future."

The restlessness had turned into an all-out frenzy. My body buzzed.

"Gwen ... you're ..." Kian placed both his hands on my shoulders and looked at me confusedly, "vibrating."

Maybe he hadn't felt the vibration in the air between us before. I didn't know what an anxiety attack or a heart attack felt like, but I was convinced I would be on the verge of both in seconds. He was so close.

While Kian looked me over for the source of the magic pulsing from my body, I let the heat from his hands on my shoulders wash over me.

"This might —"

I didn't let him finish. I stood up on my tiptoes and leaned into him, keeping just far enough from his lips to not touch them. I felt bold. A small voice in my mind blamed the English air, though I knew better. It was my strength making me so bold, and it was growing as we came closer to the land we remembered.

Our one and only previous kiss flashed in my memory and it fuelled my audacity. An instant passed as Kian considered, then pressed his lips against mine.

I could have melted right there and then. His touch cooled the ache that threatened to send me into cardiac arrest, and I felt my entire body ease. He brought his hands to my face and stroked my cheek while kissing me. I could only stand there and enjoy the moment.

"Are we ready to ... whoops. Sorry!" Garrison had opened the door without knocking then quickly shut it again. I had turned around just in time to see Seth behind him.

# Chapter Nineteen

"C rap!"

I grabbed my coat and ran out of the room. I nearly crashed into the man bringing our bags up the stairs. He was struggling with my frumpy green suitcase. Kian was on my heels, which turned into an awkward mess on the narrow stairs. By the time we sorted ourselves, I could hear Seth and Garrison leaving the hotel.

"Gwen, what's the matter?" Kian asked in the lobby.

After having unattached myself from him, the pressure in my chest was slowly rising again. I turned to face him.

"I just don't want to be caught —" I stopped. Caught doing what? Straying from my past life's path? Making a decision? "I don't want things to become awkward between all of us." I tried to ignore the mix of emotions that played out on Kian's face.

"Why would it?" he asked. "Because of Seth?" His voice was casual, but I could tell he was nearly wincing.

"It's the magic...." I really didn't know where I was going with this. "In our past lives ... I don't know...." The weakest explanation I've ever given. Kian had put on a mask of indifference but I didn't believe it anymore.

I didn't want to go into the details. No point in telling him that I had only followed him because of the waterfalls vision that turned out to be Seth, that I had only kissed him the first time because I had wakened from a dream and thought he was Seth, and that Seth was probably a Roman or a traitor. None of this made me sound good at all.

"It's not important," I lied.

Lying to Kian created a lump of guilt that sat in my stomach.

I finally managed to get Kian out of the lobby, still posing a million questions. I was just thinking about where to start looking for Seth and Garrison when I spotted them a few metres away from the hotel. Seth's back was turned to me.

"Just wait!" Garrison was saying. "Let's figure out where we're going."

Seth had obviously wanted to take off. I didn't know if he was mad, but I didn't have time to care. We had come to an unspoken agreement that our past lives would stay as such. I had nothing to be sorry for. Or at least, that's what I kept telling myself.

I jumped in on their conversation before Seth could retort.

"We should explore," I said, trying to keep my tone light and the colour from rising to my cheeks. I didn't want to think about what they had just walked in on. Pretending like nothing happened was my only card to play.

"Sure. Maybe split up?" Garrison suggested. "Cover more ground?"

"Seth, come with me," Kian said quickly.

My heart skipped a beat. *No!*

Kian would get the story out of Seth and know I had lied. I remembered his sour mood in New York. He knew there was something between us, he just didn't know what. If what I had seen were true, he would hate me. I was a traitor, and more than likely an adulterer too. My mind raced, hoping Seth would say no.

Seth didn't question it, and he and Kian walked down the cobblestone street with a quick wave to Garrison and me. I watched them go, noting their similar posture. They hunkered down against the breeze in the same fashion, moving in step. I sighed.

Garrison smiled. "I guess you're with me today."

His kindness at not mentioning anything he had seen steadied my heart a bit, but every time I thought of what Kian and Seth could be talking about, my pulse would race again. The secrets were stacking up.

The day passed quickly and the buzzing in my chest eventually dissipated. Garrison was long and lean and it was a challenge to keep up. He told me all about growing up in New York and his forward-thinking parents who let him choose his own name.

When he had begun to remember his past life at a very young age, he told them about it and they encouraged him to consult with various psychics and mediums to learn the truth about his life. Garrison laughed as he recounted his parents taking him to fortune tellers as a child.

"Here I am," he said, "maybe ten years old. Probably not even. This woman pulls out her cards and starts telling me about this past life that just didn't match with what I knew. I basically corrected her throughout the whole thing."

He was speaking and laughing while climbing one of the hundreds of staircases in the city centre. I had been out of breath and sweating for about half an hour.

The city of Chester was built on many levels, as if all of time was visible in this one place. Relics and structures from previous eras and people poked through to later periods and even the present day. The various levels of shops were connected by countless staircases and walkways, which I suspected had once been Roman aqueducts.

"So what set you off?" I huffed. "What convinced you these weren't just dreams?" I was fighting to keep my voice from revealing how out of breath and out of shape I was as he led me to yet another level of the city's ancient walls. "Do you even know where you're going?"

"No," Garrison said. "I thought you wanted to explore."

He turned around and saw my sweaty face. Smiling, he sat down on a bench for a break. I plopped down next to him. He had avoided my previous question. Running his hand through his brown curls, he stared straight ahead. I could feel an answer coming so I didn't press.

We sat for a few moments as I could feel anxiety bubbling off him. Maybe it was magic or my imagination, but the carefree and happy-go-lucky personality was gone. Was this what I looked like when I reflected on my past life? An age settled over him.

"I remembered having a good life," Garrison said suddenly. I turned to look at him but his gaze was far away in a memory. "It's hard when you have all of these feelings, and all of the … repercussions that come with having lived a whole life already. But none of it is within your control. You can't go back to that life, but you're saddled with all the baggage."

*Tell me about it*, I thought bitterly.

The sky was growing dark. The sudden change of weather surprised me, but the air felt charged. I felt like he was using magic, but I had to remember to ask Garrison about it at another time. For now, I listened. The air felt so thick around us that I didn't dare move.

"I was just a child when I saw my entire family murdered," he said flatly. I stared at him in shock. "I couldn't tell what was then and what was now, I was too young. I would live two lives — in one I would have my hippy parents who encouraged me to develop any kind of psychic ability, and in the other I would live in the past, on my own."

I didn't know what to say. My bad situation seemed just peachy compared to his.

"So what happened?" My voice came out in a whisper.

"I just dealt with it," Garrison shrugged. "The memories grew when I grew. I remembered becoming a soldier. I knew how to fight. I've actually enjoyed these lessons with Kian. Sometimes an image will float through while I'm waving that damn heavy sword around. Then my magic kicked in. I could move things, draw things to me and push them away."

I eyed the clouds moving quickly to hover over our heads. Garrison saw me look.

"That happens sometimes," he dismissed, waving a hand at the clouds. "Then," he continued, "just as I thought I was going crazy, I found Seth. This was about," he counted on his fingers, "three years ago. We tried to add our memories together — his had just started — but it still didn't make complete sense. So we just decided to wait until someone showed up one day to claim us."

Three years. Three years that Seth had known about me, and I had no idea about him. I processed Garrison's story. My naiveté seemed ridiculous now.

We spent another hour or so wandering around town. We eventually returned to the hotel for dinner. While we waited to be seated in the small dining room, Kian and Seth finally shuffled in. If it weren't for the hard lump in my heart that formed at seeing both of them, I would have laughed at their similar sulky postures.

Inside me a conflict raged. The past me wasn't turning out to be an awesome person. I felt like I needed to hide this side of me if Kian were to ever come near me again. But he encouraged me to develop who I was. And embrace it. He didn't know what I might become.

As they both walked in, I felt it clearly for the first time. Yes, it was Kian I wanted. My past life ached for Seth, but I couldn't let her win. She would take me over and turn me into her. I processed it with the clearest logic I could muster. Just like I couldn't be judged now on the merits of my past life, so he couldn't be loved for his. I startled myself with the thought. I guess my decision was clearer than I had thought.

"Good day?" Garrison asked.

I tried to act casual but was dying to know what they had talked about.

Seth nodded. "It was alright," he said.

I eyed Kian for any hint of what had happened, but his face was impossible to read.

✦

The next few days crawled by. Kian didn't seem to be interested in speaking with me and had been grumpy since our first day in Chester. I wanted to know when he would take us to where we were from, or even ask him why we were here, but he was avoiding me. He slept on the floor during our first night in the hotel, and the next day he took another room that had become available.

While Kian's treatment of me hurt, the buzzing I had experienced during our first day came back in quick bursts, where I felt like my body was being zapped with electricity. I found myself using my magic just to burn some of it off. Moving things around with currents of air, I discovered my powers were similar to Garrison's.

"Maybe we're long-lost cousins or something," he told me one day.

One evening we were watching television and news of the drought in the southern states and flooding in Florida played back-to-back. I had lost count of all the places the magicians' touch had reached. We were in Seth and Garrison's room; the two lay splayed out on their beds behind me, while I sat on the floor in front of the TV.

"How do you suppose we fight *that*?" Seth asked, waving a hand at the TV.

The footage showed people paddling boats through what used to be a town.

That question plagued me every day.

"I don't even have any real magic," Seth was nearly pouting. I turned around and gave him an incredulous look.

"Without you, we would never be able to find them. You can sense them. Know what they're going to do … right?" I tried to sound supportive.

Seth shrugged, bypassing my comments. "That or get sucked in again by a trap," he remarked glumly.

That wasn't what I had wanted to hear. Deciding it was time for bed, I stood.

"See? You scared her off," Garrison said half-heartedly to Seth.

"No way." Seth smiled at me and his demeanour melted a little. I felt a pang of guilt as my eyes lingered over his face, looking for the man inside.

*Your life to lead*, I told myself. I said goodnight and left the room.

Guilt hung over me like a dark cloud. I wanted Kian to like me. I wanted him to talk to me and joke with me like he used to. And wanting this made me roll my eyes. His marble personality made it that much more rewarding when he would open up to me and reveal the softness underneath the granite exterior. The man was like stone. But I had only come because of Seth. I had loved him for nearly two thousand years and a part of me still felt too insignificant to break the chain.

*One foot here, one foot there,* Kian had once told me. *Be careful or you'll never find your present.*

Before entering my room, I heard Kian's voice. It was the first time I had heard it raised in a long time. I immediately became paranoid about who was in his room. Before I knew it, I had crossed the hall and had my ear pressed to his door.

*Subtle, Gwen.*

"… too difficult … have a lot of magic." His voice came muffled through the door.

*Damn you, Victorian hardwood.*

After a second, there was no reply. I realized he was on the phone. I had never actually heard him speaking on the phone to one of the magicians who were sponsoring us. His attitude made it clear he followed their orders, whether he liked it or not, but now he argued heatedly.

"I won't do it." The words rang clear. Some more silence, then, "You cannot … the promise is …"

I strained.

*The promise is what?*

The door swung open and I nearly fell onto Kian's chest. He took me by the arm and ushered me across the hall into my own room, where he slammed the door shut behind us. It startled me and I sat on the edge of the bed, staring at him. He was towering above me, his long nose making him look like a bird of prey. He eyed me like an eagle would do a snake far below. His eyes were narrowed with suspicion.

"What are you doing, Gwen?" His voice was hushed but dangerous. I realized he was angry with me. It stung, since this was our first conversation beyond "Good morning" and "Good night" in a few days. He had avoided me, and now he was yelling at me. Irritation itched under my layer of dismay at his treatment.

"I'm sorry I was listening in, I just thought —"

"You don't trust me," he stated.

His tone stung some more and I didn't know how to answer. Seth must have told him everything about me that I had hidden. He must think I'm a horrible person. Something had been divulged. The paranoid thoughts circled my mind like vultures.

"What do you mean?" My voice came out in a pathetic whimper.

I didn't want to hear what he had to say. Had I been a terrible person? Had Seth told him about my husband?

"Whose life are you living?" His eyes were imploring while his voice still simmered.

"My own," I answered. The accusatory note in his tone was undeserved. I hadn't done anything wrong. Had I?

"Why are you ..." he stopped, thinking about how to continue, "being affectionate with me?"

I sat and stared, not knowing how to answer. I vowed to never eavesdrop again if this mess blew over. How had the conversation gotten here?

"Seth told me about the memories you share ... about being together," Kian prompted.

I felt a fresh wave of fuchsia flood my face as my heart began to race again. Okay, worst fears confirmed. Kian's anger had gone as quickly as it had appeared and he just looked confused. I realized I owed him an explanation, but before I could open my mouth, he went on.

"I don't know what I feel when I am around you anymore," Kian went on. "It has become difficult. I don't have any of my own magic, you know that." I nodded, waiting for him to explain. "The magic I have came from the magicians who brought me here, and only to find you. That's all I have."

There was a moment of silence when I realized he waited for me to speak. I had no idea what to say or what he was going on about.

"Go on," I suggested.

"So why choose me?" he asked. I stared at him in disbelief.

"What do you mean?"

"Why choose me? I'm powerless, yet I feel power around you. Why?" Kian continued. "I shouldn't; I have nothing but the magic given to me. You're vibrating. I can feel the energy off of you. It's hard to be near you without feeling it spread to me. It seeps into my bones and I don't even have anything to defend myself with."

I sat speechless. I loved it when he dropped the indifferent attitude, but he was flying off the handle a bit here.

"But I don't even mind that anymore," he said. "If I feel that with you, why does Seth tell me you were his? If you think you were with him then …"

I took in a deep breath. Kian's speech was like a roller coaster ride on my emotions. I was beginning to realize that he would simmer and stew, and then explode like a volcano. I needed to steady myself.

"I was," I said, though a strong portion of my mind argued that I had never been anyone's. Something Kian said sounded off to me. "I don't *think* I may have had something with him. I *did* have something with him. But that doesn't mean anything now," I said. Not mentioning the fact that Seth was probably Roman and therefore I had more than likely sold out my own people. "I know that. Meeting Seth was just … surprising after all the memories."

Kian looked utterly confused. His irritation has dissipated and was replaced by a frown.

"There is nothing between us in this life," I reiterated. "But you told me I have to figure out my memories to gain my magic. That's all."

He stood, his face growing more and more bewildered. He scowled at the wall and placed a hand on his chin. In any other situation, his befuddled appearance would have been comical.

I sighed and went on, well aware that I was quickly talking myself into a hole.

"I am realizing that this is a new life. And nothing has happened to make me …" Love? Did I dare say love? "… want to be with him. We may have been together then but —"

Kian cut me off with a raised hand. "Gwen, I don't know what kind of magic or trickery has convinced you otherwise, and it is strange that you both tell the same story, but I can guarantee you that you have never been … associated … with Seth."

# Chapter Twenty

I blinked at him like a total idiot. "But …" was all I could manage.

"I thought Seth had been lying. I know who he was, and I know you have never been together," Kian said. "That's why I was angry. I thought you or he was trying to … trick me or something." He leaned against the door and rubbed a hand over his face. "I didn't know his reasons to lie, so I watched you two. But you seem convinced of your past. I need some time to think about this."

"Uh, yeah." It was a weak defence, but I had nothing else.

My heart beat like a drum at the thought that I might have been mistaken. What if my memories weren't actually memories at all? I couldn't bear to think of it. The last grip I would have had on any of my lives was quickly slipping away. I jumped up and rushed to Kian so quickly that he backed into the door.

"Do that thing you did when you kidnap —" I stopped, "— found me. That thing where you read my memories or whatever. You'll see it was him."

Another flood of red went straight into my face as I began to worry what Kian would actually see, but he shook his head.

"It doesn't work that way. I have the magic to unlock your memories, but they are yours. What you saw then is what you'll see now. Those images were focused around you. He wasn't in them."

"How can you be sure we were never together?" I asked, suddenly skeptical.

"Because I am."

I wasn't going to get more out of him.

"Who were you arguing with on the phone?" I asked.

A change of subject was best. Arguing with Kian about what I knew in my very soul wasn't going anywhere. I'd prove him wrong. Somehow.

"We have a new location," was the reply.

I sighed and we reached for the doorknob at the same time. His face was mere inches from mine, and my breath caught in my throat. I looked up into his eyes and for a moment the world was transformed. His eyes shone brighter. Slowly, his face moulded and changed and became that of the Roman soldier at the waterfalls. Seth.

I jumped in surprise. My heart nearly leapt out of my chest, but Kian appeared not to notice anything. His expression didn't change as he pulled the door open and walked down the hall to Seth and Garrison's room.

I stood in the doorframe, leaning against the wood for support and grasping my chest.

*What is going on?* The thought raced through my mind but I had no answer.

While I still stood immobile, Seth poked his head out of his room and down the hall.

"Gwen?" he called. "Come on! Kian's doing one of his announcements."

I walked into the room, trying to act calm, though my heart still palpitated violently. But, I couldn't look at Kian in the same way. He and Seth now felt the same to me — looked the same, smelt the same. I couldn't focus on his words.

"... countryside. Be in control."

"What?"

Kian turned to me with an annoyed look but quickly looked away. He shook his head slightly when he looked my way, as if willing the confusion to tumble out.

"I said we were going into the countryside to find the next of your kind. Your memories are growing — so are your powers. So make sure you remain in control." He finished his speech and walked out of the room without another word.

"Wow, man of steel, he is," Garrison said. Seth nodded and then noticed me eyeing him. I realized too late that I must have worn a suspicious look.

"What is it?" he asked.

I looked meaningfully at Garrison, silently asking for a private minute. He got the hint but chose to only sit up in his bed and hug a pillow.

"If you're going to discuss your lovey past, then I know all about it, so no point in kicking me out into the hall."

Seth hid his face in his hands as his ears turned pink. I crossed my arms and tried to look stern, but I kind of didn't care. I surprised myself by separating the past from the present. I guess it is easier not to identify with your past life when you turned out to have been an adulterous traitor.

"Whatever," I said to him. Then to Seth, "What did you tell Kian?"

Seth looked taken aback. He must not have realized there was anything that needed to be held back. He screwed his eyes up and thought.

"I told him most of my memories were like photographic portraits. The sea. The forest. You." He shrugged. "Those few things were all I knew of my past life, other than the feelings that came with them. From those, I figured out what was going on ... I realized our story."

"And you're sure it was me?" I was nearly wincing with anticipation.

"Of course," Seth answered.

My chest eased a little and I mentally devoted some time in the near future to proving Kian wrong.

"Did I upset anyone?" Seth asked, eyebrows rising.

He was obviously referring to Kian so I shook my head to reassure him.

"He's not mad," Garrison said, joining the conversation. "It'll blow over. I see the way he looks at you."

I ducked my head, trying in vain to hide the blush creeping up my neck. I had been ignoring him watching our exchange from his bed.

"I don't know what —" I began, but Garrison cut me off.

"Yes, you do," he said. It wasn't an accusation, just an observation. I stole a glance at Seth but he seemed indifferent. Deciding to retreat, I waved goodnight and raced to my room, where a whole lot of concerns were mixed with a bunch of questions.

✦

"It's too hot," Garrison complained from the back seat.

He sat with me in the back of the rental car while Seth and Kian rode in front. The sun shone on our legs and it did feel a little like being baked inside an oven.

"I thought England was supposed to be cold, dismal ..." He trailed off, throwing his head back dramatically.

"Stop whining. The air conditioning is on," Seth called from the front.

We could hear the small car struggling to cool the air, but weren't feeling it.

Despite Garrison's dramatics, the morning had begun quite differently. He had come downstairs with puffy eyes and red welts on his cheeks that looked like burst blood vessels. A night of crying would do that. I chose not to say anything and asked Seth.

"Memories," he said. "Kian warned us. He's trying to stay in control, but it's hard."

When I looked at him questioningly, he went on.

"His family," Seth explained. "*Both* his families."

I decided not to ask any further questions because I did not want to know. I suspected Garrison's happy and upfront exterior masked something else.

"What about you?" I asked Seth.

He smiled at me then looked away. "You know …" He shrugged. I realized he shrugged a lot, as if not wanting to commit to anything he said. "Same things. Trails. Horses. Rivers. You."

The way he said it sent shivers up my spine. I wasn't sure if it was a good or bad thing. Kian pulled around with the car. It was audible from around the corner of the hotel since the car sputtered and squealed.

When we stared, he called out the window.

"Only one they had left!" he said defensively.

"Well, here's to finding a new addition to our group!" Seth had squeezed my hand and walked away, while I felt his touch ringing up my entire arm.

*What kind of magic is this?* I wondered as I let it warm and soothe me. *Idiot*, I told myself. *You're swooning.*

Kian had been in a better mood the night before, and I had a wonderful sleep. I managed to stay awake during the car ride out into the country. Unfortunately, that meant putting up with Garrison's complaints.

After two hours, the green farms began to be rather boring and I searched the car for anything to occupy my interest. After I had read the safety instructions on the back of Seth's visor about ten times, Kian finally stopped the car.

We were in a small parking lot in the middle of nowhere. The town was flat, though there were a few hills a short way away. As far as I could see, there were only some brown brick row houses, a street lined with white shops, and a small white church backing out onto an old cemetery.

One of the shops in the white street was a fish-and-chip shop and Garrison and Seth quickly rushed in that direction. I followed with Kian on my heels. I tried smiling at him, and my heart sang when he acknowledged me, but his return look was nearly a grimace. He was preoccupied. I thought back to the argument on the phone. If Kian did not want to come here, why had he?

The store looked like nothing had been updated in the last fifty years. The counters were rounded and white. The chairs were cheap metal. Behind the counter, a man of retirement age stood over the fried fish in various tin heating trays.

"One, please," Garrison said, coming up to the counter.

His eyes were wide and I smiled to myself, remembering that he was still a teenager who liked to eat, despite being an ancient magician.

"Of which?" the man asked.

"Anything! Everything!"

The man continued to look at Garrison, waiting for an answer. Realizing his joke hadn't reached the right audience, Garrison gazed up at the menu behind him.

"Haddock with peas and chips?" he asked. The man nodded and got to work.

"Me too, please," Seth added.

"Two more," Kian said, ordering for me as well.

"Where are you visiting from?" the man asked while working.

"New York," Garrison answered.

The man tsked about big cities and crime, then gave us our food and advised us not to go outside to eat because the church's procession would be coming out soon.

"Procession?" Kian asked.

The man turned to him for the first time and his eyes narrowed slightly. "You're also from New York?' he asked.

"Yes," Kian answered without a moment's pause.

"Hm," was the only reply, then, "There's a wedding today. A lot of people come in from neighbouring towns."

We took our food and went to sit down at the small metal tables. I kept feeling a pull at my chest as if I should be somewhere else but wasn't. That nagging feeling like when you're missing an exam or someone's birthday. I was missing something.

I was so wrapped up in myself that I didn't even notice the others looking just as I felt: bothered. There was something important and we were missing it.

"Why do you think French fries are called chips here and not in America?" Garrison asked absentmindedly.

"Because I don't think the English like the French very much," Seth replied, stuffing a piece of fried fish into his mouth.

"But did the French actually invent this? I didn't know they were big on potatoes," Garrison replied.

I smiled. It was just like when I had found them arguing about comic books or whatever they had been discussing. Their friendship was evident and even as I basked in it, it made me feel quite alone.

I glanced at Kian, who was picking through his food with his fork. Just like a heron examining its spoils. A thought slowly formed in my mind.

*Just like when I found them.*

I remembered the tugging sensation, pulling me closer to their location as if missing finding them was like missing your own wedding. Before I could open my mouth, Seth beat me to it. He dropped the piece of fish on his fork and stood so suddenly that the table shook.

"What —" Kian began, but he followed Seth's gaze into the crowd of people rushing out of the wedding like a flood.

There were hundreds of people all dressed in extravagant hats and fancy dresses. A mass of white, which must have been the bride, descended large stone steps with her groom as people cheered for them. A vintage car waited for them at the foot of the church.

We all stood staring out of the window. I realized we must look crazy to the old man behind the counter, but I was too busy scanning the crowd to care.

*Where are you?* I mouthed as I stared into the sea of people.

"There," Seth said, pointing. "That one."

## Chapter Twenty-One

We rushed out of the small shop as one. Faintly, I registered the old man asking us if we wanted our food wrapped up. I felt bad for being rude, but I was no longer in control. It was both frightening and exhilarating.

Just like when I had been pulled to Seth and Garrison at four in the morning, so was I being dragged to the wedding to find our fourth.

It was like gliding on air. I realized my friends were around me, but I couldn't feel myself approaching the church. The only way I knew I wasn't flying was because I could hear my footsteps on the ground.

The dragging on my body finally stopped as we reached the church and mixed with the wedding guests. I felt heavy, as if moving now took extra effort. We waded through the crowd, getting a few curious glances here and there, but people were mostly too busy to really notice us.

I still hadn't seen who Seth had pointed out.

"Who is it?" Kian asked. He was leaning over me to see the crowd. He even stood on his tiptoes, putting a hand on my shoulder to steady himself. His proximity made me warm. In the unseasonably hot November weather, I had chosen a plain tank top with jeans, while everyone else sported jeans and a t-shirt. We were hardly dressed for a wedding.

"Her," Seth said, trying not to point too obviously. I felt like a computer scanning a document, trying to take in every detail to not miss anything.

"Big hat! Big hat!" Seth said impatiently.

Our swivelling heads turned left and right.

"They all have big hats!" Garrison complained.

Finally, as my eyes surveyed the crowd, they locked on one girl as if my mind refused to move forward until I acknowledged her.

"Ooh! Her!" I blurted out. This got me more curious stares from people nearby.

The new member of our strange little group was a plain-looking girl who stood about fifty yards away from us. She was our age, as was expected, but was several inches taller than me. I realized she probably matched Garrison's height since she was on eye level with the older man she was speaking with. I assumed he was her father.

She wore her long brown hair straight and it hung nearly down to her waist. It was draped over one shoulder on a pink outfit that looked more like a business suit than wedding attire. On top of her head sat a matching hat with pink lace and netting. Full red lips and big dark eyes accentuated her long face.

Garrison, Seth, and I all rushed forward at once, causing a bit of a melee in the crowd of wedding guests.

"Wait," Kian ordered.

A small magical pull kept us back and I wasn't sure if he had used magic. I didn't even know why I was rushing. What was I going to do? Be the one to break the news to her? I hoped she knew the deal already, or else we were probably in for a wait in this little town.

Kian squinted at her dubiously. His hand had left my shoulder and it caused me to glance back at him. To my surprise, he looked at me with the smuggest expression I had ever seen. His mouth was twisted to the side and I saw dimples I had never noticed before. He seemed genuinely happy.

"What's up with you?" I asked. His expression made me suspicious. He hadn't looked so giddy when we found Seth and Garrison, and that was basically a two-for-one.

He glanced to see if the other two were looking, confirmed they weren't, and scooped me up in a quick hug. I resisted for a moment, only due to absolute shock, but then let him spin me around and put me back down.

"What's gotten into you?" I blurted out.

I felt like a memory foam mattress. His touch left an impression on me even after he'd let go. I smoothed my shirt down where his hands on my waist had bunched it up.

"Nothing," he said, avoiding my gaze, but the smirk remained.

I looked back to the girl, who was now talking to two older women. She appeared to be in a pleasant conversation when she excused herself and headed back inside the church. I thought I saw her stumble somewhat and remembered my own experience in Oregon. She was in for a surprise.

Seth and Garrison looked to Kian for the go-ahead, and he nodded once. I felt like part of some secret government mission. We subtly, as subtly as one can be in a small town where everyone knows everyone, steered our way through the crowd and into the empty church.

It was a small building, purpose-built for the town. One half was constructed from large grey stones while the other was panelled wood. Must be an add-on. We walked from the back to the front, checking the pews and vestibules. Nothing. Tucked away to the side of the church, only one place remained to look.

Seth, Garrison, and Kian gathered outside a short hallway, which led to two sets of doors. One had the word "ladies" marked outside of it. They stood and expectantly looked at me.

"Really?"

They all continued to look pointedly. I sighed.

"Fine."

I opened the door slowly and walked into the women's washroom. The girl stood at the sink, dabbing her face with a wet paper towel. The small room smelled musty and the windows let in a chill. Despite that, sweat was pouring down her face as she dabbed frantically at her make-up.

I coughed slightly, not knowing how to proceed.

She turned, startled. I saw the confusion in her eyes. The panic. I remembered what that felt like. It had sent me off the edge of a cliff. A sense of pity washed over me as I realized she didn't know what was happening, followed by guilt at being the one to turn her life upside down.

"Relax," I told her, trying to sound soothing. The panic was infectious, though.

She still stared, confusion and fear warring on her face. That's when I made the mistake of moving closer. She grabbed my shoulder and shoved me against the wall so hard that my head hit the wall and I was stunned into immobility for a few seconds. Her height and broad shoulders had overpowered me. I hadn't even put up a fight.

She bolted past me into the hall, leaving only her strange pink hat on the washroom floor.

I scrambled to keep up and ran out into the church on wobbly legs but was only faced with my confused-looking friends. None of them had managed to grab her as she caught them by surprise and burst into the church and out the doors. Upon seeing my face, Kian realized what had happened and set off after her.

"Why is the first response to run?" he called as he jogged to the doors.

I knew he referred to my initial reaction upon seeing him. Fear.

I had been gripped by fear. Maybe a small part of me knew that everything was about to change and my life would get a lot more difficult. Either way, it had been panic and fear driving me that day.

I set off after Kian, waving for Seth and Garrison to follow me. We were out of the church and around the building before I saw Kian again up ahead. I ran through the cemetery, skipping and hopping to avoid graves and loose stones. It was larger than it had appeared from a distance.

"What's going on?" Seth huffed.

We were jogging to try to keep up, but it was a half-hearted effort. The girl was fully running and I knew Kian would catch her eventually.

"Ow!"

Garrison fell over a rock and landed with a thump on a gravestone. He picked himself up before we could react and waved for us to keep going. The ground still held dew from the morning and his jeans were stained green from the fall.

"I'm fine — just dangerously exercising!"

I smiled even as I was running out of breath. I could now see Kian ahead of us running into a wood. The cemetery was fenced in, and the black iron gate was too far out of our way. Ahead of the other two, I spotted the gap in the fence.

"There!" I shouted and pointed, running ahead. Feeling like a proper spy in a chase scene, I put on some speed. Then, in an instant, I was sailing through the air.

I knew my foot had hit something hard, but it took a few seconds for the pain to set in. I hit the ground, making something ring in my foot, up to my ankle, and all the way to my knee and thigh.

I tried to stop my fall with my hands but had strained my wrists and now those hurt too. Then, the dull ache began in my foot and quickly grew to an all-out flaming pain.

"What the hell was that?" I wasn't shouting at anyone in particular, but Seth answered as he ran up.

"There was about a foot of the old stone wall through that iron fence," he said. I just stared at him but he smiled. "That's why there was a gap there."

Garrison arrived and they both asked me a series of questions to which I could only answer that yes, it hurt. Since neither of them had any medical training whatsoever, I eventually got fed up and snapped, "Can you please just stop fussing and help me move?"

I tried to keep the irritation from voice, but if I failed neither of them seemed to notice. They were a good team. They gave each other a quick glance then Garrison moved back as Seth scooped me up in one fluid motion. He was stronger than he looked. I was shocked into wrapping my arms around his neck.

I remembered when Kian had first found me and slung me over his shoulder. Always the gentleman.

Even with my weight, Seth walked towards the woods in step with Garrison. I looked at him and realized too late that our faces were shockingly close together. Something sparked. My memories? Or were they dreams? Even bearing in mind what Kian had said, I could have sworn I saw an image of us in Seth's eyes. He blinked and it was gone. I realized I was staring.

"What?" His smile felt so familiar. I could melt in it.

Maybe he wasn't the man he would grow into — or was — whatever. And maybe he had been an enemy in a past life — or I was — I couldn't keep it straight anymore. But either way, we had a history.

"Gwen, you feel —" he began. We were just entering the woods and the footing was getting tricky. Garrison took the lead.

"Heavy?" I asked. I began scrambling to get out of his arms but he held me tight. Again, his strength surprised me.

"No." Seth adjusted his hold on me and kept going as if nothing was weighing him down. "Powerful."

I remembered his ability to feel emotions and manipulate them. Could he feel magic too? Was I powerful? I had a thousand questions, but only one made it out of my mouth.

"What does it feel like?" I asked.

The woods were quiet and I felt the need to speak in hushed tones.

Seth's dark eyebrows knitted together in a frown. His long eyelashes were downcast, checking his footing along the roots and branches littering the ground. He contemplated for a bit, then looked at me with a sideways smile, reminding me of Kian's smug look.

"Like you're electrified. Buzzing. Vibrating. There's energy coming off you. I guess it's magic."

I remembered what Kian had said about feeling vibrations coming from me. He first got me to explore my magic when he had forced me to concentrate on it. I had felt the humming inside my bones, then my muscles, and then I had pushed and pummelled it to fit into my body.

Was it seeping out now? Through my skin and onto the people around me? Kian had said he felt trapped by it — Seth seemed to enjoy it. I let that thought fester until we reached a thin path.

Kian stood staring up at a tree. I couldn't begin to guess the type, but it was large enough for the girl to be sitting atop a branch about thirty yards off the ground. Pink tatters from her outfit filled the tree like ornaments. Her pink shoes with one-inch heels lay on the ground, spread far apart. I assumed she had thrown them at Kian. He saw me looking at him and the shoes.

"My training in arms has taught me to duck well," he said sourly.

I smiled at his joke. He really was happy about something.

"Hurt yourself?" he asked, eyeing my foot. His eyes darted between my injury and Seth holding me.

"Who's there?" the girl shouted.

Seth stood still with me, but Garrison approached. Craning his neck to look up, he called up to her.

"Hello!"

"Who are you?" she asked.

There was definite panic in her voice and I felt truly sorry for her. I wanted to touch her head like Kian had touched mine and let her just see it all for herself. If she didn't know by now, she wasn't going to believe any of us.

I looked up at Seth. He was the whole reason I had come with Kian. The memory of him drove me to find out more and now I didn't know what either of us were meant to do about it.

"My name is Garrison," he said slowly. Garrison was treating this like a hostage negotiation or talking somebody down from a building. "We just want to talk to you. What's your name?"

"Moira."

"Nice to meet you, Moira," Garrison called up.

Kian had crossed his arms and was raising his eyebrows at Garrison, telling him to hurry up.

"People will come looking for her soon," he said only loud enough for us on the ground to hear. "We need to plant the seed before she goes back to her life."

"Plant the seed?" I asked him skeptically. "Is that what you did with me?"

He looked guilty for a moment, and then nodded. "It makes you ... realize your potential," Kian explained.

"You also scared the hell out of me," I told him. "Let Garrison handle this."

Kian raised his arms in surrender.

"Why were you scared?" Seth asked.

I had told him and Garrison the story of my being found, and they had laughed until I thought Garrison's cola was going to come out of his nose. He assured me it was a close call. Maybe it was how I told the story that made it funny, but the panic and fear were real. I knew exactly what Moira was going through.

"What do you want?" she shouted.

Garrison looked towards Kian, but he only urged him to continue on his own.

"We ... uh ..."

Kian was smiling smugly, implying his methods were most effective. I willed Garrison to think of something convincing.

"We just want to talk?" It came out more of a question than anything else.

"What's happening to me? Did you drug me?" Moira called.

Yep. With panic and fear came paranoia. I was surprised she managed to get up a tree.

"No," Garrison yelled. "You're just having an episode. If you come down, we can help you."

"No!" was the reply.

I sighed. This exchange was getting lengthy. Finally, eyeing the path to see if anyone was coming, Kian gently nudged Garrison out of the way.

"Moira," he yelled into the tree.

"Who are you? What do you want?" Her questions were repetitive, but to her credit, she had not received a good answer yet.

"My name is Kian," he yelled. He was still glancing back towards the path, but now he had a frown on his face. It made me turn around too. If someone came now we'd be done for. "You need to get out of the tree, because the branch you're sitting on will break soon." He looked to Garrison, who nodded when he understood the plan.

"No, it won't!" Moira shouted back.

Kian nodded once to Garrison and there was a loud crack followed by a scream. Moira's cry stopped as suddenly as it had begun when Garrison caught her with his magic before she hit the ground. He said he could move things, but I'd never seen it on this scale before. I was thoroughly impressed. Moira's wedding outfit, however, was in tatters.

Garrison strained with the effort of keeping Moira afloat as beads of sweat broke out on his forehead. Still, he dropped her only a few feet off the ground. She fell and scrambled to get up, her hair matted and entangled with leaves.

Ultimate confusion played on her face as we surrounded her. She backed into the tree as if she was being hunted or attacked.

"What —" she began, but a bang sounded and forced us all to jump.

It was like another branch had snapped, but suddenly, I found myself hitting the ground with a thump. A fresh wave of fire burst up from my foot and into my leg. Seth had dropped me. I looked up at him with the intention of scolding, but stopped dead.

He was pale and looking confusedly around as a wave of red bloomed from the wound in his chest. His eyebrows were still knitted together in bewilderment when he dropped to his knees in front of me.

# Chapter Twenty-Two

The next ten seconds flew by as if my world had been fast-forwarded. Familiar gunshots rang out and I was brought back to Central Park. My heart stopped. Magicians.

Leaves dropped from the trees as more shots rang out and birds fled. Kian pushed Moira so hard that she fell about a metre from where she had been standing. She landed and rolled on to her front, covering her ears with her hands. She was crying but I couldn't hear her. Kian and Garrison then dove for Seth, pulling him behind a tree and dragging me along.

Kian hugged me to move me as we crept behind a makeshift shelter of an oak tree. As he covered my body with his, my face was pressed into his neck. I gasped and smelled the sea on him. It almost took me to a memory but then our surrounding chaos caught up. Even in the situation, I felt annoyance creep up on me. It was like a word on the tip of your tongue — just out of reach. I felt like I had almost figured out a mystery, but it escaped me.

I was placed behind the tree sitting across from Seth, who had been propped up against it. For the first time, I let the image sink in. I honestly thought I had beaten my past self's feelings for him. I was in for a surprise.

Seeing a friend get hurt, even seeing a stranger like that, I assumed was traumatizing. But this was different. My soul felt as if it was about to jump out of my body to his aid. I wanted to throw up everything inside of me. I would do anything just to help him. It makes no sense in hindsight, but everything inside just wanted to get out. It was the most terrible feeling I had ever experienced.

I remembered my dream of running through the woods searching for him. I knew it was him I had been looking for. This is what I feared most. Seeing Seth hurt tore a hole inside of me and as I turned my gaze towards Kian, who was frantically pressing against the wound to stop the bleeding. I saw Seth's face reflected in Kian's. As if in a dream, I rubbed my eyes. My emotions were playing tricks on me.

Slowly, I began to pay attention to my ears again. My body felt like it weighed a ton. I felt my throat vibrating. Was I speaking? Sounds came back and the first thing I noticed was the absence of gunshots. They had stopped. Someone was breaking the silence.

"*Gwen!*"

Garrison would have shaken me, but he was tearing strips off his jacket to press to Seth's wound. His face was as white as Kian's. I wondered what my own looked like.

"Gwen," Garrison was saying. I could tell he was repeating himself. "You are in shock. Listen to me." He paused to look at me, so I made a thoughtful face to show him I was paying attention. He needed to help Seth, not stop to look at me.

"You are in shock, but you need to move. Help Moira. Get her up. We need to go."

Inside, a voice screamed at me to start moving. It was like the message was delivered from my brain to my limbs carried on a wave of molasses. But it finally reached my muscles and I scrambled to get up.

In a rush, I realized my heart was beating a mile a minute and my hands were shaking uncontrollably. It was either an adrenaline rush or I was about to spontaneously combust again.

"Get up." I hobbled over to Moira, my foot shooting pain up into my leg. I swayed slightly from the stabs of pain but then regained my composure. No time for coddling.

My feet slipped in the fall leaves that had covered the forest floor. Half-running and half-crawling over the uneven flora, I dragged her up by her arms. Any protests died in Moira's throat when she saw Seth's prone form behind me. He had stopped moving. Stopped groaning.

As I saw her go pale, I willed myself not to look back. I couldn't risk freezing up again. How was I supposed to escape the magicians when I couldn't even protect my friends from them?

We scrambled to leave the forest the way we had come. I limped and the pain flared again. It would soon cause my entire leg unbearable pain. For now, I kept moving, concentrating on putting one foot in front of the other, and supporting my weight on Moira.

I heard Garrison and Kian working behind me to carry Seth. I couldn't look back. I could feel his presence, or lack thereof, at my back. I was coming apart at the seams. Something deep inside me knew I couldn't exist without him. I didn't know who was controlling me anymore — my past self or my current self. Either way, I needed her to get me out of these woods. I leaned on Moira and struggled through the pain in my ankle.

It seemed like ages, but we reached the church. Everyone was gone now save for a few people cleaning up. Kian signalled to take Seth into the church. We filed in through the back door, Seth and Garrison leading the way, carrying Seth between them. It was a strange sight.

They made their way to the back office, where I deftly cleared everything off an administrator's table, including a computer, with one swift movement of my arm. Kian and Garrison lay Seth down gently and I could not avoid looking any longer.

Seth's eyes were closed and his face was grey and sweat-soaked. His hair hung limply against his face. Garrison ran out of the office to get help. I put my hand on the clothes Kian had used to put pressure on the wound. They were soaked red.

My hand came away stained and I stared at it, surprised at my lack of — what? Disgust? Fear? A small part of me was happy the blood was bright red. It meant his heart was still beating. It hadn't dried while we carried him. I stifled the thought.

Pulling up chairs, Kian and I sat and huddled by Seth's head. I wiped the sweat from his forehead and smoothed down his hair. Kian kept a protective hand on his shoulder. Something instinctive drove me to put my hand on his forehead.

A bright flash of a memory danced before my eyes — I walked through a battlefield littered with bodies. The smell of it filled my nose. My first-person view of the scene included watching myself place my hand onto the foreheads of lifeless bodies, some staring, some peaceful. I was checking to see if they were cold. If not, I needed to finish the job and put them out of their misery.

I yanked my hand off Seth's face and ran to the corner of the room, where a small garbage can was luckily lined with a plastic bag. I threw up for nearly a minute before I felt like I had purged the smell and taste of the battlefield from my senses. The memory remained, though.

I put the garbage outside the office and sat back down. Kian hadn't said a word. His eyes shone bright with worry as he looked meaningfully at me, silently asking if I was fine. I nodded. A lie.

At that moment, Garrison rushed in with the minister of the church, a man carrying a large bag, and a woman. They had to push Moira out of the doorway to get in. I had forgotten about her. She was standing in the doorway, eyes wide, tears streaking her cheeks and her hands clutched to her throat.

The man introduced himself as the town doctor and the woman as his wife. At that moment, I felt eternally grateful for their lack of questions. Without mentioning the disaster in his office, the minister simply told us that everything was going to be fine, while the doctor began working. They said an ambulance would take an hour or so to arrive.

"What is your friend's name?" the doctor asked.

"Seth," Garrison and I said in unison.

"Seth?" The doctor called to Seth, peeling his eyelashes back to shine a light into his eyes. "Can you hear me?"

I held my breath until I heard his voice. "Yeah."

It was a weak response that sounded more like a grunt, but it was better than nothing. I allowed myself to breathe again.

"Are you allergic to anything?" the doctor yelled into Seth's face.

"No," he replied.

His voice sounded too far away. An overwhelming desire to touch him swept over me. I felt if I could just hold his hand and transfer my energy into him, then he would be all right.

*Just like before,* a small voice inside my mind said.

I reached for him without thinking but Kian grabbed my hand.

"No," he said sternly.

The minister gave us a raised eyebrow, so Kian took me by the shoulders and led me to one side of the office. A worn leather couch looked comfortable as it sat boxed in by two bulging bookshelves. Kian pushed me down onto it. It was cold against my legs.

"I know what you're trying to do," Kian said in a whisper. We were getting stares from the minister but

I didn't care. "You can't give him your energy. He can't handle it right now. He is in and out of consciousness. You'll just absorb his injuries and gain nothing."

Kian was still pale. His face gleamed with sweat and his bottom lip shook a little. It was a small shake but it made him seem very human. His vulnerability frightened me. He was the strongest. What did that make me?

"Isn't there some magic?" I whispered back. My voice held the high pitch of panic. "Can't we heal him or something? Fix it?"

I realized I was holding both his hands in mine.

"You can channel incredible powers," he said, "but your bodies are too human. You cannot give your energy to a mind incapable of receiving it, and you cannot heal with a force."

When I looked at him pleadingly, he went on.

"Your magic is energy condensed. A power. When you do things, you push them. Move them. Force them." Kian squeezed my hand between each example. I wanted him to squeeze it until it hurt.

*Wake me up!* I silently called to him. *Get me out of this nightmare.*

"To create a hole in the concrete, or burn a bathtub, or to move solid objects is not the same as healing a human body," he whispered. "It would be like trying to paint a miniature picture with a broomstick or put together a ship in a bottle with pliers."

I stared at the wall in front of me. The scene felt unreal. I don't know how long passed until four paramedics burst through the door. In a heartbeat, they bundled Seth onto a gurney and had him in the ambulance.

The minister gave Kian some directions on how to get to the nearest hospital. If he wanted to ask what had happened, he must have known he would not get the answers, so he stayed quiet. Instead, he turned to Moira with a questioning look on his face. She had calmed somewhat, but still shook.

"Shall I tell your father ...?" the minister asked.

Moira opened her mouth but Kian cut her off.

"She'll be back later today," he said.

The minister nodded.

Thanking the doctor, Garrison and I ran from the office. I looked back to see Kian grab Moira's wrist. The look on her face suggested it hurt, but he led her out of the office and into the car in silence. Opening the back door, he nearly pushed her in. She was frightened but didn't argue.

"What the hell happened?" Garrison yelled. His voice felt too large for the small car. There was power behind it and it made me wince. "I thought you said they would try to steal our magic! Or at least use it while we're still weak! Not try to kill us!"

"I don't know," Kian answered. His voice shook. "It wasn't supposed to happen like this."

"What was?" I asked.

Kian swatted at the question with his hand as if it was a fly then pressed both hands onto the steering wheel until his knuckles were white. Once we were on the highway, the speed of his driving scared me. We flew by the other cars as if they stood still.

Garrison proceeded with an onslaught of questions.

"I felt someone nearby," Kian answered. "Seth must have as well. But I didn't know this was going to happen. There was no reason for it to happen. Killing you doesn't get them anything. It makes no sense. "

"Why are they trying to hurt us?" Garrison yelled. "They're magicians! Surely they ..." He trailed off as Kian only shook his head. The mundane nature of guns had before only been a distraction to steal our magic. Did we do something to change their plan? Was it between stealing our souls and killing our bodies? The thought made me shake.

"If it was not a general attack on us or our magic, and they're still waiting, then it must be something about Seth," I reasoned.

"Impossible," Kian spat, ending my train of thought.

Something didn't feel right about the situation. There was something more behind Kian's panic. Why was he so upset? There was a look in his eyes I didn't recognize and it made me uneasy. More secrets from him meant more surprises for us.

We were a sorry bunch as it began to rain. Kian was staring at the road with both hands clutching the steering wheel. Garrison had his head in his hands. I was still shaking and my heart beat rapidly, but I was glad to be moving.

"Are you okay?" I asked Moira. She sat with her arms crossed protectively over her chest, staring deadpan at Kian's seat in front of her.

"No," she answered, and then turned to me with accusatory eyes. "Tell me what's going on."

There was haughtiness to her voice that I didn't like. She was ordering me and expected me to comply. Despite myself, I realized I should explain. I couldn't believe this fell on me.

"You are a part of a special group," I said, trying to find a way to get all the facts down without going into a two-thousand-year saga. "We have magic ... and ... there's these magicians trying to steal it from us. They have attacked us before to get our magic and use it to create disasters, but they eventually want to kidnap you and enslave you to them. They're also trying to take over the United States when it dissolves into chaos."

"What?" She stared at me blankly. I didn't have the patience for this.

"You know what? Just wait for Kian." I pointed a thumb in his direction. "He's much better at explaining it. That's kind of his job."

I sat back, regretting starting the conversation.

"What's happening to me?" Moira asked. The shaking in her voice made me pity her.

"Same thing that happened to me," I answered.

"And what's that?"

"Being close to someone from your time," Kian said grimly from the front seat, "like me or any of your kind, rekindles something in your magic ... or your soul, or your memories. I don't know which it is. The disorientation will pass. Your body is just getting used to a whole new side of you."

Moira nodded, wisely choosing to save her questions for later.

The rest of the car ride was spent in silence until we pulled up to a square brownstone building. Were it not for all the signs and ambulances, I never would have guessed it was a hospital. It had all the bland stoutness of an office block.

Kian had barely stopped the car when Garrison opened his door and ran out into the main administration area. I followed close behind.

"And what is the name of your brother?" the receptionist was asking Garrison.

"Seth Dougall," he answered.

The receptionist checked her computer and was frowning for such a long time at the screen that I felt my breath catch in my throat again.

*Tell me something good,* I willed her.

Finally, she looked up from her desk and said, "Is this your sister? Visitation is family only." She eyed me.

"Yes," Garrison said, nearly pleading.

"And them too?" she asked as Moira and Kian came in.

"Yes!"

She let her gaze float over us, sizing us up.

"He is in room 32A, on the fourth floor."

When I tried to follow with Kian and Moira, the receptionist opened her mouth to protest.

"They're all family!" Garrison yelled, already down the hall.

The place had the same linoleum floors, same white curtains and grey walls, and same sterile smell as any hospital would. The thought of being held here, injured and vulnerable, sent a chill through my already shaking body.

Garrison ran into the elevator, but I glanced back to see where Kian was and caught him leading Moira into an empty hospital room.

*Good,* I thought. *Let her figure it out.*

I followed Garrison upstairs, but we were stopped outside the room. A frazzled nurse hurried us away from window. Garrison was about to yell again when she shushed him.

"Your friend is in surgery. He should be out in a few hours. Until then, you can have a seat right there." She pointed sternly to a line of orange chairs that looked like they had been unchanged since the sixties. When we didn't move, she raised an eyebrow at us.

I took Garrison's arm and led him over to the chairs, sitting him down.

"Nothing you can do," I told him.

"Why would Kian take us somewhere people are trying to hurt us or use our magic?" he asked suddenly. "Twice?"

I considered it. "I don't think he meant to," I said.

Garrison shook his head. "No," he said. "Obviously someone doesn't want us to do what we're doing."

I was about to say that we weren't actually doing anything when I realized I didn't know exactly what was going on. Just then, Moira and Kian appeared from the elevators. She looked like she had just seen a ghost, or something nearly as impossible. Her eyes were wide and her face was pale. It matched ours. As Kian led her to sit down, the nurses gave her tattered appearance curious glances.

Kian placed her in the chair next to me then asked Garrison about Seth. The two walked away and talked in hushed tones, but it seemed more like dual pacing to me.

"When did you find out?" Moira asked me.

I really didn't want to have this conversation. Memories and thoughts of Seth in his past life floated to the surface of my mind. The thought that he might never get to grow into that man sent my stomach plummeting to my feet.

"September," I said.

"Oh," Moira replied. Then, "It's all crazy, isn't it?"

Her voice was hopeful. My pity for her swelled as I sensed the same tone in her voice as had been in mine. She was wishing more than anything that someone would jump out from behind a desk and yell, *Surprise!* Thus ending her terrible day. But it wasn't going to happen.

"Did you see it?" I asked. Only Kian could unlock those visions. That's what made him so convincing.

She nodded. "I just ... can't believe it's real." She was shaking her head and it looked like tears were soon going to spill out again. "There's all these things I feel and I don't know why I feel them. Kian said I would remember soon."

"Like what?" I asked. Mild curiosity.

"Well," Moira fidgeted in her chair, "don't take this the wrong way, but I don't like you."

I nodded. "That's okay. Can't win them all."

"In fact," she added, "I want to kill you."

# Chapter Twenty-Three

"**O**h."

It was the only response that came to mind. I tried to think back on everything from the last few hours to see if I had done anything to deserve it, but I doubted it. I figured it was something else my past life had to answer for.

"Kian said —" Moira began, but I finished for her.

"You'd remember," I answered. Great. "Well until that happens, can I assume you won't try to push me down a flight of stairs or something?" I stood and immediately regretted my sarcasm when I saw Moira's face. Her mouth was open and she looked horrified. She hadn't yet come to terms with her new reality. In this new world, everything was possible to her. She didn't know I was joking.

I rushed to reassure her, and when she looked slightly better, I went to join Kian and Garrison in front of a few hospital television sets.

The news played on various channels. Two stories dominated all the networks. On a few screens, images of cars being swept through towns by mudslides and people scrambling to collect items onto boats were seen under a headline about flooding in the eastern states. Kian watched intently with his arms folded over his chest.

Garrison went to join Moira and left Kian and I watching the news. It was depressing, but something caught my eye. One network changed to a computer-generated map of an island and proclaimed the biggest natural disaster in history.

"What's that?" I asked and pointed at the screen.

"Have you ever heard of Atlantis?" Kian asked me.

"Yeah."

Where was he going with this? Was he going to tell me we were going there next?

"In a single day and night of destruction," Kian turned to look at me while reciting, "the continent of Atlantis fell into the sea." He pointed to the screen. "The Canary Islands are off the coast of Africa. They sit on a dangerous fault line. Scientists are predicting that there will be a volcanic eruption that splits one of the islands in half. It will fall into the Atlantic Ocean and create a tsunami wave that will destroy the entire east coast of North America."

I couldn't tell if he was being figurative or not.

"And is that what the magicians will try next?" I asked, fearing the answer.

Kian shrugged. "It's what I would do," he replied. "But they need more power for something that big." He eyed me, seeming calmer now, and I considered his mood carefully as I dared ask the question on everyone's minds.

"Kian, what happened?"

The silence that stretched between us grew uncomfortable as I toyed with the idea that he hadn't heard me. Finally, he sighed.

"This is all my fault," he said. He turned, his brown eyes burning a hole through me. Of all the possible answers I had thought he would give, that wasn't one of them. I stood, stunned into silence, and waited for more.

"If you regain your memories and your powers, no one will be able to hurt you so easily." His voice was imploring as if he willed me to hurry the process up, but his answer still made no sense.

"Okay," I said slowly, "so why is this your fault?" As I looked at him, the answers appeared in my mind and I reached out to touch his arm. "You think it's your fault we haven't regained our full strength yet."

Kian nodded but his expression did not reassure me. I glanced at the nurses busily filing paperwork and typing on computers, realizing it would be hours until we heard anything about Seth. I was filled with a sudden frantic worry.

"Kian," I said in the sternest voice I could muster, "is there anything else we should know?" I willed the secrets to spill from his lips, but he pressed them firmly together.

"No."

The next hours were spent in silence as we alternated between pacing, watching the news, and wallowing in dark thoughts. My mind drifted between the televisions and feeling responsible for all the world's disasters, to Seth and the older man who he had once been, to Kian's secrets and back to the vision I had had in the church office. Battle. Blood. Death. It turned my stomach.

At one point I saw a man being wheeled by on a gurney. He'd most likely been in a car accident, and he was covered in blood. It nearly sent me over the edge and I reeled in my seat.

✦

*As soon as I closed my eyes to steady myself I was taken to yet another battle. I tried to open my eyes to leave the scene, but I couldn't. Instead, I noticed my hands were covered in slivers. I opened my palm to look at all the small pieces of wood embedded into my skin. My past self shrugged it off and wrapped my hand in a piece of bloody cloth that I pulled out of my sleeve. I got back to what I had been doing.*

*Leaning down on a battlefield, I pulled arrows out of bodies. The metal ends were hard to make, so it was important to collect what you could. The lifeless faces still held open eyes, and I was glad they were looking somewhere else, usually up and above me. I consoled myself knowing that they weren't looking.*

*Sometimes, the arrows stuck in the bodies and I had to keep the body down with a foot while I yanked on the wooden shaft of the feathered arrows: the origin of my splinters. Since the wood of the shaft was smooth, I wondered how many arrows I had recovered. The pack I carried on my back felt heavy with them.*

✦

"Gwen."

Kian shook me. I had been sitting with my head resting in my hands. Funny, I didn't remember doing so. When he saw my pale face, his eyebrows furrowed.

"What did you see?" he asked.

"War," I replied.

Kian looked as if he was about to say something, but then motioned his head towards Seth's room. They had wheeled in a prone form on a gurney, and a doctor stood noting something down at the foot of the bed.

I hadn't known my heart felt like it was in a vice grip, but upon seeing him in bed and alive, I felt the pressure in my chest ease.

We came into the room single file and stood on either side of the bed. Under all the tubes, bandages, and blankets, there was hardly a person visible. We were only allowed to stay for a few minutes before a doctor shooed us out and told us we could come back tomorrow.

Before we left, the doctor came out of the room to speak to us.

"Can I ask what you were doing when this accident happened?" The doctor looked us over, each in turn, over his narrow eyeglasses. His gaze lingered on Moira, who looked as if she had been hit by a car.

The silence became awkward and I realized I would have to speak.

"We were attacked. We don't know who did it," I said. I realized the police weren't here, and we weren't being investigated. A theory formed in my mind, and I figured I had nothing to lose.

"We actually didn't see our friend get hurt," I told

the doctor. "He was alone at the time. Could you tell us what happened to him?"

He eyed us suspiciously, but only for a moment. "I was hoping you might be able to tell me," he said. "We performed a surgery assuming this was a bullet wound, but there was no bullet and no exit wound."

We thanked the doctor and he left to see other patients. So that's why there were no police, and no questions. Seth's condition was a mystery. Only we knew the truth. Someone was aiming to kill us,

Outside the room, Garrison ran a hand through his curls and turned expectantly to Kian.

"What now?" he asked.

It struck me that Kian did not know. I hadn't seen him pick up the phone once. His magician wasn't giving him the directions anymore. He glanced back at Seth and reluctance pulled at his face as if he would much rather stay.

"We go back to the hotel," Kian said slowly, "and Moira comes with us. I will show you how to defend yourselves, and you will increase your magic."

"What if we don't?" Garrison asked.

"That's not an option."

✦

It was night now and I wanted more than anything to lie down and try to cast the dark thoughts of the day out of my mind. But we needed to explain Moira's disappearance first. Talking Moira's parents around was easier than any of us had hoped.

It turned out she attended a private boarding school and had only been in town for the wedding of her cousin. A few forged letters later, Moira had her bags packed and said goodbye to her parents. Her cool surprised me. She was composed and smiled as she waved goodbye. Until she got into the car.

Once she sat down next to me and the door closed, the click of the car's locks must have unhinged her. She sobbed and shook and I placed an apprehensive arm around her shoulders. She looked better now that she had washed the dirt off and changed into jeans and a plain sweater, but her emotional breakdown was unnerving.

Garrison cast wary glances at us every now and then, but Kian ignored her completely. The way he glared at the road suggested that he was in a different place altogether. I felt like I was beginning to come apart when we pulled into a motel at the side of the road. Moira's feelings resonated with me. She acted like I felt.

I cast a questioning look to Kian, who grumbled something about the hotel being close to the hospital. I picked up Big Green, my old suitcase that was still miraculously intact, and followed Kian and Garrison into the lobby.

It was a stout building made from brown bricks — like the rest of England — and the wide sign out front indicated there was a pub attached to the other side.

We silently let Kian get our rooms. He distributed keys and we proceeded down the poorly lit hallways until we reached the right doors. I shoved my suitcase in ahead of me as Moira came in and closed the door to the small room.

The yellow lighting of the hotel blended in with the yellow beds and yellow walls. It was not a particularly nice hotel, but it smelled relatively clean and it was a place to lie down. I sighed.

Moira placed her red suitcase near one of the double beds and sat on the bedspread. Her posture was rigid but she gripped the edge of the mattress with fierce determination. I lay down in exhaustion. The day's events as well as the memories had taken an emotional toll and I could only hope sleep would put a stop to it.

"What does it feel like to remember?" Moira asked me.

Ugh.

"I think it's different for everybody," I answered, not wanting to go into it. Unfortunately, the questions didn't stop there.

"What has it been like for you?" Moira prodded.

I sat up, trying not to get too annoyed. "It's confusing and gut-wrenching and sometimes painful," I told her frankly. "Your magic can come out and hurt you. Mine's nearly burned me alive on a few occasions."

Her eyes widened with fear and again I felt immediately guilty for my lack of understanding. How could I be so cruel? This used to be me just a little while ago. Kian had been patient with me and I could do my part by doing the same with Moira.

I tried to invoke some pleasant memory to share with Moira and only came up with those about Seth. I smiled despite myself. Things were different now and we were different people. But my past self had been truly happy with him on the riverbank, Roman or not, husband or no husband.

"Other times," I continued, "you can get a look into some really nice moments. Kian wants us to remember it all, though. He says that way we will be strongest."

Moira nodded but still hadn't moved from her rigid position on the bed.

"How about some TV?" I asked, trying to break the tension. Without waiting for an answer, I grabbed the remote and flipped to find an American channel. Moira's accent had made me homesick. The only one I found was FOX News. I sighed, but it was better than nothing.

An image of Washington, D.C., filled the screen, followed by American flags floating at half-mast on the capitol's iconic white buildings. A report was talking about global warming. The president spoke at a podium about working with other nations and having some goals to fight a global crisis. A panel of senators agreed with him.

I stared at each face. Kian's story sounded like a conspiracy theory, but I couldn't help but wonder about the magicians and their plot to take over America. The senators shown looked plain and boring. Did they know what I was doing? Were they all in on it? Who was the magician? Were they all magicians? Did they want us dead?

Eventually, my eyes began to hurt from staring at the screen and the news program cut to commercial anyway. I realized Moira still hadn't moved, so I decided to give her some privacy and left the room. I told myself I was doing it for her sake, not for my wanting to dodge any more questions about my past.

I wasn't ready to talk about it, not until I had myself figured out. I didn't know the woman I used to be, but I could only hope she wasn't an adulterer and traitor. Nobody wants to be that.

Outside the hotel, a few lights made to look like lanterns lit the way to a small pub attached to one side of the building. The night was quiet but cold so I walked briskly from the hotel to the heavy wooden door marking the pub's entrance. A lit path with an overhang marked the route from hotel to bar.

The smell of alcohol and old wood hit me in the face like a force. The yellow lighting, similar to the hotel, cast shadows along the narrow bar. Long, dark wooden tables with benches for seats were placed throughout. Only a few people sat with drinks in their hands.

It wasn't late, and I couldn't even remember which day of the week it was. They all blurred together now. Still, the few patrons in the pub were seated at the bar watching a game I hadn't seen before.

The televisions flipped back and forth between tennis and men in striped shirts and thick shin pads carrying paddles that made me think of running the gauntlet. I shrugged to myself and took a seat at the end of one of the long wooden tables all by myself. I tried to remember what the drinking age in England was and drew a blank. Whatever it was, I must have looked it because soon a waitress came over, asked me what I wanted, and I was sitting with a glass of wine in hand in moments.

I had only ever had red wine once in my life. But I remembered that it had put me to sleep and right now that was all I wanted. I took a sip and tried not to make a face. It was like vinegar in my mouth. Still, I took a few more sips before putting the glass down.

I stared at it sitting on the tabletop, willing myself to pick it up again. As I did, my eyes slid upwards towards the spot across from me, which had been empty a moment ago. Now, a familiar angry face glared at me with a ferocious venom that I had never seen before in anyone.

My husband.

# Chapter Twenty-Four

I think my gasp was audible to the whole room. I dropped my wine, and glass mixed with drink shattered and spilled over the wooden table. I tried to scramble to get up so quickly that my foot got stuck underneath the bench and I fell backwards. I was gasping for air and on my back when the waitress leaned over me.

"Everything okay, miss?" she asked. She seemed genuinely concerned and her round physique reminded me of my mother. I felt guilty for lying before I even opened my mouth.

"Yes," I said. "I tripped over the bench."

"Yes, of course," she replied, giving me a wink. She extended an arm and helped me up. I stood on shaky legs and cast a weary glance at the place across from me. No one sat at my table. "Perhaps no more wine tonight?" she joked.

"No more for me, thanks," I replied with a smile but couldn't help my eyes from darting around the room.

*Where did he go?*

After I had convinced the waitress that I wasn't too drunk to stand, and assured myself it had been a hallucination, I left. Pushing my weight against the heavy wooden door of the bar, I felt like I abandoned the smell of the place as if shrugging a cloak off my shoulders. I stood at the entryway, taking deep gulps of the crisp fall air.

Suddenly something pushed me and I skipped two paces ahead. Already jumpy, my heart went from zero to sixty in an instant. I turned wildly in the night, looking for the source of the attack. Nothing emerged from the darkness. I felt the pressure of two handprints on my back and froze.

A voice whispered something incomprehensible in my ear and the sensation racked my body with shivers. I doubled over, putting my hands over my ears. A force pushed them back down. More gibberish, but this time it was a man. Screaming in anger. I didn't have to understand the words to know that.

I closed my eyes tight until everything went quiet. I hadn't realized I was crying but I felt tears leaving cold, wet marks down my face.

*What's happening?*

The memories had been bad, but I had always been a part of my former self. I had always had the knowledge that this was in the past, and that body wasn't my body. That life wasn't my life. Now I felt vulnerable. I was completely alone. Was this some kind of magic or were my memories blurring with real life?

I opened my eyes and the pathway back to the hotel was empty. If I could just get to Kian I would be okay.

The fear in my body caused my legs to move quickly. I ran without intending to, knowing I must look crazy. I was halfway across to the hotel when someone grabbed me from behind and spun me around.

He held my elbow so tightly that I knew it would bruise. I looked up and saw the face I had been dreading. A voice spoke in my mind with a tone that implied hatred, not fear.

*I hoped never to see you again!* it said. It was my voice. It gave me courage even as my knees buckled and the only thing that held me up was *him*.

Just like in my dream, the man was older. Since I was so young in this life, he was old enough to be my father. Grey lined the corners of his shoulder-length dark hair and beard. His dark eyes burned with an intensity I felt sizzling on my skin. His square chin made a thin line out of his lips that looked as tight as a bowstring. The clothes he wore were from our past, and I was about to use that fact to calm myself and remember that this was an hallucination, but then my eyes floated up to the slit in his neck.

A small figurine was sticking out from his neck and the sight of it nearly made me sick, but I was too terrified. It looked like it had once been a miniature horse carved from wood. It stuck in his neck like an unnatural growth. I had just enough time to take this all in when he forced me to the ground off the path.

Large hands with numerous cold, heavy rings clasped my neck. I began to panic and grab at his arms, kicking and flailing, but his weight held me down. My heart was ready to pound straight out of my chest. I felt his thumbs pressing down on my windpipe. The pain of each tattered breath would collapse it soon. I began to see sparks in the sky. Really, they were the dots one sees when deprived of oxygen. But it gave me an idea.

I closed my eyes and tried to shut out everything around me, which was very difficult in my current situation. As I searched within myself for that spark of magic, I felt the temptation to close my eyes and lie still. Succumb. I fought it and found the flame I had fitted to my skin what seemed like forever ago.

I fed it all the energy I had left. When I had nothing more, it had still not grown as I had wanted it to. I started to draw from around me. The grass I lay on, the earth underneath that, the air around me, and even the man trying to kill me. I pulled on it all until the flame was so big that I smelled smoke around me and then let it go.

I felt my body jump with the pressure and then heard a loud crack. I sat up, stunned, thinking I had heard another gunshot. Shocked, I realized it had been me. The man was gone. I felt the place his hands had been on my neck, and it was sore.

Slowly, I inhaled, careful not to take in too much at once as the pain in my windpipe persisted. The air of England was cold and sharp. If you happened to face it the wrong way, you would get stabbed.

I finally looked around at the level of destruction I had caused. The canopy over the path had been collapsed as its supporting wooden beams were snapped in half. The crack. The grass and bushes around me were burned to shreds and smoked, but nothing was aflame. The windows nearest to me in the hotel were blown in. I was too far away from the bar to have it caused any actual damage and thought I could manage to sneak into the hotel without anyone noticing when Garrison and Kian ran out.

"What happened?"

Kian was running towards me. He took me by the elbows and I was up on my feet before I realized he was pulling me. I wobbled on unsteady legs and leaned against him for support. It still hurt to breathe and speak.

I shook my head at Kian and Garrison, whose eyes had drifted from me to the destruction around us. The smell of burning grass filled my nostrils and nearly caused me to choke on it. Patrons slowly came out of the bar with a large man leading them. I assumed he was the bar owner since he assessed the damage with an open mouth and his hands grasping what little hair he had left on his head. I was waiting for shouting when he rushed over to me.

"Are you all right?" he asked me in a thick accent.

I nodded, wincing at the pain in my throat. The man's eyes scanned me, looking for any injury. I could see the probability of lawsuits circling his mind.

"Nothing hurt you? The damn beam must have snapped and collapsed the roofing. You sure you're okay?"

I nodded again. It must not have been convincing, since I was basically hanging my weight on Kian and swooning on my feet. Nonetheless, the owner left me to look over his broken walkway and windows. I wondered how long it would take for him to realize a snapped beam could not have blown in his windows and charred the grass.

Kian silently helped me to my room. We passed the lobby and I saw that Moira had been waiting by the door, hesitant to come outside. We made a little procession to my room where Kian gently let me fall into my own bed. The pain in my neck was subsiding somewhat, but I dreaded explaining.

"Tell me what happened," Kian said soberly as he closed the door to my hotel room. He, Garrison, and Moira sat opposite me on the second bed, watching intently. I felt exposed under their examining eyes. This was the moment I had been avoiding. But I knew now that I needed help.

I pulled my legs up onto the bed and when my knees hit my chin, I wrapped my arms around them. I felt more secure in a ball, but I still didn't know how to explain.

"The truth," Kian told me, as if reading my thoughts. "Start with the truth."

"I have been seeing images of someone I think I was …" I took a deep breath, "… married to in a past life. My husband, I guess … and he is angry with me. It's like I'm hallucinating but the physical impact of it is real. I can feel him push me. He tried to strangle me."

Garrison and Moira's faces held twin horrified looks while Kian's lips were set in a grim line.

"When did this happen?" he asked.

I huffed. "You're not surprised?" I countered. When his face failed to change, I felt a fire burn inside me. "You knew this would happen?" I would have screamed had it not hurt my throat to even speak.

"I knew it may have," Kian answered. "Your souls carry ghosts. Memories of unresolved conflicts. You could have carried those memories over and have them haunt you."

Kian's words stung. He was implying this was all in my head. Just another silly over-reaction by emotional Gwen. I jumped up in agitation and hobbled over to the window. Pulling back the red curtains, I pointed to the destruction I had caused.

"Does that look like a ghost to you?" I asked indignantly.

The rush of movement had caused my hair to fall back over my shoulders. Kian didn't reply to my remark but instead stood and walked over to me, carefully pulling my hair back. His cool fingers on my neck quieted me, and I stood waiting for a response.

"That looks like your magic," Kian finally said without looking out of the window. He was still gazing intently at my neck. "But this looks like a heavy hand."

He turned me around to face the full size mirror which hung across from the dresser. While he held my hair, I saw bright yellow bruises beginning to spread. Tomorrow, they would be blue and dark. I could not be sure in the light, but I thought I saw thick veins of bruising emblazoned onto my throat in the shape of fingers.

"What did that?" Moira asked in a small voice. Her hand was cautiously near her own throat.

"Did you feel anything strange while you were trying to defend yourself?" Kian asked me, his head tilting to the side in contemplation. Had I not been in pain, I would have laughed.

*Have I noticed anything strange while magically defending myself from the apparent ghost of my past-life's husband while he was trying to strangle me in the present?*

Regardless, I thought about it. "The only thing is …" I wasn't sure if I should mention something. It might not be important at all.

"Go on," Kian prompted.

"I felt like I couldn't get enough power. Like no matter how much I tried to get to defend myself, it wasn't enough." I glanced out the window. "That's when I started to pull from around me. It burned the grass, I think, and probably broke the pathway and windows."

Kian sat on my bed, looking thoughtful. "You drew power from the earth. A gift only those with natural power can obtain," he said. I wasn't sure if he spoke to us or to himself.

"Natural power?" Moira asked.

Kian continued to stare absentmindedly but answered her. "Some are born with magic. It is their birthright. They are naturally connected to the power of the Earth and use the energy around them." He brought his hands to his face, rubbing his eyes. "Others use rituals, sacrifices, and thievery to gain their magic. Like the magicians who wish to take yours."

"You think this was another trick to scare me into using my magic?" I asked, remembering how I had thrown everything I had at the black hole in Central Park. I didn't feel as exhausted now as I had then, but the thought of them using my own magic against me still sent shivers down my spine.

Garrison surprised me by speaking. "They're following us. Aren't they?"

I felt like my heart stilled, weighing a ton all of a sudden. It was harder to breathe.

"Yes," Kian answered. "Still trying to draw out your power."

My hand flew to my throat. "How did they get that memory from my mind?" The thought of a stranger riffling around in my mind for information was deeply unnerving. I felt like I was being probed even as I stood in my own room.

"There is a magic that preys on your fears," Kian said, turning to me. "I am sure that was employed, since you kept those memories to yourself."

I thought I heard a note of bitterness in that, but Kian didn't press the matter. I realized I had stood frozen, exactly as he had left me, by the window.

"If they're waiting for us to get stronger, why hurt Seth?" Garrison was on the edge of the bed, looking ready to jump into action, but Kian only shook his head.

"I don't have an answer about Seth," he said, "but the magicians do want power. They need you to be at your full strength so that they may take the maximum amount of power from you. Killing you gives them nothing. To kill you would be a waste of the magic you've recovered. Your bodies will be dead, but your soul will escape. They would have to find you all over again. And so would I."

The thought of trying to recover two past lives in yet another future life made me dizzy. It seemed like an endless cycle.

"It seems like a big risk you're taking then," Garrison argued. "If we get our power back and they steal it anyway, what will happen?"

Kian was at a loss. I felt a need to come to his defence but did not know what to say. Arguing with Garrison was a lost cause.

"We can't do it any differently," I said. My voice still had not fully recovered. "Are we supposed to just sit idly by and let them capture us? Or what about while they cause all these disasters and people die?"

The discussion lasted long into the night and I felt none the wiser for it. Knowing that someone could cast magic over me and have my worst fears come to life was thoroughly unsettling and I found myself drifting in and out of sleep all night. I couldn't stop my mind from wandering to all of the different tricks the magicians could employ in order to get our magic.

Days passed and soon frost covered the windows when I awoke in the morning. Moira and I didn't speak often. I figured she was still settling in. Sometimes I thought I saw a glimpse of memories coming to her as she sat looking out the window with a vacancy in her eyes that implied she was somewhere far away. If she did remember anything important, she did not make it known.

We visited Seth in the hospital but for the first few days he was resting when we came and I couldn't bear to wake him. Kian assured us that Seth was safe, but I found myself inspecting every hospital attendee in the vicinity. I was also developing a neck problem as my head swivelled back and forth every time I set foot out of my room, looking for a magician who would try to steal my magic.

I felt like I had to lock myself down. Cast my body in iron like I had fit my magic into it. I couldn't ask if I was successful because only Seth could truly read my emotions and intentions. I was a little shocked to realize how much I missed him.

Kian kept us busy with sword fighting, picking up on the lessons he had tried to drill into our heads in New York. It was a welcome distraction, though I still felt a little ridiculous. I did surprise myself with the skill I was developing, and Garrison did not go easy on me. Something came to life within him as he got into the rhythm of the fight. Moira refused to participate and sat watching us.

I marvelled at how it really hadn't always been like this — even though we acted like it had. I wasn't always jumping around in the freezing rain, dodging Garrison's sword or running laps just to warm up. I had been weak and blissfully oblivious.

I also kept myself busy by writing letters to my parents, telling them about how exciting the School for Talented Young People was.

One night, when I had just finished my letter, I turned off the desk lamp and lay down in bed. Moira had already fallen asleep and I lay staring at the ceiling. Just when I was wondering if I could ever get to sleep, I felt a pull.

It was the familiar tug that made me feel I was dissolving from solid to liquid matter, yanking my eyes back into my skull and thoroughly encasing me in a memory. My slight moment of panic was lost to a sudden carelessness that overtook me. I accepted the inevitability and let myself fall into the past.

✦

*I was cold. Sitting on a rock near a small pond, I could see the moonlight cast a light over everything in sight, illuminating the scene. While quiet and serene, the landscape buzzed with life. Animals roamed the clearing while frogs and fish made the pond bubble. My senses roared to life when I inhaled deeply and found the crisp smells of the night to be refreshing and invigorating. The sounds of existence filled my ears.*

*The rock was uncomfortable, but I had chosen it over a rotting log, knowing that an unknowable amount of insects would emerge if the wood caved in under my weight. There was rustling in the bushes and my past self spun around quickly, gripping a cold hilt in one hand. I felt the weight of the sword on my waist now that I was aware of it.*

*Seth emerged from the woods and my grip relaxed. My heart began to beat a little slower as I observed him picking his way carefully over the wood and rocks to sit next to me. He was slightly younger than in my previous visions, with a shorter beard and less wrinkles around his eyes. His face was coated in a blue mud mask. It was dry and cracked when he smiled at me.*

*We said nothing. He looked up at the moon for a long time while I considered him. I could feel the magic radiating off him and it kept me warm. But I did not feel safe. We were risking being found.*

Suddenly, he turned and fished something out of his plain brown tunic, which he wore over brown pants and brown boots. He produced a gold coin and held it up to shine in the moonlight before reaching for my hand. Carefully, he placed it in my palm.

I could not tear my eyes away from his crooked smile. The smirk he wore was smug and looked very familiar. Finally, I looked down and saw a dirty gold coin imprinted with what looked like a man's head. It impressed me and I raised my eyes to smile at him when I found Kian sitting there instead.

## Chapter Twenty-Five

I awoke already sitting up.

Moira turned on her light and looked at me, puzzled, resting on her elbow.

"Just a dream," I told her, lying back on my pillow. She shrugged and turned out the light but I was wide awake, staring at the ceiling. I shook.

After what Kian had told me about never having been with Seth, the faces in my memories had begun to blur. I couldn't keep them straight anymore, but I knew what I had first felt. It was Seth in my past. Why was I getting them confused?

The morning dawned with bright sunlight, which I immediately noticed since it was so rare. Moira had already opened the window and the cool air in the room did a lot to bring me back to my senses. I wasn't sure when I had fallen asleep the previous night, but I knew I was tired.

As soon as I moved to sit, I examined the faded blue bruises on my neck. Each day I looked to see that they were going away. After a week, I had stopped shuddering when I imagined the hands at my throat.

There was a knock on the door. Garrison stood outside with a resigned look.

"Kian has us sword fighting again in the courtyard," he said. Garrison also looked as if he had gotten little to no sleep. Before I could ask about why he looked so tired, he proceeded down the hall and out of view.

I got dressed quickly and went outside, where Kian and Garrison were standing next to some sticks with strings attached to them. Moira followed me but again stopped at the benches surrounding the hotel courtyard. I recognized the long pieces of wood right away. Six summers at archery camp weren't for naught. Though I had never tried one, I had seen the antiquated longbows hanging as decoration.

"What's this for?" I asked.

Seeing Kian still brought back uncomfortable memories of my dreams last night. He had become quiet and removed from the group since Seth was shot. I longed for a moment alone with him, but it never came.

I tried to focus on the stick he held. It was a few inches shorter than me. Kian extended the stick to me and took another, which was leaning on the wall.

"Here, watch," he said.

My mood eased as I saw he had a spark in his eyes like when he lectured us on swords. I could tell it was something he truly enjoyed. I realized his eyes very rarely held that spark. My logic led me to feel a little hurt that he must not at all enjoy his mission to guide us.

Kian took his wooden stick and turned his left foot out. He pressed it against the middle part of his foot and pushed on the top, causing it to bend. He took the string that had been attached to it and looped it around the top. The string pulled tight and the wood remained curved.

"It's a bow," he said, holding the stick up proudly. "But an old version of one. It might be a little difficult to shoot, but you should try."

I enjoyed his smile so much that I didn't mention I knew how to string a bow. I was sure he had known at some point about my archery.

"Where did you get this?" I asked.

"I made it," Kian said as if it was obvious. "There was lots of wood thrown out after you destroyed the canopy over the walkway."

Right. That.

When I looked carefully, I saw the bow had details and ridges for the string, arrows, and gripping. It was well made. I picked mine up and tried to string it. The wood was new and rigid, unwilling to bend. After some struggle, I managed to loop the string against the top. I felt a small sense of achievement when Garrison couldn't string his.

When all the bows were ready, Kian gave us his arrows to shoot. I couldn't help but notice that the feathers on the ends were real and debated on whether or not to ask him where he got them. They were fletched well, too. I wondered how much I didn't know about him. What other esoteric skills did he possess?

Kian drew a line in the courtyard gravel and pointed at the opposing wooden wall of the gardener's shed, telling us to shoot. He had drawn rings on it. I somehow felt like the hotel hadn't agreed to this. Either way, I put an arrow to the string.

The familiar resistance against my fingers on the string and the firm grip of my hand on the bow gave me confidence. I had missed camp last year because of the move. It was over a year since I practiced. I pulled the string tight and brought up the bow, pulling back all the way to my chin. My time was limited since I had no glove or wrist guard. I inhaled, levelled up, brought the bow down, and released on the exhalation. My body had naturally turned to the side as I aimed.

Garrison's shot wasn't bad, but I was relieved to see my arrow close to the target. A year out of practice hadn't done too much harm. Though my arrow sailed through the air and landed close to Kian's target, he came over and positioned himself behind me. He forced his boot between my feet and kicked me a bit to get me to move my feet into a wider stance. His hands on my waist, he told me to level my body and be balanced.

"Now draw," he said.

Assuming this meant 'shoot the arrow,' I obediently did. This time the arrow hit the target straight on. Garrison huffed near me.

"Imagine a moving target," Kian told me. "Track it, slowly."

I did as I was told, though my muscles protested and my fingers on the string ached. The draw weight of the bow was too much without gloves. I imagined being a hunter, finding the target with my bow. I pulled back and let go. Again, my arrow emerged from the target's eye.

Being told to do it over and over again eclipsed the victory. Kian drilled us for hours until my fingers pulsed red. When he let us take a break, I realized Moira was gone. When Kian left to place our orders for lunch at the pub, I turned to Garrison.

"No sleep last night?" I asked him.

Since Seth had been in hospital Garrison hadn't spoken as much or been nearly as animated as he used to be. I felt like the person I had known was only that way around Seth, and I wondered what Garrison would be like on his own with no companion in sight.

"Dreams kept me up," he said solemnly. "Dreams about black."

His depressing statement made me remember what Seth had once said about Garrison's memories. We sat on the fence near the courtyard, nursing aching fingers from Kian's bows. When I didn't say anything, Garrison continued.

"Have I told you what stands out most to me from my memories?"

I shook my head. I had never wanted to press.

"I assume we have whole lives to unlock, but obviously some memories stick out more than others. Though I don't know why those in particular. A part of me thinks we don't want to unlock the whole truth. We haven't completely surrendered to the past, and so we only get snippets."

His statement made sense, though I still had no idea where he was heading with this. The conversation had taken a serious turn and I wasn't sure how to steer it back to a normal, complaining-about-Kian kind of day.

"My family was killed in a village raid," Garrison said blankly. "Then when I grew, I was a soldier and had my own family. The Romans killed them. I'll spare you the details, but I feel that knowledge keeping me back. Like it's a fence I keep turning away from. I feel like if I finally get the courage to jump that fence, I'll have all my power back."

I didn't know what to say. A pat on the back seemed inappropriate.

"After all, the magicians are determined to get us, right? We don't even know who they are, but if they're responsible for what Kian says they are, then I need all the magic I can get," Garrison said.

"Surely you've seen the worst there is," I said, fully knowing that I could not imagine what Garrison had seen. "There must be some parts of your life that were good. You should be able to get those back."

"I didn't say it was rational," Garrison replied. He squinted up at the sun. "Lunch yet?"

As if on cue, Kian came out with piles of bags from the pub in his arms. He handed them out and we ate silently. As soon as we finished, I heard the word I had been dreading.

"Again," Kian said, standing.

We groaned and took up our bows, while Kian handed out gloves.

"I found these in the small shop in the pub," he explained. "Not ideal, but it'll help protect your fingers for now."

The gloves did help and soon I found a rhythm to shooting the bows and retrieving the arrows. Pulling the shafts out from the wood still brought back memories of the war scene I had remembered when Seth was shot, but I felt I had more control now. We were just about to beg Kian for another break when Moira finally came back. She was soaking wet and stumbled into the yard.

"Oh!" Garrison dropped his bow and jogged over.

Soaked and shivering, Moira looked like a wet cat. Her hair hung limply and dripped onto her bare feet, while her coat looked like it weighed her shoulders down. They drooped and made her look rather sad. Had there not been magicians trying to kill us and steal our magic, I would have thought the sight was quite funny.

"I —" she stuttered, shivering, "I ... went for a walk ... see about magic ..." Her eyes were still wide from the shock of whatever happened. Her teeth chattered uncontrollably and we agreed it would be better to continue the conversation inside.

Up in our hotel room, Kian and Garrison waited outside while Moira changed into dry clothes and wrapped her long dark hair in a towel. When they came in, she sat on the bed and took a deep breath.

"I tried going for a walk to see if I had any magic yet," Moira said. Her tone was very matter-of-fact. I wondered if this was a coping strategy. "I stumbled and fell into a creek."

Normally, the story would end here. But not this one.

"Then," Moira became animated and accentuated her words with large gestures, "I found I could stand on the water! It was incredible! Took no effort at all! I decided to see how far I could go. A few steps later I was in the water. I don't know what happened."

I felt bad for not being more excited, but to us this was old news. While being drawn in by her gestures, I didn't see Kian's face change. He pulsed with disapproval.

"You have a magician trying to steal your magic and a friend in hospital, and you go off on your own to test your magic?" He stood and paced while Moira's eyes widened with fright. "Did you not *think* before you wandered away? You choose not to train, you risk not recovering your full strength, and do you realize that the fate of *everything* relies on what you choose to do now, in these days?"

She hung her head.

"But Gwen —" she began. I was startled to have my name drawn into this. While I agreed with Kian, he was being slightly dramatic. I wondered the true cause of his ire.

"It doesn't matter what Gwen does!" He was nearly yelling. Suddenly, he looked around to see Garrison and me in the room as if for the first time, and stormed out. Moira had tears in her eyes.

"Don't worry," I told her. "He's just worried about you."

She nodded but didn't seem convinced. I realized I knew Kian better than I had previously supposed. His mood swings and challenges all stemmed from a good place. I had to go remind him of that.

Leaving Moira to be awkwardly comforted by Garrison, I crossed the hall and knocked on the door. Kian answered and silently let me in.

"You're being unfair," I told him. When he opened his mouth to protest, I held up a hand. "You're right, but you're being unfair. Moira doesn't realize the danger or the consequences of her actions, but how can she? You haven't told her, and she hasn't seen what these magicians can do."

Kian seemed to deflate. He sat down on the bed and I came to sit with him. Slowly, he covered my hand with his. The affection between us was still uncertain, but we had grown so comfortable with each other that I didn't mind. We sat for a few minutes until he broke the silence.

"Should I go apologize?" he asked.

I nodded.

Kian got up to go, reluctantly dropping my hand. He had just closed the door to the hotel room when his phone began to vibrate on the night table. I realized I hadn't seen him pick it up since Seth was hurt. I sat, waiting for it to stop ringing. Once it did, though, it began again a few seconds later. The buzzing was getting on my nerves.

I crossed the room without thinking and flipped it open, pressing the silence button. Kian had over forty missed calls from the same number. I was curious, but I didn't want to snoop. I examined the buttons on the main screen of his phone, content with the fact that I wasn't snooping if I didn't open any of them. I noticed one of his short cuts was a camera. I had never seen him take a single photo, so I clicked on it, still trying to convince myself I was doing nothing wrong.

To my surprise, there were hundreds of photos. I had never seen him take any. I started to click through them without thinking. Sometimes, I was in the foreground. Other times, I was in the background and some pictures didn't have anyone I had ever seen before. Seth was in some and Garrison in others. Moira was in one.

Strange.

I heard Kian's footsteps coming down the hall and hastily put down his phone.

"I told her you would take her for a walk, to show her the magic you have collected," Kian said to me as he walked through the door. "I trust you to sense something not normal more than her. You should be safe. Stick to main trails."

I tried to act casual, though I felt the guilt burn on my face. I was convinced that if I stayed any longer, Kian would know that I had gone through his phone. So I hastily agreed and skipped from the room, thankful he didn't follow me.

"Be careful!" Kian called.

The task of spending time with Moira was not ideal, but it was better than feeling guilty in front of Kian. Soon I began to worry about what I would talk about with this girl who claimed to hate me upon meeting me, and all thoughts of photos vanished from my mind.

✦

An hour later, Moira dangled her legs over a bridge we had stumbled upon. The murky water beneath reflected our forms.

We had walked along a path the hotel manager guaranteed us was an old railroad. The metal had apparently been collected during wartime, and now a gravel path ran from near the hotel along various fields and over a stream.

She didn't think going for a walk was a good idea, seeing as she had just managed to dry off, but I had convinced her that fresh air would be good for her. Plus, I didn't want Kian to rope me into archery or sword fighting again. We had a few hours of daylight left, and I was determined to spend them neither shooting something nor hacking away at something — usually Garrison.

"How have your memories been treating you?" I asked her as we sat. The unseasonably hot sun had warmed the wood and I dangled my own legs over the bridge, enjoying the break.

"Fine," Moira said. Then, "But I am never sure what is a true memory and what is a dream."

I nodded. "You have to use your judgment. If you are used to having strangely vivid dreams where you're an ancient magician, then they're probably just dreams. If not, memories."

My comment got a small laugh from her and I finally felt as if she was warming to me. I dared asking the question that he been on my mind for a while.

"Why did you say you hate me?" I asked. The mood seemed to darken in an instant, but Moira kept swinging her feet over the water.

"I don't know," she said. "Honestly, I don't. But it's hard to be around you. You cause heaviness in my heart. I just want to be rid of you."

We sat in silence for a moment while I contemplated being such a burden for her. Surely I hadn't done anything wrong since we had met.

"But thank you for talking to Kian," she said in a small voice.

"No problem," I said. "He's like a strong wind. Blows cold for a short time, but then settles." I thought about that for a moment. "It's strange how well we have gotten to know each other. The memories even allow me to know people I have never met. Like my..." I paused as I forced myself to say it, "... *husband*. I feel like I know him well, too. Though I can only remember being very unhappy while married to him."

"It's still a shock to me that we were real adults in a past life," Moira countered, "and married! I know I have memories of that, and it creates a whole range of emotions I'm still figuring out."

If Moira was dealing with heavy emotions, she was being very stoic about it.

"Oh yeah?" I couldn't keep the skepticism from my voice. "And who were you lucky enough to be married to?"

She looked at me seriously. "He is in the hospital."

# Chapter Twenty-Six

I turned away to keep Moira from seeing the shock on my face. Wide-eyed, I gazed at the water running lazily below our feet. My mind was racing.

If past-Moira had been married to past-Seth, then I had a pretty good idea why she hated me. However, if she did in fact hate me, then somewhere deep inside she knew everything. I contemplated how long it would be before Moira found out and told everyone. Seth had defected to the Romans. I cheated on my husband. He had left Moira. My face burned as I fought to keep my stare on the water. How long did I have before everyone knew the truth? Kian had contented himself with believing I was misled, but Moira could confirm everything.

Understanding struck me. I remembered his smug face when he found Moira. Kian thought she would prove me wrong. He knew she had been with Seth. He thought Seth would recognize her and my erroneous feelings would disappear. He was wrong. I wondered how Kian knew some of our story but not all of it. The silence stretched between us as the sun began to set.

"We better go," I told her, standing and leading the way before she could reply. If Moira sensed my reluctance to speak, she was very accommodating. We walked back in silence or deep thought, I couldn't tell. Dozens of paranoid scenarios were running through my mind of what she would recall.

We walked up the stairs to our room just as Kian and Garrison emerged carrying plastic bags with dinner. I could smell the familiar fish-and-chips combo from the pub. Since I had hallucinated my husband and been attacked by the magic, I hadn't wanted to go back.

As per our dinner routine, Moira and I pulled out a packet of paper plates and plastic forks we had bought and sat on one bed, while Kian and Garrison sat on the other. It wasn't glamorous, but it was comfortable. Most nights. Tonight I couldn't help but keep my eyes from sliding to Moira and thinking of what she had told me. When would she remember? Silently, I willed her never to get her full memory back. And then I instantly felt guilty. If she didn't regain her full memory, the magicians would be that much closer to winning.

"I called the hospital today," Kian said as he sat down to eat. There was a smile on his face and lightness in his posture that I hadn't seen for days. "Seth is awake and has enough energy to see us now. They said the day after tomorrow we will be able to get him back."

Kian's description made Seth sound as if he was kidnapped, but I was sure that if Kian had his way, he would have healed the wound with avocado pulp as he had once done to me. Thinking of his strange tea concoctions made my stomach queasy.

"Do you think being closer to … you know … where we're from is making us stronger?" Garrison asked.

I tuned back in to the conversation with a start. I hadn't realized I was completely absorbed in my own guilty thoughts.

Kian shrugged. "In some ways," he replied. "Probably." Then he turned to me. "Gwen, what was your husband's name?"

"Augren," I answered without thinking. I clapped a hand to my mouth in surprise. "I didn't know that!"

Kian nodded, chewing on a piece of fish. "On some level," he said between bites, "facts that have been ingrained in memory are beginning to surface. I think it is helping to be here."

I tried to not bring attention to myself as I pouted at my feet. I liked my new friends. I liked Kian. And I liked the adventure. What I didn't like was my former self and how she might ruin things for me in this life.

✦

*I knelt in straw. The stone floor was cold and hard against my knees and I was uncomfortable. There was a chill that seemed to echo off the thick stone. My eyes glanced up to a hole in the wall, which served as a window. Beyond that, a grey mass told me I was looking out at an ocean.*

*"Stand," a rough voice instructed, and I stood. Before me, and older man with a long beard and a golden circlet around his neck held a long staff. His hair was grey peppered*

*with black. He sat in the only chair in the room, which was also made of stone. Around me, other people stood, looking bored or preoccupied.*

*I searched my former self for emotions. This was routine. My mind was on other things I could be doing right now. When the man, our king I assumed, turned around to consult someone, I understood my dismissal. I turned on my heel to leave but something caught the sleeve of my tunic.*

*I looked down at a young boy with a mop of black hair. He had been standing next to the king. He smiled, showing me his missing two front teeth. He held out a thistle and I took it, mock-smelling it. I thanked him and he ran away. I felt eyes on me and looked up to see Seth regarding me from the entrance, smiling.*

✦

I awoke to Moira opening the door. Garrison had been knocking. Within twenty minutes, we piled into the small car Kian had rented and drove to the hospital. I didn't know why my heart hammered in my chest.

It had been nearly two weeks since I last saw Seth fully alive and not hooked up to a dozen tubes and machines. A small part of me worried that he would be mad at me for perhaps distracting him that day. My ankle had healed rapidly and Kian even commented about my having some kind of restorative abilities. He also took credit with one of his disgusting teas. But could Seth have moved faster were it not for me?

This morning, Garrison sat quietly in the front while Moira concentrated on the landscape as we drove past. She had to duck in the small car to fully see out the window, and her long dark hair fell past her knees. I tried to imagine her as she once would have been and drew a blank. I obviously remembered some things, but not everything.

Our footsteps echoed in the clean, barren halls of the hospital. At the reception desk, however, a nurse I recognized from upstairs intercepted us.

"I thought you'd be along today," she told the four of us with a stern look. Her bright red lipstick went against her older age and the deep lines that covered her face. Her coloured brown hair was pulled back into a bun, revealing grey. "He's in with the doctor now, being given some medication and then he's due for a rest. You're going to have to come back in the afternoon."

Both Kian and Garrison opened their mouths to argue but the nurse silenced them with another stern look.

"Do you want him fit for battle or not?" she asked us.

Properly chastised, we sulked back to the car while I thought over her choice of words. I did not want to go back to the hotel and be given either a sword or a bow to practice with. Before we reached the sliding doors of the hospital, I heard a voice behind us.

"Hang on!" The same nurse puffed as she sped towards us with a flyer in her hand. She handed it to Kian and turned it over in his hand.

"There's a fair," she explained, pointing to the crude map on the back. "Just five minutes down the road. It'll keep you close and you can entertain yourselves for a few hours before returning. Distract yourselves."

She gave me a motherly pat on the back and returned to her duties. Kian looked up at me from the flyer. I shrugged.

"Why not?"

Exactly five minutes later, we pulled onto a dirt road on the side of the motorway. I forgot it was the weekend until I saw how many cars, children, and dogs filled the ad hoc dirt parking lot. A Ferris wheel could be seen in the distance. A few rides had been set up, but mostly booths and tents filled the farmer's field in which the fair was held.

I had to yell at Kian a few times as he got danger-ously close to driving over someone's pet while search-ing for a parking spot. When we finally got out of the car I felt the full force of popcorn machines, candied apples, screaming children, and yelling vendors hit me. There was so much going on, all I could do was grab Garrison's sleeve with one hand and Kian's coat with the other and drag them towards the entrance, assum-ing Moira was following.

The day was proving to be much nicer than I thought November would be in Northern England. The sun shone and it warmed my face, though I was still glad for my jacket and hat. For the first time since knowing her, I saw Moira's eyes light up with pure joy as she saw a ride which spun so fast that people were glued to their seats. Garrison shared her sentiment, exclaiming and pointing, though even looking at it made my head spin.

"You go ahead," I said to them, turning around before it made me dizzy enough to be sick. Kian caught my elbow.

"How about we meet by the entrance in an hour?" he asked.

Garrison and Moira nodded and were soon off, handing money to a man selling tickets for the ride. Kian used his grip to steer me away from the rides.

"I don't like them much either," he said as I leaned against a fence.

When I felt like I had recovered my footing, I wanted to explore the fair. We wandered along the booths and got roasted corn to eat. Every time I saw a spinning ride, I had to turn my head away.

The crowd was becoming loud and thick. I wanted to escape and used Kian's grip on my hand to pull him into the first tent I could find. Its closed curtain and small size must have been unappealing to visitors since only one family was inside. I looked around as a grin spread across my face at the irony.

Around us, dozens of chain mail suits, a few suits of armour, and lots of old-style dresses were scattered chaotically. A table of ladies' accessories stood against a tent wall next to a table of weapons. The only clear area was a throne in front of a coloured background of what I assumed was a throne room. A camera was aimed at the display.

As I watched a mother struggle to get her two children out of their tunics, a printer spat out photographs of the family in different formats.

"Care to have your photograph taken in Renaissance attire?" the man behind the camera asked. He was wearing a white-buttoned shirt with a black vest and a purple beret.

Before Kian could react, I nodded enthusiastically. He looked at me with a raised eyebrow, but I let go of his hand and went to a rack of dresses to choose one. A part of me wanted to have a picture to remember our time together. Another part thought that maybe if I saw Kian in remotely time-appropriate attire, I would remember him. I searched my brain for what period the Renaissance actually covered. Pretty far removed from our own, but I supposed the clothing was closer to our time than jeans.

My dreams of Seth fading into Kian and vice versa were now mixing with my memories. The two had become one, but I felt like it was my own mind making the confusion. If Kian claimed to have known me, why did I know not him?

I found a blue dress covered in velvet, with white silk and long white laces. I highly doubted anything like this would have existed in the time we were from, but it was a really nice dress. Checking to make sure Kian was playing along, I went behind a curtain to change.

Getting into a dress had never taken me so long. There were layers that surprised me, buttons that had no use, and too many holes for me to accidentally stick my arms and head through. Finally, when I had settled into it, I realized I needed someone to lace up the back. My choices were the man in the beret or Kian. I called for Kian.

Hesitantly, he peered behind the curtain as I turned my back. Though he cleared his throat uncomfortably, he tied up the laces with deft hands, pulling the fabric together. I couldn't help but smile like an idiot into the back of the makeshift changing room.

*This is nice*, I thought. Then, immediately, *Shut up*.

When he finished, I turned and my mouth dropped open. He looked like royalty in a silk blue tunic with a wide silver belt. While he had kept his jeans, a chain mail shirt shone from underneath the tunic and the image was complete. A tinge of disappointment washed over me as I realized no matter how good he looked, I still did not feel a single bit of remembrance. His outfit was made whole by the completely uncomfortable look on his face.

"Almost complete!" the man behind the camera exclaimed.

He motioned for us to come over to the accessories tables, where he stuck a plastic sword in Kian's hand. I nearly laughed out loud when I remembered what Kian had in his hotel room and saw his incredulous look. For me, he chose some type of fan to hold up.

While our photographer walked over to the camera to prepare it, I peered up at Kian. The outfit he wore matched him perfectly but something was missing. I looked over the table of accessories and chose a silver crown to put on top of his head. It settled on his black hair.

Kian looked at me with a question in his eyes, but I shrugged and led him over to the fake throne room screen. It was a challenge to get him to look remotely comfortable with posing and having his picture taken, but ten minutes later we walked out of the tent with a dozen wallet-sized photos.

It was a short walk back to the entrance where Garrison and Moira waited for us. We spent another while walking around together and had lunch at a booth selling turkey legs far bigger than would fit in my mouth.

I showed Garrison the pictures, and he also raised his eyebrows at me.

"What?" I asked defensively. "My idea of fun isn't being thrown around from one place to another by a machine."

"It was pretty awesome," he said.

When the crowd began to grow even larger and the lazy people who liked to sleep in on weekends got around to getting to the fair, we left.

Again, I found my heart hammering in my chest. The anticipation of seeing Seth was making me nervous, and I couldn't figure out why.

It was like déjà vu when we walked into the hospital for the second time that day. It was early afternoon and the nurses who knew us did not say anything but just watched our procession move along the hall.

We made our way to the fourth floor where I suddenly found my legs heavier than they were a moment ago. My pace slowed and I felt my hesitance slow me down like I was walking in syrup.

While the others seemed eager and sped up as we saw Seth awake and sitting up in his bed, I walked slower until I stopped outside his room. When a nurse approached me, I was thankful for the distraction.

"Only three at a time," she told me.

Her mouth was set in a straight line and I could tell she was preparing for an argument. Surprising her, I moved to sit in one of the plastic chairs and wait.

Kian turned around at the door.

"Go on," I told him. "I don't mind waiting." He smiled and moved inside, closing the door.

Satisfied I wasn't going to run in at the last second, the nurse left me in my seat and went to sort files. I let my eyes drift to the various little monitors and TV screens, the magazines arranged in a neat fan on the coffee table, and the humming vending machines. I didn't want to think about what I would say to Seth in case he was angry and I would have to think of a whole new strategy.

I didn't know how long had passed when the other three filed out, and I walked in. My pulse was thundering until I saw Seth's face.

Though still wary, I relaxed upon seeing his broad smile. There was colour to his skin again and he sat up, gesturing animatedly for me to sit. His black hair was neat and his cheeks were flushed. Most importantly, his hazel eyes had come alive once more. I realized I had been worried about seeing him as he was before we brought him to the hospital. My fears lay in him not returning to his former self, but those looked to be unfounded.

I picked my way through some kind of peel which surrounded his bed.

"Keeping busy?" I asked.

"Bored. To. Death." Seth emphasized this by mock keeling over onto his pillows. He was up again in an instant. It was nice to see him with so much energy.

"Kian said you've been practicing all kinds of fighting techniques," Seth said with a skeptical look. He had hated the training as much as I did. Only Garrison seemed to revel in it.

I laughed, telling him about what had been going on. I guessed he was hearing it all for the second time, but he listened patiently.

"What's this about you being attacked?" Seth asked, concern lacing his voice. The conversation had moved to something I didn't want to relive, so I changed the subject.

"What's that?" I asked, pointing to the mess on the floor. "Have they got you peeling potatoes?"

Seth gave me a stern look for changing the subject but let it go. He smiled and opened a drawer in the little table next to his bed. "I got so bored in here that I begged for someone to bring me something to do!" he said, taking out a small shape. "A doctor here brought me some wood and a carver."

I froze in place.

The figurine of a lion he produced was not identical to the one I had seen in my former husband's neck, but it was similar. I knew now where it came from. The image of the man from two thousand years ago with his throat sliced open by the wooden figurine filled my mind.

# Chapter Twenty-Seven

Seth was still talking. "He uses logs to heat his house so he had lots of wood lying around. I tried to make a horse but I messed up the mane so now it's a lion. Whittling is kind of cool. Maybe I'll be a whittler."

The colour must have drained from my face because he stopped and hastily lowered the figurine.

"It's not *that* bad, Gwen. You're supposed to laugh at me and tell me that it's not a profitable endeavour."

I tried searching for words, any words that would make him not worry, but it was too late.

"What's the matter?" His tone had lost its joviality.

"Nothing," I lied.

He fixed me with a stare and I melted under the pressure.

"I think I've seen those wooden figurines in my memories," I told him slowly.

Seth looked down at the lion, frowning. It wasn't a masterpiece, but it was certainly better than a first attempt. I could see his brow crease and felt a slight tingle of magic pulsing off of him. He was trying to remember. Finally, he looked up at me, sweat shining on his forehead.

"Nope," he said, and then shrugged. "I can't sense particularly doing this ever before. But I kind of like it."

"Keep at it," I suggested, not wanting to be totally unsupportive. "Make me a ..." I thought about it for a moment.

"Seahorse?" Seth suggested.

"Sure."

We talked for another ten minutes, and all the while I tried to steady my nerves. I didn't want to let the shock of realization show on my face. But it was clear that Seth had made the wooden figurine, and somehow it had ended up in my husband's throat.

*Augren*, I thought. That was his name, and it brought back no pleasant memories.

The nurse, who claimed Seth needed to rest if we could pick him up tomorrow afternoon, eventually shooed me out. We piled back into the little car and returned to the hotel. It felt disappointing to be returning without Seth, but at least he was better.

We still had some hours of sunlight left, and I dreaded how Kian would make us fill the time. Sure enough, when we climbed out and headed towards the hotel, Kian announced he expected us to meet him in the courtyard in ten minutes.

The wind had a bite to it and the sun from earlier in the day had disappeared behind clouds. I watched the sky move from comforting to gloomy. In my room, I put on two pairs of pants, two t-shirts, and one sweater. Feeling a little larger than normal, I at least had warmth. Moira watched me, amused.

"I hate the cold," I told her, settling my red knit hat over my head.

"You know, maybe if you suggested something else Kian and you could do together, he wouldn't torture you with all this fighting."

I gaped at her, opening and closing my mouth, wanting to rebuke. Her remarks caught me completely by surprise. Though we had been sharing a room for weeks, I still felt like Moira was a stranger, keeping herself closed off and remote. I hadn't considered that she might observe me like I was observing her.

"Exactly," Moira stated, satisfied with herself.

Slowly, my cheeks grew red and I wasn't sure if it was due to heat or embarrassment. I wondered if Seth knew about her and bit my tongue when I opened my mouth to ask. She would become suspicious if I carried on about it, and her suspicion might cause her to remember sooner.

Deciding silence was the best course of action, I put on my boots and went outside, with Moira following me. As per usual, she stopped at the gate to watch while I joined Garrison and Kian in the gravel courtyard.

As I came towards them, Kian suddenly moved to my left and held my arm in a tight grip.

"Hey!" I exclaimed.

He held it balanced at the point before the discomfort became pain. Kian let me go and stepped back.

"We're going to learn how to defend ourselves," he announced, smiling.

We had already done some of what he called grappling, which I referred to as my being tossed to the ground over and over again. Towering over me, Garrison had managed to knock me off balance quite a few times.

Kian showed us a few ways to get out of people holding or grabbing you. He taught us four grips and how to break them. When the sun was beginning to set, and every joint in my upper body hurt, he moved towards me again. Hugging me at the waist, Kian lifted me off the ground like some kind of Viking claiming his prize.

"Now how would you get out of this?" he asked.

I wiggled in vain as his grip tightened. Garrison shrugged and I admitted I didn't know. Kian put me down in a huff.

"You need to learn this stuff!" he exclaimed. "What if you need it? What if someone grabs you and you can't do anything about it?"

*I yell for help*, I thought. A well of guilt sprang up in my mind when I realized I had become so used to Kian's presence that I relied on his help. I didn't want to do that. I wanted to be strong enough. Chastising myself for complaining so much, I vowed to learn. After another hour, I tripped Garrison and he landed in the dirt. A surprised look flitted over his face before a wide grin spread.

"Good job!" he said as I held out a hand to help him up. He took it and stood, dusting the gravel off his pants. Even Kian smiled at me.

"It's a good beginning," he said. "It may be time for dinner."

At the thought of food, my mouth watered and I gratefully agreed. Moira had been reading a book and joined Garrison in going to the pub to place our orders. Kian showed me how to get out of another grip in the meantime.

"If I grab your shoulder here," he showed me by placing his hand in the groove between my left shoulder and neck, "you take your arm from the same side, lift it, and trap my hand."

I did as he showed me, rolling my arm over his in order to trap it. It worked and his knees buckled.

"Now," Kian said from his compromised position, "you have the advantage."

We ate our dinner in relative silence due to exhaustion. When we were nearly done, Garrison and Moira eyed each other conspicuously. I was the first to notice.

"What?" I asked.

Moira made eyes at Garrison, urging him to speak first.

"There's a trivia night with music down at the pub tonight, and …" Garrison waited for me to get the hint but I didn't. "We wanted to go," he finished.

I understood. They wanted to have fun but knew I wouldn't come. I felt guilty for their worry about leaving me alone.

"Go," I said. "It's no problem."

When we had cleared the food off the beds and into the bin down the hall, Moira grabbed her coat and Garrison left to get his. Kian remained firmly planted on the hotel bed.

"Aren't you going?" I asked.

Kian shook his head. "And miss watching hotel movies?" he asked. "Unlikely."

I wanted to kick myself for how excited I was not to be spending the night alone. Spending time in his company had made me soft. I briefly wondered what had happened to the old Gwen who spent every day alone, not caring either way. But then I remembered Kian was waiting for me to choose a movie and I went to do that, letting all thoughts of the previous Gwen escape from my mind.

It wasn't long before my excitement ran out and I was exhausted from the day's activity. While we watched a movie about a bank heist, I slowly drifted in and out of consciousness. We were sitting on the ground in front of the television and before I knew it my head had drooped to the side.

I gave in to fatigue and let my eyes close. I opened them again briefly when Kian took me underneath my arms and lifted me so that I could get on the bed. I scooted to find my pillow and was asleep in minutes. I wasn't sure if he finished the movie, but I awoke again to see Kian settling in beside me, and I didn't protest when he drooped an arm over me and fell asleep.

✦

*Extreme heat touched my skin. I felt my legs moving, and despite the pain I knew I was running towards the flames. The pounding of pressure in my head was like an onslaught against all of my senses, and I realized that for the first time I had to strain to decipher my past self's emotions. What was I doing?*

*Pain. Anger. Guilt. Fear. Regret. The emotions pulsed through me like a heartbeat. Tears streamed down my face as I ran. I smelled burning hair, singed skin, and felt as if I breathed fire.*

*The landscape streamed by me and I did not notice it. Voices called out, some angry and some concerned, but I ignored them. My eyes were set on the fire, a wall of it rising high above me.*

*My anticipation, my magic, all went towards getting through the fire. I had never encountered such a force. Never seen flames this high. Grief welled in my heart as I approached it, knowing what I would do. It had called to me and reached for me, knowing I would come. Now I was here and it would swallow me. I would not reach the other side.*

✦

I awoke gasping. Already, I was searching for the flames on my body and choking on the smoke filling my lungs. I sat up, hacking and sputtering, even as Kian ran to bring me water from the bathroom tap. I took the plastic cup and drank, the cold liquid soothing my raw throat.

When I calmed enough to look around, I realized I had set nothing on fire this time. Either I was gaining more control or it really was just a dream. The only light in the room came from the electric sign outside the pub and the open shutters revealing a full moon. The digital alarm clock showed that it was just past midnight. I could hear the slight sound of music coming from outside.

"Are you alright?" Kian asked. I could tell he was staring at me in the darkness.

I could only see his eyes glinting. He sat next to me on my bed. The TV was blacked out but still on. I assumed we had both fallen asleep while watching the movie. He got up and turned on the lights. Though the sudden brightness hurt my eyes, it helped alleviate the feeling that I was about to fall into my nightmare again.

"I think it was just a nightmare," I said.

"What about?"

I thought about how much to tell him. The emotions associated with my dream stayed with me even now that I was awake, and it was challenging to tear myself away from them. I got up hesitantly and hugged Kian where he stood.

As I wrapped my arms around his neck, I felt his hesitance and held my breath, but he returned the hug. I relaxed in his hold and relished the fact that I was not in my past life or in my dream. I was here.

Eventually, Kian offered to make me one of his teas and I rushed to assure him it wasn't necessary. We began another movie and sleep eluded me. Moira came back and Kian left. Long after she'd turned out the light and fallen asleep, I drifted off, dreading what I would encounter in my sleep.

◆

I awoke refreshed halfway through the morning. Embarrassed, I saw that I had slept nearly into the afternoon. Moira was gone with a note that she and the others were down in the courtyard. I lay for a while, thankful for the lack of nightmares. In a few hours we would go pick up Seth and everything would be back to normal.

Lazily, I drew open the curtains and looked down at the courtyard. The sun kept peeking out from in between the clouds and the scene below me looked dreary. Kian and Garrison were shooting at the garden shed again. I watched them for a while, noting how graceful they both looked. I wondered if I ever looked like that.

Suddenly, I felt a small thread of panic wind itself around my heart. A pull like the one I had felt in the park in New York City was somewhere I couldn't see. A black hole. A concentration of power. But I couldn't see anything. The magical blindness was agonizing as I pressed against the window trying to see all around my friends. Couldn't they feel it?

From the edge of the courtyard where the pub entrance was, Moira emerged carrying a box. It pulsed in my vision. I banged on the window, knowing I couldn't make it down in time. I watched, helpless, as she handed it to Kian, who recognized it for what it was. He grabbed it and threw it as far as he could and out of my sight.

Time slowed down for me as my heart beat nearly out of my chest and my banging on the window went unheard. After a second or so, a loud bang rang throughout the hotel and caused my room to shake. The window cracked and some debris and dust covered my friends below. Not caring that I was barefoot and still in my pyjamas, I raced from my room.

# Chapter Twenty-Eight

I felt like I flew as I raced down the staircase nearest to my room and out one of the side doors. With every step, I expected to trip and fall as my feet moved faster than I could think. Surprised at my own agility, I made it down to the courtyard.

The windows facing the yard were blown in and the beams on the new overhang were smashed again. The pub's door was off of its hinges and the shed that we had been shooting arrows at was flattened. My heart stopped as I saw three scattered and prone forms.

In the settling dust, I rushed towards my friends. The tightness in my chest alleviated slightly when I saw Kian slowly move to push himself up off of the ground. While his back and head were covered in dirt, the front half of his blue shirt was clean. Garrison was covered from head to toe and sat up slowly, pulling on his ears. Moira, a few yards away, was on her side and blinking dazedly. She was also covered in gravel.

I briefly contemplated Kian's clean side. He had hit the ground first. He had felt it. The concentration of power was evident to me — I had felt the pulse of it when the magicians had tried to suck Seth's power in New York and when I gathered too much just weeks ago. Desperate, I had sucked the energy from around me and concentrated my magic to get power. My panic increased when I thought of Seth.

I ran over to Kian and began to drag him up while he still struggled to stand.

"Let's go!" I shouted in his ear. He looked at me confusedly.

"What?" he yelled back.

I began to repeat myself, but when he shook his head, I gave up. I understood his hearing would be shot for the next little while so I took matters into my own hands. Propriety aside, I stuck my hand in his jeans pocket and retrieved the keys to the car.

"Seth!" I yelled into his face, jangling the keys as one would entertain a baby.

Even though Kian still wobbled where he stood, he understood my hint. As he scrambled over to Moira, hotel employees and guests began funnelling out of the pub and main hotel building. I could hear sirens in the distance.

Dread filled me as people approached us. I envisioned a lengthy questioning followed by police interrogation. When I had gathered that much magic to myself, it exploded as soon as I let it go. A theory began to form in my mind as I glanced at Moira. In the confusion, she stood still, swaying slightly. I guessed what the package had been.

I turned to see Kian taking her elbow and pushing past the crowd that had assembled around us. I helped Garrison to his feet, slung his arm over my shoulders, and followed Kian into the parking lot.

I was surrounded by a procession of coughing, stumbling, dirty people. Moira was visibly shaking and Garrison coughed up so much of the dust that he gave himself a nosebleed. By the time I got him into the car, I had enough blood on my shirt to believe I had been involved in the blast.

Kian, luckily, was intact enough to drive. Though I worried for my friends, they were still very much alive. Seth, wired to machines in his hospital room, would be a much easier target.

As Garrison shook his head to each side to clear his hearing, all while leaning back to stop the blood pouring from his nose, he attempted to speak. It first came out as a gurgle, but I could discern words on the second try.

"What-was-that?" he rasped. Then, "Seth?"

I turned to him, ready to voice my fear, but my eyes must have given it away. His jaw dropped slightly and he leaned back against the seat, looking ready to faint. Moira was in front with Kian, who still hadn't said anything. I pressed myself through the middle space between the two front seats and stared at Kian, urging him to start talking.

"It was a trap," was all he said. His knuckles held the wheel in a death grip. "Like the trap in the park." I saw his eyes glance up to the rear view mirror and at Moira, who gazed blankly out the window.

"Moira, are you okay?" I asked. She sat next to Garrison, who still had his head back in an attempt to stop the bleeding.

She nodded at me faintly, but her face didn't even register hearing my words. Worried, I turned back to Kian.

"Explain," I said. My head kept swivelling between him and Moira. She looked paler and held herself as if she was about to wilt.

"It was magic attached to an item," Kian said grimly. "The kind of magic that stole your powers in the park. Moira was meant to be drawn into it, but ..."

"She gave it to you first," I finished for him. My theory was proving correct. "It's like when I drew all that power to me and then let it go. If she held it she would have just fed it until there was nothing left."

Kian nodded but his eyes glanced up again and I realized how insensitive I'd been. I turned to reassure her but she still gazed out the window in shock.

"Why all the games?" I whispered. Suddenly, I was exhausted. The danger was too real.

"If they had wanted you dead, you would be dead," Kian replied. "If they've not killed you, then they will enslave you."

A fire rose in my throat. The anger sizzled in my blood and smoke began to emerge from under where my hands still held the two front seats. I felt like a farm animal, lulled into security by repeated close calls until I was needed for the slaughterhouse. The thought of being used against my will repulsed me.

We all sat in silence, staring at Kian. Any confidence that I had felt for my small progresses and memories evaporated and was replaced by a sense of failure.

Within five minutes we were at the hospital. Wordlessly, we shuffled out and proceeded to the fourth floor. Stares followed us as Moira and Garrison left streaks of dirt in the clean hall. I was cold in my pyjamas, which consisted of a long-sleeved shirt and shorts. I was barefoot.

My heart accelerated as we exited the elevator. It was dumb to leave Seth alone. The regret pulsed through me.

When we reached his door and found the bed empty, I nearly flew at the nurse who stood a few feet away. Before I could react, she called to us.

"He's changing into the set of clothes you brought," she said. "Don't worry."

Embarrassed that my panic was evident, I turned to the nurse to thank her. When she caught site of me, her jaw dropped.

"Do you need help?" she asked, rushing over and making straight for Garrison's blood on my shirt.

"No, I'm fine," I replied. "It's someone else's."

"Whose?" the nurse nearly wailed. The idea that someone might be covered in someone else's blood plainly seemed like a horror movie to her.

"Mine," Garrison said from behind me. His voice was still nasally due to him pinching his nose shut.

As the nurse began to fuss over Garrison and lead him away to be examined by doctors, I turned to Moira. She was still shaking.

"Who gave you that parcel?" I asked her quietly.

"Some man," she replied as a single tear rolled down her cheek.

"Do you remember anything about him?"

She shook her head. It was strange trying to comfort her since I had to look up just to meet her eyes. I noticed her hands were clasped behind her back and that she had put herself into a corner. The positioning seemed strange to me. Before I could ask, she spoke.

"What was that thing?" Her voice trembled almost as much as her body. While much taller and sturdier than me, Moira shook like an autumn leaf in the wind. "I didn't feel anything strange. Did I do something wrong?"

Kian ran a nervous hand through his hair. While we waited for Seth, the anxious energy between us grew. "It was a concentration of power," he replied. "Like the kind Gwen used to free herself from the magical attack of her memories. You didn't do anything wrong."

A shiver ran up my spine as I remembered the cold rings on the strong hands that had wrapped themselves around my throat.

"It's how the magicians move the earth and work their magic. They steal power from things around them. They are magical parasites, feeding off life strength and throwing power at the things they wish to destroy."

"When I ..." My sentence was lost as I considered what I had done.

"When you pulled the energy to yourself like that," Kian finished for me, "had you held on any longer, you would have ignited along with everything else around you."

I remembered the pressure as I lay on the ground, dying.

"Wiser and stronger magicians know how to bundle that power and put it into objects. They can control it. But that brings about another complication," he said.

"What?" I asked, but I already knew the answer. I had had enough control to push the magic away from me before the energy burst. Even with more control, that amount of bundled energy can't get far.

"They're near," Kian said, confirming my suspicions.

Sudden paranoia pricked at my back and again I felt like I was a swivel-head doll, craning my neck by trying to turn in too many directions at once. While the hospital hallway was empty, I felt like someone was watching me from around every corner.

My attention fell back to Moira, who was trying to fit herself further into the corner. Kian followed my gaze.

"What ..." He had initially assessed her for injuries when she lay on the ground in shock. She had been covered in dirt then.

Kian placed both his hands carefully on Moira's shoulders and she cringed, shying away from him. Her position left her nowhere to retreat to as he moved his hands down and forced her clasped hands out from behind her back.

The breath escaped from my lungs as I gaped in shock. Beginning between her elbows and wrists, Moira's forearms and hands resembled those of a much older person. Her fingers were all knuckle and the skin was so thin and pale it looked to be almost translucent. The tops of her hands were covered in spots and the skin hung loosely over the muscle. The sight seemed to surprise even her, and she gasped upon seeing the damage.

Kian's face immediately set in the stony stare I had nearly forgotten. He gently placed her hands back down by her sides, his gaze lingering.

"It could have sucked your magic dry, getting your body's energy as well," he told Moira. "If you had brought the package to your side or front, you would have felt those effects," he gestured to her hands, "all over."

She looked down as silent tears tickled down her face. "Can it be fixed?" she asked in a small voice. She had moved her hands behind her again, as if trying to forget them.

Kian nodded encouragingly, though the worry in his eyes told a different story. Before we could discuss more, Seth appeared with a doctor noting something in a chart. Though the morning had been terrible, I felt lighter knowing he was safe. He waved and said something to the doctor before coming over. In his everyday clothes and unhooked from the machines, I felt he was truly healed.

"Well," he announced, "thank you, travel insurance."

When we failed to laugh, he had a look around. Kian and Moira were covered in dirt, but with the training we had been put through, this could have been easily explained. Seth turned to examine me.

"It's the afternoon. Why are you still in your pyjamas?" Then, "Is that blood?"

While we waited for Garrison to be examined, we filled Seth in on what had happened and questioned him about any visitors he may have had. Seth admitted to sleeping too much to notice anyone coming and going, but the hospital had been quiet.

"Too weak," Kian finally said. "You were hurt and then put on so many drugs that you probably did not remember anything new. Your magic was beyond your reach, and anyone else's."

Seth nodded. "Nothing new," he confirmed.

"Your magic is now weaker than the rest," Kian said. His eyes rested on Moira, and I could nearly see him trying to sense how much power she truly had. His calculating gaze pierced her and she tried to retreat further into the corner.

A part of her magic, and her life, had been stolen. But how much remained? And what would be done with what was taken from her? Probably feeling outcast from the camaraderie the rest of us had already built, she had kept her memories and magic to herself. I could see the tears shining in her eyes and felt guilty once again for not making more of an effort to include her.

Garrison returned with a clean face and cotton balls stuck up his nose. He paused briefly in front of Seth, and I could see the relief as it washed over both of them. The moment deepened the resolution in me to succeed.

The truth of our defensive journey had sunk in. We were fighting for our lives. We were on the defence, needing to get stronger if only to survive. I was done being weak.

✦

A week passed. Separate hurricanes hit both Florida and California. The news coverage was so extensive that I couldn't bear to watch anymore. The hundreds of thousands of displaced people weighed on my mind. Images of drowned houses and abandoned cities flooded my dreams.

We moved out of the hotel. Though they never accused us of anything, I felt the staff and frequent guests were glad to see us go. I had still not relaxed since I found out how closely we were being watched. Moira had gotten to an arm's length of the people trying to steal our magic, and she had paid the price. She wore black gloves now to hide what the blast had taken from her. While Seth was better and Garrison eventually got his full hearing back, the week crawled by at a snail's pace. I was itching to get moving.

Kian told us that we could not make any sudden moves. That if we were being watched, it would be suspicious. My argument that it gave them longer to attack us fell on deaf ears.

After waiting a week for everyone to fully recover, Kian drove us out into the middle of nowhere, saying he was bringing us closer to our past.

"Where is it?" I asked in a hushed tone. It felt like it was a hushed-tone kind of occasion as we drove through endless narrow highways along green fields and hillsides. It was nearly December and while England did not see much snow, the cold was piercing.

I could see Kian shrug in the driver's seat. I eyed him in the rear view mirror and noticed a stubborn set to his lips.

"I have not been back," Kian said, his voice flat. "I have no spiritual ties to the earth. I was taken from this place. This is my only life."

I felt like I had just received more information than I had asked for, but I let it sink in. We made it to a small rental office in a village I had missed the name of. The houses were painted white and still had thatched roofs. Kian spoke with the man inside and eventually came out with the keys to a three-bedroom cottage.

The space was lovely and backed out onto a wide hillside. When we had first arrived in England, I felt a buzzing in my chest that I had eventually hidden away. I thought it fizzled out, but I felt it anew as soon as I stepped out of the car and inhaled the chill. I hauled my sad suitcase to the back of the cottage and into a room I would share with Moira. I sat on the bed, feeling the complex stitching on the quilt over the stiff mattress.

For the first time in a long time, I ached to speak to my mother. While I had been glad my parents were not witnessing any of my adventures, the quiet moment in the bedroom brought tears to my eyes. I sat probing my emotions.

Slowly, my dream's feelings began to sink into my consciousness again. Regret. Guilt. Despair. After a few minutes, they started growing exponentially. The speed at which I was sinking into a nightmare alarmed me and I decided I needed to escape. I came outside to where Seth and Garrison were sitting on a wooden fence in the backyard.

I followed their gaze in the direction of a large green expanse, where rolling hills had formed a steep incline. My heart still ached, but I tried to distract myself.

"What are we looking at?" I asked.

Garrison pointed over the hill, as simply as if pointing out an interesting bird. "Over there," he said. "That's where we died."

## Chapter Twenty-Nine

His statement shocked me, but it was a muted panic. As my heart sped up with anxiety, I remembered that I had known it would come to this all along. After burying my emotions, memories of my husband, and past misdeeds, I felt very little connection to the place. Grudgingly, I realized I was holding myself back. I had only myself to blame.

The cold weather was bringing tears to my eyes and I was glad for the distraction. We had driven for nearly three hours to get to this place, and the sun peeked out from in between heavy grey clouds. It was midday. We were near the seashore and the smell of salt hung in the air.

"We'll explore after lunch," Garrison decided. "I'm starving."

When we returned to the cottage, Kian was busy trying to stuff his large bags full of weapons into the cupboard. He saw me looking.

"Don't think your training will stop just because

we're coming to the end of your journey," he warned, struggling to close the cupboard door.

I didn't reply but felt a hint of sadness touch me. Kian spoke with finality, as if when we did recover our memories, we wouldn't need him anymore. What would happen when this was all over? Would it ever be over?

The smell of cleaning solution reached me and I went into my bedroom, following the scent. Moira was wearing rubber gloves on top of her black gloves and cleaning the mirrors in the room. She quickly moved on to the dresser and night table.

"What are you doing?" I asked.

She was so focused on her work that she didn't see me standing in the doorway. She jumped in surprise.

"Cleaning," Moira answered simply.

I wasn't going to get any more out of her so I gave up. I had noticed over the past weeks that when Moira became nervous, she would make herself busy. I was about to leave when I sensed a magical push at my back.

I stopped, closing the door in front of me. When the old latch clicked, Moira looked up again, startled.

"What do you know?" I asked slowly. She must have gained more magic since the attack.

Moira straightened. "I ..." she stammered. Her hesitance to tell me made me nervous. Our histories were intertwined, for better or worse. Sighing, Moira sat down on one of the narrow beds. "I know about you and Seth."

I wanted to avoid the topic but continued to probe her for details. "When did you find out?" I asked.

"After he was released from the hospital," Moira replied. "I saw how he looked at you. It made me suspicious, angry. I didn't know why. Then the dreams started." She looked at the floor.

My emotions warred with my curiosity. I didn't want to know what she saw in my past, no matter how curious I was. But if Kian was right, then we would all be faced with the truth soon enough. The tension in the room would soon prove unbearable. The matter had to be settled.

"How do you feel now?" My voice was apprehensive.

Suddenly, Moira rose and strode past me, opening the door and walking towards the kitchen. She put her cleaning supplies away. I followed her, waiting for my answer. When she had removed the rubber gloves, she turned to face me.

"I know the difference between the past and now, Gwen," she said. Despite her words, I sensed anger behind them. "I'm not going to be tricked again."

She walked out of the cottage, grabbing her coat on the way. I stood, staring after her, trying to decipher her words. Was she talking about being tricked by Seth and me in the past, or being tricked by the magicians?

"What was that about?"

I jumped. Kian was reading a magazine on the small couch and had seen the exchange. His tall frame was folded onto the short couch, its floral pattern reminding me of my grandmother's house.

"Nothing," I replied quickly and retreated to my bedroom to sort out my tangle of emotions.

✦

I lost track of the days as my paranoia kept me on edge. I kept imagining the magicians storming into our little cottage as we ate or slept. We cooked together, watched the small television together, and took long walks trying to figure out what our memories could piece together.

Kian explained the magicians did not know where to look, since their home had been elsewhere. His assurances, however, didn't do much to settle my worries — they had found us before.

Though Kian did not participate in our walks up to the top of the hill from where the grey ocean could be seen, he was relentless about the sword fighting and archery. He kept up with the self-defence as well, though Garrison was the only one who seemed to enjoy it. Moira was no longer allowed to sit out, though she complained throughout our training sessions.

After a week at the cottage, morning walks to the top of the hill became customary. I woke up, dressed, and waited for the others by the door. Soon, Seth, Garrison, Moira, and I were trying in vain to shield ourselves from the wind, but our coats were not enough against early December in northern England. It hurt to breathe as we made our way up to a small flat area on top of the hill.

The ocean looked absolutely deadly when I peeked over the edge. The fall was much higher than the one I had taken in Oregon, and the vastness of the Atlantic looked angrier somehow than the steadfastness of the Pacific. I shook my head at my giving the oceans personalities.

Garrison was pacing a small bald spot where no grass grew. He peered over the hill as if imagining the village that could have been there. Kian had called it a kingdom, but it was probably no larger than a small town. A tribe. Seth and Moira took tentative steps, making sure to cover the plateau completely. Moira had not yet told Seth about their past, and I was certainly not going to intervene.

Seth was weaker because of his time at the hospital, not just magically but also physically. Often, we paused on the hike up the hill because he found it difficult to breathe. I could see the frustration playing across his face whenever he felt vulnerable.

We had climbed up together for seven days straight. This was our seventh morning, peering over the edge, pacing the land, trying to grasp onto the past as though it were sand running through our fingers. Each time we had come, Kian would stay behind, explaining that he had no place here with us. I wasn't sure what that meant, or why he occasionally sounded bitter, but I didn't want to argue. Kian was more on edge here than anywhere else we had been. I imagined him prowling around the cottage as a bear, the fur on his back constantly up in agitation.

When the wind grew too cold, we decided to retreat to the comfort of the cottage, which, though old and drafty, felt like a warm haven compared to the top of the hill. We ate, cleaned, washed the dishes, and went to bed as if this was a routine we had had forever.

LUCY LEIDERMAN

My dreams at the cottage had slowed and played over in my head as if they flowed in syrup. I saw nothing new, just the same images and feelings playing over and over in my head as if trying to be absorbed into my psyche.

My recurring dream of floating above the hill and over the ocean gave me vertigo, and I awoke on several occasions having to place a hand on the wall behind the bed to steady myself. Our routine was making me nervous, and I had almost had enough when the change finally happened.

On the eighth day at the cottage, we awoke to a particularly cold morning. Opening the door with difficulty, I saw that the grass was covered in frost and a thin layer of snow blanketed everything. I sighed with dread. Tempted to close the door and go back to sleep, I called to Seth.

"I love snow!" he called back. I sighed again. We were definitely going outside now. None of us had clothes or boots for the snow, so we settled with wearing a lot of layers and being cold.

Kian gave me a smile as I left, knowing how much I hated the cold. "Have fun!" he called.

"Shut up," I replied.

I heard him laugh as I shut the door behind me and faced winter.

Climbing a hill covered in snow and ice while wearing running shoes isn't easy. Near the plateau, the incline got particularly steep and I found myself slipping and sliding. As I slid a few metres, I found Seth right in front of me. Moira rolled in front of him.

"I don't think this is working," she said through chattering teeth, getting up and brushing the snow off her jeans with gloved hands.

Garrison had a pair of cleats in his luggage and they worked in his favour. He had made it to the top of the hill.

"Here," he called to Moira, "grab my hand!"

He steadied himself and extended his hand to Moira. She took it and extended a hand to Seth, who took it. I scrambled to get up and tried a step forwards, but slipped again. My canvas shoes were soaked and my feet were freezing.

"Come on," Seth said to me encouragingly, "a few more steps."

He had a hand extended to me in our makeshift chain. Trying to steady myself, I focused on my footing. One step forward, then another, and I was within reach. Shaking with the cold, I looked up into his eyes. I reached out for his hand and grabbed onto it.

In an instant, I was no longer myself.

✦

*A life blurred in front of my eyes. It was like the images Kian had shown me when he first kidnapped me, but now I could see in detail the aspects of my past life. I was absorbed into the images and my senses came to life. The smells of damp earth, fresh heather, and burning wood filled my nostrils and mind with memories.*

*In an instant, I had a childhood with a father and a mother. I remembered the faces of several women who had* taken care of me. The friends who had played with me by throwing rocks into the sea on a shore of pebbles. The taste of jerky and salted meat filled my mouth as I fished and waited for the men and boys of our tribe to come back from the hunt.

Suddenly, I was older. The familiar pulse of magic coursed through my blood. The faces of the women around me became sad as cold steel was thrust into my hands and I was made a warrior for my strength and abilities. Old faces swirled as the people I encountered came and went. Uneasiness filled my heart. Something terrible was afoot.

Throughout the memories, Seth appeared. First young, and then old. Sometimes he wore a Roman uniform and sometimes we wore the plain spun tunic of our tribe. On several occasions his skin was touched with blue ink. He showed me the items he got from the Romans. Understanding dawned as I watched him leading a troop through the trees. He acted as a guide but was really leading them away from our home.

Then the earth began to roll and I was surprised to be unsteady on my feet. I had never felt anything like this before. The ocean roared and my link with the water was severed. The cool comfort that had resided in my chest since childhood was gone and was replaced by a panic I could not explain.

Weapons were needed for war. Metal was expensive. Fury rushed through me as I reached the age of marriage and was placed into the care of a man I detested. It was our king who forced me by playing on my allegiance, and while I began to hate him, I loved his son unconditionally. Seth stood next to the king, his youth a contrast to the old man's beard and heavy features. A prince. Soon he was married off as well, but I was determined to live the life I wanted, no matter *what. I would be loyal to my tribe, but my personal life was no one's affair but mine.*

*The earth would not stop rolling and soon the men in our tribe were scarce. The Romans had lost their patience, and those of us who weren't killed in battle disappeared and were feared captured by the neighbouring tribe who attacked us through their magicians. Finally, we were able to break through and capture the stone building which housed the powerful three.*

*Blood ran in my vision as we fought our way through to the small castle. The panic swelled in my chest as I feared we would be too late. Finally free of the guards surrounding the structure, our group pushed against the stone door of the chamber in which the magicians performed their unnatural rituals. There were seven of us. I spotted Moira, Garrison, and Seth in the crowd, but the other faces were unfamiliar. Garrison made eye contact with me and I knew his future self rode in this body. He saw the same thing I did.*

*Finally, we managed to move the stone and ran into the square chamber. The scene in front of me made my stomach drop to the floor. Bodies littered the ground. The slaves of the magicians had been poisoned to keep their secrets. Two bodies lay in heavy robes on a pedestal. Their long beards and hair, as well as the blue paint covering their bodies, identified them as the magicians. The two men lay with their eyes open staring at the stone ceiling, goblets in their hands. A fire was dying out, burning low around them. Heavy rings adorned each finger and golden circlets wound around their necks. We were too late.*

*Dread lurched over me as we found a slave still living. I turned my back as the information was forced from him.*

*The ritual of sending the spirit through time had been done — the magicians would wait out the threat from our tribe and the Romans and would return once more. Our group returned to our own lands, defeated.*

*The scene moved quickly to the king ordering our group to die. His voice shook and tears filled his eyes as he made the decision. The Romans would win, and he was forcing his own son to be a ritual sacrifice for our cause. The fury pulsed inside me again as I argued and was silenced. I found Seth. We disagreed with the king. We wanted to live our lives together. We made a plan to run away.*

*The night our group was to be sacrificed in hopes of defeating the magicians, we were to meet in the forest at our usual spot. I packed a few belongings and bundled a cloak around me to block the chill. My horse waited for me. I knew in my heart I would be needed here. In this time. I did not want to leave this life. Before I could reach my horse, heavy hands grabbed me from behind.*

*My husband, who had suspected me but had feared my magic, guessed my plans. He threw me to the ground and advanced. I used my magic to deter him but he was not swayed. He kept coming, and we fought. He landed a blow to my ribs and I swept his feet out from under him. I placed a knee on his chest and his head hit the ground. He came after me again and wrapped heavy hands around my neck.*

*I was weaponless. My magic would not work on him at this proximity and everything else was out of reach. Frantic, I dug in my pockets. My fingers found a wooden figurine of a seahorse. Seth had carved it for me. Its long shape made it sharp. I pulled it from my pocket and stabbed blindly. Blood spurted onto my face as I managed to lodge the figurine in Augren's neck. His eyes widened, stunned, and he fell onto me.*

*I pushed him off. No time to think about what I had done. I was late.*

*I rode hard to where the trail thinned in the forest, then jumped off of my horse and ran. Here I recognized the road. My present self made the connection. This is where I was running in all of my memories. Through the undergrowth of the forest, the familiar emotions swept over me and threatened to consume me. Finally, after what felt like ages, I emerged in the clearing but Seth was already gone.*

*When I didn't arrive, he must have thought I had gone back to the ritual. He had good reason to think that I had made this plan to protect him — sacrificing myself in the process. I had considered it but become selfish at the last moment, deciding that being together would eventually numb the knowledge of having betrayed our tribe.*

*I began to run again, though the weight of what I was about to do pressed on me and weighed down my limbs. He would sacrifice himself, and I had no reason to live if he was gone. I wanted to die.*

*I used my magic to speed my running as my breath came in short gasps to my lungs. The woods eventually began to thin and I spotted a small hill in the distance with a ring of fire burning high. People were gathered around, but no one approached. The fire spurred me onwards, fearing I would be late. I nearly flew to the top of the hill as my magic carried me. Shouts followed, either warning to stay away or encouraging me to go forward. I could see six heads beyond the fire, performing the magic together. The ritual was old. There were no guarantees it would work. I kept running.*

*As the fire sizzled my skin and I felt the heat on my face, I ignored the smell of burning hair and used my last bit of magic to shield myself from the flames. I came into the circle just in time to see Seth turn and his expression change from grim to hopeful. He extended a hand to me and I took it, joy finding its way into my soul for the first time in a long time. The fire stayed with me and I felt my magic absorb it, settling it into me. Then everything came to an end.*

✦

I awoke on the ground just as the others were beginning to sit up. Night had fallen and there was no moon to light the landscape. It took a few seconds for the cold to set in, but once it did I found myself shaking uncontrollably. We had been out here all day. The knowledge of everything I had just witnessed poured down on me like a heavy rain, and the repercussions danced through my mind.

I felt the fire inside me, just as I had before the memories ended. I used it to heat myself, and slowly my shaking abated. The feeling of a growing magic settled on me. I felt the power course through my veins. The change would have been immense for the old Gwen, but I had just seen my past play out. I had lived in my body for a lifetime, and the magic felt like home now.

Seth stood and offered me a hand. I took it. We had set off the memories by being open, by coming here and by trying to recover our lives. But the ritual had involved us linking our bodies and our magic. I realized we had all held hands and linked on the hill, out of sheer coincidence. It had opened us up to the past.

Garrison said something about wanting to climb to the plateau, and Seth and Moira went with him. I, however, couldn't wait to tell Kian. I was surprised he hadn't come to check on us. While the others climbed higher, this time on steady feet with magic pulsing around them, I headed down the hill to the cottage.

Each step I took felt like I floated. My mind felt expanded. I knew so much more now. There was no way I could retain my old human brain and absorb it all. I was more than that now. My magic coursed through my veins and I couldn't help but think that the old Gwen would find it painful. This new Gwen found it energizing.

I didn't stop to think once about if this was who I wanted to become — it had happened. Kian had led me here and I couldn't wait to tell him that his mission had been successful. We were stronger and not enslaved — yet. We had died having hope that it would all work out. This time we were going to do it right.

The fears about losing myself presented themselves as small pangs in my chest, grounding me to this life and reminding me about the importance of being human. But each breath I took brought the focus back to my senses, which were ringing with anticipation. The cold coastal wind billowed around me and I felt that with a twist of my hand I could control it, turn it into a gale or make it disappear. Control was mine.

I knew the feeling was only temporary. Once I would fit the magic into my own skin it would be like how I had gotten used to the vibration in New York. This feeling of wonder would pass and I would be faced with the reality of being hunted. Yet everything felt different now. Better. As if I had only been half of myself before.

I had absorbed my terrible past, the person I had been, the deceit, and my death. I had gone through the fire and come out on the other side. Now I was finally intact. The power made me cocky and careless. I'll admit it. But the magic fed my confidence like kindling in a fire.

I approached the cottage and was confused to find the fire in the hearth had gone out. The lights were also extinguished. Without the warmth of a presence inside of it, the small building gave off an eerie and foreboding impression.

Struggling with the latch, I pushed the door ajar and entered the tiny living space. Our stuff was shoved into every corner and littered every tabletop. The evidence of life made me feel a little less nervous in the dark. A smell hung in the air as if someone had tried to clean. I rolled my eyes at Moira's attempts and then remembered she had been on the hill with me.

I was about to turn on the lights when a rustling in the dark startled me. I stepped back immediately against the door. Kian was sitting at the table. I was relieved to find him here. I couldn't wait to tell him about my discovery. He would be proud.

I approached him but my smile faded as I saw that he was hunched over the tabletop, his head in his hands, and his shoulders shook. He was crying. My knees went weak. I didn't know how to handle the situation, and news that would cause him to break down must be something I really didn't want to know.

"Kian, what's the matter?" I tried to mask the concern in my voice.

He stood, causing the wooden chair to grate against the floor and send shivers down my spine. "Nothing," he replied shakily.

I didn't believe him in the least, so I walked in the dark until I stood in front of his silhouette.

"I get it now," I told him. To my surprise, my voice shook. "We all do. We're strong again. It wasn't about remembering how we lived, but why we chose to die."

Silence. I had expected more questioning, but nothing came.

His reaction was beginning to worry me. Why wouldn't he be happy? This was what he had wanted.

"I have my magic now. I feel it. I've got it back. All of it."

"I know," he replied shakily. "I'm sorry."

Before I could react he spun me around and held me with my back to his chest in a tight grip. Not tight enough to hurt — I felt like he was hugging me against my will. I opened my mouth to protest but he pressed a damp cloth to my face, covering my mouth and nose.

My world went black.

# Chapter Thirty

I didn't know how long I spent in the delirious stage between sleep and wakefulness. Images blurred before my eyes and my head lolled from side to side. I felt like my mouth had been stuffed with cotton. Thoughts flew by, but I couldn't grab hold of a single one to make any sense of my situation.

Finally, I opened my eyes. My mind functioned with a small level of coherence. While bright lights made me squint, I could not tell if it was day or night. Cream-coloured velvet stretching from the high ceiling to the floor covered what I assumed were large Victorian windows. The rest of the room, or what I could see of it, was just as lavishly decorated. Around me, plush sofas and armchairs were arranged, and a dark, oversized mahogany desk stood bare.

I was sitting on a hard wooden chair, and though my body ached and protested, I couldn't move into a more comfortable position. I looked down to see my feet tied with a thick coil of rope, which seemed out of place in the posh office. A rich yellow and green carpet covered the floor. I tried my hands, but those were tied too. I could feel my wrists were rubbed raw. Every small move hurt as the fibres of the robe cut into me.

I licked my dry lips and forced my mind to concentrate, closing my eyes to block out the distractions of the room and my situation. Inside, I was torn.

One half was the girl who had been kidnapped in Oregon. She was starting to panic and tears threatened to spill from her eyes. The knowledge of being drugged and kidnapped again was frightening, but the memory of Kian brought a whole new pain to her chest. Confusion, heartbreak, and exhaustion clouded her judgment. She wanted to give up.

I focused on the other half as she smouldered with a fury and determination that might actually get me through this. This was the woman who had lived two thousand years ago and whose life I had witnessed — how long ago? I had no idea how much time had passed. Her emotions were raw with being deceived and captured. Basic survival instincts forced me to assess my situation. I needed help.

The image of Seth came to my mind. His appearances melded, young and old, as my memories of him then and now made one distinct whole. I felt the magic beginning to pulse inside me as I thought of him and called in my mind. I let my last memories seep into the stream of magic, as well as my helplessness and despair. My concentration was suddenly broken when I heard a door open behind me.

"Oh no you don't, my little witch."

My eyes flung open, and it took restraint to keep from swivelling my chair in a panic. The room before me held no entrance or exit. I could hear a large door creaking behind as several sets of footsteps approached.

It was a man's voice, smooth and deep, but it held a touch of anger and magic that I wondered if I would have been able to detect without regaining my memories. His American accent with a Southern drawl made me wonder where I was.

The footsteps became lighter as my captors came onto the carpet. They stood just beyond my vision and I refused to turn and give them the satisfaction of seeing me agitated.

"She is not the child I found anymore," another voice said. "She should be destroyed. I smell the old one in her."

I couldn't help but wince at the windows. This voice was older and rougher, with an accent that made it hard to understand him. His words ended on an up note and had a strange yet familiar rhythm.

Dread crept into my thoughts. I fought the despair that threatened to show my feelings.

A spot of sun winked at me from behind the thick curtain, and I knew it was daytime — which day was still a mystery. I had been passed out for at least twelve hours.

"Gwyneth," the smooth voice spoke again, "this is what I need from you. You must understand that you have contributed to my death once already. And I have contributed to yours. So the cycle must stop."

I stayed quiet, biting my tongue and suppressing all of the questions that threatened to break free.

These men were trying to make me uncomfortable and scared. They stood behind me to frighten me, and I refused to give in. Several quiet moments passed before I heard a sigh.

"Go," Smooth Voice said.

I heard a shuffle as if someone was being pushed, and my heart sped up anticipating an attack. Instead, Kian came to stand in front of me.

I opened my mouth, ready to yell, scream, and insult. But I shut it once I realized this was just another way to rile me. A steady voice in my mind told me to stay calm. I wasn't dead yet. They wanted something. They played these games for a reason. With effort, I swallowed my accusations.

Had I not known him well, I would not have recognized Kian as he was now. The confidence in his posture was gone. His shoulders drooped and he hung his head, looking more like a bird of prey with his long nose and hunched back. He dragged his feet and refused to meet my gaze. When he stood before me, he could not delay any longer and slowly raised his gaze from my feet to my face. When our eyes met, he winced as if I had struck him.

Everything I had liked about him was gone. Something switched off in my mind and I felt a cold resolve settle over me. I steadied my gaze and felt my jaw tighten with anger.

"Gwen, I —" He stopped, dropping his eyes to the floor again. When he did not appear likely to say any more, a third voice behind me urged him with a hurried tone. At least three men and Kian held me captive.

"I don't know what to say," Kian mumbled to the ground.

It was my turn to retort. A thousand mean things flitted through my mind, but I realized I needed to gather as much information as possible if I hoped to escape.

"The truth," I spat out, "start with the truth."

He had once said those words to me, and by the tortured look on his face it was clear he remembered. No matter how I tried to control my voice, the drug and my anger made it husky and rough. I hoped I sounded dangerous. Afraid to gather magic again, in case one of the magicians behind me sensed it, I stayed prone and deadpan.

Kian refused to speak, and I wondered who would outlast the silence. Finally, I felt footsteps nearing. Two men came to stand on either side of him. A third lingered off to the side, watching.

The first two looked like normal men, though they stood out for their choice of expensive-looking suits and shoes, and the golden tie clips, chains, and watches that adorned them.

The one in the black suit had thinning black hair, which began around his ears and wound its way around his head, leaving the top bare. His eyes shone with an anticipation that made me nervous. The grey-suited man had a full head of grey hair, but his most striking feature was his piercing blue eyes. I knew right away this was the man with the smooth voice.

The magician who lingered off to the side looked out of place, wearing an oversize collared blue shirt and black pants. His long, curly black hair hung past his shoulders and a thick beard obscured the lower half of his face. Though he had tried to adapt to modern clothing, a worn and dirty heavy brown robe hung from his shoulders.

It looked like the other two had tried to dress him appropriately, but he had refused, and his strange appearance could explain why he stood apart, his eyes darting around and his fingers tapping nervously against his leg.

I assessed the men with what I hoped looked like cold calculation. Kian had said they were influential. Perhaps even government figures. If I ever cared about the news, I might have recognized them. But they were complete strangers to me.

When the silence became strained, the balding man with black hair approached me. He stopped and lowered his face within inches of mine, and I fought my own instinct to recoil.

"I can almost see her," he said. It was unclear to whom he spoke, but he also possessed an American accent with a southern twang. "Gwyneth, my colleagues and I were happy to leave you and your *kind* alone in the past, where you should have stayed. You are in our world now. It is only fair that we may use your strength."

I didn't quite understand what he was talking about but remembered Kian's words about being enslaved. When the one who had been speaking to me stepped back, I felt a small push of magic urging me to agree with him. It trapped me in his words and moulded my point of view. I pushed back at it, forcing it away from me. Being brainwashed sent the panic back into my throat.

"What do you want?" I asked through gritted teeth.

As I pushed back, the magic strengthened like a brick wall, crushing my resolve. It was strong and I didn't know how to fight it. Fear kept me pushing. Sweat ran into my eyes and I was short of breath. It felt like ages had passed but in reality only seconds. Then, as suddenly as it had begun, it stopped. Despite myself, I exhaled in relief.

"Strength," Smooth Voice said, impressed. "That was a nice show of force, and we need it." He sat casually on the desk. "The world is bigger now than when we left it quite ... abruptly," he said, smiling. His steely eyes, however, held a sharp edge. "But you know that, don't you? You're back to being that same nuisance who wouldn't let us be."

I could tell he was preparing for a story. Whatever his grudge was with me, he had been planning this speech for a long time and I decided to sit and wait, taking advantage of the time to think of something to save myself. The ropes were secure. My magic would be felt. Options were limited.

"You and your lot decided to make friends with our enemy, the foreigners who wanted our land and knew nothing of our culture. Our tribes could have united against them, but no!" His voice rose with a passion that made me uneasy. "You didn't like our ways. You did not *agree* with what we did to maintain our power. Not all of us were as fortunate as your kin. We took our powers from Alahpa. We could have saved our culture and our kingdoms, but you chose to destroy us instead. What has that gained your people? Your names and symbols have been forgotten. The Romans allowed your survivors to become the new tribe, and even they did not last to see the fall of the empire that destroyed their roots and eliminated their magic forever."

Everything he said was making very little sense to me. I was torn between listening confusedly and making plans for my escape. I committed some information to memory, vowing to look into it if I ever escaped.

Smooth Voice saw my attention straying and it visibly incensed him. "No one knows!" he yelled, shocking me out of trying to judge which floor we were on and if the window was a likely exit. "Look at you! You do not care about your tribe even now, as we prepare to take your soul and make you pay for your betrayal of our race."

My words came out before I could think about them, as if another mind spoke from my mouth. "You're a disgrace to our people!" I spat at him. "Slavery and sacrifices are not proper ways to obtain power."

His hand came up and struck my cheek before I could move. I felt a searing line of pain where his ring had cut me. Again, I fought to contain the panic and remain stoic, even as I comprehended his words and what these men intended to do with me. Kian still had not looked up from the floor, but the balding magician came to place a hand on Smooth Voice's shoulder.

"Relax," he said calmly. "It has nearly come to an end."

I swallowed the lump of fear in my throat.

This man turned to me. "You will be prepared for the sacrifice at dusk," he said matter-of-factly. "You will surrender your magic to us, and we will keep you." He eyed me in a way that made my skin crawl. His leer examined every inch of me and I was suddenly very aware of being tied up.

"If you try to escape or attempt to use your magic until that time," he continued, "we will be forced to make the process significantly less comfortable than it can be."

The magician began to walk away but turned back at the last moment, giving me a look of satisfaction. "It is nice to see you so …" he searched for the right word by waving his hand carelessly in the air, "… incapacitated and at our disposal. You are cooperating beautifully. Much more willing than in the past."

Revulsion filled my throat as his words sank in.

"Why is he here?" I asked, tilting my head towards Kian. The small action made my head ache. It hurt to speak and restrain my emotions at the same time.

The balding magician looked at Kian as if seeing him for the first time. "Oh, him?"

I wasn't expecting a direct answer but was glad for it. The anger inside me threatened to spill over as all of the possible deceitful scenarios played in my mind.

"He is here because we needed someone to find you," the magician replied. "Recognize you in your youth and bring you to us. Someone non-threatening, trustworthy, and obedient. The … connection between you is an added bonus. You would follow him to the ends of the Earth, wouldn't you?" he sneered. "Well, before now. Gwyneth, both your lives read like a Greek tragedy. As entertaining as your love affairs may be, our need for your magic is greater than our need for dramas. We have televisions here."

My mind was reeling. "Why don't you just kill me?"

The effect of the drug was beginning to pound into my brain and each of the chandelier's bulbs hurt. I was squinting, trying desperately to retain my composure.

The balding magician looked back to Smooth Voice, who smiled sadistically at my pain. This one truly hated me. He ran a hand through his silver hair and laughed as if my question had an obvious answer.

"What? Risk losing you again? I am not a fool." In a flash, his expression changed from amused to dangerous. "I know you will be my problem again when you are reborn. The ritual has put us both in the cycle."

"Let us go," the balding magician said, sounding bored. "I'm sure Gwen would like to rest before the evening. Kian, make sure she is secure."

By the way he smirked in Kian's direction, I knew it was understood that Kian did not want to get close to me. The magicians were torturing him, but I failed to feel any sympathy for him while I was bound and being readied for a ritual that would enslave me. The magician's push on my will made me nervous. I had felt strong after recovering my memories, but I was not strong enough on my own.

I heard the door open behind me and the three men confidently strode out of my vision, the strange one throwing me cautious and appraising looks. His gait was odd and everything about him suggested he had been displaced and was not adjusting to his new surroundings. When he too was gone, Kian hesitantly approached me.

Timidly, he made sure the rope around my feet was secure. He moved to my back and felt my wrists. I resented his touch and felt the anger pushing tears into my eyes. His proximity was infuriating and I hoped my feelings pulsed off me. I hoped he knew how I felt. Especially when I realized he had probably tied the ropes.

I held my breath as he secured the knots, willing him to leave. I didn't want him to see the tears that threatened to spill over. A voice outside the room called for him. Suddenly, he knelt down and I felt him close to my ear. I tried to move but both his hands were placed on my shoulders.

"Don't lose faith in me," he whispered. "I love you."

He was gone in an instant, and I heard the door shut.

I sat in the room alone, staring blankly at the gilded portrait frames, wondering if his words were in my imagination. Perhaps not all was lost.

# Chapter Thirty-One

I was left to sit by myself for the remainder of the day. As my stomach grumbled and my limbs ached, I tried to concentrate on everything I had learned so far. My head was pounding and my mouth felt like parchment paper.

Two of the magicians hated me and wanted to enslave me, using my power to further theirs. Just as Kian had said. One had wanted to kill me and get me out of the way. The strange magician did not look as well-adjusted to modern life as the other two, and the reason finally came to me.

I remembered storming their fortress, entering the chamber filled with dead slaves and knowing we were too late. The bodies, painted blue, lay haphazardly in every spare space on the floor. Somewhere, even in that instant, I knew I would have to pay the ultimate price for not stopping them in time. But we had only found two magicians. There were three. My initial reaction was right. The third was somehow transported through time.

A heavy lump formed in my chest when I put the pieces together. There had been no time during our journey to switch sides. Kian had been helping them all along. If his feelings for me did make him help me, it could not have been the original plan. So what was?

I felt like I was faced with a big jigsaw puzzle and no image to work with. Trying to put the pieces together blindly was frustrating. Where were my friends? Were they safe? Where was I?

So little of what had been said made sense to me. Whatever had happened between the magicians and me in the past could not have been important enough for me to consider it a memory worth passing on to my next life. But they obviously still held a grudge. I sighed. Another mystery. I focused on questions of the past so I could avoid thinking of Kian and causing a torrent of emotion to flood my logical mind.

As the hours rolled by, the sun began to set behind the thick curtains, and even with the gilded chandeliers overhead, the room grew dim. The sun would set early in the winter, and as the chill found me, I remembered it was December. They would come for me soon. I was too frightened to use my magic to warm myself. They could feel the power and come in again.

I was starting to tremble in the cold when the latch behind me clicked and the door opened. I was alert in an instant, again refusing to turn in a panic, even though my heart raced.

Only the two modern magicians appeared this time. The satisfaction and victory in their eyes made my stomach do somersaults. Bald Man came over to me and undid the rope binding me to the chair. My skin crawled where his hands touched me. I had a brief inclination to run before a thick and heavy blanket of magic settled over me and I couldn't move or breathe.

After a few seconds it did not dissipate and I began to gasp for air as Bald Man stood me up on shaky legs and retied my hands behind my back. When spots began to form before my eyes, the magic alleviated and I gasped for air. Their magic was far more powerful than mine, but I refused to show it.

The cold made me shiver and my legs shook from sitting. Kian's last words to me echoed as I struggled with whether or not to trust him.

We moved quietly through the large Victorian house, only the sound of my stumbling and their footsteps echoing throughout the hall. Corridors led off in different directions and I could not judge how big the building actually was. A grand marble staircase ended the wide hall, and we descended it.

While Smooth Voice walked silently behind, Bald Man squeezed my arm to keep me upright. His iron grip never let up and I fought to keep the pain from my face. I tried to look around at the gilded portraits and marble busts lining the hall, but every time my head turned I would get a small warning shake from the magician.

Downstairs, the front doors were open and led to the courtyard out front. The winter chill hit me full force, biting through my shirt and jeans. It was only as we passed through the entrance that I noticed an administrative desk by the doors and pamphlets littering the counter. A small cash register stood next to a sign telling guests the ticket prices.

I opened my mouth in shock. This was some kind of venue closed for the season.

I was pushed through the giant double doors and blinked in the fading daylight of winter. Grey frost covered the fields surrounding the house, and soon my feet were soaked, adding to the chill. The sky was clear of clouds, and the sun set low on the horizon, illuminating the frost but casting everything else in shadow.

We walked to the back of the large house, where I could see remnants of a garden maze and pond, frozen over. Nearby, a few rocks stuck out of the ground at strange angles. They formed a shape, but it was hardly a perfect circle.

They looked more like old waystones than monuments. Two figures moved among them, arranging stones in various patterns and drawing strange symbols in charcoal: Kian and the third magician.

Bald Man increased the pressure on my arm and shoved me forward. I landed on the hard ground, trying to use my shoulders to break my fall, since my hands remained tied behind my back. Kian turned to me briefly but then carried on with his work. I could not see his face.

"Ready her. Call when you are prepared," Smooth Voice said to the third magician.

I looked up in time to see Third Magician glaring at their backs as they walked away. Then his eyes fell on me. A black look settled over his face and I could feel restrained magic pulsing off of him. When he opened his mouth to speak, sounds I could not understand came out.

"Stupid girl," he finally spat at me. My confused look enraged him further but he turned back to the symbols.

Kian still worked quietly, drawing on the stones.

"Why are we here?" I asked. My voice came out shaky and quiet.

"It is holy site for the magicians," Kian answered without looking at me. "The place of death and ritual." His voice sounded bored and unconcerned.

"Shut up!" the third magician yelled. "You will be quiet!"

I lay in the frost, shaking, for another few minutes. The magician began to gather wood from a nearby stockpile and created a fire in the centre of the waystones. The heat comforted me, even if it brought me closer to the ritual they were planning. I heard him bark orders at Kian as it began to snow.

Large flakes fell onto my eyelids and I blinked them away, savouring the feeling in case it was the last time. I had rolled onto my back and watched the darkening sky. So many thoughts swirled in my mind that I imagined them as the snowflakes, melting as soon as they touched the surface of my skin.

Kian appeared in my vision. He held a long knife that looked chipped and worn. It was thin but razor-sharp. "Do not move," he said, raising his eyebrows to emphasize his words.

I felt a magical pressure around my throat. Kian had no real magic. I turned my head and saw the magician watching me with displeasure.

"He will tighten it and kill you if you try to run," Kian said in a low voice.

I lay still, lacking other options.

He cut the rope around my ankles and then gently turned me to free my hands. I brought them to the front of my body, lying back and relishing the release of tension from my back.

The wind began to howl around us and soon I was shivering uncontrollably. When Kian had freed me of the rope, he let one hand slide subtly over my cheek. My emotions warred, so I stayed still like I had promised, delaying any reaction.

Over the sound of the wind, other sounds were lost and Kian looked back to see that the magician was busy. The sky was nearly black now.

"Remember your fire," he whispered to me, moving the rope back and forth in an effort to look busy. When I squinted at him in confusion, he sighed.

"You did not possess the magic of fire in your past. It is a new development. They do not know about it. Use it when the time comes," he said, and then turned to go back to the symbols on the stones.

I thought of the last moments before we died. I ran through the fire, using my magic to shield myself, yet the fire clung to me even as the ritual was performed and I was torn from my body. It was because of how I had died that I had this new power. Finally, a surprise the magicians were not prepared for.

The magician fed the fire as Kian worked. The darkness unsettled me and I strained to listen for anything around me. Eventually, footsteps came close. As I lay on my back, struggling to ignore the pressure of the magic on my neck, the two magicians came back from the house.

Both were barefoot and wore no clothing on their torsos. The suit pants and belts looked out of place on their bodies as they settled near the fire and I could see the same strange language drawn on their bodies in charcoal. The muscular chests and arms did not fit their aging faces. They talked in hushed tones as they glanced back at me with satisfied looks. Their hands were covered in black, as were half of their faces.

"Colour her," Third Magician yelled at Kian.

I saw Kian turn with a bowl in his hands. He began to come towards me as the balding magician stuck out an arm to stop him.

"Bring her here," he said, "then do it."

The grim look on Kian's face worried me more than the words. He put down the bowl and came over to me, helping me up by my arms and leading me over to near the fire. He stood me next to the light, the flames separating the two men and me. The third magician was still inscribing on the stone, running his fingers over the symbols and redrawing them.

Kian knelt in front of me. He gave me a look that spoke to me. I could almost hear his words in my mind, telling me to relax. Stay calm. Then he began to undo my pants. I leaned forward to stop him, but the pressure on my throat tightened suddenly and I couldn't breathe. I moved back to alleviate the pain.

"Be a good girl," Bald Man called to me. As the firelight danced on his face, the look of hunger in his eyes disgusted me.

I wanted to cry and scream and cover myself, but the magical collar and the lack of a place to run to prevented me from doing so. Instead, I tried to focus on the fire. To internalize it and be ready to use it when I needed to.

Kian began to spread blue paint onto my legs. It had the texture of cement or mud, and it dried quickly, caking onto my skin. His touch calmed me, but the panic returned when he finished, stood, and moved to take off my shirt. I forced myself to stand still as he proceeded to paint me again, and I tried to remember that I wasn't completely naked and at least it was Kian touching me and not one of the magicians. He drew lines on my face with the paint, which I guessed was clay.

My blood froze when Kian stepped away and Bald Man squinted past the fire. I guessed he could barely see me, and it probably wasn't an accident that Kian had chosen this spot.

"She is not completely unadorned, is she?" Bald Man said disapprovingly. When Kian failed to move, Bald Man's voice lowered. "Do it or I will."

I could feel magic fill the air and Kian moved towards me once more, hesitantly, and shielded my body from the others, if only for a moment. He met my eyes but then closed his, squinting in pain. He looked tormented and I wondered if magic forced his movements. Slowly, he placed his hands on my hips just above my underwear. I held my breath as my heart beat wildly.

"We are ready," Third Magician's voice cut through the night.

Kian relaxed and turned back around, his body still shielding mine.

"Let's get on with it then," Smooth Voice said, waving a hand dismissively in my direction. Bald Man opened his mouth to protest but was quieted with a look from Smooth Voice.

"Later," Smooth Voice said. "I don't care what you do with her body. I want her magic. Now."

If the comment was meant to fill me with fear, it worked. I felt Kian tense. I glanced down. His hands were bunched into fists. The short moment of relief I had when Third Magician's voice interrupted my painting ceremony was put to an end.

Third Magician walked over to me and prodded me with a staff he had laid on the ground. His disdain was obvious. He did not even want to touch me. He pushed me until I was facing the fire, so close that the heat threatened to overcome me. I tried to take calming breaths but my pulse raced when the two other magicians came to each hold one of my hands.

Bald Man was on my right and Smooth Voice on my left. Third Magician came to stand between them, holding their hands and making a circle around the fire. I still had no idea what was going on, but my time was limited. Third Magician closed his eyes and began to hum.

"He is connecting to our ancient magic," Bald Man told me jovially. He squeezed my hand as if we were old friends. "Soon you will feel the magic being torn from your soul. You will be divided into two halves. Your power will reside in us, and the other part," he eyed me up and down, "will be mine. Forever. Or until I tire of you." He shrugged.

This sadistic speech was meant to enervate me. Smooth Voice still held my hand in an iron grip, but I thought I saw a small smile flit over his face.

Kian stood off to the side behind me, and I was afraid to turn. When the humming turned into words, the sound echoed unnaturally in the open night air. Third Magician's words turned into forces that resounded around us. I could not tell when it stopped being his voice and became a chorus of voices, crying out with him. The magicians on either side of me had closed their eyes and stood stock still, as if frozen in time. Behind me, someone kicked my ankle.

I guessed that was my sign. I felt the magicians were far away, in another place and time, as part of the ritual. I had a very small window to use my magic.

I began to draw energy to me and fill it with magic. I remembered the fire sticks at the club in Manhattan, what felt like ages ago. I thought of how I had ignited the canvas wrapped around the metal rods. I had fed them the energy from inside me.

The noise in the air swirled around my head until the voices surrounded me, dragged at me and I felt them against my skin. They cried out. I knew in my heart these were the slaves, captured and stolen by the magicians.

With effort, I ignored them, pushing my awareness away from the sound of the ritual and the two hands holding mine. I pushed past the cold biting at my body on one side as the fire licked up the other. Even blocking out the distractions, it wasn't enough. My magic felt small and brittle next to the force around me.

I went further, gathering energy from the life around me. I reached out with my magic, taking what I could. Kian and the magicians felt like a dead zone. I could not penetrate their energy. But the fire burned bright and I knew what I was going to do. I felt the pressure begin to build in my chest just as it had when I had been attacked at the hotel. It grew until I couldn't take it anymore.

Somewhere far away, I knew the frost beneath my feet had melted and the grass was withered. I took what I could and bunched it to me. I waited, listening, for the ritual to reach its crescendo. My blood boiled and it warmed my skin until I smelled burning flesh. The hands holding mine loosened. I was nearing my limit. I opened my eyes just in time to see Smooth Voice look over to me in utter confusion.

I released my magic into the fire, willing it to grow. The blast shocked even me as the pressure exploded within the flames, and I flew through the air.

# Chapter Thirty-Two

I hit the ground. The breath was knocked out of me but I scrambled to stand. My ears popped and the sudden cold rushed at my limbs. For a moment, all was silent. Then angry curses and yells sounded behind me. Struggling to breathe, I forced myself up.

Kian appeared and grabbed my hand. One side of his face was covered in blood, as if he had been dragged along the ground. "Run!" he yelled.

I didn't need to be spurred on. Not only did Kian pull me along with him, but the knowledge that the magicians could be chasing us bit at my ankles like a rabid dog. I ran for my life through the dark night, frost crunching underneath my bare feet.

We stopped to catch our breath when we got around to the other side of the large house. A few deer grazed in the distance, looking up at us every once in a while. We were completely at odds with our environment. While the snow had stopped and the moon began to peek out from behind the clouds, the landscape radiated serenity.

I tried to be quiet but my throat felt raw and it was still hard to inhale. Every breath pinched my lungs and I doubled over. When I straightened, Kian was looking suspiciously into the night.

"What?" I whispered.

"It's too quiet," he replied.

All was silent. Wisps of steam came from my mouth as I exhaled. Not even wind stirred. My heart froze. Suddenly, footsteps sounded all around us as if an army was descending.

"Go!" Kian shouted at me, pushing me away as Smooth Voice and Third Magician appeared on either side of him. I hesitated as Kian fought them both to keep them from chasing me. Could he win? Or would he die for me? When he motioned once again for me to run, I took off.

Like a hare being chased by hounds, I ran blindly into the night. I could sense magic in the air as the moon hid once again and my surroundings grew unnaturally dark. I stumbled over a root and soon was lost. The darkness felt like blindness. I could barely see my hand in front of my face. My imagination kicked in and I imagined my captors lying in wait for me.

I stumbled through the black for a few minutes until my hands found a wall. While comforted that I was not out in the open by myself, I was scared to be so close to the house. My pulse raced as I used my hands to feel around the side of the house. The frozen pebbles under my feet cut into me, and as the darkness consumed everything, I began to feel as if I was trapped under a blanket.

A small part of my mind began to push the blanket off me. It was hard, and I was soon sweating and dragging for breath even worse than before. But the night grew steadily lighter. Thick magic obscured my vision and I didn't have the strength to lift it.

A hand grabbed me from behind, stifling my scream as the other wrapped itself around my throat. My hands flew up to pull the attacker off me and I felt thick muscular arms. I was nearly naked and pressed against a bare chest. The stranger's heart beat against my back as horror seeped up into my throat.

I struggled in vain as I was dragged into the house through a back door. My vision cleared, and though it was still dark, I could see the moonlight reflect off of pots and pans. I was being hauled through a server's kitchen. In the short moments that passed, I tried to remember Kian's self-defence. I elbowed, kicked, and bit, but the sheer brute force of my captor was too much.

We passed through some kind of door and I was thrown into the small room. I landed roughly on the stone floor, skidding and skinning my legs. I tried to drag myself up to face the man and found my hands gripping wooden shelves. I guessed we were in the pantry, based on the dusty and empty racks. The small room was only big enough for the shelving and a small table that served as a cutting board.

I was nearly up when rough hands grabbed my hair and pulled me to a standing position. I bit back a cry as I was pressed into the shelves. My arms grated against the wall and flakes of blue chipped off. The only light came from the open door and the moonlight beyond that.

Hot breath spread against the skin on the back of my neck and my hair was moved aside. Hands began at my neck and ran down my arms as I struggled to break free. The razor-sharp knife suddenly appeared in my vision as the glow of the moon reflected from it. I felt vomit rising in my stomach and up my throat.

"I would hate to do it," a voice said in my ear. Bald Man breathed so close I could feel every exhalation and it caused my body to convulse. "But I will. I will gut you right here."

He turned the knife until it nipped at the skin on my neck, the point causing a dot of pain to spread. He then dragged it across a few inches, lightly, just enough for me to feel the blood begin to trickle onto my collarbone. I stood stock-still.

He brought the knife away and ran his hands over my arms again, this time ending at my neck. He wrapped his fingers around it slowly, squeezing. I fought to keep a whimper lodged firmly in my throat. I would not give him the satisfaction.

He released my neck and wrapped one hand in my hair. Without warning, he yanked me off the shelves and threw me into the small table. I was forced to lean over it, my hands gripping the edge.

Before I could move, Bald Man was on top of me. His left hand covered my own, and though I tossed and turned, I could not get him off. His right hand began to travel along the side of my body and over my hip. I could hear his breathing accelerate and thought I would be sick.

Suddenly, a thump echoed in the small space and the magician's weight came down on me full force. I gasped in shock, but then he was pushed off my body and landed in a heap on the floor. I turned, ready for another assault, but Kian stood over the prone form with a frying pan in his hand.

I stopped and stared for only a second before I flew at him. In that moment, it didn't matter that one magician was unconscious at my feet while two more chased us. I just wanted to hold him.

I hit Kian with such a force that he stumbled back a step before wrapping his arms around me and lifting me off the ground. I buried my face in his neck, the smell of him bringing happiness back to my heart. Any indecision or confusion was gone. My feelings were crystal-clear. I never wanted to let go.

We could have stood there, embracing, for hours. I lost all track of time as I framed my body to his and let him hold me. Kian pulled away too soon, worry lining his face.

"We have to go," he whispered. I nodded, even as a touch of disappointment echoed inside me.

As we crept through the house, I refused to think what would have happened to me had Kian not intervened. I might have been in this situation because of him, but I was not about to delude myself with thinking that I could have fought off the magicians by myself when they did find me. Not even four of us together would stand a chance.

"What did you do to the other two?" I whispered as we passed through the entranceway. I felt exposed in the wide hall even though we kept to the shadows of the walls.

"Magicians can't control your body until they control your mind," Kian whispered, taking my hand and pulling me through to another kitchen. This one was neater and looked more used. "And they can't do that until they perform the ritual on you."

"But how did you fight them?" I remembered the magic settling over me and shuddered.

"They gave me their magic to find you." Kian spoke in short snippets. This was a story he did not want to tell. "I only had a little, but I could use it to delay them and confuse them. But that's gone now."

"What do you mean?" I whispered.

"As I came to find you, I felt *him* take it back."

I understood Kian's "him" to be the third magician. A hundred questions sprang to my lips when he mentioned their supposed agreement, but I swallowed them all down. The important thing was that my power had not been torn away in some ritual and we were leaving.

I was still shaking, but now the cold felt like numbness and it was the knowledge of being enslaved that sent fear shooting down my spine. I spotted a door at the end of the kitchen and my heart began to beat faster with thoughts of escape. I reached for the handle when Kian stopped me.

He picked up a knife from the counter and turned it in his hand. With the handle, he broke the lock on the inside of the door and swung it open. Snow hit us full force. The wind blew through my bones, warning of a full-blown blizzard. My stomach sank as I thought of trudging through that weather. The wind tore the door from Kian's grasp and slammed it against the house.

Kian leaned out into the winter night and tossed the knife into the snow, where it was quickly covered. It created a stain on the snow and I turned my gaze to Kian's hand, which had been sliced when he broke the lock. Despite our situation, he smiled into the night.

"They will look for tracks but find none," he said with satisfaction. Then, taking me by the arm with his uninjured hand, he led me down a flight of stairs into a type of cellar.

The cold concrete sent chills up my legs and my teeth chattered. I was confused but didn't argue. In the cellar Kian removed a series of dusty rugs and revealed a wooden trap door. The latch looked fresh and I wondered how long he had been planning this escape. Opening the wooden lid, he placed the rugs carefully into place so that they would cover the room again once the top was closed.

I looked at him for confirmation, and he smiled. It was all I needed. Taking a deep breath, and thankful I did not mind small spaces, I climbed through the lid and down metal rungs that had been installed against the wall. My feet touched more carpet. Despite being underground, the place was warm. The musty smell of dust and dead air did not bother me after being in the cold for so long.

Piles of carpets were stacked underneath me, creating a soft floor. I tried to not think of what kind of creatures might be living inside them. Wooden shelves held random artefacts, from necklaces to binoculars.

Kian climbed down and sealed the top. Complete darkness fell until he lit a lantern. I smiled when I realized it was the kind campers used to keep off mosquitoes. The white electric light made me squint.

"The magicians are not at home in this world. It is too big for them," Kian said as he sat cross-legged across from me. "They can only sense magic. They live off it and feed on it, but there is hardly any left in this world. That's why you're so valuable to them." He peered into my eyes with a sudden intensity and I shied away.

"They want to grow their power. They aim to take control, and as they do so quietly, they may succeed." He reached out for my hand and took it in his. In the dim light, his downcast face looked to be made of shadow and his expression appeared sorrowful.

Kian took my fingers lightly and brought them to his lips. The feel of it reverberated up my arm and into my chest.

"But they will not get yours," he said it as if it was a vow. "Or Seth's, or Garrison's, or Moira's."

"Won't they find us?" My voice was hushed. The small room killed any echo and the tight space made me feel safe. It was just smaller than a medium-sized tent.

Kian shook his head. "Do not use your magic. Do not access that place inside yourself, wherever it lives. Forget it until we are through this. They can only sense you through your power. You are invisible to them as a regular human being." He looked at me with a glint in his eyes. "And despite everything, you are still very much a human being."

I thought about everything I had left behind as a human being. All of the events since being stolen away from my home by Kian had culminated in tonight, where I had nearly been enslaved by magicians.

The shudder that the memory of Bald Man's hands sent through my body unlocked a gateway of emotions. Despite an inner voice telling me to get a grip, a flood of tears and muted sobs escaped like a hurricane. All of the fear I had suppressed found its way out of my body. Kian extended an arm and held me close to his chest. I did not stop when I had soaked his shirt and cried off most of the blue paint on my face.

I was exhausted when I finally calmed, but our situation kept me from sleep.

"I betrayed you," Kian said. His voice was rough. He sat up, burying his head in his hands as if it would make the situation go away. I could only see a mop of black until he looked back to me, eyes bright.

"You did what you had to," I said. "We are safer now."

Kian shook his head. The way he winced made me nervous. "They tempted me and I agreed to do whatever they wanted. They didn't even bother to perform the ritual on me. I have no magic and they knew I was within their control." His expression held disgust. Then he turned to me and it melted from his face, revealing the most pure and innocent look I had ever seen on him. It reminded me of someone.

"They didn't count on you," he told me quietly. "They didn't know how I would fall for you."

I was curious about what the magicians had offered

and struggled to place the familiar face. But my mind was most captivated by his last words.

I pulled him closer to me until we sat side by side. The wall at my back was cold but I rested my head on his shoulder. Reluctantly, Kian wrapped an arm around me.

"I forgive you," I said.

We sat in silence until my fear gave way to exhaustion and I fell asleep. Even under the ground while being hunted, I felt better with him by my side.

## Chapter Thirty-Three

"What is this place?" I asked in the darkness.

Kian fumbled around the small room, trying to find the batteries he had put in his pants pocket for the lantern. We were underground and there was no natural light source. I strained my eyes, squinting into the black, but could still see nothing. I sighed, regretting my inability to even create a light with my magic.

"A storage locker," Kian answered distractedly. "I believe the owners of the house were afraid of having their valuables destroyed while England was bombed during the war and stored them here just in case." He struggled with the lantern. I heard plastic clicking and Kian huffed in annoyance.

"What do you think happened to the owners?" I asked.

"Don't know," he answered.

I hugged my knees to my chest as the cold set in. I yawned, the darkness threatening to lull me back to sleep.

Kian's watch alarm clock had gone off, startling me into wakefulness. I hadn't asked him what time it was, hoping to delay our departure from the small underground safe haven.

Light erupted suddenly and I shielded my eyes. Kian held the lantern and peered at me, smiling. I winced at the brightness as up my stomach growled. I hadn't eaten in a long time.

"Let's get out of here," Kian said, standing. I hesitated.

I was still mostly naked and there had been a storm. Three magicians were still out there, and they wanted to enslave my magic and me. I couldn't help but voice a concern that had bothered me since the previous night, though I was afraid of the answer.

"Why didn't you kill them?" I asked.

Kian sighed and kneeled next to me. "You weren't listening to what they said, were you?" he asked as if he was quizzing me on one of the self-defence moves. I shrugged.

"My mind was on other things," I said. Immediately, he shied away and I regretted my sarcasm. Guilt played across his face until I squeezed his hand.

"Even if I had the strength to do that," he said, "the magic that sent your soul forward has put you into a cycle, a wheel that will keep sending your soul forward until your task is complete," he said. "If I or any of you kill them, we would lose them all over again and would have no way to find them until you felt their magic growing, just like they felt yours. It's why they didn't want to kill you."

My head spun with implications.

"Wait," I said slowly. My mind worked to weave the threads of knowledge and make a whole. "What task?"

Kian looked around the room as if searching for words. "The task is the reason you work the magic in the first place. Their task was to conquer. Your task is to stop them." He smiled at me. "Call it a destiny."

"But their magic is ..." I shuddered. "Too much for me. I didn't even feel it invade my mind." The terrifying memories encircled me, threatening to break free and destroy my resolve to keep going.

His smile turned into a grimace. "Then perhaps you need the element of surprise, like I had last night. Their magic can affect me. But they had no need of it. They were convinced I would do exactly as they ordered. The only thing I had in my favour was the element of surprise. Next time will be different." He looked at the floor and bit his lip. "I've become a liability for you."

"But —" I opened my mouth to protest, but Kian turned his back and began climbing the metal rungs. His logic was not going in a direction I liked, and I made a mental note to bring this up again as soon as possible.

Kian threw open the hatch and I gasped as an even deeper chill hit me from the first cellar. It was cold before, but it grew colder as we climbed up. Kian extended a hand and helped me out of the tunnel. I itched to sit and hide, not knowing if the magicians were still here. Kian saw my unease.

"They've gone," he said. "They would have checked the house and moved on. Without your magic, you're lost to them. That's why they needed me."

Right. When everything settled, there would be time for thought. For now, I needed to concentrate on escaping, so I logged his comment away in my quickly expanding file of things to reflect on.

He left me by the open door he had smashed the night before and told me to wait. I spent several minutes, which felt more like hours, huddling into the frame of the side door, shivering. My heart beat wildly as I strained to listen for signs of Kian's return. Finally, when I heard him approaching, I ducked without thinking in case he was someone else. When I saw him re-enter, I straightened and shook off the fear.

Kian had brought me a woman's dress that looked to be from the Victorian period. It was a light mauve colour and had a high collar, with double-breasted buttons up the front. Some brown boots and a brown cloak were also included in the bundle he thrust at me.

"There is a display upstairs," he explained.

I put on the clothes and immediately felt better. I was still cold but being clothed felt like being protected. I hadn't had the luxury since Kian had stripped me in front of the fire the night before. I ached for a shower to wash the last remnants of blue clay from my skin. My stomach growled again. And food. I needed food.

When I was as bundled up as best as could be, we ventured out into the snow. Every few steps I glanced behind me convinced someone was on our trail. He saw me looking.

"Their magic is powerful, but it has limitations. They found you through your power," he said. "Imagine your magic like a window. Only you have control of the glass, but you can see out and others can see in. While your window is open, you can do more. See more. The magicians can feel you and find you. But close the curtains and you are lost to them."

Luckily, the day was calm and the wind only stirred up a light dusting of snow around our feet. As I shivered, I thought about his analogy. What if I covered the window for good? The thought was tempting, but I knew that I would not be able to. I had seen too much, and as much as I hated to admit it, my magic had become a part of me.

The sun was high above us, though I had no idea what time it was. Exhaustion set in as the hunger made my head ache. My heavy limbs stung with cuts and bruises I did not remember receiving. We walked for an hour, cresting a hill and walking down through the snow to a two-lane road. My feet were soaked.

Pulled over on the side of the road was an old farmer's truck. It was painted a faded red, and its round features gave it an antiquated look. Snow covered most of its surfaces.

Though Kian only wore a shirt, he brushed the snow off the windshield and windows with an arm, opening the door for me with a silver key he produced from his pocket. I wondered at the surprises and planning he had done. He climbed in and turned the key in the ignition.

For a heart-wrenching moment, I worried the truck would not start. It made several noises of protest before the engine roared to life. I sighed in relief, realizing I had been holding my breath. Kian turned a dial and cold air blew from the dashboard. I was about to protest, but after a few minutes hot air replaced the cold and I settled into my seat, letting my limbs relax. Kian pressed his hands against the vents and I noticed his lips were blue.

When we had let the truck warm up, he pulled out onto the road. I didn't know where we were going and was too tired to care. The warm air pulled at me and I felt lost at sea, with Kian as the captain. I didn't know the time of day, our location, or our destination, but my trust allowed me to drift off and I settled to lie down across the cabin, my head resting on his thigh.

Memories tugged at me but I pushed them away.

*Not now*, I complained, *I'm too tired.*

I felt my mind release and was asleep.

✦

*The scene around me changed as bright colours flowed down grey stone walls. I stood immobile in a small room with no roof. A stone box. At once, I knew this to be a dream and not my memory. Blues, reds, yellows, and greens took turns running down the walls around me and disappearing into the cracks in the floor as if rainbow waterfalls had overflowed. Kian stood before me.*

*"Pay attention," he said, pointing to the wall.*

*The colours turned to tapestries that ran in the same colourful cycle.*

*"Your story repeats, different but the same. Like me." He pointed to himself and sank into the ground.*

*"No!" I cried, lunging for him. He was gone. I sank to my knees as sorrow took over. Suddenly, a young boy stood in front of me.*

*"Don't cry," he said.*

*He smiled, and his two front teeth were missing. It was the same boy who had given me the flower in my memory. The one who had stood next to the king.*

*"You're going to miss it," he told me, concern wrinkling his young features. A strong jaw and long nose would make him handsome, but his round, youthful cheeks suggested playfulness. Kian stood before me once more.*

*"Pay attention," he said again. As I reached for him he turned into Seth. Then Seth turned into the older version I had seen in the past. The older man with a beard looked at me lovingly, but a hint of worry was in his hazel eyes. He shrank into the small boy and Kian's brown eyes looked back at me. The boy turned into the Seth I knew.*

*"You're going to miss it," he said to me with the young boy's voice. Then Kian stood before me.*

*And so the pattern went. It was eerie but I sat and watched, letting the dream run its course.*

✦

I awoke with a start. Kian took his eyes off the road and glanced at me.

"What's wrong?" he asked. We were still driving and the sun shone brightly over the snow. Hours or minutes could have passed.

I eyed him curiously, piecing together my suspicion as the dream vividly replayed in my mind.

"You were young when we died," I said. It was not a question. Kian's features dropped and he stared at the road, expressionless. "You were just a small boy. That's why you couldn't recognize us as teenagers. You never saw us like that!"

He nodded stiffly, his actions looking like he required much strength to do it.

"You were a prince," I continued, remembering everything he had said about the king and his father. "Seth must have been ..." I thought about it. "Your brother!"

Kian flinched. I remembered the concern on his face. His behaviour appeared to me in a new light since New York. He was trying to protect his brother. The memories and dreams had tried to tell me a story, but I was too preoccupied to notice. Though fatigued, I felt the threads pulling together and becoming a single piece like the kind that had run down the walls in my dream.

We sat quietly for long moments, but I waited. This was his story to tell. Finally, as we drove down another snowy, impossibly narrow road, Kian began to speak.

"Even when I was young, you were beautiful and for me you were like light. My brother was married. As were you. I still cannot understand why you think you were together. The love you've shown for him made me jealous."

A lump formed in my throat. This was the part I didn't want to hear.

"When the king, my father, ordered his warriors to sacrifice themselves, the decision did not come lightly. It would mean sacrificing his son and daughter-in-law."

My mind drifted to Moira.

"Seth was late. The elders thought he had abandoned our tribe, but he came in the end and the ritual began. Everyone thought you had run away. You ran in just in time, and then you were all gone." Kian's eyes shone and I reached for his hand, though it gripped the wheel with white knuckles. A scab was beginning to form where he had cut himself with the knife.

"We buried you," Kian continued and the lump in my throat grew. "My father surrendered to the Romans and they let him keep the tribe together to prevent a war." He paused as his voice began to shake and took deep breaths to steady himself. "Life was not good, but it was bearable. Our tribe began to plot with others in the north, and we would defeat the Romans. Every year they were beaten back." He took a deep breath again. "When I saw seventeen, I was going to lead our tribe's rebellion against the Romans. My father was sick. He was dying." One tear spilled over and he wiped it away quickly with his hand.

"The third magician returned. Our tribe saw two of them killed. Everyone thought he had disappeared, but he came back and used magic to make me follow him. He had woven a spell so thick I could not see through it. In this time, now, the magicians had woven the same spell. We stepped through together, and I was here. That was seven years ago."

I sat in shock. While time travel, though seemingly impossible, was the least of my worries, I hadn't really considered Kian's existence before. He had alluded to being brought here, but hearing it was jarring. The spell had kidnapped him from his own land. My experience of being kidnapped didn't rival his of being brought forward through time against his will.

"What did they promise you?" I asked quietly.

Kian pursed his lips. Anger seethed below the surface. "To go home," he said through gritted teeth. "I wanted to go home. I was told that if I helped to capture you now, I would be allowed to go back and Seth would be allowed to come with me. I was given their word." The rage threatened to boil over. "But it meant nothing."

I waited for more.

"I was beginning to reconsider. That's why they hurt him. To get him away from me and at their mercy. To keep my loyalty. The attack on Moira was to steal her power and hurt her. To show their power." He paused. "I abandoned everything, Gwen," Kian said. "The rebellion, my tribe, my father. Everything. Now I can only read speculations about their terrible fate."

"You don't know that," I tried.

Kian glanced at me, pain in his features. "They are all forgotten. Nothing more exists."

I rushed to reassure him. "They used magic on you. It wasn't your fault!"

Kian shook his head, brushing off my words. "But I could have been good here. I could have accepted my fate." He spat the last word as if it was a bad taste. "Instead I was tempted. I agreed to be compliant. To be their *servant*. I collected you. Sent your pictures and information to them. I was going to betray my own kind for an empty promise."

I remembered the pictures on his cell phone. He had truly been on their side since the beginning.

"Going back is impossible. What is done, is done," Kian said angrily. "I knew it in my heart. When I learned their rituals, it was confirmed. Still, I helped them keep track of you ... I brought you to them."

I stared at the road ahead of me. Kian's guilt and regret crashed into me and reverberated in my chest like his words echoed in my ears. Would I have done any different? Brought to this time, alone, did he have any other choice? If he had said no, he would be dead.

"I was the only one who could work with them and get close to you," Kian said, "knowing you for who you truly are. I tried to help you prepare for them, but I failed. I knew you would be the strongest after the first attack."

I mulled over his actions. Mentally picking my personal feelings for him from my brain and placing them to the side, I tried to think clearly. No matter how many scenarios ran through my mind, I could not think of anything different that would have resulted in all of us being alive and not enslaved to the magicians.

I knew that even if it wasn't for Kian, our memories would have trickled in and the magic would have surfaced. Just like when I used mine during the earthquake. I would much rather have Kian kidnap me than Bald Man or Smooth Voice. Taking a deep breath, I left Kian's actions behind me like the snow on the road.

"Gwen?"

I hadn't said anything in a long time. He was glancing over at me worriedly.

"Yes?" I asked innocently. When I smiled at him, Kian's eyes widened in shock.

"You're not angry?"

Secrets bubbled to the surface of my mind. "I was having an affair with Seth," I blurted out. "I didn't tell you before because I was ashamed. I knew I had a husband. I thought Seth was a Roman soldier, but I know now he just led them away from us. He was trying to help. Seth and I tried to run away together before the ritual that killed us. We knew we could be a better help against the impending danger than something in the unknown future. My husband tried to stop me. He was going to kill me. I killed him. Seth thought that I had changed my mind about running away and went to the ritual. I followed him there. That's why I was late."

I sat back and took a deep breath. My chest was tight against his reaction, but it did feel better to have revealed the truth. I had spoken so quickly that a part of me wasn't sure if Kian had caught all that. Finally, he nodded understandingly.

"It's a new life," I said. "You told me that. You did what you had to do and we're all alive. That's what's important. I'm sorry for what happened to you, but we need to move forward, not back."

As Kian thought over my words, I settled into my seat, digging through my emotions to see if my words matched my feelings. A sense of contentment resided in my stomach and I felt certain that I had. Everyone made mistakes. Kian had saved my life and won my heart, and that's what mattered.

"I think I have a good idea of how we can begin to move forward," Kian said as the truck came to a stop. He seemed to have absorbed the information about my past and moved on. I breathed a sigh of relief.

We were pulled into an empty gas station. A camper van was parked, but its lights were on. The evening was quickly approaching and I strained to see in the fading light. A door off to the side of the vehicle opened, and Seth walked out, followed by Garrison and Moira.

# Chapter Thirty-Four

My hand moved to the door handle but I paused, hesitant. The desire to see my friends warred with the knowledge that I would have to explain everything, including Kian's betrayal. The truck quieted.

"Why me?" I said, never letting my eyes stray from my friends as they moved towards us. Why had he taken me? Why could he not have just tipped me off?

"You are the strongest," Kian replied, his gaze focussed in the same direction. "Restraining all of you would be a drain on the magicians. Easier to pick you off, one by one."

The cold set in. Before they reached us, I had to know one more thing.

"When did you change your mind?" I asked then held my breath for a second. "When did you know that you would rescue me?"

"In the cabin. When you fell in my arms."

At that moment, Seth reached my door and yanked it open, dragging me with it. The truck's cabin was higher off of the ground than I was used to and I stumbled into Seth's arms. At least he was warm.

"What the hell happened?" he exclaimed as he wrapped me in a tight hug.

I caught myself as tears welled in my eyes. The bitter cold grabbed a hold of me now that we stood outside, but my friends crowding around me warmed me down to my soul. When I saw their concerned faces and heard the sympathy in their voices, I thought I would break down all over again.

Garrison didn't wait for Seth to let go of me and instead joined us in a three-person hug. Moira stood off to the side but smiled in relief.

"I'm glad you're okay," she said, ducking her head in my direction. I smiled in return until Kian took hold of my arm.

"We need to leave and get as far away from this place as possible," he said. The others nodded as he hushed their questions with a look.

The camper's interior was musty and old but clean. Everyone but me had to duck slightly as we stood in the living area. A small kitchenette was bordered by a closet, which I assumed was the bathroom, on one side and a few couches on the other. The colour scheme was yellow and orange, making me feel like I had stepped into the seventies. Garrison had not turned off the ignition, so I took off my coat in the warm space.

I revelled in the cosiness of it and took off my cold, wet boots, sitting down on one couch. Kian sat next to me. When the others only stood and stared, he urged them to get moving. Garrison sat in the driver's seat while Moira was in the passenger seat. Seth sat across from us on another couch. Only a thin curtain separated us from Moira and Garrison, so we pushed it aside to talk and drive.

Kian told Garrison to drive back to the cottage. It was starting to snow and the narrow, slippery roads made it hard to steer. Several times Garrison made me nervous by muttering to himself about the location of pedals and how to start the van. When he saw me staring he shot me a smile.

"Relax," he said, "I've never done this before, but I made it here, didn't I?"

When we were on the road, Seth eyed us expectantly and Moira turned in her seat, but I begged for details of what had happened to them first. Seth looked down at the carpet. When he looked back up, guilt played across his face.

"I thought you were right behind me," he said to me. "When we got to the top of the hill, I saw you were gone. I just figured you had gone back to the house." He ran an anxious hand through his hair. "We pieced it together ... random bits and pieces from our lives. I was a prince! Can you believe that? I had a brother and a family and everything. I never knew for sure...."

I could feel Kian tense but didn't mention it. Again, I knew it was his story to tell.

"But everything centred around those magicians," Garrison chimed in. Moira nodded.

"The memories of life are like ..." she thought for a moment, "exactly that. Memories. Something you think you know but remember through your senses.

Like it did happen in the past, even through the eyes of our magic. But everything with the magicians is crystal clear. In the present."

"It was just like Kian had said," Seth explained. "The ritual sent them forward in time but no one knew where. The king ..." he hesitated, "my father, thought they would be the problem of the next generation. Not two thousand years later. He decided to ... let us go."

Seth met my eyes and I was reminded of the meeting in the woods. We had both planned to run away. How different would things have been had my husband not interfered and made me late? Would I be here at all? The Romans might not have been successful. My tribe could have flourished. Kian would have had a different life altogether.

"When we got back," Seth said, "we found a note from Kian telling us to take this from the garage," he motioned all around us, "and meet you here at five o'clock." When I looked at him confusedly, Seth widened his eyes at me. "The night we last saw you was two days ago!"

It felt like ages, but I knew I shouldn't be surprised. I picked up a bag of chips they must have bought at the gas station and began munching mindlessly. I was starving. I felt the time had come for me to explain. Hesitancy wafted off Kian in waves, but it had to be done. I opened my mouth when Moira cut me off.

"Turn left here," she said to Garrison.

Kian's eyes snapped up at her. "How do you know that?" he asked. His voice radiated intensity. "Where's the map I left for you?"

Moira glanced back and immediately recoiled from his gaze. "It's ... I don't need it." She hesitated. "I see with my magic. Power. Whatever. I can change my perspective. I'm seeing through the eyes of an owl overhead." Her tentative smile and pride turned into shock as she saw the twin looks of horror on our faces.

Kian bolted from his seat but at that moment Garrison hit the brakes hard. We all flew forward. The back of the driver's seat stopped me, and Seth had braced himself against Moira's. Kian flew forward and landed by the dashboard. Garrison's seat belt had snapped taught, and he winced as he loosed it from his chest.

"What the hell was that?" I called out.

"There's someone in the road," Moira replied as she cradled her wrist.

"What?" Kian and I asked at the same time.

He picked himself up and stared out of the windshield. I didn't have to guess who by the look on his face when he turned.

I couldn't be mad at Moira for using her magic. We hadn't warned them against it. I kicked myself for stalling the telling of our story. It was a colossal mistake. Her power had acted like a beacon. I slowly made my way to stand near Kian.

The three magicians stood in front of the camper van in the dark. Snow billowed around them. A dark car was parked across the road some way back.

I found my heart in my throat again as I caught sight of Bald Man. Now it was he who stared at me with a deep hatred. Compared to his black look, Smooth Voice's glare was nothing. The third magician stood off to the side, again seeming uncomfortable with the scene. His eyes widened and he averted his gaze when he saw the four of us together.

We all stood and stared in dumb shock until Bald Man flipped his hand and the windshield popped off as if the vehicle was a toy. The angry wind billowed around us. I shielded my face from the cold.

"Gwyneth," Bald Man called to me. His tone was razor-sharp. There was magic in his voice. Even over the wind I could still hear it perfectly. It resonated around us. "Truly, you must end this now. You know I won't kill you. But I could make life extremely unbearable for you and your friends."

Suddenly, Kian crumpled to the ground next to me. His hands were clamped to his ears and he screamed in pain.

"Stop!" I cried into the night. My voice was lost in the chill. "Stop!"

Bald Man took a few confident steps forward into the bright beam of our headlights. "No," he said simply.

Kian writhed at my feet. I was panicking, as was everyone else. While Seth, Garrison, and Moira did not know what was happening, they had figured out these were the magicians. Kian groaned again and I knelt by his side, taking his head in my lap and stroking his hair while I thought. His pain echoed in my limbs as I thought frantically.

"Uh, Gwen?" Garrison's tone brought my attention back to the magicians.

Smooth Voice stood in the light, snow and wind obscuring him. He had his arms raised to the side and his eyes closed. I could feel the magic before I sensed it. The earth beneath us began to shake.

"What is taking you so long?" Bald Man screamed angrily at us. "You are thinking of fighting us?" His voice boomed. "You must not understand the full range of our capabilities. Let me enlighten you!"

The ground lurched to the side and we toppled. The storm seemed to double in a matter of seconds and the magic in the air was suffocating me. It was too thick to think or move in. I felt completely enveloped.

Kian was covered in sweat. He suffered. I felt torn in a million directions at once. I looked up and noticed that everyone looked toward me for directions. Bald Man still screamed his ire at me but I ignored him. I could feel him trying to skirt my magic and reach my mind, but I brushed him aside.

"Moira?" I turned to her as another shake sent me crashing into Garrison. The van rattled as if it was about to fall apart. "You have mental powers?" I yelled. When she nodded, I said, "Get the magician out of Kian's head." She nodded at me again and settled into her seat, gripping the sides of the van for support against the earthquakes.

"Seth?" He was next to me in an instant. "Confuse them. I don't care how or what, but get into their heads. Give me some time, okay?" He nodded and sat back down on the couch that threatened to topple over.

Lastly, I turned to Garrison. His strength of moving objects was similar to mine and I needed his help. He looked up at me, still buckled in, his nose red from the storm that had made its way to us. The wind had given me an idea and brought me back to a memory of when I had controlled it. I had dangled over a cliff edge and fought the storm. The magicians' words from the mansion came back to me.

"They stole their power with rituals and sacrifices!" I yelled at Garrison over the tempest. "The power they have is strong but artificial!" He looked confused. "You and I, our magic is natural. We were meant to do this. Like Kian said, the roots are in the earth. We can take the control back!"

Garrison nodded, but I knew it was my job to show him it was possible. I turned back to the scene before me, hoping that Seth's magic had taken effect.

The third magician stood staring at the scene before him, his eyes wide and his mouth agape. He didn't move. Smooth Voice still controlled the earth but now he frowned. Bald Man noticed me looking. He sneered and pointed at his head.

"You think you can get in here?" he yelled. He knelt towards the ground, pulling at air as if he was a mime trying to lift a great weight. My knees buckled when I felt the earth directly in front of us rise. The van was going to be flipped.

"Now!" I yelled to Garrison.

I jumped through the space where the windshield had been and onto the hood. I heard him following. It was a long jump from the hood to solid ground since jagged earth had been lifted to propel us into the air.

Bald Man leered at me. The magician was about to move towards grabbing me when, hoping my hypothesis proved accurate, I knelt on the snow-covered ground, planting my hands firmly against it.

Magic awoke inside of me and pressed on my mind. It felt heavy and pushed against my insides like the time I had gathered it to myself and released it. I didn't want an explosion this time. I wanted to reconnect. I pushed it deeper through my hands, feet and knees. I pushed it so far into the earth that I felt my awareness melt into the past.

The density of it weighed down on me and I sent soothing thoughts, taking power away from Smooth Voice and calming the earth. When my feet had stopped rocking, I tentatively opened my eyes at the same time as the magician. He looked confused for a second then saw what I had done.

A cry of outrage broke from his lips as he lunged towards me. I ducked just in time. Garrison came to help me. He pulled their dark car forward and it slid silently in the snow. As Smooth Voice prepared for another attack, he was knocked backwards from behind. Garrison ran in front of me and took on the magician. Movement in the corner of my vision signalled Bald Man coming towards me.

I threw up my arms as the wind began to form around me. Bald Man stopped in his tracks. His mouth opened in shock. I focused my magic out into the night. The snow and wind expanded as far as I could reach. I pushed further out and it threatened to overwhelm me. Feeling myself losing control, I gripped the storm around me in my mind and clamped down on it, sending it at the magicians.

A strong magical barrier pushed against me, but my feet were planted on the ground and reached down to the roots of the earth. I used the strength as an anchor. I was gaining control but I felt my magic retracting back to my body. I fed it my thoughts and feelings, urging it to blow in anger.

Memories of the magicians, being kidnapped, the ritual, and running away surged through to my magic. The night swirled around me. The magicians were losing, but not retreating.

I focused my mind on the snow and turned it to ice. Trying to aim at the magicians as best I could, I sent the ice flying like sharp daggers. The hail flew from me like an arrow from a bow as I used my magic to send it out. Power blanketed the night and I controlled it.

Small stabs of pain distracted me from my task but I brushed the sensation aside. The wind and ice spun around me until I was the centre of the storm. My hair billowed and my cloak was lost, but I was getting dragged into the power. The earth was sucking me in. I poured my life energy into the fringes of the storm, keeping it going and stirring it up. I fed it until I was lost in the noise of wind. I could not see. I could not feel. I let the last of my energy escape and dissipate in the air around me, as I fell to my knees.

At once, the air was quiet and deadly still. I fell onto my back and closed my eyes.

## Chapter Thirty-Five

The smell of cleaner touched my nose and I was startled into wakefulness. I was convinced I had been kidnapped again until my hands grabbed a quilt and I became entangled in my sheets.

"Relax."

Moira came over and sat next to me, picking up the pillow I had thrown to the floor. She placed it behind my back.

"Everyone's fine." She smiled hesitantly.

I opened my mouth to speak but no sound came out. I tried again. Only a croak emerged.

"I'll get you some water," Moira said and left our small bedroom.

I sat up, trying not to panic. Her cleaning supplies sat on the dresser and snow still obscured my view out the window. The sun hid behind low, grey clouds. Within a minute, Moira came back with a glass of water and Seth and Garrison on her heels.

They crowded my bed, asking me how I felt and

what had happened. I raised a hand to quiet both of them and then raised my eyebrows at each in turn, the universal sign of demanding an explanation.

Garrison sighed. "They ran off," he said. "I fought the steely-looking one. His magic was stronger, but he was mostly spent. The weird one ran off first. I thought you were going to tear that bald one apart." He grinned at me. When I continued to look confused, he explained.

"That storm you brewed up was deadly. We were fine, but I thought you were going to shred them to pieces. Spent all your energy, though." He ruffled my hair. I raised my hand to brush him off and winced at the sight. Small cuts marred my arm like freckles.

"Mirror," I croaked.

Seth hesitated but brought me a small mirror from the dresser.

A gasp escaped my lips, even if I had prepared myself. I was covered in little cuts that had begun to heal, but I could only hope the majority wouldn't scar. My face looked similar to when I had had chicken pox as a child.

Moira gently took the mirror from me.

"You saved us," Garrison said. I shook my head and motioned to all of us. It hurt to speak. Everyone saved us.

"No." Garrison lowered my hand back onto the bed. "You did. You had a plan. You stepped up to the challenge. We beat them this time. You knew how to …" he gestured, looking for the right words, "… get to that place. The magical place. We thought we lost you." He squeezed my hand.

"After the strange one ran and the grey-haired one lost his grip on the earthquakes and was beaten back by Garrison, it was easy to get into their heads." Seth shook his own head as if to clear it. "It was ... confusing ... but I encouraged them to leave. To forget about us. I don't know how well it worked or how long it lasted. I was barely able to get to the bald one, though. You had him surrounded."

The magic had felt as if I held it in my fingers. I had moulded it and wrapped it around the man I hated. I could barely even feel the magician behind the power I sent at him. I didn't know if I had a goal — I knew not to kill him, but what was I trying to do? I shook my own head. The night already felt like another life. I didn't like the feeling of having so much power in my grip. I didn't like the hate I had sent into the storm and at the magician. After everything that had happened, it was feeling the hate and wishing to hurt that caused me to feel least like myself.

"We're safe for now, I think," Garrison explained. "Kian said —"

Suddenly, my heart sped up in a panic. I tried to get out of bed. Seth forced me back down. I could tell he understood.

"Kian?" I asked, hoarse.

Seth looked to Garrison, and Garrison looked to Moira. The way they all avoided me made my stomach sink and my panic increase. Tears sprang to my eyes. Seth saw them and rushed to explain.

"Don't worry — you lessened the magicians' reach and Moira was able to get to him. He's fine," he said.

I sighed in relief. If I had the voice to scold him for making me worry, I would have.

"But," Seth began, "he left."

My eyes widened and I didn't have to speak for my question to be understood.

"He said he would only hold us back," Garrison continued. "He ... explained everything. He told us what happened to you, and what he did."

My hand was at my throat, trying to soothe the lump that was growing. My heart felt like a cold stone in my chest. A silence grew between us.

I waited for them to reveal their verdict on his betrayal. I reached out towards Seth, taking his hands in mine. His eyes widened.

"Yeah," he ducked his head, "he told me that part too ... it's weird ... him being the older brother now...."

Another silence stretched.

"We're not mad," Garrison said finally. "I think he did help us. He made us ready. And, if you forgave him, then the rest of us had no reason not to. But he still wanted to leave."

I ached with the knowledge that I could not see him or touch him. A hollow appeared in my chest. It echoed with sorrow and loss. I felt the tears well up again.

Moira rushed into action. "We'll give you a few minutes to rest," she said, already nudging the other two up and out the door. She gave me a smile, and for the first time I felt true kindness from her.

Though I was ashamed of it, as soon as the door closed, I allowed myself a few quiet sobs as tears spilled over. The lack of Kian's guidance and friendship, coupled with the new magic resonating inside my body, scared me. I needed someone to lean against.

The magic I had used from the earth now beat inside me in a different rhythm than my heartbeat. Though more powerful than ever before, I felt like I was about to melt into the earth and disappear. I needed someone to tell me I was real.

Eventually, I pulled myself together and decided I would have plenty of time for self-pity later. I left the bedroom and was able to pass Garrison and Moira question-free. I grabbed a piece of bread, and putting on Moira's coat came out to the front yard, where a rough wooden fence jutted out from the house and into the landscape. Seth sat on it.

"How long was I out?" I asked.

"Just the night. You used up all of your energy. When we found you looking like a horror movie, I just thought the worst." Seth rubbed his arms against the cold, even though he wore a jacket. "It felt like I lost you all over again. In my past life, when I waited for you the day we died, I thought we were going to have a life together. When you didn't show up, I thought you tricked me."

I opened my mouth to interrupt, but he went on.

"I thought you had got me away from the village so that you could sacrifice yourself and keep me safe," Seth said. "I should have had faith in you. Imagine how things would have been different if I would have just had faith in the person I loved." He buried his face in his hands. "Then when I got to the village and saw you weren't there ... I don't know what I thought. I didn't think anything. You appeared, and it was like I wanted to live again. Then I died."

I didn't know what to say. Seth raised his face and eyed me with an intensity I had rarely seen in him. I had been so focussed on my own past I hadn't considered his side of it. The look reminded me of Kian and I marvelled at how I hadn't seen it earlier.

"Just don't die again," he told me. "Okay? It was hard enough to find you again the first time."

I nodded, smiling.

"Why did he leave without saying goodbye?" I asked, taking a seat next to Seth. My gaze followed his onto the grey horizon.

"I don't think he could have said goodbye to you," Seth replied.

"Not even a note?"

"Nope."

Disappointment invaded. "Did he say where he would meet us?" I asked.

"Home," came the reply.

I chewed my lip. "I don't know what that means," I admitted. "I don't know where that is."

We sat quietly for long moments, staring out into the white expanse. I would find him, but our task was not over. The magicians had revealed a lot in their attempt to take my power and enslave my soul. I didn't want any of my friends to go through that. As if sensing where my mind was, Seth spoke.

"We're too strong for them," he said. "They need to collect more magic, but we might not be worth the trouble anymore."

"Well then it looks like we have a mission," I said. A small smile found its way to my lips, even though my heart was in despair. I felt vulnerable without Kian, but a sense of purpose helped to fill the void. At least for now.

"And what's that?" Seth turned to me, his curious eyes holding a glint of excitement.

"We find the others before the magicians do," I replied.

We had stormed the castle together, side by side. I remembered it as clearly as if it had happened yesterday. I had seen the faces of my kind. Seven in total.

# ✦ Acknowledgements ✦

I want to thank everyone whose support and encouragement allowed me to turn this idea into a reality. My friends and family who shared my excitement and enthusiasm about magic — no matter how ridiculous, and never told me I was crazy. In particular, a big and overdue thank you to Ann Dooley and Anne Connon at the Celtic Studies department at the University of Toronto. You were the first to show me the reality in the stuff of legends — and continued to patiently entertain my wild and unfounded hypotheses about the past, encouraging me to keep at it. Thank you to Allister Thompson, my editor, who was the first person in the world to read this story and the last one to see it before it got packaged into the book you are holding.

Thanks to the Ontario Arts Council's Writers Reserve Program for assistance in bringing this project to fruition.

I also want to thank every reader, since without you there would be no point in putting the stories in my head and heart down on paper.

There's a wink in this book for every one of you.